Village Teacher

neihtn

Cover photograph taken by MT in Huế c. 2007

ISBN: 978-1475101638

Table of Contents

Preface

This is a work of fiction, and any resemblance between the characters in this book and real or historical persons is coincidental.

To describe the examinations system in the following pages I relied on the following works.

Khoa cử Việt-Nam, Tập Thượng [Vietnamese Examinations, First Volume] by Nguyễn Thị Chân Quỳnh, An Tiêm, Paris, 2002

Khoa cử Việt-Nam, Tập Hạ [Vietnamese Examinations, Second Volume] by Nguyễn Thị Chân Quỳnh, An Tiêm, Paris, 2007

Lều Chõng [Tents and Pallets] by Ngô Tất Tố, originally published in 1952, reprinted by Khai Trí, Sài Gòn, 1968

Vietnam and the Chinese Model by Alexander BartonWoodside, Harvard University Press, Cambridge (Massachussets), 1988

Overshadowed by the French Indochina war from 1945 to 1954, the rebellions against French colonization toward the end of the 19th century and at the beginning of the 20th century are now usually given minimal treatment. I relied on the following publication for the chapter titled *Resistance* in this book.

Những Trận Đánh Pháp [Battles against the French] by Lãng Nhân, Zieleks, Houston, TX, 1987

To provide English translation of passages from famous Vietnamese poems, I used the following works:

The Kim Van Kieu of Nguyen Du, by Vladislav Zhukov, Canberra, Australia: Pandanus Books, 2004

The Song of a Soldier's Wife, by Huỳnh Sanh Thông, Electronic version, Institute of Vietnamese Studies (http://www.viethoc.org/), Westminster, CA 2002

Passages quoted from Mencius can be found at the following translation:

Mencius, translated by D. C. Lau (London: Penguin Books, 1970).

Throughout this novel, I have chosen to leave Vietnamese names as they are normally used in the Vietnamese language. First, all diacritical marks have been preserved since they are so important in a tonal language like Vietnamese. The order of names, namely family, middle, and first names, has been retained and not Westernized. Thus, with a name like Lê Duy Tâm, Tâm is the first name and Lê the last name. In Việt Nam, since the last name is seldom used, friends would call him Tâm, while others would address him by his title or an honorific followed by his first name, as in Teacher Tâm.

As for the country itself, throughout its long history it has undergone several name changes. Emperor Gia Long, used the name Việt Nam starting in 1804. Later the French called the country An Nam. In the early 20th century, Vietnamese nationalists brought back the name Việt Nam, and it has retained that name until now. Throughout this book, I have chosen to use the name Việt Nam, and I refer to its people as Vietnamese rather than the more pejorative *Annamites*.

Although I drew much inspiration from the cited publications, all factual or interpretive errors in the following pages are of course entirely mine.

neihtn
May 2012

The Scholar

Tâm was the first to leave Cần Chính pavilion, the ornate building within the Forbidden City where the palace examinations were held. It was the final day of the highest examinations at the national level held inside the Imperial City of Huế.

He had completed the last essay on a topic specified by the King: what reforms of the educational system would be needed to bring the nation into the modern age? Since the majority of the scholars were also teachers like him, he had thought everyone would have an easy time with the question, but his fellow scholars were still thinking or writing when he handed in his paper.

After repacking his brush and ink stone into a small bag that he carried every day to the palace, he opened the door to the small room, more like a closet, where he had spent the better part of the day. He walked past the other rooms, hearing an occasional sigh, a cough, or a groan by the occupants struggling with their words and sentences as they tried to organize their jumbled thoughts before putting them down on paper. He handed his booklet to the stern looking proctor sitting at a desk who had been watching him with a scowl on a sallow face.

The official, wearing a dragonfly hat and an expensive looking ceremonial dress, was obviously surprised and unprepared that someone was about to leave the palace at such an early hour. He leafed nervously through the booklet to verify that all the required stamps were properly affixed before finally and carefully bringing down a large seal on the last page with an unsteady hand. Once that was done, he examined the booklet once more from beginning to end. Finally, after fumbling and muttering to himself, he nodded, indicating to Tâm that all was in order, and pointed toward the exit door. Tâm bowed respectfully before proceeding in that direction.

The King was as usual nowhere in sight. It was said that Cần Chính was the place where he held Court, but he had not made an appearance since the start of the examinations, and was unlikely to do so until the results were announced. The successful scholars would then be invited to a ceremony followed by a banquet graced by his royal presence.

The very young King was closely surrounded by older Court mandarins who coached and watched every one of his comings and goings as well as his interaction with all of his subjects and with the officials of the French colonial administration. Those who surrounded the King competed with the French colonials to impose their views, their demands, and their will on the bewildered youngster, pulling him in all directions, with each party claiming theirs was the right and true path. Tâm did not envy the King in any way, and he was perfectly happy to be a village teacher.

He felt relieved the exams were finally over and wanted to go back to his inn to exercise and get rid of the aches and cramp accumulated through too many hours of sitting in confined quarters. He was staying at a modest inn near a market and one of the bridges spanning the Perfume River. Many of the other out-of-town candidates were lodged at similar inns or better ones in other areas, depending on their means. His own inn was probably the furthest out of the Imperial City, but he welcomed the long walk and in fact looked forward to it each day.

The only inconvenience was that he had to make the trip suited in the uniform, consisting of a blue silk tunic, black pants and a stuffy hat, conferred on all scholars by the King. At the peak of the dry season heat, the royal garments were stifling and most unwelcome, and he couldn't wait to change out of them as soon as he got back to the inn.

It had been several years since the last examinations were held, but the innkeepers were prepared for the influx of scholars from all parts of the country. Knowing that some of these men may eventually pass the examinations and win significant positions either in the royal administration or back in their own provinces, the innkeepers never failed to treat them with respect. For those who had ample money to spend, they went out of their way to spoil them with services mixed with favors and kindness. Even those less wealthy were given special treatment not usually reserved for ordinary inn guests.

For Tâm, a teacher from a small village in the North, his innkeeper was at first restrained when he looked at the plainly dressed young man who did not have a servant to accompany him and carried with him nothing but a bag of books and clothes. He gave him the smallest room at the end of a hall, with a bamboo bead curtain instead of a door. It could have been a maid room, but Tâm did not complain. An almost constant breeze flowed through the room, keeping it cool and pleasant enough even without the use of a paper fan.

However, as the days passed the innkeeper changed his attitude. Through the bountiful rumor mill that was permanently active in the capital, the reputation of Teacher Tâm (*Thầy Tâm*) as a brilliant scholar soon became common knowledge.

He had passed the local examinations (*Thi Hương*) at the very young age of 17, achieving all four levels and earning a licentiate (*Cử Nhân*) degree while placing himself at the top of that year's graduates. He then took over his village school from his father, and taught for seven years while continuing to study and prepare for the next levels of examinations. At the time, the French colonization of the country and ensuing wars, combined with court intrigues and politics, forced examinations in the capital to be postponed many times, and nobody could take them even if they had qualified. Finally the first palace examinations in many years were again held in Huế, and Tâm with hundreds of fellow scholars from all parts of the country converged on the capital.

Since coming to Huế, he had first taken the regional examinations (*Thi Hội*), also passing all four levels and becoming a *Hội Nguyên*, the laureate among those who earned the right to go on to the palace examinations (*Thi Đình*). His treatment at the inn had already changed for the better even before that momentous achievement.

By the end of the first week of his stay, the innkeeper knew all he needed to know about the young scholar from the North and was impressed with his attitude and comportment. Without being asked, he moved him into a larger and nicer room, at no additional cost. He instructed the servants to pay special attention to the honored guest, a promising scholar destined to the highest possible mandarin positions.

Breakfast was delivered to his room each morning. Each day, when he returned from the examination grounds, bath water was prepared for him.

Tâm protested that the original accommodations were perfectly fine, but the innkeeper was adamant. The teacher deserved nothing but the best, and the inn would do its utmost to make his stay comfortable.

When Tâm became the *Hội Nguyên*, the innkeeper had a pig killed and organized a culinary feast for the honored scholar with the inn staff and other guests happily participating. The deference toward Tâm went up another notch and he found himself revered in almost the same manner his students and their parents treated him back in his village.

He exited the Citadel, defined by the ramparts and fortifications built to enclose and protect the Imperial City, through the East gate and decided to stroll along the narrow streets. There were still a few signs of the damage inflicted by French artillery when they shelled the capital to force the Vietnamese government to open the nation's doors for them. However, most of it had been repaired or patched over. He guessed that the houses that still looked crumbling belonged to those who fled with the young King to the mountains to start the Cần Vương (Restore the King) movement. The young monarch had been subsequently captured and exiled to Algeria, but the anti-French movement went on, on the wane but not quite extinguished as yet.

Since he had nothing to do except wait for the results in the following days and possibly weeks to come, he took his time strolling back toward his inn. Only very few people were out on the streets of the capital, no doubt due to the oppressive heat of the early afternoon. From his dress and comportment, people easily recognized him as one of the scholars from around the nation who came every few years for the palace examinations. He had no choice but to wear his scholarly uniform until he got back to the inn and could exchange them for his normal village teacher attire. In the meantime, people smiled or bowed, while others just stared at him as an object of curiosity. Most people were walking like he was, and horses and carriages were rare, and those undoubtedly belonged to military officers, high court officials or to the French.

Ahead of him, he saw a woman riding a horse, followed by a maid walking on one side of her. He only saw their backs and thought the rider was of Champa origin since Chàm women, unlike their Vietnamese counterparts, were known to ride horses just like their men. The rider's head was bare, unencumbered by any hair wrap or shawl, or by the large round hat that women often wore to protect their face and complexion from the sun.

Not having ever met or seen a Chàm person before, he was curious to see what the two women would look like. Since the end of the 10th century, the Chàm people had been gradually driven out of the provinces that constituted the center of the country, but they were still concentrated in certain areas south of the capital. They were seldom seen outside of those localities, preferring to avoid contact with the people who had over several centuries conquered and destroyed the kingdom of Champa.

Yielding to his natural curiosity, he walked a little bit faster and followed the two women as they seemed to be traveling in the same direction as his. He noticed two men were also trailing them, ahead of him and much closer to them than he was. After a short while, the rider and her maid went into a side street and the two men suddenly took off running.

Immediately intrigued by their reaction, he quickened his pace. The men turned into the same side street and he lost sight of them for a moment. When he reached the corner, he saw that they had already caught up with the two women. One of them violently shoved the maid to the ground while the other tried to pull something from the rider on the horse. The maid cried out for help while the rider struggled to hold on to her saddle to keep from falling off the horse.

Tâm ran toward the group and reached the assailant still tugging at a bag that the rider was trying to hold with both hands. His momentum carried him forward as he threw his right shoulder against the attacker's back, sending the man sprawling to the ground. The other attacker was temporarily stunned by his sudden attack but recovered quickly and pulled out a dagger. The man lunged at him. Tâm made a quarter turn, grabbed the man's wrist with one hand and the elbow with his other hand. Using the man's own momentum, he continued turning as he led him away from the women. Finally, he pushed on the man's elbow while twisting and pulling his wrist, and kicked his feet from under him. The man plunged face down to the ground, landing on his stomach as air burst out forcefully from his lungs. The dagger fell off and Tâm at once kicked it as far away as possible.

The maid rose to her feet while both attackers were down on the ground. He placed himself between the women and their assailants, and then took a fighting stance facing the two men he had so easily disposed of.

The one who had held the dagger stood up, his nose bloodied, his face dirtied, flushed and beginning to swell. His companion managed to stand up slowly on wobbly legs, both hands grabbing at his chest while grimacing in pain. They looked warily at their opponent with the strange scholar dress who in a few short seconds had thrown both of them to the ground.

"Run," the one with the bloodied face shouted at his companion. He at once ran back to the main street, his companion following him closely.

Tâm turned to the women. The maid was hugging the young woman who had dismounted, and the two were watching him with terrified eyes. They both wore the same type of formal dress commonly worn by women whenever they left their homes to go outside, although that of the rider appeared to be more colorful and made of finer material. The rider looked about the same age as one of his older students.

"They are gone now, so don't worry about them anymore. Is either one of you hurt?" he asked.

"Thank you, we are all right," replied the young rider.

Her fine black hair was somewhat disheveled, unrestrained by any of the common headdresses women often wore. Her oval-shaped face was slightly flushed and her eyes were most extraordinary. Under curved eyelashes they were blue, the same color as a rare kind of water lily that grew back home in one of the many ponds dotting the countryside around his village. He felt that with those eyes she was looking right into his mind and his heart as if he were an open book, and he had to make a conscious effort not to stare at her for too long.

Realizing that the crisis was over and that they were safe, the shock on the rider's face gave way to a cautious smile as she kept looking at him, fear now replaced by amazement.

"Do you know why they attacked you?" he asked while straightening his attire and resetting the scholar hat on top of his head.

"They wanted to rob my young lady," the maid replied as she batted away the dust and soil clinging to her clothes.

"Can you get back on your horse and go home now? I will accompany you to make sure you are safe."

"We don't live too far from here," responded the young woman, peering keenly at the sight of a man in scholar attire who had fought so decisively against two ruffians. She was going to say something more but changed her mind. In a fluid and quick motion, she climbed back on her horse, glanced at him once more before prodding the animal forward.

The maid stayed close to her mistress while he walked a few paces behind them. He was elated that things did not turn out any uglier or bloodier. Until then, he never had to use his martial arts skills to actually defend himself or rescue anybody. So years of training with his uncle had finally paid off in a real life situation, one that he had until then never thought would actually happen.

People said that thievery and crime in Huế were the same as in any other big city, despite the royal presence, and this sudden attack in broad daylight proved that the rumors were not baseless. Perhaps the many upheavals and political changes of the past several years had resulted in an increase in lawlessness as government officials were too busy fighting among themselves or against the French. In any case, he did get a look at the two women, and they turned out to be Vietnamese, not Chàm, as he had wrongly guessed.

They soon arrived in front of an imposing house placed in the center of a large garden planted with many shade trees and flower bushes. The land at the back abutted the Perfume River, seen glimmering in the distance. It was a grand mansion built in Western style with brick walls and tiles, worthy of only some high court mandarin. As the two women reached the gate, a man in uniform ran forward to open it.

He decided that it was as far as he wanted to go.

"I assume this is your home, so I'll take my leave now."

Surprised, the young woman turned her horse around immediately.

"Won't you come in please? Please allow us to thank you properly for saving us from those two ruffians."

"I only did what I had to do," he said. "You are safe now and don't need me any longer."

He started to turn around.

"I don't even know who you are!" she protested. "My name is Giang. At least tell me your name and where you live."

He had already begun to walk away, but paused and smiled at her.

"My name is Tâm, and I am not from around here. I am just staying at an inn down that way," he said and pointed in the general direction of the inn where he was staying.

He resolutely strode away and did not look back again. If he had, he would have seen that she continued staring in wonder at him for some time. He also did not notice that she had ordered the guard who had opened the gate to trail him quietly from a respectful distance.

Afterwards, he was surprised that he had trouble putting her out of his thoughts. He told himself that she was in all likelihood the daughter of some high mandarin family, possibly one even related to the monarchy as so many people were in Huế, and that he was unlikely to meet her again. Yet her face, her eyes, and the faint smile she had toward the end of their brief conversation haunted him in a new and unfamiliar way. It was a long time before he finally surrendered to sleep.

The following morning, after breakfast and wearing his every day clothes, he went down to the bank of the Perfume River and hired a boat to go visit the sites of two royal tombs located upstream and Southwest of the city. As his means were modest, it took him a long time to find a small and unpretentious boat. A family of four lived on it, a couple and their two small boys. For a small additional fee, the wife said she would prepare lunch also. He agreed and stepped aboard.

"Would you like me to ask one of the song girls to come keep you company for the trip," the husband asked with a twinkle in his eyes and a big toothy smile.

Tâm was embarrassed but managed to keep his composure. He knew many of his fellow scholars had the habit of hiring song girls to accompany them on river cruises which lasted all night. They would eat, drink, and try their best to impress their female companions with their erudition by reciting or challenging each other to recite poems ranging from the Chinese Tang era to their own contemporary compositions. The women would strum along on their moon-shaped lutes or their zithers, or sing romantic songs as the mood demanded. What followed afterwards was best left to the imagination.

The pleasure seeking cruises were part of what made the capital famous, but he never had the inclination or the means to participate in one of them.

"No thank you. I am from way up North and have never been to the capital, and I just want to go see the scenery and the historic sites around here."

The boat owner chuckled and nodded approvingly.

"You don't seem to be like those well-heeled scholars who have been hiring boats almost every evening for partying," said the man as he began taking the boat out toward the middle of the river. "They are just pleasure seekers who will be bad for people if they ever become mandarins. But, I took a look at you and I knew you would be different!"

Tâm paid little heed to the compliment as he placed himself the prow of the boat, enjoying the light breeze and admiring the scenery. Overhead, the sky was a clear blue and the calm water of the Perfume River was the color of emerald.

Originating from the range of mountains not far to the West of the capital, the river went from being a series of brooks and small falls to becoming a lazy river coiled like a snake around the South side of the capital. The monsoons had not started yet, so the river was still calm and rather placid. Poinciana trees in full bloom dotted the riverbanks here and there with glorious waves of bright crimson flowers. Coming at the end of the school year, the flowers had come to symbolize the examinations season, their splendor in bloom representing the bright future of those who passed the exams. When the flowers faded and fell to form a red carpet on the ground, they would then be compared to the humiliating fate of those who had failed as their hopes and dreams came crashing down to earth.

He wondered what would be his fate this time. At the local examinations, he had fretted until the results were announced. However, he had answered without any effort all the questions asked on obscure Chinese literature and history. His compositions, both poetry and prose, came easily, written in beautiful and sharp calligraphy that few could rival. The only shock was that when he brought the good news back to the village, he found out that his father had passed away in his absence. After mourning, he took over the school and started his career as village teacher.

Having been groomed by his father starting in his early teen years, he found teaching to be as natural to him as breathing or walking. His relationship with the students evolved. When he was assisting his father, he was like a big brother to many. When he became the village teacher, despite his age, almost overnight they looked upon him with the same reverence and respect that they had accorded his father. They stopped addressing him as if they were his younger siblings, and called themselves his children. In turn, he referred to himself as Teacher (*Thầy*) rather than as Big Brother (*Anh*). Notwithstanding the change, their mutual trust and affection only continued, and became even stronger over the years.

Yet, there he was in the capital, hoping to pass the final palace examinations and thereby win some appointment at court or in a province. He had been encouraged to go by many in the village, not the least by his own mother who told him that's what his father would have wanted him to do. His father had himself taken the examinations several times but never succeeded. Had he hoped perhaps that his son would achieve vicariously for him what he could not do in his lifetime?

Tâm knew that there were candidates who continued taking the examinations well into their late years in life, and several had managed to pass them when they were well in their eighties. He could not see himself spending his life that way and hoped he wouldn't have to.

If he did pass, he had a hard time seeing himself give up teaching to become a mandarin. The few that he had known back home, and the many that he had observed in the capital, were usually sycophantic persons to those above them, while they never failed to be condescending and oppressive to those under them. Selecting mandarins by examinations was on the surface a wise and laudable process, and it worked well for many centuries in China, Việt Nam, Korea, and Japan. However, examinations did not screen out dubious character, and there were unqualified people who cheated in order to pass them. Erudition and scholarship did not always mean integrity, honor or moral probity, nor could they guarantee that a certain dynasty or regime would endure. Human vice and weaknesses affected the scholar class as much as the illiterate masses.

Another issue had also been on his mind. If he were to pass and win an appointment, he would have to leave the village to go assume a post in some other part of the country. That would have been acceptable to many of the villagers. The entire community shared in the honor of someone from the village succeeding at the examinations, especially at the national level. His village was one of those celebrated in the North for the many scholars that it had sent to serve at Court or in the provincial capitals. The names of such scholars from as far back as the 11th century were inscribed on steles in the communal house in the village.

If he were to pass this time, all the villagers would have felt proud of his achievement. It would have reflected well on the village as a whole, and enhanced its reputation for being one of the forges that nurtured and molded the nation's leaders.

Moreover, such an achievement meant the King would exempt the entire village from taxes and levies for several years, a benefit not to be underestimated under any circumstance.

However, what would happen to the village school? He had left for the capital without really thinking about or actually making arrangements for having someone succeed him as the village teacher. It could have been an intentional oversight on his part. For deep in his heart, he did not mind coming back to his students and be their teacher as he had been for seven years.

He started to pay attention to where the boat was heading. To the South of the capital he saw Mount Ngự Bình, a dark green hill flanked on both sides by two smaller ones.

To the founder of the Nguyễn dynasty, Emperor Gia Long, the three small mounts acted as a paneled screen protecting the capital. The Emperor had carefully consulted geomancers and Feng Shui masters to select the location of his capital, and they had told him that Mount Ngự Bình and two small islets on the river would help protect the capital and his dynasty from evil forces. Yet, by the time that Tâm came to Huế, the dynasty was well on its downward path and the French had conquered most of Việt Nam except for a few rebellious enclaves in the North. The country had become a colony of France, and the Vietnamese Emperor was not even allowed to use that title. He was now merely known as the King of Annam.

Soon the boat had left the capital and the imposing but largely useless ramparts of the Citadel behind. Far ahead, he saw the beautiful seven-story tower of the Thiên Mụ pagoda rise above the green canopy of the trees, including glorious poincianas profusely adorned with vivid red clumps of flowers. He made a mental note to walk up there some day.

"Teacher, would you mind if I stop to pick up another passenger?" hailed the boatman from the rear of the boat.

"That's all right by me," answered Tâm. He had not seen the man who was standing on the bank of the river and waving his hand for a ride.

As the boat glided toward the bank, the children came out to stand with him at the prow. He looked down to see two small faces observing him carefully at first, then breaking into smiles as he winked at them. Their attention soon turned to the new passenger, an older man with gray hair who, despite his age, jumped on board with ease. The man was dressed in proper street attire, with a black tunic and a somewhat faded but clean headdress. He greeted the boatman as a familiar acquaintance.

"Boat driver, where are you going today?"

"I am just taking our scholar over there to see the sights. Where would you like to go?"

"Can you take me as far as somewhere near the Tomb of Emperor Minh Mạng?"

"No problem, that's where he also wants to go."

The new passenger turned to Tâm.

"You must be here to take the examinations."

"Is it that obvious? I must look like one of those scholars with a long back and who can do nothing but eat and sleep."

They both laughed aloud before the older man sat down near him.

"I like you already. You can make fun of yourself, unlike many that I know, and that's a good quality to have. So do you think you will pass and become some high-level mandarin and make your wife and family proud?"

"Elder Uncle, I am not even married. As for passing the examinations and climbing into the ranks of government, that's for the judges and perhaps also fate to decide."

He stopped and pondered whether he should continue and say what's on his mind. The old man, dressed simply with clothes made of plain fabric, could not be a courtier or even somebody related to one. He was nodding and smiling kindly as Tâm spoke.

"I've only been here a little over a month," Tâm added. "From what I've been able to see and hear during this short time, it is obvious that the court mandarins really don't have that much influence any more in the governing of our country. The French are the actual rulers."

"You are right of course, and I am a little surprised that somebody like you would express such views," said the man. "For these examinations, scholars have been coming to the capital from all over the country, following a tradition that has existed for centuries. Most of them do not realize that their traditional learning is now irrelevant. The world has changed a lot since Emperor Gia Long, and now the powerful West can dictate its will on us with impunity. Yet very few scholars are making an effort to learn from the West. They still cling to Chinese books and classics and pretend that the world outside does not exist."

"Elder Uncle, maybe that's because Confucianism is so ingrained in our society and our culture that nobody wants to upset the natural order, just as the great sage has taught us. We keep on doing things the same way because it has worked for us for centuries."

"Yes, and that's what is leading us to our downfall."

The boat silently made its progress upstream, its keel effortlessly parting the clear emerald water. Tâm looked back toward the stern. The boat owner was sculling with two oars, his rhythmic movement seemingly effortless and graceful. The two children had gone back to play near him. Their mother could not be seen but was probably cooking for he saw smoke rising from behind the enclosed cabin in the middle of the boat.

He often heard people say that everybody in the capital aspired to become a mandarin someday, and, if they were already one, they wanted to reach the topmost ranks. He wondered if that also applied to this family which has all of its earthly possessions contained in their small boat floating on the river. The old man interrupted his thoughts.

"We are going to pass by Emperor Tự Đức's Tomb on the left bank. It is the most elaborate and beautiful of the memorials that the Nguyễn emperors have built for themselves. My father was one of those conscripted in the labor gangs forced to work on it. He died in an accident resulting from exhaustion and the brutal treatment imposed on the workers."

The old man looked away to hide his sadness. He sighed and was lost in his own thoughts for a long time before returning to the conversation.

"There was such misery and so much unhappiness during that time that it led to the Mortar Pestle (*Chày Vôi*) rebellion in 1866. However, that failed in overthrowing the emperor, and all the leaders of the rebellion were killed. Their families often were executed with them, or had to change their names, and their descendants were forbidden to take any examination for four generations."

He stopped for a moment before continuing with bitterness in his voice.

"All that for a tomb that never housed the remains of the emperor! On his instructions, at his death Emperor Tự Đức was buried in a different and secret location. Afterwards, the 200 people in the funeral procession were all beheaded so that they would never reveal the secret."

Tâm knew that the Emperor Tự Đức was often celebrated for being a well-educated man who was as good if not better than many scholars in the nation. He was a decent poet and a writer who tried to popularize literature and the teachings of the good books. How could this scholar have been so uncaring and cruel to his subjects? As if reading his thoughts, the old man continued.

"During his 36 years in power, while the emperor was busy with things like building his memorial, raising money through an opium trade with China, or suppressing the Christian religion and their Vietnamese converts, the French attacked and won over one fortress after another, even those commanded by our most capable generals. The Emperor had no choice but to cede province after province to them. He begged China to send troops to help for a few years, but that only delayed the inevitable. Now we may still have Vietnamese kings in the capital, but our nation has become a colony of France, from South to North. Just like you said before, the French are indeed our true masters."

"I wanted to visit the location, but I will now tell the boatman not to stop and just go on to where you want to go."

"My dear teacher, you won't be able to go past the entrance anyway. Only members of the royal family and their invited guests can go in. People like us may only view the tomb from a distance."

They continued toward where two small rivers joined to become the Perfume River. The older man had Tâm's full attention as he pointed out various features and points of interest along both sides of the river. Finally, they approached Emperor Minh Mạng's tomb on the West bank of the Left Tributary (Tả Trạch) of the Perfume River.

"In the seventh year of his reign, after consulting a geomancer, Emperor Minh Mạng selected a site for his tomb. It's near the confluence of these two tributaries. However, construction did not begin until almost 14 years later, and he passed away shortly after, in 1841, before it was finished. His son, Emperor Thiệu Trị, mobilized some 10,000 soldiers and workers to complete it two years later in 1843. Our country was more prosperous then, yet the whole nation could feel the burden of concentrating so many resources into a project of that scale and splendor. Workers dug up the earth to create two large lakes. They also built many temples, pavilions, plus gates and bridges connecting all of these structures. They spared no cost in acquiring building and decorating materials, some imported from far away countries. Elaborate gardens were laid out and were planted with trees, shrubbery, and flowering plants. All this for a tomb, which again may not contain the remains of the Emperor."

"I find that hard to understand," exclaimed Tâm. "Why go to the extent of having a geomancer tell you where you should be buried, only to be entombed somewhere else when you actually die?"

The older man laughed. "My young friend, when you finally get your appointment, you will soon find that nothing in the capital is actually as it appears! There is always some story underneath the surface, and maybe even another story under that first one."

The boatman eased his craft toward the bank of the Left Tributary, aiming for the space below the canopy of a group of trees perched at the edge of the water. Once the boat stopped moving, Tâm's impromptu guide for the day paid the boat driver and took his leave.

"I am going home now, but would like to talk with you again sometime. Tell me where you are staying and perhaps I'll try to come by one of these days, before the examination results are posted."

"I hope you will. I am staying at the first inn that you see when you get off the bridge. They call me Teacher Tâm. Before you go, can you tell me your name?"

"Around here people know me as Teacher Xinh."

The old man stepped off onto dry land, waved with his hand and strolled away without looking back. Before he disappeared around a bend in the path leading away from the river bank, a small hand grabbed Tâm's little finger and pulled on it. He looked down to see one of the children, the younger boy, smiling broadly.

"Mother said to invite you to come eat lunch."

After a spicy lunch of rice mixed with baby clams, with a burning mouth and a warming stomach, he looked gratefully at the couple sitting with him in the middle of the boat. The rice was the coarse and purplish variety that poorer people ate. It was liberally mixed with white baby river clams intermingled with peanuts, pieces of chopped green onions and red hot pepper. Each bowl was sprinkled with sesame seeds and fish sauce blended with lime and garlic juice. He had taken his time eating, savoring each spicy bite and finding that the more chewing he did the better it tasted. Sweat dripped from his face as he ate, and he was sure that his hosts noticed it, although they made no comment.

He marveled at the texture of the food, and the sensation of the spices which at first affronted his palate before slowly inducing a blissful sensation and a craving for more. Overall, he felt satiated, relaxed, and happy as he had not been over many weeks since he left his village for the capital.

"This is the best tasting meal I've had in a long time!"

"Ah, I wasn't sure whether you'd like this traditional dish of ours," the husband said. "I did tell my wife to make it less spicy for you, but it looks like you can handle it quite well for somebody who is not from Huế."

He slapped his thighs with delight and the children doubled up with merriment, but his wife only smiled as she cleared the bowls away to make room for tea. Even the tea that she served was excellent, strong and complex. He found that the longer he kept it in his mouth, the sweeter the tea tasted although he was sure that she had not added any sugar or honey to it.

High in the sky the sun sent its ray vertically down on the boat and its occupants, adding its maximum warmth to an already stifling midday. Tâm didn't want the boatman to have to exert himself under the merciless heat.

"I have nothing to do for the rest of the day, so we can linger here until it gets cooler before going back, unless you want to go and pick up other passengers."

"I would not mind staying here under the shade for a while," the boatman said. "We can all rest and catch a short nap. But before that I want to tell you something."

"Please do."

"I heard that teacher tell you that nothing around here is what it appears to be."

"Yes, he did."

"Well, I think you should know that he was himself a mandarin at court. A few years ago he did something bad, and as a consequence they demoted him and threw him out. He is actually not that old. His hair changed color overnight when he thought he was going to lose his head but only lost his office. Now he is just a teacher in some small village."

"Oh, and what was his crime?"

"Nobody knows for sure, but there are rumors that he was an excellent forger and used his skill to embezzle money that was supposed to be going into the construction of the late Emperor's tomb."

Not knowing what to say, Tâm kept silent as he thought about what the boatman had just related. In the capital, like in his own small village, sooner or later everyone seemed to know everything. Perhaps that explained why the government had to resort to beheading people in order to keep secrets.

He went to sit on the side of the boat, took off his shoes and dangled his feet overboard. The children came to sit beside him as naturally as if they had known him for a long time.

"I hope they are not bothering you, teacher," their mother said. "They aren't shy with you anymore."

"Don't worry. Back in my village I spend my days with children, some as young as yours."

That was how the village teacher used up most of the afternoon. He had lost his interest in visiting the imperial tombs, those grand monuments built with the sweat, tears and blood of the common people.

In the evening, he returned to the inn. His pants were rolled up halfway to his knees and, like the rest of his clothes, were completely wet. Carrying his shoes in one hand, he looked like some farmhand returning home after a day of replanting rice shoots, except that he did not feel tired at all. He was relaxed and happy after touring on the river, eating delicious food, and enjoying a few hours of fun with the two children on the boat, including at times jumping with them into the water for a swim. His clothes were still drying out and muddy here and there, but it felt like the good old times when he was growing up and played freely with the children who attended his father's school.

A carriage was waiting in front of the inn. Looking at the horse and the driver sitting idly up front, he thought that some wealthy guest had arrived, which was strange since the inn was not the kind of place for that type of patrons.

He went in and saw a dour looking man standing and talking to the innkeeper. Seeing him the innkeeper ran forward to meet him.

"Teacher, this official has been waiting for you. He asked me where you were but I had no idea. I said you left early in the morning without telling me anything, but he did not like that at all."

The innkeeper's voice had become high-pitched with nervousness and a twinge of fear. He turned to the official in question.

"Sir, this is Teacher Tâm, the scholar you were asking about."

The official inspected the one who was supposed to be a village teacher and appeared more like a laborer, except for a certain lack of humility. Those brazen eyes were directed straight at him, unblinking and friendly as if the man thought of himself as his equal! He looked the young man over from head to toe, and snickered when he saw wet clothes and the bare and muddy feet. He snarled at the innkeeper.

"You are sure?"

"That's him," the innkeeper nodded vigorously. He had also seen the condition his prized guest was in. "Teacher Tâm, you must really go take a bath and change into some dry clothes."

"I intend to anyway, but why is this person waiting for me?"

Hearing the Northern accent and seeing the deference the innkeeper was showing to the one that he called Teacher, the official finally conceded that the young man standing before him was indeed the scholar that he was looking for.

"Are you the scholar who rescued my young lady yesterday?"

Tâm did not expect the question at all and hesitated briefly.

"Yes …"

"You don't look like a fighter," the official observed in a barely audible voice before speaking louder. "Never mind though. His Excellency is requesting that you appear before him."

"Did I do something wrong?"

"He just wants to meet you."

"Then may I ask who His Excellency is?"

The man was annoyed that the question had to be asked at all. He had often thought that scholars like the one standing before him were habitually lost in their books and as a result were blissfully ignorant of the realities of life. Yet they were the ones who attained the high positions that people like him could never hope to reach. Reluctantly, he volunteered the information in the most disdainful tone of voice he could muster even though he had to address the man as Teacher.

"He is His Excellency Nguyễn Văn Hải, Special Envoy to the King of Annam. Teacher, you better go change right away as I've been waiting too long already and His Excellency must be getting impatient. I have a carriage waiting outside."

The French Mandarin

Nguyễn Phúc Ánh founded the Nguyễn dynasty in 1802 and became Emperor Gia Long after overcoming the Tây Sơn brothers who had ruled the country for twenty years before him. The Tây Sơn dynasty was a formidable foe, and to defeat them he requested and received crucial help under the form of military advisors, troops, weapons and funds sent by the King of France.

In recognition, a few of the French military commanders were subsequently granted Vietnamese titles and names. They became mandarins of the highest rank at court and were exempted from having to kowtow when they appeared before the Emperor. Some of them married Vietnamese women who came from families of high court officials, including those of royal descent.

As France's influence and colonization efforts spread, French troops were brought into the country in increasing numbers. By the end of the 19th century, they were stationed in all major cities, including the capital. The business of governing the nation was firmly in the hands of French military officers and civilian bureaucrats sent to the colony from the homeland.

The Southern part of Việt Nam was a full-fledged colony of France known as Cochinchina. The Northern part, called Tonkin, was a protectorate ruled by a French Governor with local administrative units run by Vietnamese mandarins. The central part of the country, called Annam, still had the King surrounded by his eunuchs and his court of mandarins, but the King had lost most of his power and influence, and ruled only in name. All major decisions, especially in foreign affairs, defense, and financial matters were either initiated by, or had to be reviewed and approved by the colonial administration, the de facto governing body of the country.

François Bonneau was a seasoned naval officer who spent over twenty years in the country and had participated in many of the major military campaigns which finally brought the old Vietnamese regime to its knees. While some of his superiors and fellow officers sometimes died gallantly in battle, he managed to survive with only a few minor wounds as proof of his bravery and competence.

He came from an ordinary farming family in the Southwest part of France. As soon as he could afford to, he left home and enlisted in the French Navy. Although his origins were rather modest, his *curé*, the parish priest, had succeeded in giving him a decent basic education consisting of a good dose of Latin, French and a smattering of the sciences.

With that and a mind eager to see the world and learn from it, the Navy proved beneficial to Bonneau. He steadily climbed through the ranks to become an officer just as France was taking an interest in the Far East. He took part in the major battles at the beginning of the colonization of Cochinchina, took time to learn the local language, all the while getting promoted after each battle. He became a naval captain before being finally appointed as a Special Envoy to the Nguyễn court because of his complete fluency in the Vietnamese language. He spoke it like a native speaker, and although he could not read Chinese characters well, he was completely at ease with the new Romanized script used by missionaries and their Christian converts.

His role was to advise the King of Annam and make sure that the reigning monarch would always abide by the goals and objectives of the French colonial administration. This was a relatively easy task since the King was only a child barely 10 years old when the French Resident General selected him to succeed the previous monarch, who had died of some mysterious illness. The boy was playing in the front of his parents' run down house, even though the family was of royal descent, when the Court mandarins came to take him away and enthrone him. He was dragged away against his will as he cried and begged them to let him stay home because he did not want to be King!

The Resident General, a French military man with aristocratic roots going back several generations, found it beneath him to learn the natives' language, and relied on Bonneau to convey his words as faithfully as possible to the young King and his mandarins. Bonneau did so with ease and aplomb, being the rare man who not only could converse in either language, but could also infer the deepest meaning from a word or a tone of voice even when disguised behind arcane court phrasing. In time, he became indispensable to both the Vietnamese and their colonial masters.

Without waiting for the King to give him a title or a name, François Bonneau gave himself the Vietnamese name of Nguyễn Văn Hải, with Hải, meaning sea, as a reminder of his naval past. When he told the King of his new name, the young monarch cautiously nodded his agreement. The court mandarins hemmed and hawed, but could do nothing about it.

Bonneau knew Vietnamese well enough to speak it and understand quite well what was said around him, no matter how scholarly or vulgar the speaker was. He spoke the language of scholars, loaded with an abundance of Chinese terms and phrases, with the mandarins and scholars he met in his official duties. He was equally fluent in the salty language of the common people that he met on the street, in the stores and markets, or on the battlefields.

He used his exceptional language ability to woo and marry Tăng Thị Trang, the daughter of a wealthy merchant in Cửa Hàn, the port city the French called Tourane. He had thought about going home to look for a bride in his native country, but the few French wives that he saw in the Far East seemed to be perennially unhappy and their sight convinced him that it was a bad idea. So he settled on Trang, a local beauty whom he often saw at her parents' store on his frequent trips to Tourane. The family was a member of the minority of Vietnamese Christians who, despite constant persecution by the government, managed to prosper and become influential by acting as intermediaries between the population at large and the many foreigners entering the country by the open seaport.

At first, she despised him because of the way he looked and acted, even complaining about the clothes he wore and the smell emanating from him. Undeterred, he pursued her relentlessly. After he showed that he was able to quote and recite lines and verses from folk sayings and well-known Vietnamese poets as well if not better than most Vietnamese, she began to think that he was not so bad after all.

He sealed their fate together when he used his French connections to help her family win several lucrative trading rights. He became indispensable to his future wife's family and proved himself able to help the family increase their fortune more than any of their sons or son-in-laws who were traditional scholars and mandarins. Thus, he overcame the last resistance from the members of the clan who could not initially tolerate the idea of a white man marrying one their beautiful relatives. Toward the end, some even openly expressed their displeasure that she was taking up too long to make up her mind. They were getting used to the new business profits and windfalls, and were openly fearful that he was going to change his mind and set his eyes elsewhere.

Their wedding was the largest party ever for Tourane. The French came in full regalia, resplendent in their military uniforms, their medals, and their swords. The Vietnamese showed off in their finest, with elaborately embroidered gowns and dresses made of the most expensive silk. The bride was proud of her handsome husband in his striking naval full dress uniform, and of the ease with which he was able to converse with her relatives and astounded guests in the purest Vietnamese with the proper Huế accent.

Shortly after marriage, Bonneau and his wife, who wanted people to call her Bà Trang and not Madame Bonneau, moved to the capital as his duties required him to be closer to the center of political power. Their two daughters were born there.

The first daughter, Françoise Bonneau, with the Vietnamese name of Nguyễn Hương Giang, was eighteen years of age. She inherited blue eyes from her father, but her hair was jet black and the graceful lines of her face came from her mother, with some very faint traces of her French heritage.

Her sister, Francine or Nguyễn Hương Mai, was a year younger. She retained her mother's dark brown eyes, but had light brown hair, an angular nose, and a bony face that looked definitely Bonneau. Both were fair and the younger Francine was a bit taller than her older sister.

From their very early childhood, Bà Trang made sure that her two daughters spoke Vietnamese as well as French, but their father insisted that they attended a school in Phù Cam run by Catholic priests. There they received a French education along with the children of other French expatriates and some Vietnamese Catholic dignitaries.

At home, the children spoke Vietnamese with their Vietnamese playmates, with the servants, and with their parents including Bonneau, although he often tried to speak to them in French. In school, they had to speak and study everything from religion to mathematics in French. Switching from one language to the other was so natural and instinctive to the two girls that they hardly ever noticed which language they were using. Whether their minds worked in one or the other language, they couldn't tell or cared.

On that day, while his secretary, Kham, was fetching Tâm, Bonneau and his wife were comfortably seated in the living room of the house he had built according to European standards. The ceilings were high, the windows large and tall, and there was a second story with separate bedrooms for the parents and the children. A servant was standing behind them, slowly moving back and forth a feather fan tied to the end of a long bamboo pole.

It was getting quite late in the afternoon, and Giang, sitting in a chair opposite them could not help to look out to the front of the house from time to time. Nearby in another chair, Mai was pretending to read a book but she could not help throwing disapproving looks at her sister. She had been told all about the previous day incident, more than once.

"Give it up, sister. He's not coming."

Her sister ignored her and chose to speak to their father.

"Father, how long ago did you send Monsieur Kham out?" asked Giang.

"It must have been a couple hours," answered Bonneau before turning to his wife with a wink. "But, mother, was it yesterday or today that I sent him out?"

"Oh, you are impossible, Father!" said Giang. "You should have sent Monsieur Kham out earlier to make an appointment, and then send him again to go collect our guest at the appointed time."

"Françoise, he has not passed the examinations yet. I will treat him as a mandarin when he becomes one."

Bonneau shook his head and sighed in feigned exasperation, which only made his daughter even more annoyed.

"He may not want to come, sister. He is probably filing his long nails or maybe he went fishing, and Monsieur Kham had to check each one of those boats that dock near Phu Văn Lâu."

Phu Văn Lâu or Pavillion of Edicts, situated South of the Citadel near the Perfume River, was where royal proclamations, edicts, and the lists of scholars who passed the examinations were posted. However, nearly everyone knew the reputation of the boats as floating pleasure houses on the Perfume River, and the favorite places for out-of-town visitors, including those who came to the capital to take the examinations.

"Mai!" exclaimed a frustrated Giang. She stood up and went outside to be alone and get some fresh air.

She wandered around the front garden, visiting the flowering purple bougainvillea and the coffee bushes with their green, orange and red berries. To have something to do while waiting, she started picking the ripe berries and putting them in her handkerchief.

As stipulated by her father, she, her mother and sister were dressed in Western clothes each evening. He explained to them long ago that it was a way of reminding them of the French part of their family. During the day, they could wear Vietnamese dresses, but at sundown they had to be French.

She wondered how surprised he would be to see her like she was. Through the soldier that she sent to follow him, she knew where he stayed and that his full name was Lê Duy Tâm. Her father had made inquiries at court and verified that he was one of the candidates who had passed the regional examinations and had just finished taking the palace examinations.

He was a village teacher from the Tonkin, which explained the strange sounding Vietnamese that he spoke. He was already famous for his scholarship and erudition, but nobody except her knew that he was also skilled in martial arts. She remembered the speed with which he disposed of their attackers, his fierce eyes as he stared down the two thugs who attacked her and her maid.

The same fierce eyes had looked into hers and she still remembered their expression change into one of kindness and concern. Yet he had left so promptly as soon as he saw her home, without giving her time to say anything. She told herself that she needed to see him again to thank him properly. However, it was getting late, and even at the end of a long summer day, the sky was definitely getting dark.

She heard the carriage before she saw it and a soldier ran out of his guard post to open the gate. The secretary got off first, then the village teacher. His hair was wet and glistening, tied in a ponytail in the back. He wore a simple outfit that consisted of a black but faded tunic over brown pants. She ran to him before he saw her.

"Teacher Tâm, I am so happy you could come."

His eyes showed the surprise he felt at seeing her in a Western dress. She wore a form-fitting shirt with long sleeves and a high collar going up to her chin. A long skirt covered the lower half of her body, flaring from the waist down all the way to her feet. He looked again at her face to see the pale blue eyes and make sure she was the same person he encountered the day before. Then he smiled, and she felt her heart beat a little bit faster.

"Françoise, are you going to bring your guest inside?" her father's voice boomed behind her.

So Nguyễn Văn Hải was actually a Frenchman and from all appearances one highly placed and influential at court. He was a tall man wearing the uniform of a French naval officer but without a hat. His complexion was ruddy, his face jovial, sporting a handlebar neatly trimmed and waxed. Tâm had only seen people like him from a distance, and most of them were certainly not as friendly and open as the foreigner standing before him.

Standing next to him was a Vietnamese woman with some resemblance to the one he knew as Giang. She was taller than and not quite as slim as many Vietnamese women, and she was attired in Western clothes like her daughters. Behind them was a younger woman, a sister in all likelihood, with a mischievous expression, definitely more French in her physical appearance from the much paler skin to the pointed nose and the light brown hair. Instead of being blue, her eyes were brown like those of most Vietnamese. They seemed to be rather amused by the spectacle the village teacher presented to the French mandarin's family.

The mother and the sister were looking him over, seemingly taken aback by his simple clothes, the only dry and clean ones that he could find in the meager personal belongings he had brought with him from his village. In the capital city, clothes made the man and his certainly did not fit the image of the scholar that they had expected. Nevertheless, he did look bright, perhaps even handsome, and on his hands, the nails were by no means long and curvy.

His Excellency Hải took one step forward and extended his hand.

"Teacher Tâm, welcome to our home," Bonneau said warmly in almost perfect Vietnamese.

His Huế intonation was near perfect and Tâm was stunned that a foreigner could speak Vietnamese that way. He reached out with his hand to grab and shake that of his host, adopting the Western custom that he had heard about.

Tâm bowed slightly to Giang's mother, and then followed the family inside. The room he entered was immense, unlike any that he had seen in Vietnamese homes. Giang led him to a chair and sat in another one next to him. Introductions were made, after which he became the center of attention of the entire family. The mother spoke first.

"We would like to thank you for rescuing our daughter yesterday. That's why my husband sent our secretary to invite you to come."

"Please forgive me for being late," he responded. "I went on an outing today and spent all day taking a boat trip up river and had no idea that your secretary was looking for me."

He noticed that Mai, the younger sister, somehow found what he was saying funny and was trying to suppress a laugh. Giang threw a menacing look at her sister to calm her down.

"That is quite all right," the father said. "It's my fault for not planning this better. In any case, you are here, and that's all that matters. Françoise, or Giang as you know her, told me how quickly you were able to chase away those two attackers. I want to personally say thank you for what you did."

"It's not much really. Anybody in the same situation would have done what I did."

"But perhaps not with the same skills that you showed. I know you are a scholar who has been taking the palace examinations, but may I ask if you are also a martial artist?"

"Oh no, I would not call myself that," he responded quickly. "In my family, for generations now, perhaps going back to the Trần dynasty, we have always practiced self-defense techniques passed down from one of our ancestors. I do it as a form of physical exercise under my uncle's guidance. But I never really thought I would have a need to practice what I learned from him."

The women were listening to him attentively, looking alternatively at the father then at their guest.

"That is truly amazing," said Bonneau before turning the conversation to another topic.

"The examinations are over and I know you are just waiting for the results to be announced. It may take several weeks before that happens. What are you going to do between now and then?"

"I hope to spend my time exploring the capital and its surroundings. Yesterday was my first day. I went by boat up past the tomb of Emperor Tự Đức and as far as the tomb of Emperor Minh Mạng. There are so many historic sites, monuments, and temples in and around Huế. I just hope there will be enough time for me to visit them all."

A servant came to announce that dinner was ready. The whole family stood up. Bonneau tilted his head toward the visitor.

"Teacher Tâm, please join us for dinner."

He was momentarily at a loss. He had not expected them to have dinner at such a late hour, but he could not come up with an excuse to take leave right then. The mention of food reminded him that the delicious clam and rice that he had for lunch was long gone and that his stomach was starting to protest his lack of attention to it. While he still hesitated, Giang went to stand in front of him.

"You must be hungry after being out all day. Please come."

He looked up at the blue eyes and the radiant smile, and could not find any reason to decline her invitation.

They sat down at a long rectangular table with Bonneau at the head, his wife and the younger daughter on one side, his older daughter and their visitor on the other.

Tâm was overwhelmed with the number and variety of dishes arrayed on the table. Servants were still busy placing more food on the table or serving them out to the family and their visitor. The plates and bowls were all small-sized but appeared to be of fine china quality. He had heard of the French using forks and knives to eat but did not see those utensils. Each person had a bowl placed on top of a small plate, with chopsticks on the side. The food served was fit for a royal feast, or at least he thought so since he really did not know what the King usually ate.

As soon as they were settled in their seat, Bonneau looked at him and said.

"Teacher Tâm, I usually say a short prayer before dinner. Please bear with us."

He was still looking at the father when beneath the table he felt a hand grasp his right hand and give it a gentle squeeze. He looked down and saw that Giang's hand had now clasped his and would not let go. The sudden contact left him shocked and speechless. Of whatever words of prayer were pronounced by Bonneau, he remembered nothing except that they were in a foreign language, presumably French. She did release his hand right after grace was said, and went on to act normally as if nothing had happened.

Dinner conversation was carried out in Vietnamese in deference to the guest, and it was light and inconsequential. Servants came in and out of the room, bringing even more dishes. He was plied with food by his immediate neighbor who hardly ate and instead spent time picking morsels of food with her chopsticks and putting them into his bowl.

Finally, he had to stop and claim that the food was excellent but that he was not used to such gastronomic extravagance. After that, he noticed that Giang was finally eating on her own account although she only lightly touched most of the dishes.

The head of the family ate vigorously, was able to handle his chopsticks naturally without any awkwardness, and was obviously fond of the food of his wife's country.

As the table was cleared to make room for sweets and tea, Bonneau leaned back on his chair with satisfaction. He glanced at the unusual visitor sitting next to his daughter.

Most of the natives that he was used to dealing with usually went out of their way to be submissive and toadying. In contrast, the young scholar maintained his dignity and composure. His handshake was firm, like that of a Westerner, and he did not give the impression of being overwhelmed by the strange surroundings and people around him.

Could he be one of those rebels who hated foreigners and took arms against them even though they knew they were doomed to fail? Still, after more than two decades in the country, Bonneau thought he was a good judge of Vietnamese character and he did not see the young man as a menace or a security risk.

Earlier in the day, Bonneau had made inquiries about him and, although he did not find out much, the little information that came back was favorable. The only thing missing was a lack of pedigree or backing for the young scholar who was a *hương sư,* a village teacher. His parents and family were virtual unknowns in government circles. He rose from nothing, had no influential supporter or sponsor, and would probably go back to obscurity if he failed the examinations.

On the other hand, were he to succeed, he would be another proof that the antiquated system of examinations was truly democratic and did allow the best and brightest of the nation to come out of nowhere to participate in government. If so, Bonneau would like to snatch him away and enlist him in the colonial administration. Many Vietnamese scholars passionately resented French presence and domination. If he could win over this likable young man, it would be a significant step in trying to win over the rest of the Vietnamese intelligentsia to France's causes and goals.

"Teacher Tâm, I know it will be some time before anybody finds out, but how do you think you did in the examinations?" Bonneau inquired.

"Father, it's not polite to ask him such questions," Giang scolded her father. She had switched to French in speaking to him.

"But I meant no harm, my daughter," he responded, also in French. "I may even be of help to him, if he should need it."

The young woman was still glowing, only slightly mollified by her father's explanation. Tâm, who did not understand a word of the brief exchange between the two, looked curiously at them as he tried to guess what the argument was about. Finally, he decided to answer Bonneau's question the same way that he usually did.

"I did my best in the examinations, but it will be up to the judges and fate to decide the outcome."

"Yes, indeed. We'll just have to wait to find out," said Bonneau. His thoughts then drifted to a subject that had been dear to him and to his superiors in the colonial administration.

"Since you are a teacher, I would like to ask you something else. Are you by any chance acquainted with the Romanized script for writing Vietnamese, the one that Christian missionaries invented over two centuries ago?"

Tâm replied without hesitation.

"I have heard about it, and I am quite interested in it. However, until now I have not found anybody that could teach it to me, or any good way to learn it by myself."

"Well, you should know that in this family, only my wife knows how to read and write Chinese characters. I don't, although at times I wish I could in my dealings with the Emperor and the court mandarins, but that's another matter."

He waved his hand to reject the dark thoughts that threatened to take him off track.

"Our two daughters refuse to learn Chinese, saying that it is too hard and it would take too long. Then we insisted that they learn how to read and write Vietnamese using the new Romanized script. My wife and I both know the script quite well. So she teaches it to them at home, while they go to school for the rest of their education in French. They have done that for a few years now, and they are just as good in French as in Vietnamese, for the alphabet is practically the same between the two languages."

He turned to his two daughters who both looked at Tâm and nodded their heads to confirm what their father had related. Bonneau got up and said.

"Please come with me and I'll show you proof of what I just said."

His curiosity now fully awakened, Tâm followed the father. Bonneau opened the door to another room and, as soon as his guest entered after him, he closed it. They were in a fairly large room, with an immense desk covered with nautical memorabilia taking center stage. The wall was richly paneled and one side of it was covered with a big map of Southeast Asia. Bonneau sat behind the desk and invited him to take a chair. He opened a drawer to pull out a piece of paper and took up a tube that he uncapped, revealing a shiny metallic nib at the end of the tube. He looked up, saw Tâm's gaze fixed on it and explained.

"This is something an American captain recently gave me. It's a fountain pen with its own reservoir of ink stored in the tube. It is very convenient to write with because you don't have to continually dip it in an ink bottle."

Tâm was captivated by the Frenchman's pen, silently making comparison to his brush and ink, when Bonneau interrupted his thoughts.

"Teacher, tell me the first few lines of any Vietnamese poem that you like. I will write them down on this piece of paper using the new script. I am ready whenever you are."

Tâm thought for only a few seconds then started to recite the first lines of the popular "Kim Vân Kiều" by Nguyễn Du.

"Those are famous lines indeed! Just give me a little time to write them down," Bonneau said good-naturedly.

Tâm noted that he wrote quickly from left to right, and the characters that flowed out of his pen had no resemblance to the Chinese characters he was accustomed to. The strange looking writing instrument functioned as Bonneau described it, for not once did he reach out to any ink container and yet the ink flowed smoothly and evenly from its tip.

When Bonneau was finished writing, he dried the paper with a curved blotter then got up, went to the door, and called for his elder daughter to come in. Giang entered the room, a questioning look on her face. Waving the piece of paper on which he had scribbled six lines, he challenged her.

"My dear daughter, will you read this for us?"

She took the paper from him, glanced at it briefly, then turned to face Tâm with a twinkle in her eyes.

"I love this poem! It is so beautiful."

In a soft but clear voice, she then read the lines that her father had written down on paper.

Trăm năm trong cõi người ta,
Chữ tài chữ mệnh khéo là ghét nhau
Trải qua một cuộc bể dâu,
Những điều trông thấy mà đau đớn lòng.
Lạ gì bỉ sắc tư phong
Trời xanh quen thói má hồng đánh ghen.

(Were full five-score the years allotted to born man,
  How oft his qualities might yield within that span
      to fate forlorn!
  In time the mulberry reclaims the sunk sea-bourn,
  And what the gliding eye may first find fair weighs mournful
      on the heart.
  Uncanny? Nay – lack ever proved glut's counterpart,
  And minded are the gods on rosy cheeks to dart
      ceslestial spite...)

Bonneau looked triumphantly at his visitor.

"You see! Didn't she read every line, every word?"

"This is very impressive," Tâm replied then turned to Giang. "How long did it take you to learn this new script?"

"Not long at all. Both Mai and I were very young then, and we were learning French at the same time. Mother knows the new script and used it to teach us how to read and write in Vietnamese, while the priests at school taught us French and Latin."

"And how long do you think it would take for someone like Teacher Tâm?" her father asked.

"Perhaps a few days, or a couple of weeks at most," she replied. Impulsively, she turned to her father with an eager face.

"How about if I were to teach him the new script? I can do it."

"You are certainly quite capable of doing it. That's if he doesn't mind being taught by a child like you."

"Father, I am not a child! Oh, you are impossible!"

She ran around the table and gave Bonneau a hug as he winked at the village teacher.

That was how he started learning the new script, under the daily tutelage of a young woman half Vietnamese and half French, in the living room of her home.

At first, he tried not to show the mixed emotions that he felt. He wanted to learn the new script, thinking that he would eventually teach it to his own students back in his village. However, he felt uncomfortable associating himself with the family of one so prominently connected with the colonial regime. What would people say? What would they call him, a traitor? All he wanted to do was to learn something that he could later use for his own students' benefit.

In the past, there were generals who learned military tactics by observing how French troops drilled and attacked. The same generals then trained Vietnamese soldiers and adopted modern weaponry to fight successful battles against the French. One of them even learned how to make guns for his men, copying the design from Western models.

On the other hand, those who continued to cling to old fashioned military doctrine, or even worse, to superstition or astrology, were never able to put up much of a fight against the French, losing their lives and those of their followers in the process.

He did not consider his attempt to learn the new script to be the same as cooperating and abetting the enemy. The French wanted more people to learn it, and perhaps they saw that as a way to get rid of the antiquated Chinese inspired system of education. That was not necessarily a bad thing, he thought. It was a goal that he could agree with. He as much hinted at it when he wrote his final composition a few days earlier.

"Teacher Tâm, you are day dreaming instead of concentrating on your studies!" her voice gently chided him. "What are you thinking of? Who are you thinking of? Is there someone back home waiting for you?"

He shook himself off his reverie and returned to copying the new alphabet characters and the short phrases that she had written out for him. He had mastered the alphabet in little time, as well as the fountain pen that she had borrowed from her father for him. He did not ask for it, but she somehow knew he was intrigued by the mechanical writing instrument and simply handed it over to him to use.

"What are you talking about?" he said. "I was only thinking of the strange coincidence that brought me here."

"So there is no one back home waiting for you?" she persevered.

"Oh yes, there is."

He stopped writing and looked up in mock seriousness. A fleeting look of alarm appeared on her face and the blue eyes blinked several times.

"My old mother is the one waiting for me."

She lowered her eyes and turned away as her cheeks colored, and then returned to the book she was holding on her lap.

Giang was the other dimension in his life, one that he had not planned for when he set forth from his village to go to the capital. She had been a gracious host and a delightful teacher during the few days that he spent at her house.

Her mother, her sister Mai, and some servants stopped by occasionally, but for the most part, they were left alone. From the beginning, he had insisted that he would only spend an hour or two in the morning with her. He gave his full attention to the lessons and made excellent progress, pleasing both of them very much. More than once, she had asked him to stay for lunch or dinner but he had always declined.

What was he going to do when there was nothing more for her to teach him and the lessons ended? From the very beginning, this kind and sweet young woman had made a determined effort to make him feel welcome in her house. She had not grasped his hand again and held it like she did on that first day, but he knew well enough that their daily interaction had taken a deeper meaning with time. He had heard that Westerners were more open and expressive, and Giang could certainly be considered a young Western woman, even if she looked Vietnamese.

"What are you reading?" he asked.

She looked up from her book.

"It's a little novel from Alphonse de Lamartine, a French writer from some twenty, thirty years ago. It's titled *Graziella*."

"And how do you like the book?"

"It's quite good so far, but I think the ending is going to be sad. I wish you knew French, and then I could let you read it also. You may enjoy it too."

"I've been thinking of learning French as soon as I master this new Vietnamese script."

"Will you need a teacher then?" she asked eagerly.

"It will be easier if I had one."

She put her book down.

"Do you want me to teach you? I have all the books you'll need. I even have a grammar and vocabulary book in three languages: our own language, the author calls it Annamite, then Chinese and French. You will like that. I am pretty good with French myself, according to the Jesuit priests at school. I think you will also learn it very fast, from what I've seen you do these past few days. You only need to be told once, and you remember everything perfectly."

"I may have only a few weeks left, do you think that will be enough time?"

She laughed and teased him.

"I will tell my father to ask the King to order the judges not to announce the results for a long time, at least not until I am finished with you."

"You can't do that. I will run out of spending money and will definitely have to go back to my village! Seriously, you should ask him whether it's all right for you to teach me French."

"He will have no objection. Consider it done!"

After a while, she stopped reading again.

"Have you done any more sightseeing as you said you would?"

"Not yet, I've been thinking about it, but I wanted to make sure I learn this first. Lately, after your lessons, I've spent my days practicing writing and reading the books in Vietnamese that you lent me."

She thought for a moment and was going to tell him something but changed her mind and kept quiet.

The following day, as he was preparing to leave for his daily lesson with Giang, the innkeeper came to his room. The man was quite excited but spoke in a low voice, almost a whisper, although there was nobody around them.

"Teacher, there is a young lady waiting for you outside. Her maid came in and asked me to let you know she is waiting for you."

After a slight pause, he winked and added.

"You are a very fortunate man indeed."

Thiên Mụ Temple

They were standing in front of the inn, the maid nervous and apprehensive, while Giang seemed calm.

"Teacher Tâm, today let's go sightseeing instead of studying," she said as soon as she saw him.

There was not going to be any study at her house, and all he could do then was to suggest the Thiên Mụ temple, a place he already wanted to visit. She readily agreed, and after she told the maid to go home, they left the inn.

They walked side by side on the bank of the Perfume River, along the South wall of the Citadel. The temple was to the West of the city. She was wearing a hat with a wide circular brim and a five-panel tunic over black pants of the same material. He found her more attractive and more natural with those traditional garments than in her Western dresses.

"Have you been to the temple before?" he asked.

"Oh yes, many times. Even though we are Catholics, my mother has been taking Mai and I to the temple every year. It is a beautiful and peaceful place, and she goes there to donate to the abbot and his monks. Many years ago, her family used to be devout Buddhists, even though most of them are now Catholics. The abbot is one of her uncles."

"What do you do when you get there? I thought that your faith discourages involvement with other religions."

"That may be so, but my mother doesn't always listen to the priests. For her, unless she does something bad, God will not mind whether she visits a Catholic church or a Buddhist temple."

"And what do you do at the temple, you and your sister?"

'Usually we end up just following her around. When we were younger, we roamed the temple grounds, played hide and seek, or ran up and down the stairs until our legs gave out. When lunch was served, we ate our fill of the vegetarian food, especially the sweets. Sometimes we also teased the novices, and we liked to pick on the younger ones."

"I can just imagine you doing that. You and your sister must have added a few more months or years to their training each time you go there!"

"That is not so!" she protested in mock dismay. "They don't mind our teasing at all and just laugh with us. Of course, if we see the older monks we keep very quiet and reserved. We also avoid even looking at the wooden sculptures of the fierce temple guardians near the entrance gate. They are truly scary."

"I wonder what you would do if you were visiting the temple in my village. It has only one abbot who is my uncle, and no novice, only a deaf mute old man who helps maintain the temple and the grounds. There won't be anyone for you to tease."

Her curiosity was awakened at this revelation.

"Really? A temple with only one monk! Do people go there?"

"Yes, there are some people who do, and so does my family. I go there not so much to worship, but to exercise. My uncle is the one who taught me our clan's martial arts, and I go to practice with him regularly."

"Then I will have you to tease, Teacher Tâm, and you will have to keep practicing for a long time before you can be ordained."

The light bantering was relaxing both of them and they covered considerable ground without even noticing it. They were soon past the Citadel.

The houses became scarce and were replaced by luxuriant vegetation in a gamut of green intermingled with red, purple and yellow. Tall grass, ferns, bushes with beautiful flowers, and trees grew on both sides of the road, spreading down all the way to the river itself. The road sloped up toward the hill where the temple was situated. Giang tried to fill him in on the historical facts surrounding the temple. Her Jesuit upbringing and the stories passed down to her through the maternal side of her family allowed her to give Tâm a concise but factual account.

"Thiên Mụ is the name given to a legendary old lady dressed in red that appeared at the site more than two centuries ago. She predicted that a powerful lord would build a temple there for the nation's prosperity. In 1601, the building of the temple was started by Lord Nguyễn Hoàng, an earlier ancestor of the current Nguyễn dynasty. Through the centuries, a succession of lords, emperors, and kings expanded and rebuilt it many times. The most beautiful structure is the Từ Nhân tower, erected during the reign of Emperor Thiệu Trị. It is the tallest in the country and the royals and commoners alike have penned many poems and songs about it. You probably know some of those poems, Teacher Tâm."

The hill was not steep, but when they arrived at the gate they were no longer talking. At the foot of the stairs leading to the tower, Giang momentarily stopped to catch her breath. Without thinking, he took one of her hands in his. She turned her head to look at him, her cheeks slightly flushed. Her eyes blinked in the sunlight which only enhanced their blue color. She smiled happily, squeezed his hand and leaned against him briefly. Then they began their climb of the 15 steps leading to the court where the tower stood.

At the top, they turned around to look down at the glorious vista of the river placidly encircling the hill before turning South and disappearing toward distant mountains partially hidden behind white clouds floating against the blue sky.

After admiring the scenery for some time, they began walking through the temple, going from one level to the next, visiting the gardens and looking at the various buildings but not entering any. The monks were holding their mid-morning prayers and the grounds were deserted. They heard monotonal chanting accompanied by the rhythmic tapping on a wooden fish punctuated now and then by the metallic sound of a bronze prayer bell being struck. Only in the communal eating hall were there people moving around, presumably the monks and novices who had to prepare meals.

Without any warning, they heard a deep and strong voice behind them.

"What is my young lady Giang doing today at our temple?"

That question was followed by a hearty laugh. They stopped and turned around to see a middle-aged monk in a yellow robe walking toward them. His tonsure shimmered in the sunlight as his hair was entirely white, but he had a cheery countenance and the gait of a man much younger than his age.

"He's the abbot," whispered Giang. They each joined their hands together and bowed deeply to the monk. When that was done, Giang straightened herself and looked mischievously at the old man.

"Venerable abbot, it's all right to call me young lady any day, but today you must not."

The monk stopped in front of her, frowning and scrutinizing her face to guess what she was trying to get at.

"Today, you must call me *Cô Giáo* (Teacher) Giang, because I brought along my student." She pointed to Tâm. "I am teaching this young man how to read and write in the new Vietnamese script. Then once he has mastered it, I will be teaching him French. So, yes, Cô Giang, if you please."

The monk looked from Giang to Tâm, blinking his eyes several times to make sure he was seeing right and understanding correctly.

"Ah, you are putting me on, little Giang. He is older and bigger than you, how could you teach him anything?"

"Then student Tâm, you tell the abbot whether anything I said is not true," she said and looked in mock severity at her student.

"Yes, Venerable abbot. I am her student and she is indeed my teacher," he dutifully declared with a big smile.

"So, you see, you were wrong in not calling me Cô Giang today."

"All right, I stand corrected Cô Giang, since your student supports you."

"So, the next thing is you must make up for your mistake. We are both starving, and my student has been complaining, so, Venerable abbot, do you think that you will let us share some of the delicious vegetarian food from your kitchen?"

"Of course, of course!" the abbot laughed. "Follow me, Teacher Giang, and student Tâm."

He continued laughing as he led the way to the temple eating hall.

Tâm was about to protest to Giang that he had not complained about anything, but she already guessed what he was about to say.

"You didn't say you were starving, but I wanted to be sure the abbot would not leave us out here by ourselves while he and his monks savor their food inside." To his consternation, she had raised her voice with that statement while walking right behind the abbot.

"I heard that!" the abbot shouted. "But the Buddha's teachings do not allow me to be offended."

He exploded in an ever louder laugh.

She took his elbow and squeezed it quickly.

"He is my mother's uncle, remember. I always give him a hard time and he likes me that way."

"She's absolutely correct, Teacher Tâm," the abbot roared. "Her mother told me about you a few days ago, so I already knew."

Giang let out a long sigh.

"That spoils it all. Here I was thinking I could surprise you a little bit, Grand Uncle."

"Cô Giang, you and your student can still come inside and you can tell me more about what you have taught him all this time."

Afterwards, as they left the temple to go back to the city, he asked her.

"Giang, when you were on horseback the other day, you were going home. But where were you coming from?"

"I thought you would be asking about that sooner or later," she replied. "We have time, so I'll show you instead of telling you. Just follow me."

They left the road along the river bank and took a side street which took them up a steep hill. Halfway to the top was a house that had seen better times. The walls were blackened with moss or soot and the roof was missing a tile here and there. However, the garden around the house was well maintained and planted with flowering bushes and all sorts of vegetables and fruit trees.

A child stood up in the front garden and shouted "Cô Giang!" then ran up to meet them. Soon other children emerged from various places in the garden and converged on the visitors. An old man with a shaved head also appeared, squinting and smiling broadly.

The children, boys and girls of various ages, clustered around Giang, chirping happily and tugging at her clothing to pull her in various directions. The old man shushed them until they finally quieted down.

"My young lady, what brings you here today?" he asked, clasping his hands and bowing slightly.

"Uncle Thanh, this is Teacher Tâm," she said by way of introduction. "He wanted to know where I went to last week, so I wanted to show him this place."

Turning to Tâm, she continued.

"This is an orphanage that the Thiên Mụ temple opened a few years back, right after the French soldiers sacked and pillaged the capital. Many people died and most of the orphans here are their children. Uncle Thanh is the caretaker in charge of daily operations here. He is not a monk despite his shaved head. There are also two real nuns helping in the back, and my sister and I try to bring a few things here from time to time. As you can see, they grow most of their food, except for a few things like rice. So last week I used my horse to bring them a bag of rice, salt, sugar and a few other essentials. At other times, I try to bring some medical supplies that my father obtains from the French military. You know, when those two men were trying to rob us last week, the sack one of them tried to snatch from me was mostly empty and had nothing of value since all of its contents were brought here."

The old man looked at her then at Tâm before adding his own comments.

"Teacher, she gives us many of the things that we desperately need. The children make toys and sell them at the market, together with any surplus crop from our gardens. We use the money they earn to buy some of the things we cannot grow or make ourselves, but it's never enough to meet our needs."

"I also come here to play with the children," added Giang as she was dragged away laughing by several children who insisted she had to go see what they were making in the back.

Uncle Thanh nodded appreciatively and spoke to Tâm.

"They adore her. She helps us tremendously, not only with what she brings with her, but also by merely being here regularly. She's like an older sister or a young mother to them."

He led Tâm inside the house and gave him a tour of the simple accommodations. There were two large rooms, one where everyone slept on bamboo beds of all sizes, large and small, and another one where they took their meals. The kitchen and storage rooms were in the back. A well in a small courtyard provided water. The house and its simple setup reminded Tâm of the village school that was his home.

"Are you a teacher from around here?" the old man asked. "You don't sound like anybody I know in these parts."

"Actually I am a village teacher from way up North. I am just here as a visitor."

"That's too bad, because we need someone like you. The young lady tries to teach them how to read and write, but she cannot devote all of her time to it."

"Is she teaching them the new Romanized script?"

"Yes indeed. Some people say it is too easy compared to Chinese characters, but at least the children are learning something."

Tâm was amazed, realizing that Giang had already taught all these children and that he was not her first student. No wonder that she was so confident and capable. She definitely knew what she was doing and anticipated all his questions when he was learning to read and write the new script.

After a few minutes, Giang came back surrounded by a bevy of small children, some holding on to her arms and her dress. She looked down at them and said.

"It's getting late, and this was an unexpected visit anyway. Teacher Tâm and I should be going now. I'll come back another day."

A small girl clinging to her but looking at Tâm with two big eyes asked.

"Will he be back also?"

Smiling, Giang pointed to Tâm.

"You ask him."

He bent down to the little girl's level and stroked her cheek. She giggled but did not shrink back from his touch. Without waiting for her question, he said.

"Little girl, I will be back."

They returned to the city reversing the path they took in the morning. The sun was still high in the sky and the afternoon was hot. Beneath the hat that Giang was wearing, he saw a thin layer of moisture at her temple and he knew that he was perspiring too.

She chatted and pointed out to him points of interest along their way. It made time go faster, and without even noticing it, they were already at the gate of her house. A soldier ran up to open the gate.

Tâm was about to say goodbye, when the maid came out of the house to meet Giang at the gate. The woman let out a continuous stream of questions and admonitions.

"Where did you go? Your mother was so worried about you. She scolded me for not staying with you, and letting you out of sight for so long. Lunch is still waiting for you, but it's almost certainly too cold by now. Your face is all flushed and your clothes are soaked!"

Giang tried to calm the maid down.

"I took Teacher Tâm to the Thiên Mụ pagoda. We already ate there with my Grand Uncle. You know that it is not too far from here, but it still took some time to walk there and come back. We also went to the orphanage."

Tâm then realized that more than half a day had already passed. "Let me come in and reassure your mother that everything is fine, and apologize to her for taking you away too long."

"Please come in if you want to, but you don't need to apologize to her. She won't scold me if that's what you are worried about," she said as they went through the gate.

"Do you know how to ride a horse, Teacher Tâm?"

"I've only been on a horse once, when I was very young," he answered, wondering what she was leading up to. However, she said nothing more.

Later that day, after taking a bath Giang was in their bedroom combing her wet hair as her sister looked on. Mai had noticed her older sister's changed mood after she returned from the outing she took with the young scholar. Although their mother was unhappy for having lost track of her daughter for several hours, she did not voice her disapproval, especially once she was told that they met and had lunch with her uncle the abbot. For her part, Giang was in a dreamy mood even as she was drying her hair with a towel and combing it.

"Sister, you should have told me you were going to the temple. I could have covered for you with mother."

"I didn't know where we were going to go, not until he said he wanted to see the Thiên Mụ pagoda."

Mai made a show of clearing her throat.

"I wouldn't have dared go with him by myself, at least not without asking mother. You are so much bolder than I am. He's all that you've been talking about lately. Don't think I haven't noticed it, my dear sister."

"What about you and that French officer, my dear sister? Don't think I haven't noticed your puppy eyes whenever he's here."

Mai let out a long sigh.

"Giang, he only comes once in a while, and always on business with father, and he pays no attention to me, whereas your scholar is not so indifferent to you."

"I don't know about that."

"You mean, about how he feels about you? If I were you, I would ask him the next time I see him. Ha!"

Giang was absorbed with her own thoughts for a long time before she spoke again.

"I will not ask him. He can tell me, when he wants to. I will wait."

After a few days, they went back to the orphanage with Giang making another delivery of several large bags of foodstuffs. Instead of her maid, she asked Tâm to come along and they walked with her horse up to the orphanage. Uncle Thanh and the children greeted them with the same enthusiasm. The older children quickly unloaded the horse, and soon the children and Giang disappeared toward the kitchen, leaving Tâm standing alone with the caretaker.

"Uncle Thanh, what can I do to help you today?" he asked.

The old man shook his head.

"You don't have to do a thing. Just by coming here is already such a treat for the children. They usually yearn to see the young lady, and now that they also have you, they could not be more pleased."

"You know, you should put me to work. At home, I have to tend to our vegetable garden and take care of all of our plants, so I am very familiar with what needs to be done. In fact, I've missed my gardening work since coming to the capital."

They walked toward the back of the orphanage where vegetables grew on long rows of mounded earth. The children were nowhere to be seen. As if reading his thoughts, Uncle Thanh explained their absence.

"The children are assigned duties in the garden, but they are probably inside crowding around the young lady. She always bring them soft sesame and peanut cake or other kinds of candy, and they can never have enough of those sweets."

"Well, in that case let me try to finish what they started. I see that somebody was weeding but was only partially done, so I'll try to pick up where they left off."

The old man protested one last time.

"Only if you really want to, because you don't have to do anything."

Tâm removed his tunic and was going to drape it over a tall bush, but Uncle Thanh took it from him.

"I will hang this inside for you," he said then left.

Tâm rolled up his sleeves, picked up a hoe, and started weeding. He enjoyed the feeling of the familiar task and soon found his rhythm, moving expertly along the rows. The garden was well maintained and each row was covered with vegetable plants at various stages of growth, probably to spread out the harvests and avoid overabundance at any one time. Absorbed in his work, he did not notice a little girl who had approached and was watching him. She followed him like a shadow until he finally saw her and stopped.

"Ah, it's you, little one."

She smiled and her big eyes shone even brighter, pleased that he had not forgotten her. She was chewing on something, probably a piece of sesame candy he thought.

"What are you eating?"

"Candy," she replied as she extended her right arm and opened her hand. In her palm was a piece of candy. "This is for you."

"Ah, thank you, but I don't want any. You keep it for yourself."

"She said to give it to you." It was obvious she was referring to Giang.

"Did she? Then I am giving it to you. You can keep it and have it later."

The little girl insisted.

"No, I want you to eat it."

He could not say no anymore and took the candy.

"What's your name, little one?"

She made sure that he put the candy into his mouth and started chewing before she answered.

"Found."

"What? Your name is Found?"

"Yes, Grandpa Thanh found me at the front door, so everybody calls me Found," she explained as if that was the most natural name to be given to her.

He grabbed the top of the hoe handle with both hands, rested his chin on it, and looked at her then at the silvery Perfume River in the distance. He tried to imagine the circumstances of the mother who had to abandon her baby. Was her family poor and starving, or did she have some other reason? The baby had grown into such a cute little girl. What would the mother say now if she were to see her little girl? And the father, where was he?

"You found yourself a little girl friend today, didn't you, Teacher Tâm?" asked a smiling Giang. "She didn't forget you from last time, and when I gave out candy, she asked for one extra piece so that she could give it to you."

"She is so cute, and with such a strange name," he responded.

"Nobody knows where she is from, or who her parents are. Her mother or someone anyway, left her at the door one day when she was just a baby just several weeks old."

"How did she survive at that age without a mother to feed her?"

"Uncle Thanh had quite a time finding some new mother in the nearby houses that was willing to share her milk and feed her every day. Fortunately, they found one that was in the process of weaning her own child and consented to do it, in exchange for rice to feed her own family. The baby turned out to be very good and did not cry very much. Anyhow, she survived and thrived, and she has been here ever since."

His heart was still heavy when he thought back to the last image he had upon leaving the orphanage.

"She looked so pretty even when sad, because we were leaving. How could anyone abandon such a child?"

The days after that, he came back to the orphanage every chance he got. Uncle Thanh asked him to conduct classes for the children. He taught them popular verses and told them about the lives and times of legendary heroes of Việt Nam. He even drew maps on the ground to show them where different parts of the country were in relation to Huế.

One day, he was so absorbed in his story telling that he didn't notice that Giang had arrived and had been watching him for some time. When their eyes met accidentally, she nodded, smiled, and then hurried away to some other task. He remained in place, looking dreamily at the space that she had left. After a while, he felt a gentle tuck on his sleeve.

"Teacher, tell us the rest of the story," said the little girl named Found.

Judges

The judges were scholars who had passed the examinations in the past and were now serving in official capacities at court or in various Ministries. They were selected by the Minister of Rites, who organized the examinations for the King. After selection, the judges were sequestered from the official start date until the day when the list of those who passed was approved and officially posted.

They stayed in a section of the royal pavilion where they spent their days waiting and grading papers. They discussed their work among themselves, ate and slept in rooms reserved for them, watched over carefully around the clock by royal guards. During the entire examination process, they were not allowed to have contact with their families or with anybody else outside of the proctors who patrol the grounds.

Depending on the year, the number of scholars taking the examinations in the capital ranged from a few dozens to hundreds. Each one had to hand in eight essays covering topics issued from a list of questions submitted by the highest court ministers and approved by the King.

When they handed in their papers, the top of each page where they had written their names was cut off and a sequential number was assigned to each paper. The list of names and assigned numbers were in the custody of two military officers. They kept the list but could not answer any question about it since they were illiterate. This reduced the risk of tampering by any corrupt judge, but it did not eliminate it.

After all papers were graded on a scale from zero to ten, custodians took them to two different judges who compiled a preliminary list of scholars ranked by their total grades. The papers of the top-ranked scholars, each now properly identified with their authors, were then submitted to a panel of five higher-level judges. These judges reviewed them before they made their final recommendations to the King. The final judges had the power to change the grades and the rankings, if they thought that someone had been unfairly treated and deserved a better or worse grade.

At times the King or the Emperor, especially if he was a man of learning in his own right, would himself read the papers to assess the caliber of the scholars about to be granted important positions in the government. There had been instances when he would reach past the top scholars and select from lower-ranked ones or even from among those who had been failed. This occurred when nobody from a region or province, especially the area surrounding the capital, made it to the final list. The nation's leader just wanted to insure that the loyal subjects who lived closest to him around the capital were not left out, even if they were not as bright and erudite as those from more distant provinces. On the other hand, he could also fail a finalist if he particularly disliked that person for any reason, such as having a parent or an ancestor who was in political disfavor or had somehow offended the royal family.

The current King was still too young, and too uneducated in the eyes of many, to do more than approve the list of scholars recommended to him by the final judges. Bonneau and the French Resident-General were in audience and stood before the young monarch sitting awkwardly on his throne. Bonneau as usual provided all the translation that was needed. He suspected that the King and the mandarins in their silk robes and dragonfly hats surrounding him knew at least some rudimentary French, and quite possibly more. But they obstinately spoke only in Vietnamese and he had to interpret for the Resident-General, his superior, who could not and would not speak the native language.

The two men, in their military dress uniforms with medals and decorations dripping down their chests and ceremonial swords hanging at their sides, stood ramrod straight in front of the King surrounded by his ministers. Bonneau tried to soften the Resident General harsh tones, without diluting the meaning of his superior's demands and questions.

"Your Majesty, we have been advising you for several years now to do away with the examination system. Yet they are still being held at this instant, and the affairs of government have slowed down considerably since so many of your top mandarins are involved in them. Our question to you is this: what do you expect to do with the scholars who will be selected?"

Bonneau translated the statements made by his superior in his best Huế accent, sometimes adding more than was actually said in French. He did not want any confusion or misunderstanding of his country's policies, but he also did not want to sound too blunt or too confrontational. France was omnipotent, and could pretty much do as it pleased her interests, but he had lived in the country long enough to know that there was nothing to gain by humiliating the head of a nation, even if the person holding that title had little substantive power.

As soon as he stopped talking, the Minister of Rites, Trịnh Toản, a severe looking elderly mandarin, responded without waiting for the King's permission. This was not the first time that he did so, nor would it be the last. Minister Toản considered himself an unofficial Regent and usually spoke out whenever he wanted to.

"Our examination system has existed since the year 1075 under the Lý dynasty, when, may I remind you, your country was still in what you call the Dark Ages. With it, we have always been able to recruit the best minds among our scholars to serve the nation. Over the past several years, the examinations were not held because of the chaotic times during which your country managed to impose its will on ours. However, now that normalcy and peace have returned, His Majesty has decided to have them held again. The government needs a new infusion of talent to replace those who have departed because of age or war. We know that many of the scholars who have come to the capital for the examinations are undeniably the men that are needed to help His Majesty govern. The very high quality of their examination papers attests to that."

The Resident-General was annoyed. He had heard the arguments many times before, couched in even loftier phrases, but it boiled down to one principal idea: the examination system worked very well in the past and it would continue to be used indefinitely. He raised his voice even more, momentarily frightening the adolescent King, and Bonneau translated.

"The Resident-General is saying that your country, especially in the North, has not yet known peace. The remnants of the Black Flags are still a nuisance in several provinces. The Cần Vương rebels, who include members of the royal family, are still strong in some parts and make a mockery of your reign. Without France's generals and troops, you would not have a country to rule. So, please tell us how picking scholars by testing their memorization of Chinese texts that are thousands of years old is going to help you govern better."

Minister Toàn ignored the Resident General's tone and condescension. He threw a disapproving glance at the King. By a combination of marriage and blood, Toàn was proud of his royal pedigree. He was a generation above the King, an uncle close enough that he could get away with bullying the King, unlike the father the youngster had, a man who had no backbone and was the reason the French had picked his son for the throne.

The young monarch looked at him sheepishly and sat up straight on his throne as if a teacher had just rebuked him. Satisfied that the King had regained some control of himself, the Minister turned back to the two French officers, his eyes staring at them beneath bushy eyebrows, the tails of his dragonfly hat fluttering in the back of his head.

"Unlike other Western countries, by tradition our scholars are as well versed in military strategy as in literature and some of these learned men do become our best generals. From the current crop of examination scholars, His Majesty will select one of them to lead an expedition against the pirates and the rebels, and restore peace to the North."

The Resident-General smirked at the allusion to his lack of literary achievement. He and his officers were practical men who had earned their commissions and titles in campaigns and battles, but the ministers arrayed on both sides of the King still considered them barbaric.

Even Bonneau, who spoke their language and was familiar with their poetry, was still a boorish man in their eyes. Wars were won by strategy, planning, leadership, daring acts of bravery on the battlefield, and technological superiority. France was winning every battle and all these mandarins could think of was to recruit even more scholars. Yet, the old Minister had made the bold promise to pacify the rebels, and he wanted to make sure that will indeed be done.

"We will work with the mandarin that you select to ensure his mission's success. When he marches off with his troops to the Northern provinces, I will have some of my officers and men accompany him."

The image of the young scholar whom his daughter had befriended flashed through Bonneau's mind. The Minister of Rites noticed the fleeting smile on the Frenchman's face and made a mental note to find out why later.

Without kowtowing to the King, another affront that the Vietnamese had to endure, the two French officers turned sharply around and walked out of the royal audience room. A small retinue of lesser officers and secretaries were waiting for them outside and followed them out of the palace.

The two officers climbed on a waiting carriage, which whisked them away, leaving small clouds of dust behind. At the insistence of the Resident-General, they left in grand style by the South gate, another insult, since that gate was reserved only for Emperors or Kings to use to exit or enter the royal grounds.

Kham, Bonneau's secretary, was preparing to mount his horse to rejoin his boss and the Resident-General by way of the Eastern gate, the one used by everyone else, from mandarins to commoners. He did not have the courage to exit by the South gate as the Frenchmen deliberately did. However, before he could get away, a royal guard came running and waved for him to stop.

"His Excellency, the Minister of Rites, wants to see you," the man shouted.

Minister Toàn knew Kham well. He had encouraged the man, once a minor clerk in his ministry, to take a position on Bonneau's staff. Kham was to ingratiate himself with the Frenchman, and report to the Minister what was happening inside the colonial administration.

Kham had also been told to learn French and try to eavesdrop on his employer's conversations with his French fellow officers.

The secretary, however, was finding it hard to learn the foreign language, and made slow progress in that direction. But the Minister was willing to bide his time and was satisfied enough with whatever Kham could report so far through mere observation and participation in Bonneau's activities.

That was the least he could do against an adversary that he considered cunning and dangerous. The Special Envoy was a rarity in his command of the Vietnamese language, one that few of his fellow countrymen bothered to learn. With it, he served the colonial government effectively, giving his superior a good insight into the intricacies and nuances of court politics. Toản was convinced Bonneau also had spies at court, and that, through his Vietnamese wife, he knew quite a bit more about capital politics than even some of the mandarins themselves.

"Secretary Kham, have you been reporting to me all that's been happening in your work with that Frenchman?"

"Yes, I have, Your Excellency."

"Everything, you are sure? What about his personal life? Anything unusual?"

"No sir, no scandal. He is completely faithful to his wife."

Kham was thinking furiously to guess at what the Minister was driving at. He wanted to please the old mandarin who had saved him from obscurity and allowed him to earn a decent living and yet still convince himself that he was working in his country's best interest. Suddenly sweat began to appear on his face as he realized that he had not yet reported on something.

"Your Excellency, about a week ago his older daughter and her maid were attacked on the street not too far from their house."

"I heard about that," said Toản, without betraying any emotion.

"A man rescued them and chased away their assailants. The day after that, I was told to go and invite him to their residence for dinner."

The old man fixed Kham with a puzzled expression but remained silent.

"He looked like a commoner to me, more like a peasant than a scholar, but somehow he got along fine with the family, especially with the older daughter. Since then he has come almost every day to learn the new Vietnamese script with her as teacher."

"Did you find out who he is?"

"He is a scholar from the North. He is in his mid-twenties, his name is Lê Duy Tâm and he took part in the recent palace examinations. He has nothing that may distinguish him, nothing that I would consider worthwhile. He will probably not pass, from what I can tell."

"Secretary Kham, you only report to me what the facts are, and nothing more. When I want to know your opinion, I will ask you."

Toàn chastised his informant because he had recognized the name as one of those on the final list of scholars.

The Minister of Rites oversaw the entire examination process. Only the King himself was a higher authority, but with such a young King, Toàn had the actual and definitive say on such matters. He had convened a meeting of the five final judges and asked them to bring the stacks of papers that they had graded and passed. At this stage, all the papers had been matched to the candidates' names. Outside of the six mandarins in the room behind closed doors guarded by the proctors, nobody knew who was on the final list to be submitted for the King's approval.

"Who can tell me how many scholars made it to the final list?" Toàn asked. He already knew who they were but wanted to hear it directly from the assembled judges.

One of the mandarins, a silver haired man from the Ministry of Justice, answered right away.

"Your Excellency, only ten have been deemed worthy of passing the examinations: two from the North, six from the Center, and two from the South."

"That is a good distribution by region. It shows the dominance of our capital and its neighboring provinces in these matters, thanks to the high caliber of the scholars that have been nurtured here."

He knew that insecurity in the North had prevented a significant number of scholars from travelling to the capital to participate in the examinations. As for the South, a full colony of France, the elite class there was turning to French education and few wanted to come to the capital to try to win degrees that were no longer worth much in terms of power or wealth. However, he kept these thoughts to himself and asked his next question.

"Of the ten that you have judged to be the topmost, which one stands out as the best of the crop?"

The judge who had spoken earlier did not hesitate.

"Your Excellency, one of the two men from the North is clearly better than all of the others."

The other four judges nodded their unanimous assent. Minister Toản did not like what he heard, but he had no choice but to continue with his line of inquiry, knowing what was to come next.

"What is his name? Tell me why you found him so clearly better than the others."

"You Excellency, he is Lê Duy Tâm. All five of us have read his papers, as well as those of the rest of the scholars. His essays stand out not only because of their obvious erudition. There is no doubt that he knows the Four Books and the Five Classics at least as well as the others. But he is able to be very concise while covering all the required points, almost as if he were one of those who wrote the Song commentaries themselves."

Minister Toản knew that the scholars had to explain the meaning of several aspects of the Confucian texts. He had selected the topics himself, making sure that they included several esoteric ones that he suspected few would know about, unless they had read the commentaries by Zhu Xi of the Song dynasty.

"His prose poems and verses are also exemplary," continued the judge. "He did not violate any rule and he incorporated in them the correct allusions, proverbs, idioms and quotes from past classical Chinese authors. Still he managed to convey in no uncertain terms that he is a Vietnamese writer and not a mere imitator of the Chinese. None of the other scholars would or could do that, and therefore we judged him superior to them. His final essay on the reforms needed for our educational system, even though a little too idealistic and impractical in many respects, should be presented to the King for his review."

So they liked his originality and his independence from Chinese tradition, thought the Minister. He wondered what they would think if they knew that their choice scholar was now involved with a French family and might even work for the French in the future.

Toản could already guess that the final essay was about discarding the old and adopting the new Western ways so that future generations of Vietnamese would give themselves over to foreign culture, religion, while losing their morals and their traditions in the process. Of course, the essay would not exactly say that, but that's what its unwritten implications would be.

Yet the shortsighted mandarins under his employ who served as examination judges failed to recognize the threat, just because the writer of the essay had an easy way with words and could produce exemplary turns of phrases. The Minister seethed with fury but tried his best to keep it under control. He was already seeing the beginning of a plan to deal with the problem in his head.

"Hand me all of his papers. What you have told me about him has aroused my curiosity. Over the next few days I want to read what he wrote to see whether I will arrive at the same conclusions as yours."

"Certainly, Your Excellency. We would be honored if you do so."

The judges had expected the results to be announced so they could be released and allowed to go home. They were tired of their isolation and missed their families. However, they could not defy the Minister's will and they had no choice but to stay sequestered in the palace for a little while longer.

The Minister of Rites walked out with the examination papers he wanted tucked inside his robe sleeves. The rule was that no paper left the palace until after the results were announced and the examinations declared over, but who was going to challenge him?

For two days Minister Toản read the papers, some of them several times, carefully, from beginning to end, then back to the beginning. He remembered years ago when he was a young scholar sitting in his tent under the harsh summer sun or in the rain, trying to write his examination papers. He conceded that it probably was not as easy for him as for this young scholar from the North. He had to struggle to come up with each word, each sentence, one by one, slowly and painfully.

This young scholar, from what he could tell, was thinking in whole sentences, perhaps in complete paragraphs. His calligraphy, the best he had seen in a very long time, showed a steady hand and an evenness worthy of the best artists. The characters exhibited consistent ink coloration, and though each was formed correctly and there was no amateurish flourish, there was still some originality in the way each brushstroke was begun and completed.

He had heard that the scholar used his martial arts to subdue and chase away the attackers of Bonneau's half-breed daughter. It was quite possible that his physical training had a bearing on the way he used the brush for writing.

So, how was he going to fail such an accomplished scholar? Toản mulled over his options for another day from dawn until stars began appearing in the night sky. He ate little and went to bed only to toss and turn next to his mystified young wife.

She watched him carefully, not knowing whether she or something else was the cause of his bad mood. After his wife's death, he had picked her, a woman of humble origin to share his bed. She was pretty, younger even than his son, but once his eyes fell on her, her family had no choice but to grant the wishes of such a powerful mandarin.

At first shy and easily intimidated, she had gradually learned to know him and anticipate his moods and desires. With time, her self-confidence grew as he became accustomed to depend on her at home while she strived to please him and indulge his littlest whims and demands.

However, he had not confided in her what was bothering him. He practically snarled when she tried to ask him about it. She too had things to hide from him, but she was sure he would never find out about that. Whatever was bothering him could only come from his work. She decided to bide her time, knowing that soon enough, one way or another, he would tell her.

After a sleepless night, Toản woke up before dawn and sent for his most trusted guard. The man climbed out of bed and came running while adjusting his uniform.

"Go find me Teacher Xinh and bring him back here this very morning," he instructed the guard.

The surprised man opened his eyes wider than normal to look at the Minister. He had no idea who Teacher Xinh was, let alone where he could find him. The Minister saw the look of confusion and shouted impatiently.

"He lives in a village near Emperor Minh Mạng's tomb. Go down to the river and ask any boatman to take you there. Go! NOW!"

The Beach at Thuận An

L earning French turned out to be a bit more challenging to Tâm than he had originally feared. It helped that he already knew the alphabet, but he was dealing with a completely foreign language. The words and their writing were not too difficult, as his nimble mind enabled him to remember each word's spelling with relative ease.

French grammar was complex with its gender and tenses, its declensions and different spellings of plural and singular forms, and it took him considerable effort to begin finding order and logic in French grammatical rules.

The hardest part, however, was that he had to learn to produce new sounds and utter words totally unfamiliar to him. From the very beginning, pronunciation had been especially difficult for him. He hesitated, tried, stumbled, and tried again and again.

Thankfully, Giang was a patient and tireless teacher who never stopped encouraging her student. Her sister Mai joined their group from time to time to help with pronunciation drills or verb conjugation. Playfully, she seemed to enjoy breaking the monopoly her sister had on their guest's time and attention, but she too was honestly trying to assist him with his learning. The two sisters took turns making him repeat French words and sentences day after day. He found himself practicing his drills as he walked back to his inn, but they continued to correct him frequently during the sessions at their home.

Giang let him borrow as many books as he wanted and every day when he came back to the inn he poured over them well into the night. He used the dictionary in three languages the most as he tried to read the other books. At first, the foreign words danced in front of his eyes but with patience and an innate ability to master languages, they finally began making sense to him.

During a break, he could not help expressing his frustration.

"I am taking too much of your time and making hardly any progress. Now I know how my own students back home felt when they struggled with their assignments."

Giang was understanding but nevertheless shook her head.

"Teacher Tâm, you are doing very, very well," she said. "In fact you are doing much better than anybody I know. Take secretary Kham, he has been trying to learn French for at least a year, but I think you are now advancing beyond his level, and that's only after a few weeks. Every time I see you in the morning I know that you have retained all that Mai and I taught you the day before. It's just that there is so much to learn, and we are trying to accomplish in a very short time what should normally take months and years."

As an afterthought, she added wistfully. "I only wish that they keep delaying the announcement of the examination results, so that I can spend more time with you."

Later, before he went home, she told him almost casually.

"Tomorrow, I will come by your inn very early in the morning and we will go on another outing."

"I wouldn't mind going back to the orphanage," he responded without hesitation.

He had gone back there with her once already and enjoyed being among the children as if they were his own students back home. While Giang was busy taking inventory of the provisions and talking with the old man running the place, he at first tried to help with the gardening. But the children would not let him do much of that kind of work, preferring instead to make him sit and tell them fairy tales or stories about historical heroes. He did not mind playing that role again to take a break from his own struggle with French.

However, this time Giang had a different idea.

"We'll return to the orphanage for sure, but tomorrow we'll go to a different place, for the whole day. I will tell my mother in advance so that she won't have to worry like last time. And, my dear student, you can still practice French as we go. I'll make sure to remind you of that."

He laughed at that last warning.

"Teacher, don't I deserve a break once in a while?"

She turned away to hide a smile.

"I was only afraid that you would insist on staying in town to study."

"So tell me where we are going that will take the whole day?" he asked.

"Would you like to see the ocean?"

Tâm got up early the following day eager to be leaving with Giang for the seashore. Although the Pacific Ocean had been nearby for a good portion of the way down to the capital from his village in the North, he had never actually been close to it, only catching glimpses here and there whenever the road skirted along a coastal area. Even then, he was in a hurry to get to the examinations and did not want to take the time to go near the waves, something that he had always wanted to do but just kept on deferring to another occasion.

Although its sources came from the Trường Sơn range of mountains Southwest of Huế, the name Sông Hương (Perfume River) was given to the river formed by its two tributaries at Bằng Lãng. From there it flowed leisurely for no more than 18 miles before discharging itself into the Pacific Ocean at a small fishing village called Thuận An. From where they started in the city, the distance to Thuận An was a about nine miles. Tâm was prepared to walk that day and was not too surprised when he saw Giang waiting for him while standing beside her horse in front of the inn. The relatively young animal, a filly, was carrying on its back a basket and a bulging burlap bag tied together and thrown across the saddle.

"I brought some provisions for us," she explained. "It will be a long trip."

She was in a cheerful mood and wore a light yellow tunic over black pants, her hair tied loosely to the back and held together by a ring of yellow and white frangipani flowers. After she turned the horse around, he stopped by her side and pointed to the animal.

"I can walk the distance, but you should get on the horse."

She shook her head resolutely.

"I will walk with you. I don't want people to think that you are my manservant."

Seeing that he was still showing some misgiving, she declared.

"It's not that far, I can do it. Remember that I am used to walking from my house to the orphanage, which is also a fairly good distance."

She took the filly's reins and began walking, leaving him no choice but to follow her. They stayed on the road that kept close to the right bank of the river. The sun was low on the horizon and the early morning air was still cool and pleasant. For the city's inhabitants, the day had barely started, but they saw boats drifting downstream toward the ocean, with people on them busily preparing their nets and fishing equipment. Other boats were moving in the opposite direction. Giang seemed to be familiar with the activities and explained.

"The boats coming back have been out fishing all night along the coast. They are bringing in their catch to sell at the markets in the city. The others are just starting to go fishing now. Later on, maybe we can hail one of them and see if we can buy some fresh catch for lunch."

They moved easily along the deserted road under the shade of the pine trees that grew on both sides. A cool breeze blew in from the ocean, gently swaying the branches and their needles. The scent of the pine trees permeated the air surrounding them as they walked side by side, having almost forgotten about drills and practices. Once in a while she pointed out features in the landscape in Vietnamese and asked him for their corresponding French words. He managed to get the majority of them right.

Over the sound that the horse's hooves made on the road and that of their own footsteps, they heard the songs and calls of a multitude of birds as they hunted for their food or called for one another. Once in a while, high in the canopy where the sun rays tried to pierce through the thick pine needles, they could see a brief fluttering of wings as birds darted from a tree branch to the next.

"It is so peaceful out here and I feel re-energized. This trip is an excellent idea of yours, thank you Cô Giang."

"Don't even mention it, Teacher Tâm. I am glad that you wanted to come with me. Most people I know, even my own sister, would rather stay at home and out of the sun."

As they neared the ocean, they began to hear the distant sound of waves crashing lazily against the as yet invisible coastline. Giang pointed ahead to the river on their left. A small boat was moving inland and heading in their direction.

"That boat over there seems to be trying to come to shore."

They slowed down to watch the boat gliding silently toward them.

"Teacher, Teacher!"

The voice of the boatman was directed toward them. Tâm realized that he was the same one that he had hired to take him to see the imperial tombs. His two children were standing at the prow waving. A few minutes later, their smiling faces were looking at him and Giang as the boat gently scraped the river bank before coming to a stop. The boatman gave the young couple a curious look over, but other than that did not express any surprise. He refrained from asking the village teacher about his companion.

He dug his oar into the bottom of the river and tied the boat to a tree stump. His wife was sitting near him, holding a fish trap still glistening wet. She smiled warmly at the young couple, while her children ran to Tâm and hugged him. He laughed and hoisted each up in the air over his head. After he put them down, they stood clinging to him but eyed shyly the young woman that they had never seen before. Giang patted them on their cheeks and they giggled with delight, sealing their acceptance of her.

Tâm addressed their father who was striding toward him.

"Have you been out fishing this morning? Did you catch anything?"

"We sure did," the boatman answered proudly with a big toothy smile. "We netted some river clams and caught some fish and prawns."

Giang was immediately interested.

"Do you have anything you can sell to us?"

The boatman pointed to his wife. "She's going to make dumplings with the prawn. Teacher, if you want to try another delicacy from the Center, you should try these dumplings! The young lady knows what I am talking about."

Giang gave the reins of her horse to Tâm, eagerly climbed on the boat and went to squat near the boatman's wife to look into the fish trap. The boatman and his wife treated Giang with the utmost politeness and respect.

"Those dumplings are very tempting," Tâm said. "But we are on our way to the beach right now."

"Well, maybe some other day then."

The boatman paused and swerved his head to look up and down the bank of the river. Satisfied that there was nobody else around, he leaned forward and lowered his voice.

"Do you remember Teacher Xinh, the man you met on my boat last time?"

"I sure do. What about him?"

"A few days ago, I had to ferry him back to the capital. He said that he had been told to report to one of the King's ministers. He was worried and uneasy during the whole boat ride."

"I hope he did not get into some kind of trouble."

The boatman readily dismissed the idea.

"I don't think he did. But here's why I wanted to stop you the moment I saw you today. A few days after I dropped him off in the capital, Teacher Xinh came to find our boat and asked to be taken back to his village. He was gloomy and wouldn't say anything to me. When he left the boat he kept mumbling something about the examinations. He even let out some vile swear words that I don't want to repeat."

"What do you think he meant? I had no idea he was involved with the examinations."

"Who knows what he meant? But since you had taken the examinations, I thought I should warn you. Something is going on."

"Ah, perhaps that explains why they are taking so long before announcing the results."

As they finished talking Giang came back with several prawns, still alive and squirming despite being tied together. She proudly held them up.

"Look at what I bought! That's going to be our lunch today!"

"Just like that, raw?" He had heard of Japanese eating raw fish and shrimp, but he had never tried it yet.

She laughed. "No, of course not, Teacher Tâm!"

"But where can we cook them?"

"You'll see. You'll just have to wait until we get to the beach."

The boatman winked at him in mock sympathy.

"Well, Teacher, it appears she knows more than you do on some subjects."

"So, you and the young lady are going to the beach then?" he asked while preparing to push off from the bank. "It's a nice day for it, not too hot, not too windy. Enjoy the beach then, I'll let you know if I hear anything else."

The boat moved away from the bank. The boatman's wife, after being paid handsomely by Giang, was smiling happily. The children looked disappointed but bravely stood and waved to them until they could no longer see their faces in the distance. Afterwards, the boatman chuckled and observed to his wife.

"I did not expect to see Teacher Tâm with a girlfriend. After all, he's so unlike the other scholars who come on river boats like ours and spend the money their wife or family gives them on song girls."

The forcefulness of her response jolted him.

"My dear husband, open your eyes. She's not at all like those girls for hire. Her bearing, the way she talks, her polite manners, those things mean that she's from a good family. And see the way he treats her, with respect and an attitude worthy of the good scholar that he is."

After a slight pause, she sighed, not sadly but only because she knew that life in the big city could be challenging and full of surprises.

"He has really fallen for those blue eyes, and she in turn seems to genuinely like him. I just hope their families will not object or separate them from each other."

The boatman was baffled but, from past experience, knew not to disagree with her. He was the one who talked to everyone and saw everything on both sides of the river. On the other hand, she hardly ever spoke to anyone outside of their small family, yet her observations on most people and events have usually turned out to be much more perceptive and accurate than his.

"What did he mean when he said he would tell you if he heard something?" asked Giang.

"I'm not sure," he replied. "He probably doesn't know either. He was guessing that something is happening that might delay the announcement of the results of the examinations."

She was at once puzzled and concerned.

"How could he know about that?"

"That's it, he doesn't. It's just that someone, one of his passengers, has been acting strangely and rambled incoherently about the examinations. In fact, I actually met the man. We shared the same boat when I tried to go visit the imperial tombs. He's also a teacher like me. I have no idea why he would be involved with these matters. However, there's nothing we can do about it now, so let's keep going."

For a while, they walked in silence. He could see her frown as she thought of what the boatman had revealed. He also felt a little perturbed and tried hard not to show it. However, the damper on their mood proved to be only temporary. The fresh and pure ocean air flew in from the coast and soon helped them leave their uneasiness and worries behind.

They made good progress the rest of the way. He was amazed that Giang did not once complain or asked to stop for a rest. Instead, she made sure to check on him from time to time as if she was afraid of losing him if he got tired and fell behind.

They reached the beach before noon. He had never been so close to the ocean before and its vast expanse overwhelmed him. He stood and scanned the horizon almost devoid of clouds from North to South. The unbelievably long beach seemed to stretch forever in both directions. Giang, who had been to the beach before, took them to her favorite spot, one shielded from the back by pine trees and open in front to a gently sloping cove. The ocean was calm, sending languid waves onto the golden sand.

He removed his shoes and ran down to the edge of the water. Sand bubbler crabs scurried about and ran into their burrows as soon as he drew near them. The ocean air smelled fresh but briny, quite different from what he had been used to. He breathed in deeply and felt reinvigorated.

He saw that Giang had already secured her filly to a pine tree. He hurried back to help her unload the two bundles that she had brought. They contained several green coconuts, with their tops precut, ready to deliver their juice, and packages of food wrapped in banana leaves. There were also two large rectangles of cloth, one that she laid out on the sand close to the tree line. She asked him to tie the other to tree branches to use as a shield against the sun and to provide them some shade. While he was doing that, she gathered dried twigs and started a fire in a shallow hole that she dug in the sand.

They sat down and drank juice from the coconuts to quench their thirst after the long morning walk. She patiently waited for the fire to die down before placing the prawns one by one on the red embers. They burned, sizzled and when they turned orange red and black, she took them out. After they cooled down a little, she shelled them and placed the still steaming prawns on a package of sweet rice brought already cooked from home. Condiment was sea salt mixed with red pepper. She handed out chopsticks and they began eating. The morning long walk had made them hungry, and the impromptu meal tasted heavenly. They finished it off with sweet and juicy mangosteens that she had also brought.

"Giang, this is so good, and the way you made is so simple. How did you know how to plan all this?"

She was pleased with the compliment.

"Well my family has been here a few times before so I knew just what to bring. I was also aware that if we left early enough we could meet the fishermen as they return from their early morning trip and bring their catch to sell in the city's markets. With what I prepared and brought from home, we could have bought either fish or shrimp for our lunch. Or clams, but you already had rice and clams the other day, so I thought we should try something else."

The sun was now at its peak, and so was the heat. They tried their best to stay within the shade provided by the cloth that he had hung up and by the swaying pine trees. The sandy beach stretched out in both directions as far as the eye can see. There was nobody else on it and the only humans were on the fishing boats bobbing further out on the ocean. The breeze kept blowing in from offshore, a little bit stronger and creating small whitecaps further out from the shoreline. The sky had a few clouds but they looked harmless since the monsoon season had not yet started. He stood up.

"Let's go for a walk!"

She grabbed his hand to pull herself up. They started ambling barefoot, following the shoreline to the North. He saw in the distance the remnants of the two forts guarding the North and South side of the river at Thuận An where the Perfume River met the sea. The forts were crumbling and looked abandoned, but there was a tricolor French flag flying over the Northern one.

"Was your family living in the capital when the French came to attack Huế?" he asked.

She had not expected the question, thought for a moment and finally answered in a measured and detailed manner.

"Around this time several years ago, this was the way the French came to conquer the capital. Their ironclads shelled the two forts guarding Thuận An. The forts fell and as many as 2,500 Vietnamese soldiers died fighting. In the aftermath of the battle, French marines even bayoneted and killed wounded Vietnamese soldiers, even though the French did not lose a single man and only suffered a dozen wounded. The way to Huế was wide open for them."

"We were living in the Northeast corner of the citadel then. My father had worked hard to convince the old Emperor to open the door of the country to the West, to France. He said that the more he tried, the more obstinate the Emperor and the mandarins around him became. On at least one occasion, he really feared for his life. The fact that my mother was a Christian convert did not win him any friend at the court either."

"The Nguyễn emperors, even the first one who had relied on French support to gain his throne, did not want any foreign influence. But in 1883, before the battle of Thuận An, Emperor Tự Đức passed away, and a succession of weak kings were enthroned. The battle that occurred here, and the threat of total destruction of the capital and the entire dynasty, forced the government to sign the Treaty of Huế. The South was given as a colony to France, while the Center and the North became protectorates."

"Two years later, some mandarins led a revolt against the French and fighting started in the capital. The royal cannons shelled the French quarter, and Vietnamese troops surrounded the French garrison. We were still small, and my sister and I screamed every time the cannon balls whizzed overhead or landed near our house. However, after the initial surprise, French troops counter attacked and won the upper hand. For several days, they killed and pillaged the entire capital, including the Forbidden City and the innermost royal sanctums.

Thousands of Vietnamese soldiers and civilians lost their lives. My mother even feared for our own lives. She would not let Mai and I go out of the house for weeks, until my father reassured her that all was perfectly safe again. "

As an afterthought, she added. "The majority of the children that we saw the other day at the orphanage near the Thiên Mụ temple lost their parents during that time. My father has always said that we should help them in any way we can."

Their conversation took them closer to a delicate subject that he had wanted to discuss with her but had not yet found the appropriate moment to do so. He watched her in profile to see what her reaction was going to be.

"Giang, since you are half Vietnamese and half French, how do you feel about all this?"

She thought for some time, and then turned toward him. Her blue eyes looked into his with sincerity but also with a hint of sadness.

"Do you know that all my life I have considered myself Vietnamese, despite my father and his efforts at making us French, including having us wear Western dresses in the evening? A year ago, he took us to France for the summer. I was at first very eager to go. I wanted to see these places he had been telling us about for years. I wanted to see and know ordinary French people. But once my curiosity was satisfied, I couldn't wait until we got on the ship going back to Việt Nam. I was so unhappy and homesick the whole time I was there."

She laughed briefly at her own words before continuing.

"My father, believe it or not, feels the same way. He prefers living here rather than in his own motherland. However, he also told us something that I want to repeat to you now. There is no chance that this country can stand up against France's might. It has been weakened too much by centuries of civil wars, by the corruption of the Nguyễn dynasty and by the nearsighted policies of the current ruling class."

She closed her hands and made them into tight fists, bringing them up to her chest in a prayer gesture.

"I wish that things could have been different, that we could be more like Japan and less like China. My father said that Japan, after having opened its doors, is rapidly becoming a modern country equal to any of the Western nations. In China on the other hand, the Manchu dynasty is still in power, but it is rotten to the core, and the West has carved up that big country to exploit it anyway they want. They call China the sick man of Asia. We are like China, the little brother of the sick man, and just as unhealthy. It can be done, but it will take many years before we can be strong again. In the meantime, it is better for us to stop trying to fight the French. We should open our doors and concentrate our efforts on learning as much as possible from them and from the other Western powers."

He had been silent and had watched her as she spoke. She sounded at least as well or better informed about the politics of their times than most people he knew. Her parents and the Catholic priests who taught her should be justly proud of her. He also did not fail to note that she always referred to Việt Nam as "our" country, and to France as a foreign nation.

"What about you? Do you think my father was right?" she asked suddenly.

He looked out to the ocean and the waves continuously crashing against the sandy beach. It was a subject that he had thought about often, without talking about it with anyone.

"He is right, and there are probably many among us who will agree with him. Our country has clearly lost its independence. Our kings, who are now hand-picked by the French Resident General, rule probably nothing more than the few subjects, the eunuchs, and the sycophants who surround them. There are rebellions in many parts of the country, but they can't be very effective given the poor state of our country and the lack of unity and leadership. Whether we want to or not, the French are here to stay."

"Then, may I ask you whether you would be willing to work with the French colonial administration?" she asked, and then hurriedly added. "You don't have to answer if you don't want to."

He stopped and turned around to look back behind them. She followed his movement. Their footprints were visible on the wet sand. There were two sets along the shoreline, his were the larger ones, hers the smaller and delicate ones. The footprints never overlapped or even touched one another, but there was no doubt that they were walking close together and going forward in the same general direction. They turned around once more and resumed their walk.

"I spent years, practically all my life, preparing for the examinations. Before I came to the capital I had visions of passing them and being rewarded with a royal appointment. I imagined myself serving our people by being a good mandarin who could bring order, justice, and prosperity to at least some small corner of the country."

"I now realize how naïve I was. I feel like one of those sand bubbler crabs always building its nest only to see it wiped out by the next wave from the sea. For the past several years, I have been taking examinations, one after the other, and really have accomplished very little. My knowledge of the Four Books and Five Classics, or Tang poetry, helps me pass those examinations, but they have little relevance to what our country actually needs."

"Other scholars think that they are superior to those who have not studied like them, but I don't share their sentiment. Giang, you have seen more of the world than I have, and you have an education that is more practical and more appropriate to our times. You, and not I, are the type of person that Việt Nam needs."

"In the current state of our country, some people are clinging to the old regime, because they don't want to lose the privileges their families have enjoyed for generations as retainers of the Nguyễn emperors and kings. Others are fawning over the French because they see that the new rulers are able to provide them with similar privileges for generations to come. Everyone is saying that they are doing so only for the sake of the country and the people. But of course they are all serving their own self-interest, and I don't wish to be like them."

"So you would not want to work for the French? Even for someone like my own father who loves this country more than his own?"

He observed her from the corner of his eyes. She was facing forward, her eyes focusing perhaps on the distant horizon, her expression pensive, almost apprehensive.

"I think there are good and bad men in any country, any government. If the French were to plunder our country as their soldiers did in Huế, I will not work for them and will oppose them in any possible way. If they are at all like your father and have an interest in helping modernize Việt Nam, I will gladly work with them."

She sighed and looked down, slightly shaking her head.

"I agree with how you feel, even though somehow it does not make me happy to hear you say that. My father told us that among the French who are here or will be coming in the future, there are adventurers and cast-offs who only look out for their own selfish interest, men who will exploit, steal and plunder. Others are arrogant racists who firmly believe in France's *mission civilizatrice*, her sacred mission to civilize the world. They are certain of the superiority of the West and the supremacy of the white race. I am just afraid that the bad will outweigh the good, and that will discourage people like you from embracing what good the West can bring to our country."

They continued in silence, having said as much as they could about that subject. Kings and generals would come and go, insurrections would flare up and subside, and history would take its course, influenced by factors beyond their power to control or affect. They were only two people drawn together by fate first, then by mutual admiration and an unspoken attraction for each other, and they knew they had little power and influence to affect much beyond their own lives and destinies.

After a long pause, she came back to the question that had started them on their political discussion.

"And you, Teacher Tâm, do you consider me Vietnamese or French?"

He chuckled then answered. "You are more Vietnamese than French, that's for sure. For me, you are and will always be Giang, not Françoise."

She would not let him off so easily. "Teacher Tâm, which part of me is Vietnamese, and which is French?"

"First of all, you look Vietnamese, except for those blue eyes," he started, and did not want to add that it was those same eyes, so pure and so beautiful, that fascinated him from the time he first met her.

"Please go on, Teacher. I am waiting."

"You also think of yourself as primarily a Vietnamese. Also your gestures, your comportment, and your entire behavior are surely Vietnamese."

"So you think I am not as crude and barbaric as those foreign devils?"

He smiled and shook his head.

"No, not at all."

After a short wait, she gave him a gentle reminder.

"You are not finished yet, right? You still haven't said what part of me is French like?"

"This is where I know I am on shaky ground, since I really haven't dealt with that many foreigners, in fact with no foreigner at all until I met you and your family."

"Tell me anyway."

"From the very first time I met you, there has been something different in the way you have treated me. I don't really know what it is. You have been sweet, kind, and so understanding toward me."

He said those last words slowly, stopping at each one as if he were groping for the right word to use.

She tilted her head to look at him at an angle.

"So nobody else has been sweet, kind, and understanding toward you?"

"Not in the same way."

"No young lass that you left behind in your village before coming to Huế?"

She immediately blushed and lowered her gaze as soon as the words left her mouth, but soon lifted her eyes again to peer into his and wait for his answer.

"No, nobody whatsoever."

She regained her composure, and pressed on with her original question.

"So, why am I French like? Is it because of how I treat you?"

"I did not mean to imply that. It's just that you are so unlike any Vietnamese that I have ever known. You and I come from such different social background. Your father is standing right next to the source of real power behind the throne. My father was a poor village teacher who only left me his school and a few students. You live in a mansion, while I live in the back of a small village school."

"We are from two different worlds whose paths somehow crossed a few weeks ago," he went on. "If it were not for those two thugs who tried to attack you, we would have never known each other. The tie between us is totally accidental. Yet, you have somehow made it become more than that. As we say in Buddhism, there must be some karma in our previous reincarnations that have brought us together in this life."

They did not say anything for a long time, thinking over what they have said about their lives. They walked in the surf along the never-ending seashore, enjoying the relative coolness of the water compared to the hot sand. Gulls flew overhead and flocks of sandpipers took off or landed around them.

"I like this concept of karma," she said. "My mother and her friends refer to it often in their conversation, even though we are not Buddhists, and now I can see why."

"Sometimes only karma can explain what happens to us, whether good or bad," he said. "For example, people are now saying that our country is going through its difficult times because of what our ancestors did to the kingdom of Champa and its people. Over seven centuries, Vietnamese kings, lords, and generals have managed to practically wipe out an entire civilization in their conquest of the South."

She could only nod her agreement to his point. The heat and implacable sun made them retrace their steps and come back under the shelter of the pine trees. As they sat down, he noticed blisters on both of her feet. He pointed them out to her.

"Giang, you can't walk home with those blisters!"

"I know, but I think that by the time we go back they will subside and heal. How come you didn't get any on your feet?"

"I walk everywhere and the bottom of my feet has hardened like buffalo leather," he replied with a twinkle in his eyes. "For the trip down to the capital, I was with a group of other scholars, some with their own hired porters, and we walked every day for over a month."

"It's such a long way! I can see now why you are nothing but skin and bones," she teased him, and then added as an afterthought. "Let me to tell you about something I saw in France. It is what they call trains. They are long cars that run on iron tracks, pulled by a machine using power from what they call a steam engine. We rode a train from the port of Marseilles to Paris, the capital of France, and it took us only a day to cover a distance much longer than from here to Hà Nội. And we could eat and sleep on the train, sitting on very comfortable seats. If only we had such a train in our country, you wouldn't have had to walk for such a long time coming here to take the examinations."

"I've heard of those before, but had never met anybody that actually taken a ride on one."

"You haven't been to the South yet. My father said that they started building the first railroad there in 1881. Four years later, it took its first passengers from Sài Gòn to Mỹ Tho. What's even better is that in Europe, they are now starting to have carriages which are pulled not by horses but by machines, or engines, similar to those pulling the trains, except that they are much smaller. Father said that it won't be too many years before those automobiles, as they are called, will make their appearance in Sài Gòn."

He only had a vague notion of what she was describing, but he wanted to hear more.

"Tell me what else you saw in France that we don't have here."

"Let me think," she said. She stopped for a brief moment, trying to summon up her memories, her eyes gazing downward before she brightened up and continued.

"I did not see these, but people were saying that there were inventors working on making machines that could fly. They said that perhaps by the beginning of the 20th century these machines will be able to carry people, not just one but many people, faster than trains and higher even than those birds we see floating in the air out in the ocean, maybe as high as those clouds up in the sky."

They both gazed upward, trying to picture what the future flying machines would look like in the blue sky. Would they have wings and flap them like the seagulls gliding across the sky? He had no idea. He didn't even know what a train looked like.

"Cô Giang, you never cease to surprise me with your knowledge of the world out there."

Pleased with the compliment, she smiled and lifted her face to enjoy the sea breeze, her eyes half closed. Without looking at him, she gradually lowered herself onto the cloth they had spread over the sand.

"I am going to take a nap, and you should do it also. It's too hot now to go anywhere, and we need to rest before going back to the capital later in the afternoon."

Sensing his hesitation, she pointed to the cloth area on the next to her. "There is enough room for both of us. I promise you I will keep silent during our nap."

He carefully lay down, making sure he would not touch her body, and closed his eyes. He felt and smelled her presence. The light fragrance of frangipani mixed with her human scent was a new and profoundly moving sensation for him.

A month earlier, he would have never imagined that he would be spending a day at the beach with her, or with any female for that matter. He wondered what people back home would think if they saw their village teacher at that instant lying on the beach next to a young woman whom he had only met a few weeks earlier. What would her own people say if they knew what Giang and he were doing so far away from the capital and from any other human being?

When he first met Giang, he had been curious about her, then charmed by the attention she had given him. She showed little inhibition toward him, whether it was during her daily lessons, or when they went to the orphanage or on an outing.

In a society where the rule was that unmarried men and women should be physically separate, even while doing the simple act of giving or receiving objects to and from each other (*nam nữ thọ thọ bất thân*), she had no false modesty and was not afraid of violating the rule. She had seized his hands on more than one occasion, but those acts were natural, spontaneous, unaffected, and devoid of any impure thought or intention. Because of that, he sometimes thought of her as a younger sister. Yet whenever he saw her, he could not bring himself to see in her the sister he never had. Hidden somewhere in his innermost thoughts, he wanted her to remain the sweet person that she was, the kind of friend that he had until then never dreamed of.

Outwardly, he was much more reserved with her. As a Confucian scholar, he knew he should have made a deliberate effort not to be so close to her. Yet he did not pull away, nor did he say no. His rationalization was that whatever physical contact there was between them had happened without premeditation or planning. Furthermore, nothing more had happened and his emotions and thoughts about her were as pure and honest as on the day when he rescued her from her attackers. He was attracted to her, yes, but she could have been just another good friend. The fact that she was a member of the opposite sex was not relevant. At least that's what he thought as he drifted slowly into sleep.

He remembered what the boatman had told him earlier that day. He saw himself transported back to the boat, going upstream to the capital. There was another passenger on board. He thought at first that it had to be Giang, although he only saw a dark and indistinct shape. He called her name, and the dark shape turned around. It was Teacher Xinh, who had on his face a smile more akin to a grimace, with menacing eyes, his hand holding a dagger, the same one the thugs used to attack Giang. Without warning, Xinh lunged at him. He stepped back to one side as the dagger flew by the front of his shirt. Against his instinct and training, he turned around to warn Giang and push her out of the way, when he felt his back pierced by the dagger. He cried out in pain and called out her name again.

"Wake up, wake up, Teacher Tâm!"

He opened his eyes and saw her bending over him with an alarmed expression.

"You must have had a bad dream. I was dozing when I heard you call for me, and there you were thrashing about as if you were fighting somebody."

He sat up and felt his back.

"I dreamed that someone stabbed me from behind."

She moved around to his back. She saw what look like a small pebble where his body had made an impression in the sand. She lifted the cloth, felt under it and brought out a small white seashell in the shape of an elongated cone with a sharp and pointed end. She giggled and showed it to him.

"You slept on this shell. That's why it felt like someone stabbed you."

He laughed and vigorously shook his head to get rid of his bad dream.

"And here I was thinking that this person I met the other day on the boat actually attacked us."

"Who was it?"

"He's another village teacher from around these areas, the same one that the boatman told me about earlier. Maybe that's what led to my daytime nightmare. In any case, let's not worry about him anymore, and I'm sorry to interrupt your nap like this."

She came around and knelt down next to him. Without looking at him, she asked.

"You called for me in your dream, didn't you?"

"Yes, I wanted to find you and warn you. I saw you, and somehow I took my eyes off the attacker, and he came at me, and …. In any case, it doesn't make any sense now. We are both here, alive and well, on this beach."

Her voice became almost a whisper.

"So you thought about me in your dream?"

He seized one of her hands and squeezed it gently.

"Yes, and also most of the time when I am awake."

It took them just a few minutes to prepare for their return to the capital. He put on the filly's back a cloth bundle with everything that could be packed. Once that was done, he looked at her feet as she tried to put her shoes back on.

"Those shoes will be painful on your feet now. Don't put them on, because you are definitely riding back instead of walking."

She nodded in agreement. Still barefoot and holding her shoes with one hand, she climbed on the filly. After securing her shoes to the pommel, she took the reins, but, to his surprise, did not cue the animal to start walking. Instead she announced her intentions quietly but clearly as she faced forward, avoiding a direct look at him.

"I can't let you walk if I am riding. Please climb up and sit behind me. There is enough room for both of us."

He didn't move. He knew then why she had asked him on their last outing whether he could ride.

"We'll be all right. You can just hold onto me from the back and I'll guide the horse."

He hesitated, thinking of what would happen if people saw them riding together. She sensed what was bothering him and insisted.

"I will not go anywhere until you come up here. We will ride until we get closer to the city, and then, if you want, you can walk the rest of the way."

He had no choice but to agree to her request. He climbed on the horse, straddled the saddle and wrapped his hands around her. She shuddered and gently tapped his clasped hands. Then she laughed gleefully, dug her heels into the horse flanks, shouted "Ha!" and they moved forward.

The scent of frangipani flew back from her hair into his face, engulfing him once more. Her lithe body was even slimmer than he had thought. The novel physical contact with her at first overwhelmed and even frightened him. However, after they had only gone a short distance, he stopped fighting his feelings, discarded his inhibitions, and found himself welcoming the new intimacy between them.

As they emerged from the line of pine trees, a pair of cranes flew up from the marshes and headed toward an unseen nest. The filly flinched but Giang brought it under control easily. She pointed the large birds out to him.

"People say those cranes mate for life and are always together no matter where they go."

"Yes, indeed. Back home, the villagers say that they symbolize loyalty and faithfulness."

The maid ran to her as soon as she dismounted and handed her horse to a guard.

"Miss, you better go to your mother right away! She's been waiting all day for you."

Giang stopped in her tracks.

"Why? Didn't you tell her that I went to Thuận An?"

"I did! As soon as she got up. But she was not happy at all and have made life miserable for all of us all day."

As they walked back to the main house, Giang handed to the maid the bundle she brought back from the trip and her shoes.

"Can you take these to my room, please?"

Without waiting for an answer, Giang went into the living room. Madame Bonneau, or Bà Trang to her Vietnamese friends, was sitting on a couch with Mai, two cups of cold tea and a half empty tray of sweets between them. Mai signaled to her older sister with her eyes to be on her guard.

Bà Trang voice was at first even and unemotional.

"Giang, where have you been all day, and with whom?"

"Mother, I went with Teacher Tâm to the beach and you know it takes a few hours just to get there."

"All I've been hearing from you lately is about him. What are people going to think when they find out where you have been with him today? Have you lost your mind? I allowed him to come to our house because he did rescue you from those attackers, but it does not mean that you have to compromise your reputation with him!"

"Mother, nothing shameful happened between us, not today, not any other day! We just walked on the beach and talked, that's all."

Giang went to sit on a chair next to her sister, but turned her head away from her mother.

"And who is going to know that? What am I going to tell your father when he comes back? We didn't mind the other day when you went to visit the temple, but this time you overreached yourself."

She saw her daughter shoeless. Her voice was now strong and merciless.

"Look at you, what happened to your shoes? Did you forget them on the beach? Did you lose your shoes as well as your mind?"

"Mother, I just couldn't wear them because I got blisters on my feet. The maid took them to my room."

Bà Trang was not mollified at this last revelation. She paused and tried to regain her calm. She remembered that many years ago she had spent a similar day with the young French officer who later became her husband. But she knew what she was doing, whereas her naïve daughter obviously had no clue of the damage her behavior could bring to her reputation.

For some time now, she had been thinking about the future of her two daughters. Some of her friends joked with her that Giang and Mai had a wide field of candidates, Vietnamese and French, for marriage. However, she knew in reality that the field was much more limited than anyone could think. Many Vietnamese families shied away from having anything to do with mixed ancestry or métis children. Meanwhile in the French community, there were not that many eligible bachelors that she would consider worthy of her daughters. Of those whom she deemed eligible, some also openly discriminated against métis. Such was the case of that lieutenant St Arnaud that her daughter Mai was interested in, he who would barely look at her.

She had begun a quiet campaign to find a suitable prospect for her eldest daughter among the upper-class families of the capital. A number of excellent prospects had been identified, and some were sons of court ministers or other high-level mandarins. She was looking for suitable ways of letting Giang be seen and known in those circles, but this young teacher from the North had thrown her plans askew.

Clearly, her daughter had taken a romantic interest in him, without any thought to his social status and to the future. He was obviously poor and had nothing to his credit other than a few successes in examinations. Even then, who knew whether he would pass the palace examinations that he just took? In the past, some of the most brilliant scholars had been known to fail, not once but several times before they finally gave up trying. The other important consideration was what her uncle, the abbot, had told her about him. Many times before, he had forewarned her about certain things, and on many occasions he had been absolutely prescient and accurate.

She saw that her daughters were whispering to each other, probably sharing some secret about the older one's foolish escapade. She clucked her tongue to regain their attention.

"Starting today, I don't want this village teacher coming to our house anymore."

"Mother!" Giang exclaimed instantly and stood up as she turned to face Bà Trang.

"You have no obligation to teach him anything. I am sure he only used those lessons as an excuse to come see you."

"You know that's not true!" Giang argued, her face becoming pale underneath the suntan she got on the beach. "It was father who came up with the idea of teaching him the new script."

Bà Trang lifted her hand to stop her daughter, determined to impose her will and end once for all what she considered to be her daughter's fleeting summer romance.

"It doesn't matter whose idea it was. But no more talk! From tomorrow, I want you and your sister to go down to your aunt's fabric shop at the Đông Ba market. It is time that both of you learn something actually useful instead of those romantic notions floating around in your heads. You will become your aunt's apprentices and she will teach you her business. And once you no longer have any contact with him, you'll forget about him. Trust me. It will be easier than you think."

Mai, who had so far kept out of the argument, was suddenly interested with her mother's decision.

"I do want to go work in the shop at the Đông Ba market. This summer has been so far been quite boring."

"Whether you want to or not, both of you will start tomorrow. There is nothing more to discuss. I will tell your father, but I know he will agree with me."

She stood up and, after a warning glance at Giang, left the room. She pretended not to see the large teardrops that had started to roll down from her daughter's beautiful blue eyes.

François Bonneau could not believe what his wife had told him. They were in their bedroom where he was changing into his evening clothes, out of earshot of the rest of the household.

"You are telling me that the village teacher is banned from this house to protect Giang's reputation, and you are putting both of our daughters at a stall in the Đông Ba market where everybody can see them. That makes no sense to me."

His wife patiently explained.

"That's the whole point. I want my daughters where prospective suitors can see them. Who will know who they are when we keep hiding them behind the walls of this house? At the same time, they will learn a trade and acquire some business smartness to counterbalance those fanciful and useless notions that the Jesuits have taught them."

"Why are you so against Teacher Tâm? What has he done to fall out of your grace?" Bonneau asked. "To me, he's a decent and honest man, more so than most people I know."

Bà Trang sighed, a pained expression replacing the confrontational attitude she had maintained with her husband.

"He has done nothing to your daughter, at least I hope so. But my uncle at the Thiên Mụ temple told me that he will only bring sorrow and heartache to Giang, and that's why I don't want her to get involved any further with him. We have discharged our obligation toward him, and we owe him nothing now. Let him go out her life. I don't want her to have an unhappy future."

"So that's why," Bonneau snickered. "Your uncle, the abbot, with his powers to see into the future, is the cause of it all."

He continued sarcastically. "First of all, he is not infallible, you know that, right? People make a big deal about some of his predictions that turn out to be accurate, and they always forget that he has made many more that are way off the mark. He said that the Nguyễn dynasty would endure for many centuries, and look at the sad shape the monarchy is in right now."

"Secondly, in the case of Giang and Tâm, you are actually fulfilling his prediction by pulling them apart. I haven't seen my daughter yet, but I am sure she's is totally distraught by what you have done."

His wife, however, had the last word.

"She is my daughter too. As a woman and as her mother, I know what's best for her and I know what I am doing. You let me handle this and keep out of it."

The following morning, the innkeeper brought Tâm a package of books wrapped tightly in a square piece of cloth.

"Teacher, the young lady's maid said to give this package for you," he said.

"Ah, thank you."

He was going to ask whether the maid was still waiting or had left, but the innkeeper anticipated his question.

"She went back as soon as she handed me the package."

Tâm turned the package over several times before untying the cloth. Inside he found two textbooks in French, with a small note tucked between the cover and the first page of one of the books.

In a neat cursive handwriting that he recognized readily, she wrote in Vietnamese:

'I am writing this quickly to let you know that I am not allowed to see you and help you with learning French any longer. I will find a

way to see you somehow, I don't know when. Soon, I hope. In the meantime, keep and use these books to help you in your studies'.

'Going to the beach with you made yesterday unforgettable. Its memories have kept me from feeling completely wretched. Don't worry about me though. Keep yourself well'.

'Giang'

Her name was slightly blurred by a teardrop that fell on the paper. He pictured her trying to write as she was crying, and blamed himself for having ultimately been the cause of it, for letting emotions overpower his judgment. He had known it would come to this eventually, and he should have tried to stop seeing her sooner. Selfishly and thoughtlessly, he had ignored all the warning signs, and led her down the unfortunate path they had taken.

Examinations Rules

Starting with the Lý dynasty (1010-1225), examinations were held in Việt Nam to select the mandarins needed to run the government. Of course, passing examinations was not the only ticket to official positions. Having never taken or passed an examination, some could still be selected to important positions by the ruler or by his top mandarins. They only needed to be well connected either by birth or by marriage; or they could also have rendered some extraordinary service to the regime or the nation.

Overall, however, examinations were the path that was open to all, women and musicians excluded, aiming for a lucrative career in government. To be a mandarin was the ultimate goal of many men. In the pursuit of that goal, they were fully supported by their parents when they were young and by their wives after they got married.

Even poorer families allowed their male children to spend years studying while the rest of the family toiled and struggled to support them from an early age well into adulthood and beyond.

Wives willingly endured hardship and deprivation to enable their husbands to do nothing but study. Whenever examinations were held, the men would use what little money their wives had hoarded to travel to distant cities and spend weeks or months taking the examinations and waiting for the results to be officially posted. If they failed, they would go home to resume studying and try their luck again at the next round, always relying on their families for sustenance and funding.

In principle, any man who wanted to become a mandarin could study and take a series of examinations that will determine whether he was qualified for a post at the local, regional, or national level.

No one was born a mandarin. However, anybody lucky enough to be reincarnated into a family of mandarins and scholars would more than likely have the means to study and participate in the examinations.

In the capital, there was a National College where renowned scholars taught royal princes and the sons of prominent government officials. Those privileged students received stipends and rations of rice while attending school. Unless they committed some grave offense, these mandarin sons were usually guaranteed high-level governmental positions, especially if they managed to place well in the examinations.

Conversely, those from poor families seldom had an opportunity to receive the education needed to compete in the examinations. For them, escape from the subsistence life into which they were born was thus theoretically possible but actually very hard to achieve.

There were schools at the village levels taught by respected scholars who either had failed the examinations or might have passed them but chose to teach instead of getting involved in the country's politics. Such schools often graduated excellent examination candidates who not only passed them gloriously but also went on to become some of the best administrators or military commanders throughout history. However, village schools were private institutions that received no support from the government, and village teachers had to depend on the students' families to pay them with money or in kind.

The Vietnamese examinations system was derived from the Chinese model, from form to content. Prior to the Lý dynasty, Vietnamese scholars had to go to China to compete in examinations held in that country, subject to arbitrary quotas imposed by the Chinese emperor.

To avoid such discrimination, starting with the Lý dynasty, examinations began to be organized in Việt Nam, with modifications and adaptations from the Chinese model as suited the Vietnamese rulers' whims and inclinations. Still, in the end, the system retained most of its original Chinese characteristics until it was abolished by the French in 1919 toward the end of the Nguyễn dynasty.

Under that last dynasty and throughout most of the 19th century, examinations fell into three main categories.

The regional examinations, *Thi Hương*, took place at the main city in a region. Those who passed all of the stages of these examinations were called *Cử-nhân*, or recommended man, roughly equivalent to a Bachelor degree holder in modern times.

The *Cử-nhân* scholars from the entire country could choose to go on and participate in the metropolitan examinations, *Thi Hội*, held every few years in the capital under the Nguyễn dynasty. In rare cases, an exceptionally talented person who did not pass the regional examinations could still be granted a royal dispensation and allowed to sit in the metropolitan examinations.

Those who passed the metropolitan examinations went on to compete in the palace examinations, *Thi Đình*, held shortly afterwards in the same location.

The palace examinations were considered the final stage of the metropolitan ones and were designed to rank the scholars by their intellectual prowess. Those who sailed through this last stage were called *Tiến Sĩ*, or presented scholar, approximately equivalent to the holder of a Doctoral degree. The top ranking scholars were given land holdings and were appointed to the highest offices, including ambassadorships and ministerial posts. Those below won less impressive but still coveted positions, such as Prefect or Governor, at regional levels.

The examinations usually consisted of four stages, each concentrated on a particular subject matter.

The first stage covered the Four Books and the Five Classics, all from the Chinese tradition, to test the depth of scholarship of each candidate.

The second stage involved Chinese-style classical poetry and prose poems to ascertain each candidate's capacity to write masterful poetry within strictly regulated verse structure and rules.

In the third stage, the candidates wrote essays on classical Chinese literature topics to prove their knowledge of Chinese history and politics, as well as their familiarity with traditional commentaries by famous scholars.

The last stage generally required an essay on a policy question about historical or current topics of interest to the ruling monarch.

To succeed, a candidate had to earn at least a passing grade in all stages. Initially there were four grades: excellent, good, passing, and failed. Afterwards the grade system was refined into finer increments, eventually adopting a scale from 0 to 10. Under French rule, the scale was changed to be from 0 to 20. The grades from all four stages were added together to determine the ultimate ranking of the candidates.

Those who failed to pass some of the stages, without committing any disqualifying violations of the examinations rules, were given more minor positions and the chance to retake the examinations in later years.

On the other hand, those who failed all the stages or were completely unqualified could be stripped of their offices and be forbidden from taking future examinations. The local officials who did not properly screen unqualified candidates and allowed them to participate in the examinations were also disciplined.

Failing the examinations, whether at the regional, or metropolitan and palace levels, was due to various factors. They ranged from the obvious ones such as insufficient preparation, deficient scholarship, or simply an inability to thoroughly memorize the classic texts and their historical commentaries.

Not much creativity or originality was demanded from the candidates, and rote learning was inculcated into them from a very young age. It was by no means easy to pass the examinations at any level, and there were famous cases of brilliant and renowned scholars who failed to pass despite repeated attempts over the course of many years, sometimes well into old age.

Because the stakes were so high, there were as many ways to cheat and pass the examinations as there were reasons for failure. The honors and lucrative appointments conferred on successful candidates ensured that people throughout the centuries always managed to come up with ingenious ways to beat the system. On the other hand, many examination rules and procedures were specifically set up and refined over time to defeat the efforts of those who tried to cheat.

Coming to the examination grounds with pre-written papers was a cardinal offense. Candidates were searched and anything they brought with them was subject to inspection. Even a piece of paper with innocuous characters on it led to punishment by caning, expulsion and immediate disqualification.

Once inside and taking the examinations, candidates were naturally forbidden from communicating with one another, verbally or otherwise. To make sure that this rule was strictly enforced, at local and regional levels, candidates sat in their own tents erected on the examination grounds. The tents were surrounded by walls dotted with high towers where soldiers constantly stood guard. Since the metropolitan and palace examinations had fewer candidates, they often took place inside a royal pavilion. The scholars were assigned small rooms, provided mats to sit on and a small wooden desk for writing, but they were watched even more closely since there were fewer of them.

Wealthy candidates every now and then tried to beat the system by hiring someone else to take the examinations for them. To prevent such substitutions, candidates had to declare their names, birth dates and places, and certain biographical characteristics, such as any official title or position they held, so that their identity could be verified without any doubt. Written certifications of a candidate's identity by local authorities were required when there was any doubt.

Still there were cases of candidates disguising their provenance so that they could participate in regional examinations to which they were not entitled. Examinations were not held every year or at the same time throughout the country, so a candidate that missed one and did not want to wait for several more years could try to go to another location with forged identification papers.

Assuming that a candidate was genuine and bright enough to handle the questions on the examinations, he could still be ensnared by a final rule, *phạm huý*: nowhere on his examination papers was he allowed to use, intentionally or accidentally, taboo names of the ruling dynasty. Such names and the Chinese characters representing them were never to be used without modifications.

Before the first day of the examinations, a list of taboo names was posted at the entrance for all candidates to read and remember. The list was divided into two broad taboo categories.

The primary category consisted of the personal and official names of the monarchs. All these names were to be absolutely avoided, or had to be changed to a different character with a similar meaning or the same sound.

A secondary category was more varied and broader. It included the names of the king's mother and his ancestors going back a few generations, the names of royal palaces and pavilions, and the names of the birth places of the monarchs and their royal consorts. Such taboo characters had to be modified by altering them slightly, usually by adding an extra stroke or removing one or several strokes.

A scholar in the 1847 metropolitan examinations used the words "gia miêu chi hại" meaning "harm to good rice" in his essay. Unfortunately Gia Miêu happened to be the name of the ancestral village of the Nguyễn dynasty. The scholar not only failed the examinations, but also lost his *Cử-nhân* degree previously won in the regional examinations.

Other rules required that scholars, when they referred to Heaven, should write that character three lines above the normal line. When they referred to the King or a part of his body, those characters were to be placed two lines higher. Finally, when they referred to the King's accomplishments, those words should be written one line higher.

To prevent cheating and collusions with examination judges, there were rules that specified how certain characters should be exactly written. Deviations from those rules, for example by adding extra strokes or not writing all the required strokes, could be construed as some special code to enable judges to recognize a candidate's exam papers. If and when caught, such deviations were sufficient to cause the offending candidates to be failed.

Handing in a sloppily written paper was also forbidden. Someone who made too many corrections or spilled ink on their examination booklets could be suspected of making secret signs so that bribed judges would be able to recognize their preferred candidates' papers.

Each scholar was required to count how many characters they corrected or erased in their paper. Then he had to write the total number of such characters, not to exceed 10, at the end of his paper.

In 1900 an 82-year-old scholar forgot to write down his total number of corrections. He lost his second place finish at the examinations, and could have been failed completely. However, in consideration of his advanced age, he was allowed to pass in the next to last place of his promotion.

Handing in a paper where too much space was left blank was another severe violation. It showed that the candidate was insufficiently prepared. Both he and the mandarin official who screened him and allowed him to participate in the examinations were punished. The candidate was automatically failed, and the official could be demoted or docked months of pay as a result.

Handing in a paper late automatically disqualified its author. The paper would not get graded, but the judges would still review it to see if any rule violation was committed.

All papers had to be read and graded by more than one judge. This was intended to prevent possible collusion between candidates and judges since it was thought to be harder to bribe several judges rather than just one. It also allowed for a review process intended to catch all mistakes and rule violations, and to minimize individual bias against the candidates.

Woe fell equally on the candidate who carelessly used a taboo word and on the judge who missed the violation when he graded the paper. Punishment for the candidate ranged from immediate failure, followed by caning, demotion, banishment, and, in extreme cases, by outright beheading.

The names of those committing name taboo offenses were posted on a separate list, made crudely out of bamboo painted white with the names of the offenders written in black.

For the judge who overlooked the violation, punishment could be demotion, docking of wages, and prohibition from ever grading examination papers again.

Teacher Xinh was sitting before the Minister of Rites. Between them, spread out on a small table, were the examination papers of Lê Duy Tâm, the village teacher that he had met only a few weeks before.

Many years ago, Xinh, a skillful forger, used his talent to embezzle funds reserved for the construction of the late Emperor's tomb. When found out, he managed to escape death only by bribing all the officials responsible for prosecuting him. Some of the officials were involved in the same scheme but covered their tracks by reducing his crime to a matter of sloppy bookkeeping. He escaped the executioner's sword but was demoted and banished from the capital. Since that time he had been earning a living as a village teacher until Minister Toản summoned him.

The task given to him was beyond belief. He had to read through the examination papers and find a way to fail the man he knew as Teacher Tâm.

The papers had already been graded excellent by all the official judges, but the Minister of Rites was the final arbiter and he wanted the young scholar to be disqualified and punished. He told Xinh to forge any of the examination papers and introduce a name violation where there was none.

Toản did not say why he had to go to such extreme, and Xinh could only guess that somehow Teacher Tâm had offended the Minister. He had no way of knowing that the two had never met and that the offense was fundamentally between the court minister and the arrogant French Resident General supported by his capable subordinate, François Bonneau.

"Your Excellency, I have read through all of these papers. He did not commit any violation whether in prose form or in poetry."

The Minister looked at him severely.

"Are you telling me he never used any of the forbidden names, even the secondary ones?"

"This candidate was very careful," Xinh replied. "He avoided using any of the taboo names so that he did not have to modify a single character."

He did not add that he was more than impressed with what he had read. Tâm not only had a good grasp of the language and its rules. He had an exquisite talent for choosing the right historical allusion, the proper metaphor, and the right rhythm to represent a certain nuance and offer the exact imagery that he wanted. Over several days, Xinh read, savored, and admired the scholar and the artist embodied in the papers spread out on the table before him, often forgetting that his assigned task was not to praise but to condemn.

"This is where you come in," the Minister interjected. "Copy one page of his papers and introduce a subtle name violation somewhere in it."

"Your Excellency, I can try, but it will not be easy. By changing a character, I will change the meaning of an entire sentence or section. Any scholar worth his salt will see that he couldn't have chosen that character to write. The judges will certainly question why something that was so obviously wrong had not been caught by any of them."

The Minister became annoyed at Xinh and immediately wanted to put an end to their discussion.

"Don't you know that I am fully aware of that? You just do your best, I know you will, and I'll take care of the judges. Remember also that you will be very well compensated."

That was a signal for Xinh that his audience was over. Many years ago, Minister Toản had saved him from execution in the embezzlement scandal. He owed the Minister his life and he could not possibly refuse to carry out what he had been very plainly ordered to do.

The evening of the same day, Minister Toản had a late dinner with his young wife. As usual, he ate in silence while she, having eaten beforehand, only served him his food and kept him company.

She related to him the latest gossips going around the capital. Most of them, he ignored as idle speculations from people who had too much time on their hands. As an example, she told him that it was rumored that the King delayed announcing the results of the examinations because too many of the successful candidates were from the North. This could have been true many years ago, but this time he knew the exact cause for the delay.

He continued eating without saying a word and ignored her chatter. However, his ears pricked up when he heard her talk about another kind of rumor.

"They say that people have been jamming the roads leading to the Đông Ba market these days. I will want to go see for myself what it's all about."

He guessed that she had already known and was just waiting for him to ask for the details.

"And what is it about?"

"Apparently there are two new lady merchants at one of the silk shops. They are two young women of real beauty and the city's mandarin sons have been flocking to their store, parading in front of it to take a peep inside or to try to impress those two young ladies. Some are even spending their money and buying silk they don't need. You can imagine that the shop is doing a very good business as a result."

The old man leered at his wife who was actually younger than his son.

"How can there be anybody more beautiful than the lady who is having dinner with me?"

"My lord, you are always too generous with your words. I am like a flower a little bit past its prime, but these two young women are supposed to be without equal. I wouldn't be surprised if one of these days some young gentleman won't actually swoon in front of their shop."

The Minister put down his chopsticks and extended his right arm. She promptly lifted a tea cup and placed it in the fingers of his hand.

"Do you know who they are? They just cannot appear out of nowhere!"

"People say they are the daughters of the French Special Envoy to the court."

"So they are his daughters!" he exclaimed.

"It is said that their mother had kept them out of sight pretty much since they were born, but recently decided to let them learn the silk trade at her family's shop. The family is quite wealthy, as I am sure you know."

"Indeed, thanks to that French husband of hers who has been guaranteeing them a virtual silk monopoly between Cửa Hàn and our capital."

She did not care much for the business aspect of her gossip and went on.

"The younger one has the looks of a Westerner with light brown hair and a long nose. She is right at the front of the shop, greeting customers and sweet-talking them into buying silk. Her face and the way she laughs fascinate quite a few, and young men engage her in conversation just to hear pure Vietnamese coming out of a foreign mouth. The other one is much more reserved. People say she's Vietnamese in everything except her eyes, which are blue. She stays at the back of the shop and keeps herself busy with the books."

The Minister raised one of his eyebrows.

"So which one do the young men like more?"

"They say the young men cannot have enough of the younger one. But the older one has some serious admirers, even though rumors have her already attached to someone already."

He already suspected the answer to his next question, but he wanted to confirm what Bonneau's man, Kham, had already reported to him.

"And who is that someone?"

"I've only heard that he's some scholar of humble origin who is here to take the examinations. People have seen him with the older daughter on several occasions. Despite her Vietnamese looks, she's behaving more like a Westerner and seems to care nothing about being seen with him."

She sighed, thinking about how the Minister of Rites once passed by her humble house, saw her, and within a matter of days had her sharing his bed. There was no courtship and nothing romantic about it.

She looked at the old man in front of her, his eyes half closed, his face wrinkled, his gray hair sprouting absurdly from his dragonfly headdress that he insisted on wearing inside the house, his hand caressing his wispy beard on which a grain of rice had become obstinately stuck. How she wished he had been some poor young scholar who had at least talked to her once or twice before consuming their marriage.

She thought about her husband's son who was even older than she was. He's the one who had been buying silk that he didn't need, and had servants bring it back to her as gifts.

"Your son is among those who have gone down to look at the two new beauties."

The old man opened his eyes and frowned at her. He knew for some time now that Bonneau's wife was discreetly inquiring about possible husbands among the sons of prominent mandarins for their daughters. His still unmarried son was one of those young men that the

Special Envoy's wife considered a prime candidate. Behind a façade of indifference, Toản had actually been carefully weighing the matter.

His first reaction was that he did not want to dilute his family's blood by marrying his son to a girl with a French father, no matter how beautiful she was. He was sure his ancestors would reject such miscegenation outright. On the other hand, Emperor Gia Long, the founder of the dynasty, had allowed Frenchmen to marry Vietnamese, and their offspring were not so rare in the capital, and some even held official titles in the government. French soldiers, as they roamed the countryside in the many military campaigns, also sired mixed blood children, but those could never be considered at the same level as those in the capital who were the product of proper unions between consenting parties.

That she was a Christian also worked against her. Although Toản was not by any means a devout Buddhist, considering himself more of a Confucian, he hated Vietnamese Christians as much as he hated the French. If his son were to marry one of Bonneau's girls, who was going to maintain the family's altar? His ancestors originated from a small village near the old Northern capital, Thăng Long, where they lived for centuries until they moved South in the 16th century and settled in the region around Huế. The Northern branch of the clan still worshipped the common ancestors at altars set up in the ancestral village, while he, as the most prominent representative of the Southern branch, had a similar duty at the main altar in his own residence. His first wife, and now the second one, never failed to burn three incense sticks every single day in memory of the ancestors, and he wanted his future daughter-in-law to continue that tradition. What would the ancestors say when no incense was burned or offerings made on their death anniversaries?

Still, after his initial rejection of the idea, Toản had reconsidered, without telling anyone. From decades of immersing himself in capital politics, it was second nature to him to always reassess any issue and try to weigh the alternatives each time.

Despite his hatred of the French, the old Minister was foremost a survivor who had come through several royal successions with his head still on his shoulders and his family fortune intact. While others openly or secretly took arms against the colonizers, he was a member of the growing faction at court who had concluded that the French were in Việt Nam to stay, with the King being a mere figurehead. So while he made an outward appearance of disdain and obstinacy against the colonial administration, he was also looking for ways to work with it, at least indirectly and as discreetly as possible. A marriage of his wayward son to the daughter of the Special Envoy was not out of the question, with miscegenation or religious issues taking a secondary importance.

His son, Trịnh Dần, also was another factor that he had to consider. He was the Minister's only son, the last child after a string of daughters, all of whom had been properly married away. The lad had inherited from his mother a sturdy build as well as a less than spectacular mind. Despite Toản's best efforts, including the hiring of several tutors, his son was a far cry from being considered a scholar.

Dần certainly could not have sat in any examination. He preferred to spend part of his time training with his father's bodyguards, fancying himself as a martial arts fighter. The rest of the time, he partied and went around importuning young women from all walks of life, including those supposedly well protected behind family customs and traditions.

The Minister did not want to dwell on this for he himself was a womanizer in his youth, but he knew that the situation could not continue indefinitely. He was looking for ways to make his son settle down, and if Dần indeed took a fancy to one of the Bonneau's girls, he would perhaps give up his dissolute life. If everything worked out, Toản as well as his son could gain in stature. The Minister could be an important ally of the French, while Dần became the son-in-law of one of the most influential Frenchmen in the country.

A perverse current of thought crisscrossed the old Minister's brain. It would be nice if Bonneau could be deprived of his favorite village teacher at the same time that either one or both of his daughters came under the spell of his son. In his youth, the Minister used to think of himself as something of a terror to the capital's families with nubile daughters, and his eldest son was living up to that fame. Perhaps I could give him a little assistance this time, the Minister thought, and the grin that appeared on his face made his wife shiver despite the heat.

It was late afternoon and Teacher Xinh was on the boat taking him back to his village. He sat near the prow and watched as the calm river water flowed by silently. He was drained of energy after the two weeks he had spent at the Minister's residence. Except for one trip back home to get a change of clothes, he had not seen his family and had not slept a peaceful night.

He had finished his task and respectfully declined the offer of compensation for it. The Minister had not insisted and that suited him fine. He did not want to burden his conscience even more by accepting to be paid for doing what he found so abhorrent.

He had copied one page of an essay by the young scholar he met on this same river, and replaced a character in it with one representing one of the King's numerous names. He had carefully chosen the character, and the switch did change the original meaning, but it did not make it meaningless or absurd.

A cursory reading of the essay would not have picked up the new nuance resulting from the change. The important thing was that an examination judge would have immediately picked up the taboo name violation. It was an obvious mistake that any scholar could have easily avoided if he had committed to memory the long list of taboo names posted in front of the Cần Chính palace where they sat for the examinations. That kind of mistake could and did happen, but certainly not to someone at the level of Teacher Tâm.

He was going to go home and try to forget about it. He would not tell his mother, his wife or his children of what he did. He would resume his teaching, saying nothing of it to his students. He would avoid his neighbors and acquaintances.

The only one he would tell anything to would be his father. As soon as possible, he would go to the grave, burn three sticks of incense, kneel down to pray, tell him what he had done, and ask his father to forgive him for that act. He would never visit the capital again under any circumstance.

"Teacher Xinh, you sure are pensive today," the boatman hailed him. He was the same one that had ferried him and Teacher Tâm upstream a few weeks before. "Is something bothering you? You look like you are going to a funeral."

Teacher Xinh smiled bitterly. Somebody might in fact die or be punished so severely that his life would not be worth living.

"I am just thinking about life, and how sad it can be at times."

"You scholars always have your heads in the clouds anyway," the boatman laughed. "You should live our kind of life, and get to worry about nothing except where your next meal is coming from, day in day out."

"You don't know how much I actually envy you, boatman!"

There was another passenger and, although the man was not watching him, he knew that he could not have missed any part of the conversation. He was a swarthy man, of a stocky built, wearing a conical hat that hid most of his face. He sat with his back to the boatman and his face turned to the far bank, away from his fellow passenger. Sensing the man's aloofness and unfriendly attitude, Xinh thought that it would be better not to say anything else and resumed his silent soul searching.

He and the second passenger got off at the same place and they both began walking on the meandering path that led from the riverbank to his village. The stranger followed him from a distance, hardly making a sound. If he had not seen him when he disembarked, he would not have known that someone was behind him.

The setting sun was casting long shadows over the path that went through an old bamboo grove then out to an open dirt road. The latter wound its way through fallow land and rice fields spread out over low rolling hills. His village was in one of the shallow valleys still unseen from where he was.

He wondered whom his silent companion would know in his village. The next community was many more miles beyond his, and it did not make sense that the man would walk that far. Not wanting to be unfriendly, he almost wanted to turn around to ask where the man was going, but changed his mind at the last moment. Something told him to be wary and to keep to himself.

When he reached his home, night had fallen. The house was completely dark for his family went to bed early like the rest of the village. As he announced himself and knocked, the stranger caught up with him but continued walking into the darkness. He breathed a sigh of relief and waited for his wife. Soon he heard her remove the door bar and the door opened. He saw her face breaking into a smile.

Before he could enter the house, he felt a blinding sensation on his back that went all the way to his heart. It was so painful that he could not even scream. Pictures of his family flashed through his mind as he collapsed. He was dead by the time his body hit the ground.

Before his wife recovered from her shock, the stranger stepped over Xinh and in one swift motion slit her throat. After she fell, the man moved through the house and murdered the children and Xinh's mother in a similar manner. Finally, he dragged Xinh inside, set fire to all four corners of the house, and disappeared running into the night.

At the Đông Ba Market

Phu Văn Lâu was a beautiful pavilion erected in 1819 and placed directly in front of the South gate of the Citadel. It was a square structure consisting of two stories supported by 16 columns. There was no wall at the first level, creating an airy and unpretentious look unlike other buildings inside the Citadel's ramparts.

Phu Văn Lâu was where proclamations and edicts from the royal government were posted for all to see. Whenever examinations were held, the list of those who passed was also put up there. Inscriptions on two stone steles enjoined passersby to dismount and take off their hats before reading the edicts or the list of successful scholars.

Tâm had wandered away from his inn and, without meaning to, his feet had taken him to Phu Văn Lâu. He knew that there was no posted list yet because otherwise the place would have been mobbed. Not only the candidates themselves, but also their friends, families, and perhaps the entire city of Huế would come by to see and read the names.

He had not heard from or seen Giang since the day he received her books and note. Since then he had tried to continue his studies of French with the books that she gave him, but found that he could not concentrate as well as he used to when he was with her.

Strangely, isolation decreased his attention span as the feeling of guilt kept returning to haunt him. He tried to block her out of his mind, but it was of no use. He told himself that he should never have involved himself with her to the extent that he did. But something else within him kept clinging to the hope that somehow their destinies were not fated to cross path only once.

Just South of Phu Văn Lâu and right next to the Perfume River was a smaller pavilion, Nghinh Lương Đình. In the hot summer months, the royals would come there and board a dragon boat to cruise on the river. They could also just sit under the pavilion to admire the view while commoners were kept from a safe distance so that they could never set eyes on any royal face. The place was normally deserted, but even then commoners were not allowed to go near it.

Tâm skirted carefully around it to get to the riverbank. Once there he followed it toward a group of moored boats. He had not talked to anybody for days and wanted to look for the friendly boatman that he had already met twice. From afar, he thought he had recognized the boat and once he got closer, the same boatman called out to him with his usual toothy grin.

"Teacher, do you need to go anywhere?"

"No, sorry, not this time. I was just taking a stroll, but I thought I might see you here. How's business?"

"It could be better, but I can't truly complain. Yesterday, I took Teacher Xinh home. He still looked unhappy."

Tâm nodded but he was already busy waving to the boatman's children who came running to him. At their insistence and encouraged by their father, he climbed on the boat and bent down to pick up the younger one who had his arms extended to him.

"You'd make a good family man, Teacher," the boatman said.

He laughed. "It's going to be a while before I become one."

"So what's the young lady doing these days?" the boatman immediately inquired. "How come she's not with you?"

He shook his head. "To both questions, I must say that I don't know. I haven't been in touch with her lately."

The boatman nodded in sympathy, wondering if there had been a lovers' spat, although the young teacher did not seem to be the type to quarrel so easily.

Tâm remained silent, distracted by the children who were trying to show him their toy animals made out of strips of bamboo. Their father seemed intent on asking their visitor a question that had been on the back of his mind. News and rumors travelled along the river as fast as a boat could go downstream, and he had heard of something that should be of interest to the young scholar.

"Teacher, I heard that there are two new silk merchants at the Đông Ba market. They are two sisters, with one of them looking like a Westerner."

Tâm turned away from the children to stare at their father. So that's where she has been, he thought. He knew there was more information coming and waited for the boatman to continue.

"Their presence has created quite a stir in the market, and the young men in the city are tripping over one another to go by their stall and look at them." He laughed at his own humor before directing his next question to Tâm.

"Would the young lady of the other day be one of the sisters?"

"Frankly, I wouldn't know. I haven't been to the market since I've been here."

"Heaven! How can that be? Everybody must go to the Đông Ba market at least once in their life! Let me take you there right now."

"Thanks, but ..."

He was torn between wanting to go see her, or staying where he was and putting an end to it all. Should he try to catch a glimpse of her when she's not allowed to have any contact with him?

"You did not quarrel with her, did you?"

He smiled at the question.

"No, of course not!"

The boatman continued.

"Then how about coming with us? My wife wants to go buy something at the market anyway."

Tâm hesitated, looking forlornly at the vast expanse of the river. The boatman, sensing his unspoken wish, made the decision for him.

"Let's go Teacher. The market is closing down soon."

He immediately pushed off his boat so that his guest could not change his mind and jump back on the river bank.

She was adding up the day's entries in the shop's record book a second time when the maid spoke up.

"It's getting late, miss. We need to go home before it gets too dark."

Giang shook her head and signaled the maid to keep silent. She refused to use the abacus and was doing the arithmetic in her head as the Jesuits had taught her. The day's entries were many, requiring her total concentration.

She had started a book to keep records, writing it in the new Vietnamese script and using Arabic numerals for numbers. It was a crude form of bookkeeping, but better than nothing. Her aunt kept almost nothing on paper, and even if there were records to speak of, they would have been in Chinese and useless to Giang.

Since coming to the shop, she had let her younger sister handle the customers out front while she stayed in the back, taking care of the records and managing the help to keep the shop stocked with merchandise. Mai, vivacious and good-natured, had taken to sales like fish to water. Her looks charmed the customers and her incessant chatter easily convinced them that they had to buy something, anything.

They were running through bolts of silk at a rapid place as flocks of people were coming to buy every day. Giang knew the young and well-dressed men came and spent freely because they wanted to ogle Mai and banter with her. But the steady comings and goings of customers prevented Giang from leaving the shop during the day, and she hoped that once the novelty of their presence in the shop wore off, she would be able to spend her time as she pleased.

She wanted to sneak away to see Tâm and was getting frustrated that she had not yet managed to do that. She worried about how he had been since the day they went to the beach. Despite what her mother had predicted, not seeing him only made her miss him more.

Eventually they closed up the shop and went home. Mai and the maid led the way, while she followed behind them carrying her book and the day's earnings in a money belt tied securely around her waist. The shops were shuttered and the market was deserted. Even the street vendors had gone home or moved away to other sections of the city to sell their sweets and snacks.

After having gone just a small distance, they saw that their way was blocked by a group of young men. They were affluent looking, probably scions of wealthy and influential families. She counted five of them, standing idly as they observed the three women walking toward them. The maid turned to ask Giang a question but saw something else and said instead.

"There are two more men behind us."

"Let's keep walking," Giang said without looking behind.

As they neared the first group, she recognized one of them as someone who had been in the shop many times, buying silk without bothering to bargain and haggle over prices as people normally did. The others were also customer faces that she had seen at least once. She felt more confident in her ability to handle them.

Soon they reached the group in front of them. The young men showed no intention to yield the way but instead adjusted their clothes, smoothed over their hair, straightened their headdress, and waited.

"Young ladies, it's not a good idea to walk outside at this time of the day," said the one that Giang now called Buyer Number One in her head. "Would you care to let us accompany you home tonight?" He ended his question with a snort that his companions found funny as they guffawed in unison.

The maid responded sternly.

"Please stand aside so that my ladies can pass. We don't need anybody to escort us."

Buyer Number One made a shoving motion that the maid instantly recoiled from, almost losing her footing.

"Miserable servant, I wasn't talking to you, so get out of the way! I am addressing myself to this lovely miss who has been selling me beautiful silk, and to her sister who has been keeping coy in the back of the shop."

The five crept closer step by step to the three women. Giang stepped in front of her sister and the maid.

"Make way and let us go through," she said firmly.

The leader of the men stopped and made a show of looking her over from top to bottom.

"Do you know who you are dealing with, young maiden?"

"I don't care who you are. Just step aside."

He circled around the three women while his friends maintained a solid wall blocking any movement forward. He nodded his head up and down.

"In your shop, I had to pretend to look at the merchandise. But now that I can admire you, I see that both of you are very, very lovely indeed, from head to toe."

"You are nothing but a lout!" Mai exclaimed.

He had learned a few words of French and now used one of them to impress her.

"*Mademoiselle*, is this any way to call a good customer like me. You know what, now that I've taken a good look at both of you, I much prefer your sister."

A calm and familiar voice rose out from behind the women.

"Whoever you are, stop bothering these three women and let them go home."

Giang recognized at once his voice even before she even turned around.

Once the boatman pointed it out to him, Tâm had been observing her shop from afar until it closed and the three women left to go home. He followed them from a distance, uncertain as to whether he should make his presence known.

He saw what happened between them and the five men who blocked their way home. He quickened his pace and reached Giang just as the one who said he was a customer moved closer to her. He stepped up to put his right hand on the man's chest and stopped him.

"Who are you?" Buyer Number One asked as he tried to bat Tâm's hand away.

"I am a passerby who saw your brutish behavior and bad manners. Have you no shame?"

He used his left hand to gently move Giang behind him, placing himself between the three women and their persecutors.

"Did you hear that, my friends?" Buyer Number One said and feinted a turn toward his friends. Suddenly, he reversed his turn and came back with his right hand balled up in a fist. He directed it directly at Tâm. His father the Minister had insisted that he trained in fighting techniques with the guards at his house, and this was going one of those times when he could put all that to good use.

Tâm shifted quickly to the side and out of the way of the incoming fist. With his left hand he redirected his attacker's hand downward. At the same time, with his right hand he delivered a quick and hard punch to the side of his opponent's face. The man's momentum carried him to the ground where he cried out in pain.

"Move back," Tâm shouted at Giang and her companions, while he kept the four young men still standing in sight. However, they were too shocked to see their friend groveling on the ground. They had heard him brag many times of his fighting skills and now had a hard time believing that he was actually defeated in the blink of an eye. They stood cowered and silent, forgetting to come to his aid.

As Giang moved with Mai and the maid away from the scene, waiting to see what would happen next, she saw a dark form from somewhere behind them dash toward the village teacher.

"Watch out, Teacher Tâm!" she screamed.

Tâm felt a rush of air before he saw the attacker. He spun swiftly on his feet and stepped back to get out of the way. A dark shape flew by him at the same time that he felt a stinging sensation on his chest. Instinctively he threw his leg out tripping the man and sent him to the ground next to the one who was already there and trying to get up. He retreated a few steps, stood ready for the next confrontation, and saw the dark shape getting up at the same time that he was helping the other man do the same. The latter was as surprised as Tâm was.

"You, what are you doing here?" Buyer Number One asked.

"Young master, I was on my way home when I saw you here. Are you hurt?"

The young master ignored the question and pointed an unsteady finger at Tâm.

"That scoundrel attacked me. Teach him a lesson. Kill him for me!"

The swarthy man, holding a dagger in his right hand, faced Tâm. He was short, dressed in black clothes, with the bearing of a martial arts fighter or perhaps a soldier. He advanced cautiously, the point of his dagger wiggling from side to side. He feinted several times in different directions, before finally charging forward.

Tâm turned his body, parried the knife downward with his left arm, and again used his right fist to strike the man's face. He next moved toward his opponent, pinning the knife-wielding arm while using his elbow to hit his opponent's chin. He continued using his right arm to force the man's head down and slammed him to the ground. With the man on the ground and dazed from the sudden shock, he pressed one knee against the man's head and the other against his back, and then used his hands to disarm him. By that time the man had ceased all resistance. Tâm stood up, now holding the knife. He waved it in the direction of Buyer Number One and his band.

"Who's next?"

They ran away, leaving the attacker in black lying semi-conscious in the dirt. After a long minute, the man struggled to a kneeling position, a mix of confusion and fear on his face. Half of his face was swollen and turning a dark red. One eye was almost closed and his nose was bleeding. Without warning, he kowtowed in the direction of Tâm.

"Please spare me!" he said and remained prostrated on the ground.

"Just go away," Tâm said.

The man slowly stood up, took several wary steps backward before turning around and running away from the scene.

Tâm watched him for an instant, and then breathed in deeply to calm himself down before turning to face Giang and her companions. The three were watching him, still surprised at the rapid turn of events and amazed at how fast he had neutralized his two attackers. Giang stepped gingerly toward him, her eyes fixed on his chest.

"You are bleeding," she suddenly shouted and ran to him. He looked down and saw that the top of his tunic as well as his shirt underneath was torn open. A red stain was already visible through both garments.

She sent her sister and the maid home to get some medical supplies while she accompanied him back to the inn. By the time they reached it, the stain was much larger even though he kept pressing a handkerchief that she gave him over his wound.

Inside the inn, she enlisted the help of the incredulous innkeeper in a whirlwind of activities. Within minutes, Tâm found himself sitting on the bed in his room stripped of his tunic and shirt, his upper body wiped clean by Giang with hot water. She had him hold and press a clean piece of cloth over the shallow but long cut. Meanwhile she alternated between sitting beside him and getting up to go to the door to see whether her sister or the maid had returned, wringing her hands and returning to look at him with concern.

He felt like a sick child who was being pampered.

"Giang, it's just a surface wound and I am not going to die."

She sat next to him and took his free hand into hers.

"You could have been killed if that man had come any closer with the dagger! I missed you and thought of you so much already these past few days. What would I do if you were gone forever?"

Embarrassed at her sudden outburst, she turned away to hide her face. He pulled on her hands to make her turn back. Gradually her resistance faded and she leaned toward him at the same time that her face turned and came close to his. Her eyes were moist with tears.

"What about you, did you think of me even once?" she asked softly.

"No," he answered and waited for her puzzled reaction before continuing. "Not once, but all the time, every day."

They heard someone clearing her throat at the door. It was Mai and the maid who had made good time coming back to the inn because they used the family horse carriage. Mai had a package in her arms and an impish smile on her face.

"I hate to interrupt this touching moment, but if you don't bandage him now with what I brought here, he may bleed to death, and you will indeed never see him again. Or his hand will be permanently stuck to his chest, and …"

"Mai!" Giang raised her voice. "Stop talking gibberish and come here help me."

Giang first cleaned his wound with a stinging liquid from a bottle that Mai had brought. Next the two sisters applied a dressing and held it in place with a bandage wrapped around his chest and neck. Once that was done, Tâm put on a clean shirt, but they would not allow him to leave his bed or do anything else.

"You need to rest, and we have to leave now before our parents become worried about us." Giang said. "I'll try to come back later."

He had to lie down on the bed before the two sisters would consent to leave. They gathered his torn and bloodied tunic and shirt and took them away. At the door, they turned around to look at him one more time. An awkward silence followed until Mai spoke up.

"If you are not going to do it, I will!"

"Do what?"

Mai shook her head.

"Oh Lord, these first-born are always so clueless!"

She went back into the room, sat down next to him, lifted his head, cradled it with both of her hands and looked him straight in the eyes. He had no time to react.

"Teacher Tâm, thank you for what you did today," she said and planted a moist kiss on his cheek.

She stood up and gave a panicky Giang a gleeful look.

"There, we can go now."

"How dare you!?" Giang exclaimed.

Mai sauntered past her sister with a triumphant grin on her face. The maid could not contain herself and burst out laughing.

Minister of Rites

The Minister of Rites, Trịnh Toản, and the examination judges, all in flowing robes and dragonfly hats, stood slightly bent forward on both sides of the King and the Head Eunuch behind him. They were there to present the results of the palace examinations and get the monarch's approval on the list of candidates who passed.

As he sat on the throne, the young King looked lost and unhappy. He hardly said a word, much less a sentence, unless it was to approve or disapprove something on the advice of his ministers or the Head Eunuch.

There were many factions at court, each trying its best to influence and steer the King in their direction. However, in the matter of examinations, the only faction was the one that the Minister of Rites led. The King had no choice but to agree to their recommendations. Still, the audience with the King and the presentation of the results were formalities required by customs going back several centuries, and the Minister of Rites would not have done it in any other way.

Minister Toản had seen his chief guard, face battered and one eye swollen shut. The guard assured him that he had taken care of Teacher Xinh. He did not say what happened to his face and the old Minister didn't want to pursue that matter since the guard occasionally suffered bruises and sprains in training with other guards or with his own son. The fact that his son later appeared with his face similarly battered confirmed the old Minister's thinking. His young concubine chuckled oddly when he told her about it, but she did not say anything. Toản forced himself to put those images aside to concentrate on his audience with the young monarch.

He began addressing the King in a sonorous and commanding voice.

"Your Majesty, only nine have been deemed worthy of passing the examinations: one from the North, six from the Center, and two from the South".

The young King looked at him impassively. Minister Toản glanced at him, and then continued.

"This is perfect as it represents the reality of the distribution of scholars throughout our nation. The North, which used to be dominant a century ago, is now in decline. The South, under the exploitation of the French, is in a similar state, namely going downhill. What that means is that our next generation of mandarins will be among the most qualified since they come from the best scholar families who live in and around the capital."

The thought of his own son not being such a scholar crossed the old Minister's mind, but he dismissed it immediately. His son was more interested in women than scholarly studies, and that couldn't be helped at the moment.

He held the list of chosen candidates and looked firmly into the King's eyes.

"Your Majesty, there is one more matter that we must report before we present you with this list."

The King was not surprised. Trịnh Toản often behaved as he were the King's father, admonishing him and even surprising him with some indirect criticism at times. He was literally terrified of the Minister, but there was not much he could do about it. He could not yet trust anybody, except the immediate members of his family who were still too new to court politics and had no political ally to advise them. He was not even sure of the royal eunuch, another old man with a ruddy complexion, who was constantly at his side. In fact, the French Resident General and that special envoy who could speak Vietnamese have turned out to be the only people he would trust. They did not lie to him, even if some of the things they said in his presence could be perceived as harsh, arrogant or disdainful of his status of King.

The old Minister saw the fleeting look of fear or perhaps revulsion on the young monarch's face, but he steadfastly went on.

"One of the scholars has committed a grave offense by violating the proscription on using one of your royal names."

Even he had lost count of how many names he had, the King thought. How could somebody else be required to memorize them so as never to use them?

His full name began with the dynastic names of Nguyễn Phúc. A poem written by Emperor Minh Mạng determined the next name. Since he was a fifth generation descendant of the Emperor, the fifth word in that poem, Vĩnh, had to be used. Finally his parents gave him his own personal name, one that could no longer be pronounced without a slight inflection or be written without a modification of its Chinese character.

Those close to him used to call him by a vulgar nickname his parents had given him to confuse and ward off evil spirits, but a King could never be called that.

When he was crowned, two dozen honorific and glorified names were chosen for him by the ministers. He could not even remember what they were, but Minister Toản standing before him was telling him that some scholar had dared to actually use one of them without modification.

"Your Majesty, the offender is a mediocre scholar from the North who should never have been allowed to participate in the palace examinations."

Their heads bent, the judges glanced furtively at their neighbors standing next to them. The Minister of Rites had shown them the examination paper containing the offending word, and told them that they should have been punished for not having detected the violation on their own.

Punishment included having their salary docked for a year and possible demotions to lower ranks. It meant the end of their mandarin career at court. However, the Minister also said he would overlook that matter if they were to keep quiet and let him present the results to the King in his own way.

They could see that he was going to deflect any blame to lower provincial mandarins who had organized the regional examinations and allowed their best scholars to go on to the palace examinations. Minister Toản was willing to lie and defame the one scholar whom they considered the best of the crop, but he said that he did so to protect their own hides. One skeptical judge had dared to ask to look at the examination paper a second time, but the old Minister simply glared at him, excoriated him at length and denied his request.

"Your Majesty, this is a very grave offense. According to the rules, it is the same as treason and punishable by death."

The King visibly blanched, several judges gasped, and the rest shuddered as if a cold winter breeze had blown through. Even the Head Eunuch, who was normally reserved and imperturbable, could not refrain from raising his eyebrows.

Everyone in the audience hall knew that punishment for name violation was never that severe. Those guilty usually were caned, banned permanently from taking any examination, and demoted or fired outright if they held a government position. That the Minister of Rites had elevated it to a capital offense was extremely unusual.

"Therefore, Your Majesty, we respectfully present to you the list of those who passed this year's palace examinations." Minister Toản, the only man who remained calm and collected, continued. "We ask that you approve and affix your seal on the list. We also ask that you order that punishment be carried out for that mediocre scholar guilty of the crime of name violation. His name is on the second of the two lists I am now presenting to your Majesty."

He extended his hands in front of him to present the lists to the King. The Head Eunuch promptly stepped forward, took the lists, and then returned to his position behind the throne. The audience was coming to an end and the lists would be dealt with later, after the Minister of Rites and the judges left.

"Must he be executed?" the King managed to ask in a voice barely heard around the room. It was the voice of a child who did not speak often, and only when he was allowed to.

"Of course, Your Majesty. We need to set an example for posterity. We have to let everyone know that the use and abuse of royal names are not inconsequential matters. Nothing less than death by beheading can be commensurate with the magnitude of this crime."

The Head Eunuch bent down and brought his face close to the King's ear. Those in the room thought that they heard a high-pitched woman's voice whisper something to the King, but they could not make sense of what was said. The King closed his eyes to listen and remained motionless for several minutes to muster his courage. He opened his eyes again, and his voice was quivering and still weak, but everyone understood what he said next.

"We would like to give this matter some more time before making a final decision."

"The audience is over," announced the Head Eunuch. "You may leave this hall now. You will be told to come back later when His Majesty commands you to."

Trịnh Toàn and the judges kowtowed to the King five times then walked slowly backward until they went out of sight of the royal gaze.

Both the King and the Head Eunuch were lost in thought after the audience. The Head Eunuch had served five kings, most of the time standing in silence behind them, catering to their personal needs and desires.

Emperor Minh Mạng had imposed strict limits on what the eunuchs could or could not do to avoid the excesses of their counterparts in China where at times eunuchs actually controlled the fate of their nation and usurped the power of the emperors they were supposed to serve.

The Head Eunuch therefore had little influence outside of the walls of the Forbidden City. However, he had accumulated a lot of information and facts by his mere presence behind the throne, listening and observing how the monarchs and their courtiers interacted. He was also a literate man and a scholar in his own right with access to all the books in the royal library.

When the King was brought to the palace as a terrified boy, the Head Eunuch had taken it upon himself to advise and educate him. The boy's parents were incapable of doing so, the courtiers were only interested in fighting among themselves, and the whole scene played perfectly into the French's plans for having a puppet at the head of a nation that they had colonized.

"Your Majesty, the Minister of Rites was misleading you when he said the name violation offense is punishable by execution. This kind of violation is always hard to avoid, and last century, the scholar Lê Quý Đôn had even proposed that those rules be abolished. In fact, in 1772 he deliberately used the names of the Lê emperor and the Trịnh lord at that time in the topics given out at one of the regional examinations."

"So why are we now enforcing those rules again?" asked the King.

"I suspect it may have something to do with our dynasty wanting to be different from the Lê. Your ancestors were also very keen on adhering as much as possible to the Chinese examination traditions. Emperor Minh Mạng often read the papers of winning Chinese scholars and compared them to our own to make sure that our scholars measured up to them."

"Even then," the Head Eunuch went on, "I have never heard of capital punishment for name violations. Yes, there have been executions, but they were for people who committed other crimes such as falsifying examination papers in order to pass unworthy scholars."

"This was the case of Nguyễn Tú in 1834. He received the death sentence, his accomplices were either jailed or demoted, while the scholars in questions were stripped of all their titles and never allowed to take examinations again. Then in 1841, Cao Bá Quát, an examination judge in our capital, was guilty of correcting some poems that contained name violations so that their authors could pass the examinations. He was condemned to death by decapitation. However, Quát was a legendary scholar who had earned a reputation for unrivaled intelligence and erudition from a very young age. Recognizing this, and reasoning that Quát was only trying to help others and not cheating for his own benefit, Emperor Thiệu Trị commuted his sentence twice and he was only demoted and exiled."

The Head Eunuch added as an afterthought.

"If we were to follow Chinese traditions, we must not forget that Emperor Xuan of the Western Han dynasty changed his name, which contained two common characters, to a different name with rarely used characters. He wanted to make it easier for scholars to avoid committing name violations."

The King was a still in his teens, but showed more wisdom than most of his courtiers was willing to grant him. His next question went to the crux of the matter.

"Why then does the Minister of Rites want to punish this unfortunate scholar from the North?"

"Your Majesty, he may have some personal grudge against that man or perhaps he is using him as a pawn in some broader scheme. Things in this city are never what they appear to be at first glance."

"Then tell me what I should do. I don't want the Minister to have his way, but I also don't want to change the examination rules at this time."

Bà Trang inserted into her mouth a small roll made of slices of area nut and lime wrapped in betel leaves and started chewing vigorously. The maid was preparing some more wraps and placed them one by one on a small lacquer tray. The Special Envoy's wife absent-mindedly watched her hands move skillfully back and forth between a basket full of fresh betel leaves and areca nuts, a small pot of lime, and the lacquer tray. She only indulged occasionally in betel chewing as her French husband disapproved of it. She needed it occasionally to lift up her spirits and give her an extra surge of energy to tackle the problems of life in a mixed Vietnamese French household with two nubile daughters who were as headstrong as they were naïve.

"So, you came back from bringing him some food, while my two darling girls *forgot* to tell me about their encounter with him, after I had told them never to see him again."

"My Lady, he saved us from those thugs who bothered the two young ladies. And he was wounded by the bodyguard of one of those thugs."

"I know, I know," Bà Trang said. "No need to remind me. That's why I haven't said anything to my daughters yet. Where are they now?"

Her daughters had not mentioned the incident at dinner in front of her and her husband. Yet, from their unusual silence and furtive glances to each other, she knew something was going on and set out to find out the truth from her maid afterwards. That her husband was kept in the dark was fine with her.

"My Lady, they are at the Đông Ba market," the maid sighed. Although she had to report everything to the mistress of the house, her sympathy had been shifting lately to the side of the two sisters, and, she conceded, to that of the village teacher who had saved them twice already.

"And has that young mandarin son reappeared at their shop?"

"Not yet, my Lady. I don't think we'll see him until his swollen face returns to normal." She turned her head to hide her smile, hoping her mistress would not see it.

Bà Trang promised herself that she would find out who the stranger was. Probably the son of some official or a very wealthy merchant, making him a good son-in-law prospect, she thought. He appeared to be besotted with either Giang or Mai, so she already had half of her work done for her.

The one thing she wanted to do next was to isolate that village teacher and put Giang out of his reach. That was not going to be easy, but she had faced worse problems than a daughter's passing infatuation with an insignificant village teacher. She stopped chewing and directed a red stream of gooey into a brass spittoon.

Secretary Kham once again found himself in the presence of the Minister of Rites. He saw that the old mandarin was even angrier than last time. He suspected the mood had something to do with the examinations results that the whole capital was now waiting for impatiently. His French boss had asked him why the court was taking so long before posting the examinations results. Since he was standing before the only man who would know, he was looking for a way to see whether the old Minister would give him any insider's view on the matter. However, Toàn's first question surprised him.

"Tell me about this scholar from the North that's intimate with the Bonneau's family. What is he up to these days?"

"He has not been coming around to their house, Your Excellency. The servants are whispering that the Frenchman's wife has told her daughters to cut off all contact with him."

The old Minister tapped his fingers on his chair' arms finely inlaid with mother of pearl.

"And why is she doing that?"

"I can only guess that she has set much higher criteria for prospective sons-in-law, and he cannot come close to meeting any of them. Unless he passed the examinations, his yearly income as a village teacher probably won't be enough to buy one chair like the one Your Excellency is sitting on. Perhaps, she is setting her sight on someone much higher and with a better pedigree."

Minister Toàn wondered whether Kham knew about the latest incident his son had at the Đông Ba market, when he moved too aggressively on the Bonneau's girl. The young man was unable or unwilling to tell him who had done it to him, and his chief guard could only confirm that he had met a man with better fighting skills than his. The old man was still furious about it. He felt the bruise on his son's face as if it were on his. Throughout his life, he was always free to pick and choose his sexual conquests and nobody had ever dared attack him for that, even with a feather.

"What does the husband, Bonneau, think?"

"Either he does not care or doesn't know what his wife is planning. I suspect it is the latter. He was very impressed with the village teacher, and still is."

The old Minister snorted and dismissed Kham with a wave of his hand. He would give anything to see Bonneau's face when he found out the predicament his favorite scholar was going to find himself in.

Interlude

Tâm woke up feeling slightly feverish. He tried to go about his normal activities and attempted to study, but by mid-morning he had to lie down. His body was burning and he drifted in and out of consciousness as he slept restlessly. At times, he felt the presence of someone in the room and a hand pressing something cool over his forehead or wiping off the sweat from his face. Toward evening, he woke up again and realized that finally his fever had broken and disappeared. The bandage over his chest appeared to be dry and his wound was no longer throbbing with spasms of pain. He heard footsteps, got up to go to the door but felt dizzy and had to sit back on the bed.

The innkeeper came in, frowning and concerned, and looked him over carefully.

"Teacher, you slept for two whole days. Did you know that the young lady was here during most of that time?"

"Two days I slept? And, she was here?"

"You didn't know, did you? You were feverish and delirious. She was really worried. She sat by your side and wiped you down every few minutes to keep you cool, while I had to go empty and refill the wash basin time and time again."

"I felt someone was in the room, and so it was her."

"She didn't leave until you were sound asleep, and that must have been just before dawn." The innkeeper shook his head in sympathy. "I know it's none of my business, but I doubt there is anyone else, except maybe your own mother, that would care for you as much as she did."

He examined the bandage carefully then switched to another topic.

"This morning, her maid brought you some gruel also, and I'll go heat it up and bring it to you a little bit later. She wants you to eat to regain your strength. You know, this young woman is taking over and running me and my inn now."

The innkeeper laughed, his merry eyes becoming thin slits. Giang had demanded a great deal from him and his inn, but she had also compensated him well.

"From now on, you must rest and try not to get into any more scuffles."

Later, Tâm was sitting at a table in the small restaurant at the front of the inn. Before him was a large bowl of steaming gruel and a plate of fresh fruit. Ravenous, he ate with gusto, but could not stop thinking of how much more involved he now was in his relationship with Giang.

When he was banned from coming to her house, he had blamed himself for being dishonest with his emotions. What was he thinking, coming to see her every day and going on outings with her? His instinct told him from the start that there was no future in their relationship because their social statuses were so far apart, and yet he gave free rein to his emotions instead of keeping them in check like he always did at home. He was supposed to be the teacher, someone that students looked up to as their ideal of Confucian scholarship and morals.

He had the excuse of wanting to learn a new way of writing and even a foreign language, but did the end justify the means? Then again, why did he venture to see her at the market and get himself into another altercation? On the other hand, if he had not gone, could he bear the thought of that mandarin son putting his hands on her?

The attention and the care she had shown to him only showed that she felt deeply about him, as much as he did about her. However, was he ready to go along that path, one that he didn't think he would have to face so soon? If not, how was he planning to disentangle himself? Could he ever turn the clock back and start over? How could he avoid hurting her? Before leaving his village for the capital, people had jokingly warned him about the passionate women of Huế. Was Giang that kind of woman, one that would let her heart and not her mind govern her actions? What about him? He cared for her, perhaps more than he was willing to admit, but what was really motivating him, his heart or his mind?

"Teacher Tâm, what are you doing there? Composing a poem, day-dreaming, or maybe thinking of someone?"

He turned toward the sound of the familiar voice. It belonged to Chí, the son of the Village Chief back home. He was standing at the entrance to the inn, a chubby and nattily dressed man who looked as if he would fit right in with the mandarins in the capital.

Since he became a student under Tâm's father at the village school, Chí had been both a friend and a rival. They played together, at least when they were young, while inside the classroom Chí tried his best to snatch the number one ranking from Tâm, but could never do it. Subsequently, he left to study under another teacher in Hà Nội, and seldom came back to the village. However, he also came to the capital to sit for the same examinations, and Tâm had seen him there but only spoken to him very briefly.

Chí scanned around the room, his eyes and a slight pout expressing disapproval.

"I've been looking all over for you. Finally, somebody mentioned that you may be staying in this part of town, and here you are. You should have come and join us on the other side of the river, where it's much nicer and friendlier than here."

He winked at those last words, full of hints and suggestions.

"This is perfect for me," replied Tâm. "Have you heard about when they are going to post the results?"

"Alas, no! There are all kinds of rumors, but probably not one of them is true. What are you worried about? You are going to be the top man anyway. As for me, I am just glad to have some extra time to enjoy life in this city."

Chí took a seat opposite him and stared at him curiously. Tâm knew that his friend was looking for him to get at some information he wanted. From the times they were still in the village school together, the pudgy Village Chief's son never came to talk to him unless he needed some favor or wanted to know something.

"I've heard that one of our fellow scholars is vying for the attention of a beautiful young lady from a very powerful family in the capital. They say he may be competing with some court minister's son. Did you know about that?"

"No, I never heard of that rumor, until now."

He guessed right away that Chí was speaking about Giang, but he was not going to confirm any rumor about her. Besides, it was the first time that someone had told him about a mandarin's son being interested in her, and so his answer was strictly correct.

"I didn't think you would, since you don't mingle with people like the group I am staying with. But it's interesting, isn't it? Romantic intrigue in the midst of palace examinations, right here in the imperial city! Who would have guessed it?"

Tâm attempted to change the subject.

"So, how do you think you did in the examinations?"

"I did my best, but one can never tell. I did notice that you were always the first to leave the Cần Chính palace, while the rest of us were tearing our hair out looking for ideas and words. My main concern during those weeks was that if I left too many blank pages, I could be accused of insufficient preparation and be caned!"

They both laughed until Chí pointed to the table.

"I see that you had a nice breakfast, or maybe it was lunch. Not too bad for a village teacher in the big city! Well, I'm going down to the river and hire one of those boats. Some of us are planning an evening on the river today. Would you like to join us?"

He stood up without waiting for an answer, already knowing what it would be.

"No, thank you. But let me take a walk with you. I need some exercise."

Tâm got up and made an effort to be steady on his feet so that his friend would not notice anything unusual about his physical state. Fortunately Chí already had his mind on his pleasure trip on the river and paid scant attention to him.

When they came near the river bank, Chí went to join a group of his friends, while Tâm strolled in the opposite direction hoping to see his friendly boatman. As he walked away, he overheard Chí exclaim to his group.

"It's not him, it can't be! Look at him, he can't even afford a decent tunic to wear."

Another voice was just as loud.

"So we'll have to keep investigating until we find the lucky guy."

Tâm walked on, unaffected by their conversation. Soon he arrived at the familiar spot where the boatman usually moored. Sure enough, husband and wife were on deck apparently mending a fishing net in the shade of the tree to which their boat was tied. The boatman saw him first and stood up.

"There you are Teacher! We were just thinking about you. Come on closer so I can tell you a few things."

Intrigued, Tâm approached but did not climb on board.

"How have you been, boatman, how's business?"

"Same as always. But, listen, Teacher Xinh and his family are dead."

He was jolted by the shocking news, now understanding the sadness he saw on the boatman's face.

"What? How can that be?"

"Their house burned down and they couldn't escape the fire. All four of them perished, incinerated."

"What a horrible tragedy," Tâm shook his head. "I should go pay my respects, even if I don't know him that well."

"Are you wounded?"

The boatman's question came out of nowhere. Tâm stared at him for a moment and hesitated.

"How did you …"

"I saw you fighting the man who attacked you from behind. I was going to get off the boat and come to your help, but you had already disposed of him before I could take one step."

The boatman's admiring eyes made Tâm feel embarrassed.

"Then I saw the young lady accompany you home. You were holding something against your chest, so I thought perhaps you were wounded."

"It's not too bad now, nothing to worry about."

"Did you see who attacked you?"

"Yes, some man who was quite dark and wore a black outfit."

The boatman thought about the swarthy man who got off with Teacher Xinh on his last trip.

"People say he is one of the bodyguards for a very powerful mandarin."

Back at the inn, he opened the books she had given him and tried to resume his French study. He kept being distracted by a sense of unease and foreboding. Was it the news about Teacher Xinh, or the lack of news about the examinations, or the growing weight on his conscience about the precarious state of his relationship with the daughter of the French Special Envoy? He held his head in his hands and closed his eyes.

He didn't know how long it had been when he heard a soft knock on the door. He turned around and before he could get to the door Giang opened it and came into the room carrying a package.

"You are up!" she said and stopped in front of him, anxiously looking him over. "Why are you sitting in the dark? I thought you were sleeping or still sick."

He stood up and went to her.

"I feel much better today, and I actually went out for a walk. The innkeeper told me you watched over me constantly while I was ill. You must be very tired."

She shook her head.

"I am fine. I was worried about you and I needed to make sure you were all right."

He wanted to ask her more, but she gave him her package and went to light up the oil lamp on the table.

"I brought you some new clothes in this package. I had a new tunic and shirt made to replace your old ones that were torn. Please try them on so I can see whether they fit? The seamstress used the measurements from your old clothes, but I want to be sure."

He knew that there was no point to deny her request, so he complied. As he stood and took his shirt off, she looked at his bandage and told him to let her change it. She carefully unwrapped the old dressing and started cleaning around the wound once more. He felt her cool hands moving over his chest and back, and he shivered at the unfamiliar sensations. She stopped.

"Am I hurting you?"

"No ..."

He looked into her anxious blue eyes. Her voice was barely audible.

"What is it?" she asked weakly.

He reached for her hands. Soon her hair with the scent of frangipani was in his face. Their arms found each other and their love blossomed, pure, unaffected and unwavering, in the darkness of a small inn room at the edge of the capital city. For fear of hurting him, she only gripped his arms with all her might. He bent toward her ear and whispered tender words that he sometimes read in poems but until then never knew their true meanings.

Motherly Interference

Tăng Thị Trang was born in Huế but grew up in Cửa Hàn, the city that the French called Tourane, their way of pronouncing its Vietnamese name. It was a coastal city with a natural harbor some 60 miles south of the capital. Her family had prospered there mainly through trading with the foreign vessels that came to the city's port, when the old port of Hội An some 20 miles further down the coast became silted over by the alluvial discharges from the Thu Bồn river.

The first Emperor of the Nguyễn dynasty, Gia Long, in consideration for the crucial support the French had given him in attaining power, gave them exclusive trading rights through the port of Cửa Hàn. In reality the French came and went through all of the country's harbors from South to North without much opposition from the local governors or from anyone else.

In 1835, Emperor Minh Mạng, who succeeded his father, decided to limit French influence by decreeing that the only port open to French ships was Cửa Hàn. The city flourished even more under that special exemption. Shipbuilding and repair vied with commerce, crafts, and the processing of agricultural products to make Tourane the wealthiest city in Central Việt Nam.

Trang's father had taken the local examinations and failed twice before he realized that his mind and his heart belonged to a business career. He moved his young family to Tourane where he opened a small shop buying and selling handicraft products. Over the years, that small shop became a large trading house dealing with ships from many foreign nations, importing anything from silk to guns, and exporting

Vietnamese handicrafts and agricultural products for markets as far away as Japan and Europe.

The family, once ridiculed by other clan branches for leaving the scholar tradition, became the clan's main support. Her uncles and aunts who remained in Huế could barely eke out their living from the minor positions they held in the royal government. While they never forgot to remind Bà Trang's father that they were intellectually his superior, they also never turned down the money and gifts he gave them each time he went to visit their homes when he was doing business in the capital. Naturally, the gifts were also intended to grease his way into the bureaucracy and help his business.

Growing up in this environment, she developed a marked dislike for scholars. In traditional culture, scholars were placed at the top of the social ladder, followed by farmers, artisans, with merchants at the bottom, in that exact order. To her though, scholars were like leeches sucking on the blood of the other three classes, while at the same time proclaiming their moral and intellectual superiority. They ruled and governed with no purpose other than making sure they always stayed at the top of the ladder.

In Tourane, a city with a sizable Christian minority, the family converted to Catholicism, and their young daughter, Trang, started going to a school taught by French priests. There she learned French and mastered the new script the missionaries used to write their translation of the Bible and other religious texts into Vietnamese. The Jesuits also taught her some mathematics and a little bit of science, letting her glimpse at how advanced and powerful the West was. The education she received only convinced her further of the backwardness and hopelessness of the scholars who hung on to the Chinese classics that even China was in the process of discarding.

Her relatives looked down on her father, and by extension on the rest of his family, while at the same time expecting to benefit from his largesse. Whenever she visited them, she saw their patronizing smiles and condescending attitudes, but she also noted the carefully tailored tunics and dresses, all made from silk that her father gave them as presents.

Her father provided even some of the food on their tables, especially those delicacies coming from foreign lands. He told her not to mind their relatives' attitude, since the business was benefitting from all the connections and influence that they provided him, but his advice did nothing to lessen her bitterness.

When the time came to choose between a young French naval officer and a promising scholar who was the son of a local mandarin, she chose the former, against the wishes of her own parents. It turned out to be a wise decision since Bonneau opened many new doors to her family business. Once the young Bonneau proved of immense usefulness to their business, the parents conceded that her choice of a husband was indeed wise and prescient.

The only disadvantage, if it could be termed such, was that the couple had to move and go live in the capital when Bonneau was appointed Special Envoy to the King of Annam. It was a well-deserved post for the French officer who, through sheer will and the ability to learn and adapt to a foreign culture, rose up through the ranks. That he was fluent in the language and had a wife who was a native only enhanced his credentials to the boy King as well as the French Resident General.

In Huế's society, where a title, especially one so important as Bonneau's, was a prized possession commanding respect and envy, Bà Trang's stature suddenly took off. Her uncles and aunts hastened to get to her door and beg for an audience while admiring the splendor of the colonial house and the soldiers guarding it. Suddenly, the underestimated girl of a failed scholar, a merchant, became the wisest woman in town.

Even her uncle, the abbot at Thiên Mụ temple, who had ignored her before, found the strength to overlook her Christian faith. He made himself a regular presence in her house, spending more time visiting there than any other place, and offered his niece advice on all subjects. The two grandnieces that he had neglected in the past became his favorite ones.

He fussed about their health, their education, and their happiness. He plotted their future, especially after they grew up and became two of the most fetching young ladies in the capital. Nobody lower than a mandarin son or a rich merchant could be worthy of his grand nieces. That is why he was so disappointed when Giang introduced the village teacher to him. He did not like what he saw, and afterwards made his opinions and his predictions about the young man perfectly clear to her mother.

Bà Trang had indeed been obsessed with the abbot's dire prognosis of her daughter's relationship with the poor scholar from the North. She convinced herself that if Giang persisted on seeing Teacher Tâm, she would be destined for a future as chaotic and filled with misfortunes as that of the ill-fated Thuý Kiều in Nguyễn Du's famous epic poem.

In the quietness of their bedroom, she waited until Bonneau had settled in comfortably in a chair by the window. He liked to sit there and puff on his pipe before finally going to bed. Normally, she would also sit near him, enjoying the fragrant smell of the pipe, happy that her husband had not taken up opium.

"I am planning on going to Tourane with Giang," she announced without preamble. "The two girls are doing quite well at the silk shop and we'll have to get some more products as a result."

Bonneau was only mildly surprised. He knew that his daughters were intelligent and capable of running the business, each complementing the other. Françoise was the back shop manager who could keep the books, organize and motivate the help, while Francine was at the front wooing customers and getting them to buy as if there were no tomorrow.

"Are you taking your older daughter along to teach her the business?"

"Certainly, that's exactly what I am planning. In Tourane, I will take her with me and introduce her to all of our suppliers and contacts there. She will learn how business is really carried out. She has probably picked up a few things already, but there are still many aspects of our business that she doesn't know. This will be a good learning trip for her."

"When do you plan to go?"

"That depends. Do you know if one of the French ships is scheduled to go to Tourane very soon? If not, we'll go by road over the Hải Vân pass."

However, she did not care for travelling via the pass with the approaching monsoon. The pass at its highest point was quite often literally in the clouds (Vân), while its lowest points skirted the ocean

(Hải), and she did not relish the thought of being on it when the weather was bad.

Bonneau also did not want his wife and daughter to have to take the land route.

"I think there is one ship leaving this week, but let me check tomorrow and I'll let you know the exact day."

She was relieved. "I'll tell Giang to get ready and be prepared to go any day then."

"How long will you be gone? If I knew, I could find out what ship you could board to come back here."

She wanted to keep her daughter from the capital as long as possible, the longer the better.

"It could be a few weeks, but don't worry, I can ask around in Tourane when we are ready to go back. We plan on bringing back a good amount of silk and other goods, which may take some time to buy and get ready for shipment."

Rank had its privileges and she knew that the French ships could not refuse passage to the wife of the Special Envoy, even if she had a long train of baggage.

Bonneau frowned and observed his wife through the smoke. His instinct told him that her planned trip had a deeper purpose than business training for their daughter. People in the capital often said that things were never the same as what they appeared to be. He had been in Việt Nam for more than a quarter of a century, and had been married to the woman sitting opposite him for almost as many years. He knew her well.

"Are you going there for any other reason?"

She threw him a surprised look that was anything but genuine.

"No, what are you talking about?"

"Are you still fighting your war with that young village teacher, the one that Giang cannot stop thinking about despite your ban?"

Even though the household kept quiet about it, secretary Kham had told him that there had been another incident in which the village teacher had to fight to stop several mandarin sons from harassing his daughters. He was also well aware that Françoise had taken medical supplies and bandage from his medicine chest to treat the wound Tâm sustained in the fight. He had discretely replenished the chest and hoped that she had everything she needed. For some time now, he was beginning to doubt his wife's wisdom in trying to keep Françoise away from the unusual young scholar from the North, but he was not yet ready to question her openly about it.

His wife attempted to use a compliment to avoid answering his question.

"You are a very smart man, Your Excellency. It's no wonder that the Resident General picked you to be Special Envoy to the King of Annam. You can see right through all the natives, including me."

"Especially you, Madame, since I've known you the longest," he chuckled. "Anyway, I hope you know what you are doing with your daughter. Don't you do anything to break her heart. Remember that your parents were totally opposed to me at first."

"That's true, but I was much different from her," she insisted. "You never took advantage of me, not that I would have let you, even if you tried. But our daughter is still too young and quite immature. She needs to be stopped before she loses herself completely to that village teacher."

She stood up to emphasize her last sentence.

"And I will never let that happen!"

Shortly before noon the following day, Bà Trang arrived in the family carriage at the Đông Ba market. She got off and immediately headed at a fast and resolute pace toward the shop stall where her daughters were. When she saw her mother arriving in haste, Mai turned away from a customer and exclaimed.

"Mother, what are you doing here?"

Out of breath, Bà Trang only waved dismissively and went to the back of the shop to find her older daughter. Giang was seated at a small table, recording into a ledger book the latest inventory and sales figures. She looked up in total surprise.

"Mother! What's the matter? Why are you here? Did something happen at home?"

"No, no. Your father just told me that there is a ship leaving for Tourane this afternoon, and I would like you to come and get on the ship with me. We are going to Tourane. I thought we wouldn't be able to go for a few more days, otherwise I would have told you earlier. Drop everything and come with me right now."

Giang stood up, confused and thrown off guard.

"Mother, I can't go like this! I haven't prepared anything. Why are we going all of a sudden?"

"I already packed what we need in two trunks, for both you and me. All is ready, we just need to go now, and we have to hurry. The ship is not going to wait for us."

"But, why do you want me to go?"

"You are keeping the books so you should already know why. The shop's merchandise is being depleted at a fast pace ever since you and your sister started here. That's good and it means both of you know what you are doing. However, now we need to go buy more products, especially silk and even some trinkets, and bring them back here to sell. This will be a good opportunity for you to meet our suppliers so you can learn how to select their merchandise and negotiate their terms. You'll also get to know how to have things packaged and shipped back here. This part of the business is just as important as what you two are doing here, and I want you to come with me so you'll have some experience with those matters."

During her long explanation, Mai had come into the small back shop room. As soon as her mother stopped talking, she said.

"Let me accompany you if she doesn't want to. I wouldn't mind seeing Tourane again."

"You will next time, but for now I want you to stay here and take care of your father at home. Hurry up, Giang, we are leaving this instant!"

She pretended not to see her daughter's distress and proceeded to walk out to the front of the shop. After a few steps she stopped, turned to scan around the shop and waited for her older daughter. Giang looked at her sister, grabbed her hand and dragged her deeper into the back shop.

"Mother, I'll be right there," she shouted. Once out of sight of their mother, she fixed her eyes on her little sister who was as surprised as she was.

"Can you go see him tonight on your way home, and tell him that I am going to Tourane?"

There was no doubt whom she was referring to, and Mai responded immediately.

"Is he expecting you? You've been seeing him every day!"

"Hush, I don't want Mother to hear us. Just tell him so he will know and won't worry about me. Tell him I had no idea this trip was going to happen and that I'll be back as soon as possible."

Mai could not resist making fun of her sister.

"Why? So that he will wait for you and pine after you every day? What's in it for me?"

Giang's eyes started to fill up with tears.

"You can never stop teasing, can you? Promise me you'll do it."

Mai relented before her sister's pitiful face.

"I was just kidding! Of course I'll tell him, I promise. Don't forget that I like him in my own way too."

Giang went on imploring. "And if he needs something, anything, you … help him. Do what I say and I'll bring you back a nice stone carving from the Marble Mountains."

"Now that's more like it. Nothing is for free you know, not even between sisters."

She finished by winking at Giang and hitting her lightly with an elbow.

"Go, go now, and try not to let Mother see you cry. Go …"

Relieved, Giang wiped her eyes and cheeks dry, breathed in deeply, composed herself, and then walked out to her waiting mother.

After her sister left, Mai no longer felt as spirited as she had been up to that point. She handled customer inquiries listlessly, no longer teasing or making fun of some of the male customers who dropped by the shop and pretended to buy silk. By midafternoon, the crowd thinned out at the Đông Ba market much earlier than normal, so she and the maid agreed to close up the shop early.

Later, when they left, the air was still hot and the monsoon clouds that had started to gather up in the sky showed no sign of bringing any relief soon. The maid looked up and said.

"I hope the lady and the young mistress will get to Cửa Hàn before there is any storm."

Mai nodded in agreement. "Me too, but I am not too worried. Those French ships have steam engines and can travel very fast in any kind of weather."

Without any warning, she turned to the maid and asked her point blank.

"Have you been reporting to my mother where my sister has been going every day after she leaves our shop?"

The maid looked down to the ground. Her face reddened and she stammered.

"Yes, I had to. Your mother questions me every day when I come home. She wants to know anything that happens, especially things about your older sister."

Mai glared at her.

"And what exactly have you told her?"

"Only the truth! I told her that the young mistress went to see the teacher, but only to tend to his wound and look after him, and nothing else."

The maid saw that Mai was getting angry by the minute, glaring at her with accusing eyes. She tried to mollify her.

"Mistress, the teacher is an honest and virtuous man. He would make a very good mandarin when he passes the examinations."

She did not dare to add that he would also be an ideal life companion for either of the two sisters, especially Giang.

"If so, why did you act as a spy?"

"Your mother left me no choice. I had to tell her everything, and I also thought telling her the truth would convince her that there wasn't anything improper happening between your sister and Teacher Tâm."

Mai laughed dryly. "Well, now see what you have done. She's been sent off to Cửa Hàn and we have to go tell him that he won't be able to see her anymore, for real this time."

The maid scrunched up her face and sighed.

"It's so sad, but maybe it's karma, it's their fate."

"Ah no, don't you talk like that! What did my sister do to deserve such fate?"

The maid was surprised by the fervor with which Mai said that last sentence. Her Buddhist beliefs and life's own teachings have conditioned her to accept her ample share of adversities and misfortunes, but apparently, her young Christian mistress was not of the same mind.

"Please forgive me. I didn't mean to say that."

As they neared the inn they saw him walking back to it from the direction of the river, carrying in his hand what looked like a giant grasshopper made of plaited reed leaves. He was as surprised as they were, but seemed happy to see them. Seeing the mood on their faces, he inquired immediately.

"What brings you here at this hour? Isn't it too early for you to close shop?"

With her eyes, Mai signaled for her maid to keep quiet as she answered his questions.

"We closed up early because my sister wanted us to come tell you ...." She did not finish her sentence, struggling to find the appropriate words, not wanting to sound too harsh.

Tâm sensed her mood, heard the ominous tone, and saw the hesitation.

"Did something happen to your sister?"

"No ... yes," Mai stumbled in her answer then quickly let the truth come out. "She had to go to Tourane with our mother and will be away for some time. She wanted me to come tell you that."

He turned his face away while his hands toyed with the toy grasshopper.

"How long will she be gone?" he asked.

"I don't know," she replied and tried to give a plausible explanation. "She went with my mother to buy supplies, so it may be for a good while. It was something that my mother decided at the last minute, and Giang was as surprised as can be. She had to leave right away and had no time to come here and tell you herself."

He nodded to indicate that he understood more than what her words conveyed. His eyes were directed toward the river, fixed on some distant point. They thus stood, silent, each not knowing what else to say. Suddenly, they heard the familiar voice of the innkeeper who, from inside the inn, hurried to the door.

"Teacher, what are you doing here? Where have you been all day?"

Tâm seemed to welcome the sudden interruption.

"I went to the orphanage and spent most of the day there," he answered and waited for the innkeeper to explain what he was so excited about.

"That's why you are holding that grasshopper," the innkeeper beamed with understanding. "The orphans are good at making these toys to sell at the market."

Tâm turned to Mai and gave her the toy grasshopper.

"Yes, and one of the children insisted on giving me this one that he had just made. He said it was for your sister."

The innkeeper, however, was not to be distracted.

"Teacher, haven't you heard? They have posted the examinations results at Phu Văn Lâu. Everyone is going there to look at the names. You should go find yours also." There was no doubt in his mind that Teacher Tâm would be on the list, and probably at the top of it.

"That's why the Đông Ba market emptied itself so early today," Mai exclaimed turning to the maid. The latter, however, did not seem to hear her. Her eyes were riveted on something else coming from the river bank.

"Soldiers are coming."

They all turned to look at what the maid had alerted them to. A column of soldiers clad in black uniforms and wearing conical helmets, was marching toward them. They were carrying rifles and were led by an officer riding a horse. Tâm and his small group stood transfixed as the soldiers headed straight toward the inn. Curious people were starting to come out of the neighboring houses and establishments to find out what the noise was about.

When they were still a house away from the inn, the officer shouted an order. The soldiers divided into two groups and ran toward the inn. They spread out on both sides of Tâm and his small group. The innkeeper fidgeted as the officer approached them. In a loud and powerful voice, the man ordered:

"Tell the innkeeper to come out."

"I am here, Your Excellency," the innkeeper said in a quivering voice.

The officer tried to control his horse, which was unnerved by his own shouting.

"Do you have a man named Lê Duy Tâm staying at your inn?"

Instinctively Mai grabbed Tâm's arm preventing him from stepping forward and answering the officer. He glanced at her briefly before turning to the officer, and said calmly.

"I am Lê Duy Tâm."

The mounted officer seemed surprised to see him standing there right in front of him, especially with a foreign-looking young woman behind him. However, he recovered and raised his voice to sound even louder.

"Lê Duy Tâm, kowtow and accept His Majesty's pronouncement."

He raised his hand as a signal and two of his soldiers came running to stand on both sides of Tâm, pointing their rifles at him.

Mai let go of his arm, bringing both hands to her face as she gasped in astonishment. The maid and the innkeeper started shaking with fear. Tâm paled visibly as he stared at the officer then slowly knelt down in the dirt as the muzzles of the rifles followed him downward.

"Kowtow and do not lift your head until I give you permission!"

With their rifles the two soldiers motioned him to perform what the officer commanded. He put both hands against his forehead, bent to the ground and left his head resting on his hands down there.

"Lê Duy Tâm, for the crime of committing *phạm huý* (name violation) in the palace examinations, you are hereby committed to the royal prison where you will await punishment to be determined by His Majesty. As of this moment, you are in the custody of the guards of the Ministry of Rites."

Tâm could not believe what he had just heard. Avoiding name violation was one of the basic principles that he had consciously observed every time he sat for an examination. He was even more careful this time, reading and committing to memory all the words in the long list of prohibited names posted at the entrance of the examinations pavilion.

He was absolutely sure that he did not use any of those words in his compositions. How could he have missed one? The only way that could have happened was if a word was added later to the list without him knowing about it. But he looked at the list every day before entering the examinations pavilion to take that into account, and he never saw a new word added to the original list.

"Lê Duy Tâm, stand up and accept the cangue!"

Tâm rose from the ground, his face now flushed and his mind a jumble of conflicting thoughts and clashing emotions. Behind him Mai kept saying in French "Mon Dieu, mon Dieu...," while her maid was terrified and speechless.

"What is *phạm huý*? What kind of crime is that?" Mai desperately asked of no one in particular.

The innkeeper, who knew something about examinations from the scholars who have been guests at his establishment, replied in a low voice.

"That's when someone uses any of the names of the King in an examination paper without modifying it properly."

There were even more people now looking on, including all the help from the inn who left their chores and duties to rush to the front door. Others from further away were also drawn to the scene by the presence of the soldiers and the sharp orders of the officer. Some of the newcomers looked like scholars on their way to or coming back from Phu Văn Lâu. They were talking and pointing at Tâm who was now the center of attention.

Two more soldiers stepped forward carrying a cangue to be fitted over Tâm's neck. The cangue was a restraining device, usually a square or rectangular piece of wood placed around the head of a prisoner. It had a hole in the middle that encircled the prisoner's neck and left the head protruding over the wood. When the cangue was large and heavy, the prisoner had to support it with both of his hands to be able to stand. If the cangue was large enough, the prisoner lost the ability to feed himself. Another type of cangue, and one used in this case, was a short and lighter contraption that looked like a short ladder and was made of sections of wood. The middle section went over the head and around the neck, leaving little room for any movement. The prisoner's hands were tied to the two ends of the ladder to prevent him from using his hands to free himself of the device.

Parading a prisoner wearing a cangue through the streets was the ultimate in public humiliation reserved for the worst criminals, political prisoners, or defeated and captured enemy fighters. On the orders of the Minister of Rites, Tâm fell into the first category, with the only consolation being that his cangue was not heavy enough to bend him over under its weight.

As the soldiers finished tying his hands, he thought one of them looked familiar. The man had studiously avoided looking directly at him, but stole a furtive glance at him at the same time that Tâm recognized him as the swarthy man who had attacked and tried to stab him near the Đông Ba market. A flash of malevolence appeared in the soldier's eyes, but he turned away after finishing his task.

Before he was led away, Tâm had only a second to look at Mai, not knowing what to say about the calamitous turn of events.

"Mai, please don't let your sister know about this," he implored.

"I have to tell her!" she said right away. "She will never forgive me otherwise. I will also tell our father, I will. Don't worry!"

Then she shouted desperately at the officer.

"Where are you taking him?"

The man looked at her suspiciously, not knowing what, if anything, he should tell a foreign woman who spoke fluent Vietnamese. After a slight pause, he turned away without answering and gave the order for his soldiers to start moving.

They led him away in front the hundred or so spectators who had gathered around the inn. Most kept silent at the pitiful spectacle of the disgraced scholar walking with a cangue around his neck, with armed soldiers following him closely. Some were wondering about the enormity of the crime that caused him to be treated no better than a common criminal.

Mai herself wanted to run home to see her father and ask him to intervene on Tâm's behalf and somehow end his predicament. Would he do it? Was it even possible? She had no idea, but she was not going to let up until something was done. She did not know much about examinations, but what had happened in front of her eyes definitely did not appear right. Somewhere, somehow an injustice had been committed.

Reprisal

The blows started as soon as the prison doors closed behind him. He found himself in a dimly lit hallway lined with two rows of sturdy timber columns. Before he could see anything else, he was violently pushed head first to the floor. With the cangue around his neck and his hands tied to it, he could not break his fall and hit the ground hard. He tried to crawl forward but a series of well-placed kicks forced him into a fetal position where the only thing he could do was curl up his legs to protect his face and upper body. He could tell that only one man was kicking him while the rest of the guards remained out of sight. His attacker grunted each time to impart the maximum force behind each kick.

Tâm's head was leaning against one of the columns as he braced himself against the kicks. Someone behind it whispered.

"Don't resist! Play dead!"

The kicks were increasing in intensity and Tâm did not need much urging. Bursts of pain shot up from wherever the kicks landed. Before the effect from one died out, the next one was already exploding from its point of contact, sending waves of pain into his body.

He went limp, telling his body not to flinch or otherwise react. He thought of his mother and was happy that she could not see what was happening to him. He thought of Giang and hoped she would never have to witness the punishment he was receiving. He thought of his students and the children who sometimes looked at him with adoring eyes. They too should never see the humiliation he was enduring.

When he came to, he found himself inside a large cell being tended to by an emaciated man with gray hair while other men looked on. The cangue had been removed from his neck. He heard the sound of thunder rumbling and rain falling on a roof, and saw lightning illuminate at brief intervals the small barred window on one wall of the cell. The monsoon had finally arrived. Pain signals were coursing through his body with almost the same intensity.

"He's coming to," a voice said. "I thought he would be gone much longer."

"He's a strong one," the old man said, then spoke to him. "Teacher, you must drink this and rinse the blood out of your mouth."

A hand propped him up and another one brought a bowl to his lips. He was thirsty and drank the liquid, forgetting to spit it out. He looked at the faces surrounding him, all showing pity and concern, and encouragement. He recognized the old man's voice as the one telling him to play dead.

"Who are you?" he asked.

"All of us are the King's prisoners here," the old man answered for the group. "We know your story."

He wondered what they had heard about him and how the news could travel so fast that even prisoners in a jail knew.

"None of us believe that you made that mistake of misusing the King's name in your examinations," the old man continued. "You must have fallen out of favor with somebody highly placed, and he is making you pay for it."

Tâm tried to sit up to look at the men surrounding him. The cell was badly illuminated with the only light coming from an oil lamp hanging from the ceiling in the middle of the hall outside the cell. Once his eyes became accustomed to the poor light, he saw that his companions were all older men wearing clothes that had become rags hanging on their skeletal bodies. Nevertheless their faces and especially their eyes showed intelligence and kindness.

"How long have you been here?" he inquired.

"Some of us have been here for several years, especially those on the other side of the hall. Most of us on this side have been here for less than a year."

He was about to ask what their crimes were, but the old man went on.

"We just chose the wrong sides during the various royal succession battles. We are the lucky ones who were spared from being executed."

With his chin, the old man pointed to his companions as he continued to speak.

"We are also the forgotten ones. Some of the people who put us in here have themselves been executed, but nobody is stepping forward to tell the jailers to free us. The young King may not even be aware of us, not that he would want to free us even if he did."

Several nodded sadly while others sighed.

"What about your own families?" Tâm asked, thinking about his mother.

"Scattered out of the capital, and sent back to their ancestral villages after losing everything we had," the old man replied and went on to reassure the village teacher. "But in your case, for the kind of crime they say you committed, your family should not be affected. The thing is, they probably don't even know you are here, since you are from so far away up North, right? The news will eventually reach them, but it will take at least several weeks if not months."

Tâm did not want his family to be aware of where he was at that moment. He wanted to find a way out of the sorry state he was in, so that he could at least clear his name and go home as a free man. Meanwhile the old man was still talking and explaining the new prisoner's situation to his fellow prisoners.

"The fact that this teacher has been thrown in here with us means something. They know that he cannot be executed. This kind of offense against the King is not punishable by decapitation."

The other men in the cell nodded their heads and looked at Tâm as if to reassure him. The old man did the same but his eyes were angry and fierce.

"However, look at him. He is bruised everywhere and his face looks awful, swollen and turning purple and black. Luckily for him, he did not suffer any broken bone. Still, if he were a weaker man, he would have been whimpering and moaning right now."

The old man stared at him, an eyebrow raised on his forehead.

"They don't ordinarily treat a scholar like this. Humiliation by parading you through the city with a cangue around your neck should have been more than enough. But beating? No. Do you have any idea whose pride or feelings you have offended?"

All the events in his life from the last day of the examinations coursed through Tâm's mind, the sweetest moments with Giang as well as the most mortifying ones leading right into the prison cell. He thought about what his uncle, the ascetic monk, had taught him about karma and the cause-effect of one's actions, not only between one's prior life and the current one, but also within the same life. He could see that all the men were waiting for his explanation.

"I really don't know who I have offended. But several days ago, I tried to stop a group of mandarin sons from importuning three women, including two young ladies. It was not a pleasant situation, and I ended up having to fight one of them as well as one of his men, probably a bodyguard. That man seems to be the same one who roughed me up today."

The old man had deduced most of what Tâm chose not tell them. In life people fight for power, money, or the favors of a woman, and it was an easy guess as to which category the village teacher fell into, and who his enemy or enemies were.

"Then you are up against some Court minister, a very powerful man, and I don't think he's finished with you yet. "

The previous night's monsoon had only increased the humidity without decreasing the temperature by much. Huế was already sweltering as the French Special Envoy strode into the audience room. His visit had not been planned, and the hour was much too early for the court, so he had to wait while the eunuchs went to bring the young King to the throne.

The usual complement of Court ministers was not in attendance, and Bonneau paced back and forth while waiting. He'd rather see the King alone, even at the risk of breaching protocol and etiquette, something that he and his boss had unfortunately done too often.

Bonneau was alone and promised himself that he will try to be more civil and observe protocol as much as possible. He had actually left his sword in the carriage as a token gesture of goodwill. After all, he was only acting on his daughter's word after she came running home the previous evening to tell him that the village teacher had been arrested by the King's guards.

In the morning, he sent out his secretary Kham to find out more about the arrest, but he had not yet heard from him. He could have waited for Kham to return, but lately he had begun to doubt what the sly man was reporting to him. In this case, Mai saw what she saw, and there was no doubt about that.

That was what motivated Bonneau into seeking an audience with the King. He wanted the monarch to issue an order, if not to free the village teacher, then at least to bring his case out in the open and hear what crime, if any, he had committed. Bonneau suspected this was another one of those instances where a combination of politics and intrigue had conspired to destroy a man's reputation. It would not have been the first time, or the last, in the city of Huế.

He heard footsteps and turned around to see a retinue of eunuchs escort the young King to the throne. His Majesty was fully dressed in his ceremonial clothes, but his hair was still wet under the hat that he had hastily donned. A drop of water coursed down the King's right cheek and he nervously wiped it away as he sat down, with his personal eunuch standing behind him at his right. Bonneau bowed deeply before straightening himself. He went at once to the core of the matter on his mind.

"Your Majesty, I am told that last night your men arrested and imprisoned a scholar who had come to participate in the palace examinations. Since I personally know the man who was arrested, I would like you to indulge me and allow me to ask: why?"

The King showed genuine surprise and turned around to his eunuch. The two conferred rapidly for a moment in low tones. The only words that Bonneau managed to catch and understand toward the end was "ask", repeated several times. Finally the King turned back to his visitor.

"Tell me the name of the scholar."

"His name is Lê Duy Tâm, Your Majesty."

Again the King turned back to his eunuch who now looked flustered. Without waiting for his monarch's permission, the man spoke directly to Bonneau in a high-pitched voice.

"We are told that this scholar misused one of the King's names in an essay that he handed in at the examinations. Even though this is a grave offense, no order has yet been issued to arrest him. His Majesty is still reviewing the case. Are you sure of your information, Special Envoy?"

"I know people who witnessed his arrest late afternoon yesterday. They said that he was led away with a cangue around his neck."

Another hurried exchange took place between the King and his eunuch. Both appeared agitated and Bonneau suspected right away that somebody had ordered the arrest without the King's consent or knowledge. There were as many factions at court as there were ministers, generals, and royal relatives, and the French colonial administration knew that the young King had not yet managed to bring them under his control. The old eunuch standing at his side again took control of the conversation.

"Do you know where the scholar was taken to?"

"People saw him being led into the Forbidden City."

"If so, it's just a matter of time for us to find out where he is. We will let you know as soon as we find him."

"Your Majesty, we are concerned about his fate. May I accompany and assist whomever you are going to send to search for him?"

The King nodded and the eunuch voiced his monarch's agreement.

"His Majesty grants your request. In a short time, some of my eunuchs will meet you outside and go with you on the search party."

Bonneau again bowed deeply and even tried to take a few steps backward before turning around and leaving the audience hall.

In the morning, the same guard who had beaten him the day before came to take Tâm out of the jail. The man said nothing and frowned as he surveyed the black and purple bruises as well as the swelling on the prisoner's face. Satisfied with the results, he once more placed the cangue around his neck and led him out. The rest of the prisoners looked on with surprise mingled with pity and a few even fell to their knees and began praying. Many indeed thought the village teacher was going to be executed.

His tormentor walked in front while another guard followed from behind. Tâm's body ached all over, but he found that he could walk almost normally except for the occasional spasm of pain. He kept telling himself that the pain did not matter since his life was going to end soon anyway. He wondered what his last thought would be, and the images of his mother and Giang kept coming to his mind. He did not want the guards to see him crying and forced back tears that threatened to blur his vision and spill down his face.

He noticed that they went out of the Forbidden City. Soon they were leaving the Citadel walls and moving in the direction of the Đông Ba market. He was wondering whether his execution would be witnessed by all the people who were thronging the market at that hour. Already passers-by were stopping to watch his small procession advance.

However, well before they reached the market, the head guard suddenly turned toward a mansion. The front door opened and Tâm was led into a courtyard where a horse-drawn carriage was being prepared for travel. It looked quite similar to the one he had seen at the Bonneau residence, and it was an obvious symbol of the power and influence of the mansion's owner. He remained in the middle of the yard while his tormentor went inside.

Tâm looked around him. The mansion obviously belonged to some high-level mandarin. There were guards posted at each corner and at the main gate, and the horses tied to the carriage looked healthy and sturdy. The garden was well cared for and rivaled the one at the Bonneau's residence. The path leading from the front porch to the main gate was lined with lush rose bushes on both sides, and there was not a single faded flower on any of them.

A movement at the partially open front gate caught his attention. Through the slight opening, he saw a small girl holding a bunch of toy animals made of reed leaves. She was staring at him curiously. Her expression changed to one of shock as she recognized him. Before he had time to react, she ran away. He recognized her as Found from the orphanage and guessed that she was on the way to the market to sell the toy animals. He desperately wished that she had not seen him in his sorry plight, but it was too late. A loud voice interrupted his thoughts.

"Don't you wish you could be out there?"

He turned around and saw the leader of the group of mandarin sons harassing Giang a fortnight ago. The man, dressed in fine clothes and grinning from ear to ear, was standing next to another man who was an older version of himself, in all likelihood his father, and an attractive young woman. The father squinted and appraised Tâm through the narrow slits of his eyes. The head guard ran out to where the prisoner was standing and barked an order.

"Kneel down and kowtow to His Excellency!"

Tâm did not budge.

"No need for that," the old mandarin growled. "He will be dealt with in due time. But, son, why is he here?"

"Father, I figured that since we'll be in Tourane for a while, our guards could use some help in cleaning up the horse stables in our absence."

For the benefit of the prisoner, Trịnh Dần, the son of Trịnh Toản, the Minister of Rites, added.

"Village teacher, wouldn't you rather be here anyway? The stinking prison is too overcrowded and the bed bugs will eat you alive if you are not too careful. Ha, ha, ha ...."

Father and son laughed in unison, but the young woman did not join them. She lowered her gaze and looked away. Minister Toản, sensing her displeasure, turned to her. Obviously, she was the old man's wife, although she appeared to be younger than his son.

"Please go in and don't let this bother you. We will be gone just for a few days, and I will bring back some nice gifts for you."

She nodded and retreated inside the mansion, but not before throwing a hateful glance at Trịnh Dần that neither her husband nor her step-son noticed. The two men climbed up into the carriage and with a shout from the coachman, the pair of horses attached to the front began pulling it toward the main gate.

Tâm had to jump quickly aside as the carriage flew by and disappeared in a small cloud of dust beyond the wide open main gate. Through the larger opening, he glimpsed Found who was now standing on the other side of the road. She stood up on her toes and managed to catch his eyes, smiled, and waved to him before the main gate again became shut.

By noontime, he had cleaned as much as he could from the stables. The guards were surprised that he had completed his work so quickly. They had been neglecting the stables for quite some time, hoping the Minister's son would not notice. For Tâm, the gardening work he did every day at home made everything look easy, even when he had to cart away enormous amounts of manure and straw soaked with horse urine. His cangue had been removed for the day and he was able to move around without being weighed down by it.

However, he had not had any food since the previous day and the vigorous physical work made his body crave for nourishment. Since coming to the mansion he had only managed to drink some of the well water that he used to thoroughly clean the stables. His clothes were soaked with sweat and he actually smelled worse than the few horses still remaining at the mansion. The guards assembled for lunch in their quarters and allowed him to rest. However, they provided him neither food nor drink.

Tâm went to sit in the shade of a row of hibiscus bushes. He peered at the clouds overhead trying to guess when the afternoon monsoon would come. His throat was parched, his stomach was growling. In desperation, he plucked a hibiscus flower, and with trembling hands peeled off the sepals, and sucked on the mildly sweet petal end. Whatever minute amount of nutrients they had were infinitely better than having nothing. As he was savoring the nectar from the flower, he heard from behind him a small voice call out.

"Teacher Tâm!"

He looked carefully through the branches and leaves. Found was standing outside in the street and calling out to him through the hibiscus bushes. Once she saw that he had seen her, she bent down and disappeared from sight. A few seconds later, she reappeared at his side, having somehow crawled her way through. She sniffed a couple of times but otherwise ignored the smell coming from him. She knelt, rummaged through her clothes and brought up a package wrapped in banana leaves. She opened it carefully and offered it to him with both hands. It was black sweet rice sprinkled with ground roasted peanut and cane sugar.

"Eat this, Teacher. I sold our toys and bought this for you."

He turned to look behind him but saw nobody outside the mansion or the guard's quarters. He was going to ask how she found him, but already she had taken a small amount of the sticky rice and inserted it into his mouth. He smiled at her and gratefully chewed the delicious rice. He held the wrapped rice in his trembling hands, and his eyes swelled up with tears as he ate, blurring the vision of the little girl fairy who had come to offer him nourishment. She kept smiling and feeding him, one morsel at a time.

Suddenly her eyes went wild with fright. He looked up at the same time that a woman knelt down beside them. It was the Minister's wife. She winced as she saw his condition from up close.

"What have they done to you? Was failing you at the examinations not enough? Do they have to destroy you physically also?"

She added quickly.

"I noticed that the guards didn't give you any food, so I was going have something brought to you. But I see that your friend got to you first. What a good-hearted little girl!"

Both Tâm and Found observed the well-dressed woman, not knowing what to say. She had a gentle face on which the most alluring feature were two large eyes that were at that moment fixed on the little girl.

"And who is this charming friend of yours, Teacher Tâm? How did she come here?"

He could not fail to note that she already knew his name. He almost asked her how she knew about him, but instead answered her question first.

"She's an orphan I came to know recently. She was selling toys at the market this morning and saw me being led here this morning when the Minister and his son left. I hope she won't get into any trouble for bringing me some food."

The woman shook her head, brushing his concern aside.

"How old are you, little girl?"

Found raised five fingers, having lost her tongue at the sudden apparition of the beautiful lady who smelled so nice and wore such magnificent clothes.

"What's your name?"

Tâm had to help her as she remained silent.

"We call her Found, and that's what she goes by."

"Found? That's her name?"

"Five years ago, when she was a newborn baby, somebody left her at the orphanage near the temple at Thiên Mụ. She doesn't have any other name."

"O Lord, have mercy upon me!" the woman exclaimed. She put a hand over her heart while her other hand moved to seize Found's little hand. Still spellbound with the Minister's wife, the orphan did not recoil from the touch. Long minutes went by without any of the three saying anything.

Tâm observed the Minister's wife and Found, each looking dreamily at each other, the little girl completely absorbed by the woman that she thought was a fairy, and the woman somehow deeply moved by the elflike girl. Suddenly the woman knelt down on the ground, hugged Found in a tight embrace as tear drops rolled down her face. She rocked back and forth and sobbed openly. Caught in the sudden burst of emotion, Found was speechless and looked at Tâm, asking him with her eyes what was happening.

A soldier who had finished his lunch walked out of the guard's quarters and stopped in his track when he saw the group on the ground. Seeing him, the woman resolutely rose to her feet.

"Why didn't you feed this man? How do you expect him to work without any food?"

"My Lady, the Chief told us not to feed him," the man blubbered.

"Does the Chief want to starve the man to death, after beating him like this?" she exclaimed, pointing at Tâm. "Listen to me now, this man is not to do any more work until I say so."

The dumbfounded guard bowed and nodded. She next turned to the two upturned faces looking at her from the ground.

"Please follow me inside, Teacher Tâm and you also, little one."

After a bath with hot water that a woman servant provided, Tâm changed into clean clothes laid out for him. He wondered whose clothes they were, but he had little choice in the matter since his own had been taken away by the servant who kept mumbling that they were disgusting.

Before he could put the shirt on, the servant asked him to sit down and proceeded to carefully apply generous portions of salve over his facial bruises and cuts. When she was done, she declared with glee.

"There, this salve should help you feel better now. Cô Giang would thank me if she were here."

He looked up at her in surprise at the mention of Giang, but the servant was already beckoning for him to follow her. She led him to a parlor and closed the door after him once he entered the room. He saw Found sitting next to the lady of the house in a large chair. The little girl was still awed by the strange surroundings and clung instinctively to the woman. However, as soon as Tâm entered, she jumped off and ran to him.

"I have to go home."

He bent down and took her in his arms. As she nuzzled against him, he spoke to the Minister's wife.

"She has to go back to the orphanage before they become too worried about her."

The woman did not respond, absorbed in her own thought for a moment. Her eyes, fixed on Found, betrayed alternatively love, guilt, and worry. Finally, she stood up and went to stand next to Tâm. She drew him a distance away from Found then spoke softly so that nobody else could hear them.

"This little girl is my daughter. The Minister forced me to marry him six years ago. Right after that, he went on an inspection tour of the North to check on the examinations being held that year. The tour took almost a year. After he left, one night his son came back drunk from a party. He broke into my room, took me by force, even hitting me in the process because I fought back … and, I became pregnant. Once I could not hide the swelling in my stomach any more, I used my mother's illness as an excuse and went back to stay with her in our village until I gave birth to my daughter."

She gazed lovingly at Found who looked at the two grown-ups with innocent eyes.

"I am a Christian and abortion is not allowed even if I had wanted to. After giving birth to her, I came back here, but I could not leave her with anyone. My mother had passed away shortly after I gave birth.

As for the rest of my family, my brothers and sisters, nobody wanted to have anything to do with what they called the fruit of my shame."

She stopped, closed her eyes and frowned as if she was reliving the drama of that time when her whole family rejected her.

"I came back to the capital with my child and left her at the doorstep of a house in a good neighborhood, hoping they would take her in. Since then I have passed by that house many times but never saw my baby among the children playing in front of it. Today, when this little girl came here and when you told me about her, I think I know what happened. The owner of that house must have taken her and abandoned her at the door of the orphanage."

"How can you be so sure she's yours?"

"I am certain. If you carefully look at the top of her head, beneath her hair you'll see that she has a small birthmark about the size of a small coin. She had it when she was born, and it is still there. Earlier, I confirmed it myself when you were getting cleaned up."

He thought back to the incestuous relationships between princes and royal concubines or consorts, relationships that led to the downfall of many dynasties, including the Lê dynasty that preceded the Nguyễn. Was Found the innocent result of a similarly immoral relationship in this Minister's household?

"Then, this little girl is the Minister's granddaughter?" he asked.

"Yes," she replied, her eyes now pleading with him. "Please don't let anybody else know about this. One way or the other, I will take care of my daughter. I just don't know what my husband would do when he finds out. He's an evil man, as you probably know from what he has already done to you. But I will deal with him and his son."

Despite Bonneau's reassurance and optimism, Mai did not feel comfortable with the situation. Nobody knew where the village teacher was, even after her father, with some of the King's eunuchs, went to the royal jail to inquire about him. All the guards could tell them was that Tâm was thoroughly roughed up when he was brought in and that the same soldier who delivered the punishment came back the following morning to take him away. No one knew where the two went.

The next step had been to check with the Minister of Rites, but secretary Kham reported that the Minister had left for Tourane on a carriage, with the only passenger being his son. After that dead end, no one could come up with any suggestion as to where Tâm was. The King's eunuchs went back inside the Forbidden City to report to their superior.

Mai suspected that Tâm was still somewhere in the city, and she had already sent their maid to Tourane by road to inform her sister of his arrest. She hoped that upon hearing the news Giang would come back to the capital at once. They could then put their heads together and figure out a way to find and help Tâm.

The weather, however, was not cooperating, and the daily monsoon rains were sure to slow down any travel, by land or sea, between Tourane and Huế. Inside the capital, already some low-lying streets were getting flooded It never dawned on Mai to wade through the waters and go visit the orphanage, which was on high grounds. There a little girl could have told her where the missing village teacher was.

He spent the night in the guard's house, thankful to be sheltered from the monsoon rain and wind that raged on until the following day. The guards let him occupy a corner of their cramped quarters and did not mistreat him. Since they had no order to take him back to the royal jail, the concubine told them to take him in for the night. They did not fail to notice that she had given him a new sedge mat and a fine blanket to use for bedding.

As night fell, he sat on the mat in a lotus position, breathing in and out deeply and tried to put his mind at ease following the painful events of the past two days. He closed his eyes, rested his hands on his knees, relaxed gradually and felt tension slowly leave his body. After half an hour, he reopened his eyes. The guards had observed him in silence, awed by the display of self-control and meditative power. He stood up and rearranged his blanket to prepare to lie down on his makeshift bed. One of the guards approached him, offered him a hot cup of tea and engaged him in conversation in respectful terms.

"Nobody told us about you until you came here this morning. We don't know what crime you have committed but apparently, the Minister's lady thinks you are a good man. We hope you'll forgive us for neglecting you earlier today."

"I understand," he responded. "You are not to be blamed for anything. I know you must carry out your orders as good soldiers do."

One by one the curious guards slowly moved toward him and sat down around him. The guard who had spoken to him and appeared to be their leader was still curious.

"So what did you do? You don't look like the type that goes around committing murder or stealing from people."

Tâm smiled bitterly. "I am just a village teacher from the North who came down here to take the palace examinations. They say that I misused the King's name in one of my compositions, and that's why I was arrested yesterday as soon as the results were published."

With that, the attitude of the guards began showing even more respect and consideration for him. They inquired about his village, his school, and about his successes at past examinations. They told him about their background and their families. He asked them about their work and learned that they rotated between guard duties at the Ministry of Rites and at the Minister's personal residence, and generally disliked both places. The guard leader, a naturally curious man, wanted to know more.

"How could they treat you, a scholar, in this manner? You were beaten pretty badly before even coming here, and once you were here, the Chief guard had you clean the stables."

"I don't mind physical work," Tâm said philosophically. "I usually enjoy it and do it quite often at home. Some of the greatest heroes in history have been people who tilled the land or tend after animals."

"That may be true, but today you were forced to do it. The Chief guard didn't seem to care much for you, and he had to find some humiliating chore to assign to you. A few weeks ago, another village teacher came to the Ministry, but unlike you, he was very well treated. He was received by His Excellency himself and was provided with good food and anything he needed. We were told to attend to his needs, not that he requested much."

Something in what the guard said intrigued Tâm. He tried not to be obvious with his next questions.

"He must have been highly regarded as a scholar. Do you know what he did for His Excellency?"

"I only saw him writing for many days, and he used a lot of brushes and ink. But since none of us can read, we have no idea of what it was all about."

"So how long did he spend at the Ministry?"

"He came twice, and each time he only stayed for a few days. The last time, he was leaving for home apparently after finishing his work, and he didn't look very happy. I thought that His Excellency didn't like his work or perhaps didn't pay him for it. But His Excellency was in a good mood, and he was not angry at all."

Tâm remembered about a week or two earlier, what his friendly boatman had related to him about Teacher Xinh boarding his boat and looking very despondent. He began to try to tie together the different pieces of information and thought the beginning of a connection to this own plight.

"Who was he?" he asked the old guard.

"We just called him Teacher, just like we do with you. He definitely isn't from around here. After he left for the last time, we never saw him again."

In the morning, he got up at the same time as the guards did. They had stopped treating him as a prisoner and let him move about freely inside the yard. He took the opportunity to go through his exercise routine as the guards stood around watching. When he was finished and went inside the guard house, the guard leader said.

"Teacher, seeing you practice, I remember a while ago, the day after that other teacher left to go home, our Chief guard came back in the evening with the young master. Both had been roughed up by somebody and their faces were swollen, but they wouldn't tell us what happened. We thought maybe they had been sparring with each other and got carried away."

Tâm nodded without saying anything, knowing very well what had actually happened. At that moment, a servant girl entered the guard house and respectfully addressed him.

"My Lady told me to ask you to come to the upper house."

He found the Minister's wife sitting at a table on which steaming bowls of food were arrayed. She smiled and invited him to sit down and share breakfast with her. They started eating in silence. As usual, she was skillfully made up and looked striking. He also noted she was in full control of herself and her comportment and gestures were precise and resolute. After a few minutes, she stopped eating and said.

"I have decided to go to the orphanage today and claim my daughter."

He looked up, put down his chopsticks, and picked up a cup of steaming tea. He blew on the tea while waiting for her to continue. He had been thinking about Found since the previous day, and was wondering what was going to happen next.

"My daughter should live in this house. She has as much right to be here as I do. I will not let her be an orphan for the rest of her life."

He wanted to ask her what she was going to do about her husband and her stepson, but she had anticipated his questions.

"I will tell the Minister the truth, and he can do whatever he wants with me. His son violated my body against my will. Six years ago, I was a scared young woman, and all I could think of then was to try and hide my condition. Now my conscience is clear, and I am prepared for anything that may happen when the truth comes out. He can send me back home if he wants to, but he cannot throw his granddaughter out in the street. She has done nothing wrong. She has committed no sin."

She was no longer the teary woman that he saw yesterday. Her maternal instinct had been awakened and overnight she had transformed herself from the role of an accommodating young wife to that of a mother determined to fight for her child. He felt happy for Found. However, what she said next stunned him.

"The Minister is now taking his son, the rapist, to Tourane to ask for the hand of the Special Envoy's girl, the one who loves you so dearly."

He stared at the concubine and started to say something but could not come up with any word. Emotions converged and clashed inside him. Suddenly the real reason for Giang's abrupt departure came to light for him.

During all the time he had known Giang, neither of them had told anybody of their feelings for each other. To hear another person, the Minister's wife, say that Giang loved him was a total surprise. He had honestly thought that their relationship had been known to only a few persons. His surprised expression brought a faint smile on the concubine's face.

"Do you think that nobody knows about you two? This city has eyes and ears everywhere, and your romance with her is becoming well known. Servants, boatmen, and innkeepers talk, you know. Don't worry though. Even if some in the mandarins do not approve, the common folks have only sympathy for you. I am one of those on your side, even if the Special Envoy's wife and the father and son of this house, all three of them, are conspiring against you. I will see to it that the story of how Found came into this world will become known throughout the city."

Before she could go on, the maid hurried into the room and blurted out.

"The royal guards are here with the King's Eunuch."

They stood up, surprised by the sudden turn of events. A man wearing a high-rank purple and blue eunuch uniform entered the room on the heels of the servant. He did not pay any attention to the young woman and addressed himself directly to Tâm.

"Please follow me, Teacher Tâm. His Majesty has pardoned you and decided to let you go free. We are taking you out of here."

He did not force Tâm to prostrate himself on the ground to receive the monarch's pardon. As he spoke, two royal guards came in and placed themselves on both sides of Tâm not to arrest him but to provide him with a protective escort. After giving a signal to the guards, the Eunuch turned around and walked out. Tâm understood that he was to follow him and glanced at the Minister's wife. She recovered from her initial surprise and smiled to him, delighted at the news of his pardon. As he walked out, she only had time to say.

"Thank you for bringing Found to me. I will forever be grateful to you."

Out in the yard the Minister's guards stood in a straight line in front of their quarters. A dozen royal guards were grouped together near the residence's main gate. They parted respectfully in the middle to let the Eunuch and Tâm proceed to the gate.

When he was outside, he saw that a small crowd of curious onlookers had assembled on the other side of the road. He recognized among them the Special Envoy's secretary, Kham. Tâm nodded his head slightly, but Kham did not react and his face was as cold and unfriendly as it had been on previous occasions.

With the Eunuch leading the way, he and the soldiers fell in step and the procession moved forward. After a short distance, he became aware that nobody had placed a cangue around his neck.

They took him to his inn and once there, the Eunuch turned to face him. His eyes showed genuine sympathy and compassion for the unfortunate village teacher.

"Teacher Tâm, you are now free to come and go as you please. Unfortunately, at this time your name cannot be added to the list of those scholars who passed the examinations. You may decide to go back to your village, or to stay here until we finish our investigation. It's entirely up to you."

Perplexed, Tâm asked.

"Your Excellency, I thank you, but can you tell me what the investigation is about?"

A familiar voice answered from behind him.

"It's to determine whether you actually committed the offense of using His Majesty's name in your examination papers."

He turned and saw secretary Kham who had followed him to his inn without being noticed. Kham had the same stern expression that he always showed, except when speaking to his employer, Special Envoy Bonneau. The Eunuch officer did not seem to mind that Kham had answered Tâm's question and even confirmed the answer with a slight nod of his head. Obviously he knew who the secretary was.

"Teacher Tâm, consider yourself fortunate that the Special Envoy has spoken to His Majesty on your behalf," Kham continued evenly. "Without his intervention, you would have suffered a much worse fate."

Before the secretary could go on, the Eunuch shouted an order and his soldiers did an about face and turned in the direction of the Citadel's walls.

"I will let secretary Kham fill you in on the rest of the story. I must now return to the Forbidden City."

Without acknowledging the bows of both Tâm and Kham, he turned around and he and his men marched off. A small crowd of onlookers had begun to assemble, and, as soon as the small column of soldiers left, they crowded around Tâm. The innkeeper elbowed his way through the small circle to be close to him.

"Thank Heaven, you are back. But look at what happened to you! Teacher, please, please … come inside and let me tell them to prepare a hot bath for you."

The innkeeper could not help staring at the black and blue marks on Tâm's face. He was wringing his hands and making hissing noises as if he himself was enduring the pain. He shooed away the curious onlookers and opened a path for Tâm to walk into the inn.

"There is no time for that," growled Kham.

"But, why …, why not?" the innkeeper managed to say, his eyes watching the Special Envoy secretary with suspicion.

Instead of answering him, Kham came face to face with Tâm.

"You have been freed by His Majesty's eunuchs without the knowledge or consent of the Minister of Rites, who is right now on a trip to Tourane. Who knows what will happen when the Minister finds out about this? There is only so much that the King can do for you, and he has already done a lot by letting you go free. The Minister is one of the most influential and powerful men in the capital, and he could easily persuade the King to let him handle your case in his own way. You should seriously think about leaving the capital immediately before the Minister comes back."

Tâm looked away toward the Perfume River and said nothing. He thought about a little girl named Found, and about her mother, the young wife of Minister Toản. He remembered what she said about the Minister's son, Trịnh Dần, and the timing of his visit to Tourane while Giang was also down there.

Secretary Kham went to stand even closer to Tâm. He lowered his voice but his words resonated in Tâm's ears.

"Don't think for a moment to stay here because of the sympathy the Special Envoy's daughter may have for you. She is beyond your reach, and even more so now that you have been disgraced in the examinations. You must already know that the Special Envoy's wife is adamantly opposed to you. She is determined to marry off her daughter to someone closer to their social status. Who can blame her? Hasn't she banned you from coming to their house? Can't you see that there is no future for you in this city? Go back to where you belong and do not try to ruin a fine young lady's life anymore. She has suffered too much already because of you."

Kham's eyes were shining and full of hostility. Before she left for Tourane, and without letting her husband know, Bà Trang had summoned him. In no uncertain terms, she had given him the order to go tell the village teacher to keep away from her daughter. The secretary had no trouble agreeing with her and carried out his order with genuine glee.

The Minister had hinted openly at his son's interest in the older Bonneau girl, and had been asking him about the situation between her and the annoying village teacher. Without being told, Kham had given himself the task of sending Teacher Tâm back North to remove an obvious rival of the Minister's son and clear the way for him. Therefore he did not mince any word, and meant everything that he said.

Tâm was fully aware of the change in tone and in the manner in which Kham was talking to him now. The usual forms of respect for a scholar teacher had been dropped, and he was being addressed in crude terms more suitable to a criminal. Even the innkeeper, who had overheard bits and pieces of Kham's admonitions, was shocked by their callousness. What a contrast with the day when the secretary came inquiring about Tâm, and the deference he showed at that time!

Ever since his arrest, Tâm knew that his ambition and the dreams he had brought with him to the capital had been shattered. It was also evident to him that he had to start burying deep inside himself the novel emotions and feelings that the last few weeks spent with Giang had evoked in him. It was time for him to leave the capital and go home.

"I will be leaving soon," Tâm told the innkeeper. "Let me go in, pack my clothes and books, then I will be on my way. I will of course settle my account and pay you what I owe."

The innkeeper waved his hands vigorously.

"Teacher, you don't owe us anything. The other young lady took care of everything the day of your arrest. In addition, I have packed all of your belongings and put the bundle in your old room, which is still unoccupied. Won't you at least rest and stay one more night, Teacher?"

Thinking of Mai settling his account, he realized that he was now further indebted to her and to Giang. He thought about how to thank them, but shook his head, both to himself and to the innkeeper.

"I'll just get my bundle and go now. It's still early in the day and I can walk on the Mandarin Road and get to the next town before nightfall."

Tourane

The streets of Tourane were filled with people, and its shops and inns were crowded with foreign as well as Vietnamese customers. From the harbor to the city center, artisans could be seen bent over the tools and the products they were making for export to Korea, Japan, Indonesia, and all the Western countries whose ships and armies were conquering Asia. Dock workers, bent in half under heavy crates or enormous jute bags, labored all day long to load or unload ships.

Following her mother, Giang went to textile storefronts and warehouses to look for Japanese and Chinese silk prized by the upper classes. Silk weaved and embroidered in Việt Nam had been exported for over a thousand years, but foreign silk was the kind sought after in Huế. She herself wore tunics of silk weaved in Hà Đông, near the old capital in the North, and the wealthy customers who came to the Đông Ba market stall had often admired their looks and quality. However, once she told them that it was made in a village in the North, many lost interest and demanded to see and buy foreign silk instead.

Like she used to when she was a small child, she followed her mother, keeping quiet and making the proper bows to various people. However, her mind was back in the capital and she kept worrying about Tâm. Did he ever find out whether he passed the examinations?

Her mother had told her that they were to attend a banquet that evening in honor of an important Minister who was in town for a visit. Giang pleaded to be excluded from attending it, but a withering look from her mother had settled the matter right then.

"In business, opportunities for meeting high government officials are to be prized. Even if you have to hold your nose, you still must attend these banquets and act as if you are enjoying them to the fullest. This Minister is like a Regent to the King, and cultivating good relations with him will be very beneficial to us."

Giang could only sigh, and her mother mellowed a little.

"You will meet some interesting people there, and, I promise, you will not be bored."

Toward early afternoon, the monsoon fell heavily in the region. Strong winds caused the rain to come in waves, some almost horizontal at times. The loud drumbeat of water drops falling on thousands of roofs vied with that of clacking thunder to strike fear in children, animals, as well as adult humans. Just as Bà Trang fretted about the storm keeping their guests away from her banquet, the monsoon shifted toward the mountains leaving behind only minor floods throughout the city. Half-heartedly, Giang had to change clothes and get ready to accompany her mother.

They were the first to arrive at the banquet hall, in a prominent inn at the heart of the city but far enough from the docks to avoid drunken ruffians and foreign sailors. There was really nothing to worry about since the Governor's office had sent a contingent of soldiers to stand guard and provide security for the important government officials who would be arriving at the inn.

As hostess, Bà Trang was pleased with the hall and the lavishly decorated room and tables she had reserved for the occasion. There were very few customers around, since most were kept away by the weather and others were discouraged from entering the inn by the stern government soldiers standing guard all around it.

She busied herself by ordering the innkeeper to bring out his best foreign wines and liquors. She made sure that the serving maids were ready at the main door to greet the guests. If she were a mere merchant, she would have stood by the entrance herself, but as the wife of the Special Envoy, she only needed to stay in the banquet room and rise to greet her guests when they arrived. Seated at her side, Giang was maintaining a stoic composure, and Bà Trang was too busy to be overly concerned with her.

The Governor was the first to show up, a middle-aged man resplendent in a ceremonial dress embroidered with a colorful dragon flying through clouds over churning sea waves, turtles, dolphins, and lesser creatures. Flanked by a small staff, he met Bà Trang half way as she scurried toward him. After exchanging formal salutations and some small talk with her, she led him to his seat. Passing by Giang, he smiled and stopped briefly.

"So this is the young beauty from Huế who has come down to visit us. You will be capturing many hearts in this city, isn't that so?" He laughed aloud and resumed a nonchalant walk toward his seat followed closely by his attendants.

Before Giang could react, there was a small pandemonium at the door through which two men, led by excited maids, walked in. The first was a shriveled old man with gray hair sticking oddly out of his official dragonfly hat and wearing a ceremonial court dress no less striking than the one the Governor had on. Minister Toản squinted to look at those already in the room with myopic eyes, his head bobbing up and down like that of an owl.

Behind him was a younger man, stylishly dressed and well-fed, the very symbol of wealth and indulgence. The Minister's son, Dần, scanned the room and his eyes settled on Giang as soon as he saw her. He smiled crookedly and tilted his head to get a better look and assure himself that she was the same young woman he had seen at the silk stall in the Đông Ba market. In the carriage that took them to the inn, his father had hinted as much without revealing her identity. Dần had been detached about it, especially since the entire trip so far had been a string of events that he found extremely inane and boring. However, finding himself in the same room with the beautiful young woman he had long coveted suddenly made the whole trip worthwhile and he silently thanked his father for dragging him along.

She immediately recognized him as the leader of the band of mandarin sons who had harassed Mai and herself a few weeks earlier. She felt her cheeks becoming flushed as her whole body reacted with indignation and anger. She felt betrayed by her mother for bringing her into the presence of the man she had hoped to never see again after the altercation near the Đông Ba market. The same man who had commanded his guard to strike and wound Tâm. She could not believe that her mother had arranged for the banquet so that she would have to meet this vilest example of humanity. She began to think of ways to leave the room and get as far as possible from the banquet and the inn.

Bà Trang, oblivious to her daughter's emotions, shepherded the two new guests to their seats, the Minister in the center, flanked by the Governor on one side and by his son on the other. She sat down opposite them at the round table and with her eyes forced her daughter to take her place next to her. Lesser mandarins in the Minister's retinue and from the Governor's office went to two separate tables laid out on both sides.

Like weaving loom shuttles, serving maids began scurrying in and out of the room to bring trays of food and drinks under the innkeeper's supervision. As wine flowed freely and food was served in abundance, the noise level in the room rose quickly.

Dần remained silent and could not keep his eyes away from Giang. Her beauty was even more striking than at any other time he had managed to peek at her in the back of her shop, and he found himself dumbstruck. At other banquets he would have started with the drinks before diving into the food while taking every opportunity to paw the serving maids. This time, he was abnormally subdued, constantly adjusting his headdress and his tunic collar.

Giang kept her eyes downcast and her hands in her lap, paying no attention to him or to anybody else at the table. Minister Toản stole glances at her while trying to listen to what his neighbor the Governor was saying.

The Governor did not fail to notice the attention directed toward the young woman. That afternoon, he had been told that the Special Envoy's wife had sent men bearing several heavy gift boxes to his residence. He knew that they were for several favors they wanted from him, one of which he could grant right away. As prearranged with Bà Trang, he decided to start playing the matchmaking role that he had promised he would perform.

"Your Excellency, the examinations must be over, for I see that you can now take time to travel with your son to our city, to take care of some family matters perhaps?"

Minister Toản was not obligated to explain why he was at the banquet, but he did not mind this time, considering who was hosting it.

"Actually, I am still kept quite busy in the capital, but Bà Trang asked me to come to Tourane and give her advice on some business matters."

The Minister used the French name for the city, hoping to attract the attention of the half-French daughter. Meanwhile, his son managed to regain partly his faculty of speech. His flirtatious comment in the direction of the young woman sitting in front of him was delivered in an abnormally unsteady voice.

"As for me, I … wanted to follow my father to come admire with my own eyes … the person who is reputed to be the most beautiful young lady of Huế."

Giang started to get up to leave, but her mother seized her hand under the tablecloth and forced her to remain seated.

The Governor raised his wine glass.

"Well said, very well said. I have heard about Your Excellency's son, and indeed he is living up to his reputation as one of the courtliest men of the younger generation. Therefore, I would like to propose a toast to our hostess, the Special Envoy's wife, and to the beautiful daughter that today she has allowed us to be introduced to."

Bà Trang let out a little laugh and waved her hand.

"Your Excellency, Governor, we are the ones who are thankful for your presence here today. We consider ourselves most fortunate that you have taken time out of your busy schedule, and braved the monsoon, as well as thunder and lightning, to come here share this plain meal with us."

The banquet and the gifts were far from trivial, but she thought they were commensurate with the favors she was seeking, and the alliance she was contemplating with one of the most powerful family in the country. She could see that the Minister had taken a good look at her daughter and had not shown any outward objection. His son was obviously smitten with Giang and could not keep his eyes away from her. The Governor, an eloquent man with a silver tongue who had been properly induced with gifts, was also doing his best to help. The only person she was worried about was her own daughter.

Minister Toản was tired well before he came to the banquet room. For the past few days he had made the rounds of his subordinates and friends in the city and there had been nothing but lavish receptions and sumptuous meals from the time that he got up to the time that he went to bed. The pace of activities had begun to affect him. He was bored with the endless and pompous speeches people felt they had to deliver in his presence. He was starting to feel nauseated at the sight of the banquet dishes arrayed in front of him. After a while they all looked alike and the food no longer had any taste to him. He barely touched it. He missed home cooking and the loving care of his young wife.

However, as he sat across from the Special Envoy's wife and her daughter, he was not concerned about the food. Many years ago, Tăng Thị Trang looked very much like her daughter did now, minus the blue eyes. Before he was married, and while he was still a relatively minor mandarin, he had fancied her and had almost asked his parents to send a matchmaker to her house. What stopped him was the fact that she was a Christian. Being married to her could have held back his career, or could even have led to a disgraceful demotion to some remote tribal village in the mountains. Instead, he settled for a more conventional wife while she went on to marry a French officer.

Two decades later, many more Vietnamese had converted to Christianity and the French were in full control of the country. Being Christian was no longer a burden on anyone, and in fact could be of help in the colonial administration. Even some court ministers and high government officials had been declaring themselves as Christians, or had married Christians and been converted through marriage. Even his second wife was one of them. Toản sighed at the thought of how the world around him had changed.

Two decades later, he and the wife of the Special Envoy were seated at the same table, and he could not help but notice that his son had lost his wit ever since he saw the daughter of the woman his father would not marry. Dần was no longer the merry and loquacious ladies' man that he usually was. He had changed into a simpleton with eyes fixed on the girl across the table, unable to say anything intelligent. He still ate and drank copiously, but he forgot to laugh at the jokes that the Governor was telling. The Minister was seeking for a way to give his son an advantage when the Bonneau girl spoke up unexpectedly.

Ever since the Governor mentioned that the Minister was able to come down to Tourane because the examinations were over, Giang had been yearning to know whether Tâm had passed them. Since meeting him, she had come to realize that he was the most intelligent man that she had ever known, even when she took into account her father, the benchmark she had used for judging. The way he had set himself to study French with her help and the few books she lent him clearly showed his unusual ability with languages. If he showed the same kind of mental prowess with his traditional Chinese studies, there was absolutely no reason why he should fail the palace examinations, especially after he had distinguished himself by placing first in the metropolitan examinations. Still, she needed to find out for sure from the old Minister sitting opposite her.

At the side of his father, the Minister's son was the exact opposite of Tâm. His pudgy face betrayed all the signs of an indulgent life. He looked physically dominating, but she also knew that Tâm, who was smaller and lighter, had bested him easily and decisively in just a few seconds. She also thought she had recognized the man who had come to Dần's rescue, the one who had tried to stab the village teacher from the back. He was probably one of the Minister's attendants, a swarthy man dressed in an officer's uniform, who was now sitting at one of the other tables.

Preoccupied with the observations and thoughts that were crisscrossing her mind, Giang hardly touched her food. She was looking for an opportunity to ask the Minister about the examinations and was patiently waiting for the Governor to stop his small talk and his jokes.

Finally, the Governor decided it was time to join the others in taking a few bites and the table temporarily became hushed as conversation and laughter were replaced by the clicking of chopsticks and the sounds of slurping or energetic chewing. Giang saw her opportunity and turned to the Minister.

"Your Excellency, did I hear the Governor say that the examinations are now over?"

"Of course, young lady, they are over," Minister Toản said with a surprising eagerness. His eyes blinked furiously and a big smile spread out on his face. "The results have already been posted at Phu Văn Lâu and those who passed have been celebrating and will be returning to their cities or villages in triumph."

Giang was hanging on to his words. He stopped to savor the moment before continuing.

"The unworthy ones, those who did not pass, of course also left the capital, except for one."

The whole table was now paying attention. Sensing the sudden change in mood, the other two tables also fell silent. Giang closed her eyes, and suddenly the image of Tâm waking up in pain from his bad dream on the Thuận An beach appeared in her mind. She reopened her eyes at the same time that the swarthy guard officer turned around to listen to the Minister deliver his shocking news. He was indeed the same man who had lunged at Tâm with his dagger.

"This happens at practically every examination. Once in a while some scholar, through carelessness or perhaps out of arrogance because he thinks of himself as without equal, commits the unforgivable offense."

Minister Toản took his time, moving his eyes slowly from Giang to her mother, then the Governor, and finally to his son before scanning the other two tables to make sure that no one would miss his words.

"The offense is the use of one of the King's names without alteration. It is a mistake that could have been easily avoided because the list of prohibited characters is posted for all to see at the entrance to the examination grounds."

He settled his eyes triumphantly on the person he most wanted to hear what he had to say. Giang was starting to pale and her eyelashes were batting a little faster than normal. He glanced at his son whose upturned eyes were showing signs that he was beginning to understand what his father was doing. The lad had finally awakened from his self-induced daze.

"A man from the North, where the quality of scholars has been declining for some time now, did indeed misuse one of the King's names, whether through negligence or intentionally, we'll probably never know. In the past, an offense like that was punishable by death. We don't know whether this is going to happen in this case since the King has not yet decided what to do. However, the scholar, a poor and insignificant village teacher, has been imprisoned as soon as the results were made public. I made certain of that before I started on this trip."

Before he even finished speaking Giang had stood up covering her mouth with both hands. She looked like she was about to throw up as she hurried out of her seat and ran out of the room. Her movement was so sudden that her mother did not have time to react. Bà Trang, who had begun to smile as she guessed the identity of the scholar, almost stood up herself to go after her daughter, but she needed to ask the Minister one last question to be absolutely sure.

"Can you tell us the name of the scholar?"

"Certainly, Lady Special Envoy," Toản's chortled loudly and the joy of revealing that last bit of information spread triumphantly over his beaming face.

It was very late by the time Bà Trang arrived back to her parents' house where she and Giang had been staying since arriving in Tourane. She wanted to scold Giang for leaving the banquet early, forcing her to apologize profusely to the Minister and the Governor. But her daughter was staying in the same room as her grandmother, and not wanting to disturb them, she went to bed quietly.

Actually, she was very pleased with how the evening had turned out otherwise. The Minister and his son were thrilled with Giang, despite her childish behavior. Nothing was said openly, but it was understood by all that there was going to be more to follow-up on when they all returned to the capital. Exhausted but pleased with the evening and with herself, she slept soundly and did not wake up until almost noon the following day. When she got up and went out to the kitchen, she was surprised to see her maid surrounded by members of her parents' household who had been up much earlier.

"What are you doing here? Aren't you supposed to be in Huế?"

"My Lady, Miss Mai sent me down," the nervous maid answered. She looked disheveled, and tired, as if she had braved the monsoon to arrive in Tourane.

"Why? What for?"

"She sent me down to tell Miss Giang that Teacher Tâm has been arrested. I left several days ago, but the monsoon was very heavy and we could not get through the Hải Vân pass until the storm finally stopped."

"Never mind that. We already know about him failing his examinations and being arrested. Why did Mai have to send you here to tell her sister about that?"

The maid was briefly dumbstruck. She thought she was bringing fresh news from the capital, but her mistress apparently already knew about it. Then she remembered something that Bà Trang could not have known.

"My Lady, His Excellency the Special Envoy has interceded with the King on Teacher Tâm's behalf."

That set off another flurry of questions that the poor maid had no answer for. Bà Trang did not welcome the last piece of news and wanted to extract all the information she could about this unplanned turn of events. The maid, however, could not tell her anything beyond what she had already said. She had been away from the capital for several days already, and anything could have happened during that time.

Bà Trang sat down on a chair already weary and irate at the news that the maid brought. Then she thought about Giang whom she wanted to scold for leaving the banquet so unceremoniously.

"Where is my daughter?"

The maid looked at her with alarm.

"My Lady, she left at dawn."

"What do you mean?" Bà Trang slapped her thigh and dreaded the answer that was coming. "Is she not in this house?"

Instead of the maid, a familiar voice answered. A stooped woman, bent with age, entered the room but remained near the door, her chin pointed in the direction of Bà Trang. Despite her frail looks, her mother's voice was clear enough for all to hear.

"My granddaughter went back to the capital to see what she can do about the village teacher."

Bà Trang jumped up from her seat to face the old woman.

"Mother! You let my daughter leave, just like that? Are you serious?"

The grandmother calmly countered.

"I did not let her. She left on her own, and there was no way anybody could talk her out of it. She's just like you when you wouldn't listen to anyone and decided to marry that Frenchman."

"But, you let her leave without me? By herself? Oh Lord, why is this happening to me?"

The old woman shook her head in exasperation.

"Not by herself. I gave her a carriage with two horses and a coachman. The monsoon has stopped for now, and if she travels all day, she will be able to reach the capital before the rain comes in the evening."

As an afterthought, she added sadly.

"As for invoking the Lord, it is more appropriate for you to look into your karma and see whether you have brought this upon yourself."

Separation

As her grandmother predicted, Giang reached the capital in late afternoon before the monsoon resumed pouring its daily quota of rain on a city already steaming in the heat. She was worn out and still scared from the trip over the Hải Vân pass. When she climbed aboard the carriage, she had urged the coachman to travel as fast as possible. She promised him a big reward and so their carriage flew. He was a devoted member of her grandmother's household staff and gave his best to accomplish the mission that the patriarch had given him: take her granddaughter quickly and safely to the capital. Fortunately for them, the monsoon had temporarily stopped and the sun, hidden at times behind heavy clouds, did not shine too harshly.

The pass with its twists and hairpin bends was a challenge every inch of its two-mile long length. At times, she had to close her eyes and force herself not to look down while her driver maneuvered the carriage and urged the horses on. The ascent from Tourane was bad enough, but the descent toward Huế was even worse, even after the stop they took at the top to rest, feed, and water the horses. While it did not rain, the humidity was high and she could feel it seep through the scarf she wore on her head. It also soaked through her clothes, and she shivered uncomfortably for the last part of the trip.

All she could think of was Tâm, and the image of him being thrown in jail with a cangue around his neck haunted her. In her worst nightmare, she could never have imagined it. How he must have suffered, she thought. She blamed herself for going to Tourane with her mother, as if her presence could have prevented his arrest from happening. She should have been stronger and should have resisted her mother. Who knew, if she had stayed in the capital, perhaps things could have been different?

She was sure some injustice had been done. To bring it to light and rescue him, she had immediately thought of her father, the only one that could be of any help in such matters. That is why she left the absurd banquet that her mother organized for the horrible Minister of Rites and the vulgar man that was his son. The thought of those two revolting characters further strengthened her conviction that what she did was right, even if it meant flouting her independence right in front of her mother's guests.

As soon as the carriage came to a stop, she rewarded the coachman generously and climbed down. She felt faint but summoned her last reserve of energy and hurried into the house. Before she reached the main door, it opened and a surprised secretary Kham greeted her.

"Mademoiselle, what are you doing here? I thought you were in Tourane with the Special Envoy Lady."

She walked past him and continued toward the stairs, but shouted back.

"I just came back now to see my father. Is he home already?"

"Yes, he's in his office."

She hesitated then decided not to go to her room to change. She went directly to the office, knocked and opened the door as soon as she heard his voice. Secretary Kham followed her in. Her father and Mai looked at her with surprise, with her sister being the first to speak as she ran to her.

"Giang, you came back already! Did you speak with our maid?"

"Yes, she told me everything," Giang replied. She turned away from her sister and approached her father. "Father, you have to do something about Teacher Tâm."

Special Envoy Bonneau looked at the pitiful sight that his older daughter presented with her disheveled hair, wet clothes clinging to her frail frame, a face showing obvious signs of strain and those blue eyes on the point of tears. He realized then that her feelings for the village teacher amounted to much more than a passing summer romance. He himself had liked the young man from that distant village in the North from the moment he first met him. He found it an interesting experiment to see his daughter teaching him the Vietnamese Romanized script, and then French. In the back of his mind, he thought that Tâm, after passing the examinations, would be appointed to an important post in some province. He would then be gone from their lives, and his wife, Bà Trang, would no longer have to worry about Giang being entangled with him. Now, seeing the distress that Giang was in, he knew he had been very wrong and had underestimated his daughter. He tried his best to appear calm and in control.

"My dear daughter, don't worry. I have already interceded with the King, and His Majesty has agreed to pardon him."

Giang exhaled and smiled wanly, relieved by the good news. Despite her exhaustion, her face brightened as she asked her next question.

"What do you mean by pardon? What crime did he commit?"

"The matter is being investigated, but it will take time before it can be resolved. There is some doubt whether he did anything wrong, and there is a possibility that he was the victim of some political intrigue. But it takes time to investigate these matters, even with the support of the King. In the meantime, he is free."

Bonneau smiled and lifted both of his arms into the air, mimicking a bird in flight, hoping to relieve the tension in the room.

"Where is he now?" Giang faced her sister as she asked the question.

Mai shook her head. "I don't know where he is. I just found out about this a few minutes before you came in."

Their father pointed to his secretary.

"Kham here can tell you about Tâm. He was present when they freed him."

Secretary Kham cleared his throat, looked at the Special Envoy then at his older daughter. His French was heavily accented but he had little trouble making himself understood.

"A few days ago, men from the Ministry of Rites arrested him and put him in jail. They beat him up severely then sent him to the Minister of Rites' residence to clean up stables. Fortunately, that did not last too long, because the King's eunuchs came the following day to set him free. He wanted to stay in the capital to clear his name, but I suggested that it would be safer for him to go home and let the King deal with the Ministry of Rites later. I told Teacher Tâm that it would be better for him if he were not to seen around the capital until the matter is cleared up. He took my advice and left at once to go back to his village."

"He left? When?" Giang's voice was weak, barely audible. She closed her eyes and waited for the answer, like a condemned person waiting for her sentence.

"He left several days ago, right after he was released."

"Françoise!" exclaimed Bonneau. He jumped up and kicked back his chair to rush toward his daughter.

"Giang!" Mai shouted.

She ran toward her sister who had crumpled to the floor where she lay unmoving.

Special Envoy Bonneau checked on his daughter every morning before leaving for work, and every evening when he came home. She remained feverish for several days, would not eat anything, drank little, kept her eyes closed most of the time, and refused to talk to anyone. She made no effort to acknowledge her mother when she returned from Tourane.

Bà Trang was determined to reprimand Giang for returning to the capital without even telling her, but changed her mind when she saw the state that her daughter was in.

A French military doctor was called in. He took her pulse and prescribed medications, then left shaking his head. After a few days she seemed to improve slightly but remained unresponsive most of the time. The maid was able to feed her a small amount of congee every day, and Mai was sure that her sister acknowledged her from time to time. But that was the extent of her interaction with her surroundings and the people around her. The rest of the time, she slept or kept her eyes closed, and had fitful dreams during which she mumbled unintelligible sounds and words. It was as if she was living in her own world.

For several weeks, the doctor came back once a week to check on her, not adding any new prescriptions and telling the family to continue the same treatment. One day almost two months later, he gathered the parents in front of him and told them very frankly that his services were no longer needed.

"She is a healthy young woman and will recover physically from her temporary illness. However, she is going through some kind of neurasthenia, and I have no medicine that can help with that. As a physician, there is nothing more I can do for her. Only she can pull herself out of her semi catatonic state. Only she can deal with whatever brought about this whole thing, and frankly, I am sure you know more about that than what you have told me."

After the doctor left, Bonneau led Bà Trang and Mai into his study and closed the door behind them. The three sat down around his desk, and Bonneau began to speak as he reached for one of his pipes. With unusual coldness, he fixed his eyes on his wife, and she sensed that he was unhappy and perhaps even angry with her.

"The doctor was right. We all know why Giang is in the state she's in. I don't want her to hear what I am about to tell you, for I am afraid it could make her condition worse."

"How could she be worse off than in her current condition," Mai protested. "Just look at her!"

Bonneau raised one hand.

"Hear me out," he said and paused for effect. His eyes were sad as they focused on Mai.

"First, on the subject of the young man from the North who came into our life this summer, and who now has a special place in your sister's heart, despite your mother's objections and machinations."

His wife raised her eyebrows, and made a hissing noise to show her irritation, but she wisely chose to remain quiet as Bonneau turned to her with a disapproving scowl.

"The King's men think that Teacher Tâm examination papers were tampered with. After reading all of his papers, they concluded that the offense that he was accused of committing is just impossible for a scholar of his caliber to commit. The only possible explanation is that someone changed a character in one of his compositions. However, we don't know who did it. What is curious is that the examination judges are all staying mum about this case. The only one who brought it to light was the Minister of Rites. Under normal circumstances, one or two judges should have discovered the violation first. They would have shared their findings with the other judges, and their collective recommendation for failing the offending scholar would have been presented to the Minister, then to the King."

He paused to make sure that both Bà Trang and Mai understood fully what he told them. His wife was silent, but their daughter sighed audibly to express her frustration.

"I do not like this Minister at all! He is a monster!"

Her father nodded, and then continued.

"Minister Toàn, who is charged with overall supervision of the examinations, is not cooperating with the King's men in their investigation. The King is too weak and incapable of making him change his mind or behavior. As it stands currently, without some proof or evidence, there is nothing anybody can do for Teacher Tâm. The Resident General is fully aware of this situation and it gives him one more argument he will use to ask the King to do away with the antiquated examinations system. In the meantime, it was in fact a wise idea for Teacher Tâm to return to his village. The Minister of Rites is a very powerful man, and he could still try to do him harm if he were to remain in the capital."

Bonneau puffed on his unlit pipe, and then continued.

"Some time ago there was a report of an entire family perishing in a suspicious fire in a village outside of the capital. The head of the family is a disgraced mandarin who was caught embezzling royal funds a few years back. He was a skilled forger who used his talent to falsify official documents in order to steal the money. Just prior to the fire, he spent about two weeks at the Minister's residence working on some secret project for him. Then he went home, and his house burned down with him and his entire family perishing in it. This happened right before the Minister discovered that name violation in Teacher Tâm's examination papers."

He took his pipe out of his mouth and waved it in the air for emphasis.

"If hundreds of tomb builders could be slaughtered to protect a tomb's location secret, could this man and his family have been killed to protect some other secret, one that had something to do with our village teacher's examination papers? I think so, but unfortunately there is no witness and no evidence."

"Father," Mai interjected. "You should send secretary Kham to that village and find out more about this. Maybe it is related to what happened to Teacher Tâm."

Bonneau sighed. "It wouldn't do any good. By the way, you must not have noticed that Kham has not been around for a few weeks. I dismissed him."

"You fired him?" asked a surprised Mai. "I cannot trust that man and don't like him at all, but why?"

Her mother, however, showed no emotion at the news of the secretary firing. Bonneau glanced at her before continuing.

"There are many reasons. I've long suspected him of being a spy for the Vietnamese government, reporting to them what he could see or hear when he worked for me. Secondly, he has been quite reluctant to tell me many things on this matter, things that affect Teacher Tâm as well as us. I got the impression that he knew all the sordid details behind it, but kept them to himself. I now know that he is related to the Minister of Rites, and may have been taking his marching orders from the old fox while pretending to serve me."

Bonneau turned to face his wife squarely. Bà Trang looked away to avoid his eyes, pretending to be indifferent to what was being said.

"Finally, he took it upon himself to tell Teacher Tâm to go away in terms that he had no right to use. I recently went to the inn where he was staying, to see if I could find out more about the circumstances of his sudden departure. I met with the innkeeper who told me that Kham practically chased Teacher Tâm out of the capital. He repeated to me all the insults Kham hurled at that poor young man. It was shameful and he had absolutely no right to use such language, unless he had been instructed to do so."

He looked again at Bà Trang, but she kept averting her eyes and continued to maintain a stoic silence. His head veered back to Mai who was now thoroughly absorbed with her father's revelations.

"Your mother has been working for some time now to steer your sister away from Teacher Tâm. I confess that I was complicit in that because I pretended to be too busy at work to keep myself from getting involved. I don't doubt that your mother always have the best intentions in the world for both you and your sister. Unfortunately, this time her maternal instinct did not serve your sister well, as recent events have shown us."

"What events are you talking about, father?" Mai asked. Since Giang fell ill, she had stopped going to the stall in the Đông Ba market and had lost contact with the world outside of the family compound.

"The young man, the son of the Minister of Rites, who was at the contrived banquet that your sister attended in Tourane, has disappeared from sight. Some of my sources told me that he went to Cochinchina."

"What does it matter where he went?"

"They say that he had an argument with his father, the Minister, and that he will probably never come back to the capital," Bonneau explained. "Meanwhile, at the Minister's residence, a little orphan girl has been adopted by the Minister and is being raised by his second wife. People are saying that the girl's father is no other than the Minister's son, and her mother is the Ministers' wife."

As Mai gasped audibly, Bonneau raised his voice, addressing himself directly to his wife.

"So, is this the kind of person we want our family to be associated with? Never! Should we have been more conscientious in investigating his background before we pushed Giang toward him? Absolutely! There were obvious warning signs about him, like that time when he led a band of similarly debauched friends to harass the two of you at the Đông Ba market. However, because *we* wanted to uphold our class and its privileges *we* ignored those signs and gave him a pass and officially introduced him to our daughter."

His emotions got the better of himself and he took a moment to regain his composure. In the meantime, two large tear drops rolled down Bà Trang's face. She wanted to ask him to stop, but could not find the courage to do so. He paid scant attention to her imploring eyes.

"If you, Mai, and your sister had let me know at that time, I would have given him a lesson to remember for life."

As Bonneau said those last few words, he looked at his sword hanging proudly on the wall behind his desk, trying to remember the last time that he had to use it.

"So a brave and innocent village teacher has suffered a grave injustice, one that we have no way to redress. Some people may say that his life is forever ruined, but I don't think so. He has been running a school since he was seventeen, and he has developed a wisdom beyond his age. He has a vision of the future that the vast majority of the scholars in this capital city do not share, but he will do well. I only regret that he won't be close by so that I can watch him succeed and prosper."

He thought about his sick daughter, lying on a bed upstairs, unresponsive and perhaps imprisoned permanently in her own world. He was a man of action, but he could not think of anything that he could do to help her.

How could a summer that started out so well end up with so much unhappiness? Was his wife's uncle, the abbot, right with his prediction after all? As a man from a Western civilization proud of its modern achievements, he rejected the abbot's fortune telling. Yet, in this case, the old monk had been proven right, so far. Lost in thought, he did not notice that his second daughter had quietly left the room.

Mai went upstairs to visit her sister. She was debating whether to tell her what their father had just related to her and their mother. She thought that maybe the news about the creepy mandarin son disappearance would help cheer her up. When she opened Giang's bedroom door, she was shocked to see that her sister was standing up, a little shaky, pale and thin. It was certainly a welcome change from the horizontal position she had been in most of the time over the last couple of months.

"Sister, you are up, thank God! Are you feeling better?"

Giang smiled for the first time since she fainted at the news of Tâm's departure.

"Yes, I do feel much better now."

"Let me run down and tell our parents. Are you sure you are fine?"

"Yes, of course. He's finally home."

"What are you talking about? Whom are you talking about?"

"Teacher Tâm. He's back in his village, safe and sound."

Resistance

Situated roughly mid-way between India and China, throughout history Việt Nam has been visited by sea traders from India, Siam, Europe, the Middle East, Malaysia, Indonesia, Japan, Korea, and of course China. In the 16th century, the Portuguese were the first Westerners to set up shops in the port of Hội An in Central Việt Nam. A few years after them, the Dutch did the same in northern Việt Nam.

Missionaries followed the traders and began trying to convert Vietnamese to Christianity, especially after they were driven out of Japan in the early 17th century under the Tokugawa shogunate. The Romanized Vietnamese alphabet was a direct result of efforts by Portuguese missionaries to transcribe the Bible and other religious texts into the local language. However, it was a French Jesuit priest, Alexandre de Rhodes, who finalized the new script with the publication of his Vietnamese-Portuguese-Latin dictionary printed in 1651 in Rome.

The spread of Christianity in the country met with ruthless suppression by almost all of Việt Nam's rulers. The persecution of missionaries and Vietnamese Christians was widespread, except for one brief period during the rule of Nguyễn Ánh. He was the founder of the Nguyễn dynasty who had to rely on French military assistance to defeat the Tây Sơn dynasty and gain power.

As long as Nguyễn Ánh, or Emperor Gia Long (1762-1820), remained alive, he neither encouraged nor forbid Christian missionary work. During his 18 years on the throne, foreign priests and their new Vietnamese converts were relatively free to move within the kingdom.

Even a grandson of the Emperor, who was the prince in the direct line of succession, had converted to the new religion. However, the conversion cost him the throne because Gia Long selected as his successor another prince in a secondary branch, a man who was anti-Christian and distrusted foreigners profoundly.

After Gia Long passed away, his chosen successor, Emperor Minh Mạng (1791-1841) resolutely cracked down on the new religion. To him, and to the ruling mandarin class, Christianity was evil and posed a grave threat to traditional culture and values.

Foreign ships entering Vietnamese ports were searched and missionaries were denied entry. Religious books translated into Vietnamese were seized and burned. Vietnamese Christians were forced to abandon their new faith while rewards were given for the capture of both foreign and domestic priests. Priests and converts who would not renounce their faith were tortured and executed.

In 1835 a French priest, Joseph Marchand, was arrested along with the remnants of the Lê Văn Khôi rebellion in the South of the country. After having Marchand and his fellow rebels slowly tortured to death, the Emperor ordered increased efforts in the suppression of Christianity.

Under Minh Mạng tens of thousands, possibly as many as 100,000 of Vietnamese Christians and their priests, foreign as well as Vietnamese, were thus martyred, some in the most horrific circumstances. Despite this, Christianity kept spreading throughout the country and Vietnamese continued to congregate in Catholic churches, including some built underground, in ever greater number. Meanwhile, the persecution of missionaries and their converts gave France a ready excuse for intervening in Vietnamese affairs. It also furthered the French's goals of establishing first a trade route to China, then a colony in Indochina.

Emperor Thiệu Trị (1807-1847), a mild mannered man, succeeded his father Minh Mạng and at first reduced the intensity of anti-Christian activities. In 1847, France sent two warships to the harbor of Đà Nẵng to ask for the abolition of anti-Christian policies and for Vietnamese to be free to practice Christianity. While waiting in port, the French wrongly perceived that they were going to be attacked by several Vietnamese boats that had moored nearby. They opened fire and sunk all of the suspect boats. Emperor Thiệu Trị immediately reacted by further forbidding all missionary activities, and instructed that Vietnamese Christians be punished severely.

Anti-Christian sentiments worked hand in hand with other xenophobic tendencies among the Nguyễn monarchs and their regime. Foreigners who had been welcomed under Gia Long soon came to be distrusted and the regime rejected all foreign influence whether motivated by religion, trade, or politics. The country literally closed itself to the barbarians from the West. It stagnated for several crucial decades while its foreign enemies only grew stronger and bolder.

Emperor Tự Đức (1829-1883) began his reign in 1847 by decreeing that Christianity was a religion that went against nature because, among other things, it ignored the cult of ancestors. He directed that foreign missionaries be captured and drowned. Vietnamese priests were forced to renounce their faith, or risked being sliced in half if they didn't.

In 1851 the first foreign missionary was decapitated and his remains thrown into a river flowing out to the ocean. Three other suffered a similar fate in the following year. One of them was a childhood friend of the French Empress, Eugénie de Montijo, a Spaniard and wife of Napoleon III.

Under orders from Napoleon III, French forces, supported by troops provided by Spain, began in 1858 to attack and occupy cities from Cửa Hàn, or Tourane, in the Center to Gia Định in the South. In 1862, the French forced the government to cede to them three major Southern provinces and to allow them unfettered navigation on the Mekong River. The Vietnamese government also had to agree to let French and Spanish missionaries proselytize freely, and to allow Vietnamese to convert to the new faith without fear of persecution.

In 1863, Phan Thanh Giản, Grand Counselor to Tự Đức, led a Vietnamese delegation to Paris to ask Napoleon III to return the three Southern provinces to Việt Nam. The negotiations failed, but the Counselor took the opportunity to observe firsthand the scientific and technological advances achieved by France in the midst of the Industrial Revolution. When he returned and reported his observations to the Emperor, the monarch was dismissive, and the kingdom's xenophobia went on unabated.

In 1867, the French attacked again, wanting to take over the three other remaining provinces in the South. Phan Thanh Giản, who had been appointed Governor in the South, knew his forces were no match against the French and chose to avoid unnecessary bloodshed. He surrendered the fortress at Vĩnh Long and ordered his subordinates to offer no resistance. He then went on a hunger strike and finally took his own life by taking poison.

Thus in the space of five days, the last three provinces of the South fell into French hands and the entire South became a French colony.

In 1873, a force of fewer than 200 French soldiers and Chinese mercenaries under Francis Garnier launched a surprise offensive and took over the old capital of Hà Nội after only one hour of fighting. The Vietnamese commanding general, Nguyễn Tri Phương, was wounded and captured. He refused treatment and starved himself to death over the following month. During that time, four Northern provinces fell into French hands.

In order to fight the French, the regime had to seek the help of the Black Flags, a group of Chinese bandits under Lưu Vĩnh Phúc (Liu Yongfu) who, under pressure from Imperial Chinese troops, had spilled over from Southern China into North Việt Nam.

Royal Vietnamese forces joined the Black Flags in attacking Hà Nội under French control. Even though they were routed, a group of Black Flags soldiers managed to ambush and kill Garnier. A month later, the French returned the Northern provinces to the Vietnamese government.

In 1882, French forces again assaulted Hà Nội under the pretext of protecting French civilians. They took over the city in less than three hours of fighting. The Governor, Hoàng Diệu, chose to hang himself rather than fall into enemy hands.

Emperor Tự Đức, as a consequence of smallpox contracted during his childhood, had no direct descendant. Upon his death in 1883, he was succeeded by several nephews who were young, weak, and too easily overwhelmed by palace intrigues.

His first successor, Dục Đức (1852-1883), only lasted three days before being jailed by courtiers who accused him of ignoring mourning rites and of moral depravity. He was left to starve to death in jail.

The second successor, Hiệp Hòa (1847-1883), ruled for four months before being forced to take poison because he was accused of being too conciliatory toward the French.

The third, Kiến Phúc (1869-1884), was enthroned against his wishes at the age of 15, and eight months later died after a prolonged illness.

In 1883 the French attacked the port of Thuận An to force the Vietnamese court to sign the Treaty of 1883 which established Central and North Việt Nam as French protectorates. Thus, in practical terms, while only the South was an official colony of France, the entire country had become a French colony for all intents and purposes.

The younger brother of Kiến Phúc succeeded him in 1884 and became King Hàm Nghi (1871-1943) at the age of 13. Only a few months later the court faction that elevated him to the throne launched a surprise attack against the French stationed in the capital.

After their initial surprise, French troops regrouped and managed to beat back the Vietnamese royal troops. The French pursued their attackers, killing thousands of soldiers and civilians in the process. They invaded the Citadel, penetrated the Forbidden City and went on a rampage of killing, raping, and pillaging. The young King had to be evacuated and fled the city with barely a hundred soldiers and attendants.

In the following three years, Hàm Nghi had to move from one province to another to escape the French. In 1888, one of his men betrayed him and led the French to his final hideout. He was taken directly to Thuận An and immediately put on a ship that took him to Algiers. He lived there in exile until his death 55 years later.

While fleeing from the French, in 1885 Hàm Nghi issued a proclamation urging Vietnamese everywhere to rise up against the French. Mandarins, scholars, and military officers from all parts of the country answered his call. The Cần Vương resistance movement thus began.

The most prominent resistance leader was Phan Đình Phùng, a mandarin native of Hà Tĩnh province, famous for his integrity. He was a talented scholar who passed the palace examinations of 1877 as the laureate scholar. Following that remarkable achievement, he held a series of positions, culminating with that of Censor, which gave him the right to investigate and criticize any official, including the King.

The role of Censor naturally earned him many enemies among the mandarins. In a typical instance, a royal edict had decreed that all Court officials were required to attend training sessions to learn how to shoot with Western rifles. However, most did not bother to attend the training and the Censor reported to the King that nearly all mandarins found ways to excuse themselves from the shooting lessons. That and other similar incidents earned him the monarch's trust, but the mandarins were resentful of his influence and many plotted to have him removed.

Ironically, just before the Cần Vương uprising, he was dismissed and sent home by the real power behind the throne, Regent Tôn Thất Thuyết. The Regent suspected that Phùng disapproved of his machinations to put on the throne a man of his liking, namely King Hàm Nghi. However, when the Cần Vương proclamation came, Phùng put personal enmity aside and cooperated fully with Thuyết in organizing resistance against the French.

One of his first actions was to hunt down and kill the traitor who had betrayed King Hàm Nghi to the French. Next he attacked two Catholic villages accused of collaborating with the foreigners. However, his forces were routed and his brother captured by French colonial troops who rushed to the rescue of the villages. Phùng refused to turn himself in to the French in order to save his brother. Admiring him for his resolve and strong moral character, many scholars and local heroes enthusiastically joined the ranks of his armed groups.

His most accomplished follower was Cao Thắng, a military genius who helped him organize and train volunteers. Cao Thắng was able to use captured French weapons as models to manufacture some 300 rifles. Unfortunately, he did not know how to rifle the barrels of the guns, which as a result could not shoot as far and were less accurate and effective than the foreign-made guns. Nevertheless it was an achievement that no one else in the nation could have accomplished at the time.

Overall, the human and logistics support needed by the rebels never matched what the French could afford to field in terms of troops and resources. Thus, despite an initial popular support, the rebels were essentially fighting a hopeless battle. The rebels found it harder and harder to fight against the French who were at times joined by royal troops commanded by mandarins loyal to the French-appointed kings in Huế.

Soon the rebels could no longer afford to confront French forces in set piece battles. They switched to guerilla warfare while the French kept building outposts and expanding their influence deeper into the countryside.

In 1893 Cao Thắng himself was killed in an attack against a French outpost. With the loss of such a gifted commander and with dwindling support, the guerillas' days were numbered. Two years later, in 1895, Phan Đình Phùng was killed in a battle against royal Vietnamese forces. His forces quickly disintegrated, and its leaders were captured and executed.

In the Northern province of Hưng Yên, Nguyễn Thiện Thuật was a mandarin and a capable military commander who had led successful campaigns against Vietnamese and Chinese bandits, and had fought the French when they first came to North Việt Nam.

In 1882, when Emperor Tự Đức sent an emissary to tell Thuật and his allies to lay down their arms and stop opposing the French, he and his fellow mandarins refused to obey the order. Some quit and went home in frustration, but Thuật called for armed resistance against the French. His reputation as a scholar and able administrator earned him many followers and his forces soon extended from his home province all the way to the Northwestern border with China.

Using guerilla tactics, Thuật and his troops inflicted defeat after defeat on the French in a series of battles from Hưng Yên to Hà Nội and Hải Dương. Still, as the years passed, the efforts to keep such a militia fed and supplied with weapons and ammunitions proved to be too overwhelming. The rebels were finding it increasingly hard to hold on to their bases.

Thuật went to China in the hope of getting help from Vietnamese exiles and from the Qing government. Little did he realize that the Qing dynasty was itself in its last throes. China was under severe foreign pressure and was in no condition to help itself, let alone another country.

Thuật spent the rest of his life in China and died there in 1926. Once he left Việt Nam, his movement crumbled and its remaining leaders scattered or were captured and killed.

Hoàng Hoa Thám, joined an uprising against the French in 1874, when he was only 16. By 1892, he had become the leader of a militia based in the Northeast province of Bắc Giang in the district of Yên Thế.

Over the next 30 years, the "hero of Yên Thế" became the nightmare of French colonial troops, winning and losing against them in many battles, including one that pitted more than 15,000 colonial troops against his forces.

Despite setbacks and bounties for his capture, Thám always managed to avoid being taken prisoner. When defeated, he usually disappeared to come back months later and resume his attacks against the French. He lasted until 1913 when three Chinese mercenaries managed to poison him, and then delivered his head to the French.

Việt Nam could not escape the yoke of French colonization, and the blame rested largely on a succession of Nguyễn monarchs who turned inward when confronted with the realities of Western power and influence. Perhaps they were initially preoccupied with dousing the fires of multiple rebellions throughout the land. Some of those uprisings were instigated by retainers of the previous Lê dynasty who viewed the Nguyễn as usurpers. Nevertheless, by the middle of the 19th century, the real threat was foreign and the best way to counter it was to open up the nation and try to learn as much from the West as possible, as Japan and Siam did. Instead, the Nguyễn rulers declared Việt Nam closed to all foreign influence, and rejected anything even remotely connected to the West.

The scholars and mandarins who served the regime were no better than the rulers. In order to preserve their social status and privileges, the vast majority clung to traditional Confucian values and customs. They believed that the country should keep following the Chinese model, and that China itself would help Việt Nam militarily and politically if and when needed.

With a view of the world dominated for over a thousand years by the larger and powerful neighbor to the North, no one realized that China was rapidly falling and eventually would not be able to help itself let alone anyone else.

Men like Phan Đình Phùng were the rare exception. He wanted the country to emulate Japan or Siam, and to learn and adopt Western science and technology. However, he was a lone voice that went largely unheeded by his fellow mandarins and the monarchs that he served.

The Cần Vương movement initially rallied the nation against the foreign invaders from the West. However, some of its proponents used anti-French sentiments as an excuse to exterminate Vietnamese Christian converts. The Vietnamese Catholics had little choice but to turn to the French for protection. Thus, a significant and growing segment of the population came to see that their well-being and survival rested on cooperation with the foreigners. Eventually the regime in Huế fell under the control and supervision of the colonial administration and was compelled to relax its anti-Christian policies and stop its persecution of the growing Christian minority.

Once King Hàm Nghi was exiled to Algeria, resistance fervor waned and the Cần Vương movement faded. No foreign power was willing to help the rebels fight off the French. Western powers were busy carving up the Middle Kingdom, and no Asian nation, least of all China, could provide anything more than asylum for Vietnamese fleeing from French pressure and attacks.

The monarchy and a court still existed in Huế, even though kings were appointed by the French. Mandarins throughout the nation had to pledge allegiance to the King and to the colonial regime if they wanted to keep their positions and continue to enjoy their ranks and privileges.

French colonialism started in the South and within a few years signs of modernity and progress began to be visible. The first railroad and train were inaugurated in Sài Gòn in 1885, and the fertile Mekong river delta was transformed into a veritable rice basket. The Southern part of the country became economically superior to the Center and the

North, a position that it would keep holding well into the 21st century, despite wars and political divisions.

While he was only several days from home, Tâm had to stop at a riverbank to wait for a ferry boat to take him to the other side. He looked for shelter in a small inn nearby to escape from the rain which was falling in heavy squalls. When he came down a few months earlier, the river was a gentle and modest stream the color of jade. Now, swollen by the monsoon rains to twice or three times its previous size, it was flowing fast and furious, its water enriched and colored a reddish orange by alluvial particles of silt and clay.

An old woman, perhaps the owner of the inn, brought him a pot of tea and a dish of boiled peanuts to munch on. After a while, he saw a boat appear in the rain mist that had settled over the river. Two ferrymen were fighting hard against the current to bring their boat right to where he was standing and waiting before. They hurried into the inn as soon as they had their boat tied securely. He hailed them before they found a place to sit.

"Are you going across again soon?"

He was answered with a question from the older of the two men.

"Is there anyone other than you, Teacher?"

He had recognized Tâm as a village teacher and was addressing him respectfully.

"No, only me."

"Then would you mind waiting for a while? More people may show up later and this way we also get to take a little break and rest."

"I am in no hurry," replied Tâm. "We can wait as long as you like."

The bank of the river was almost devoid of trees and shade. A few months earlier, there was a steep drop from the bank to the edge of the water. Now it was possible to step from the bank into the boat directly without needing a plank. He wondered what would happen if the river ever overflowed its banks. The man who had spoken up earlier interrupted his thoughts.

"You came down this way a few months ago with a group of scholars, didn't you, Teacher?"

Tâm was rather surprised at the man's keen memory. The band of scholars he came with on his way to Huế had somehow made an impression on the ferrymen, but he didn't think he had stood out so obviously.

"Yes, we were on our way to the examinations in the capital."

The man politely skipped over the obvious fact that the unheralded return trip for Tâm meant that he had failed.

"You must be going back to teach in your village then. I wish you were going to ours. We don't have a school and there is no place where our children can get an education."

"Why is that so? Isn't there a teacher in your village? Or isn't there a school somewhere nearby?"

"Our village is too small to afford a teacher, and the nearest town with a school is too far away for the children to walk there and back in one day. Besides, the town is now being fortified by the rebels and, sooner or later, the French will come attack it."

Tâm was aware there were still some pockets of anti-French rebels, but this was the first time that someone had mentioned a specific location to him.

"Does this rebel group belong to the Cần Vương movement?"

"They do indeed. They are led by a high court mandarin who answered the call of King Hàm Nghi, and most of the rebels are patriots from this province and the surrounding areas. None of us like the French and many have joined the group to fight the enemy."

"Have the French ever attacked the rebel town before?"

"They haven't yet. On the contrary, the rebels themselves have been attacking French outposts to capture weapons and kill a few French soldiers at the same time. Their raiding parties are led by a daring commander who has so far managed to win every fight. Unfortunately, the French are going to retaliate, probably as soon as the monsoon is over, if not before then."

"Who is this commander? Have you ever met or seen him?"

"Everybody knows him around here. He's quite popular and goes by the name of commander Chính."

Tâm spent the rest of his time asking questions about the rebels and their commander. He suspected he knew who the hero commander was, but in the end, he kept his thoughts to himself.

Sometime later, three travelers arrived at the inn by the ferry crossing. They carried only light bundles and packages, were neatly dressed and did not look like they were from anywhere nearby. A young woman, pretty and seemingly good-natured, asked the ferrymen.

"Are you going to cross soon?"

"As soon as the rain stops," answered the older ferryman.

She had the accent of the people of Huế, and hearing her Tâm could not help but think of Giang. He looked curiously at her, and she returned his gaze without any affectation. Suddenly, she burst out laughing.

"Are you going home, Teacher Tâm? You must be coming back from the palace examinations, right? I remember watching you that day when the Minister of Rites guards came to pay you a visit."

He flinched at the reminder of that shameful day, and decided there was no point in trying to save face. There were hundreds of people watching him having a cangue fastened around his neck before being marched off to the royal jail. Their faces were a blur to him and he wouldn't have been able to recognize her anyway even if he had noticed her then.

"So you were there that day... I am indeed on my way home, after things didn't work out as I had hoped. I will once again be a teacher in my village."

She nodded sympathetically but admonished him.

"You should not feel any shame for failing the examinations. You know, people do not actually believe that you are guilty of whatever they accused you of, this silly thing about using taboo royal names. In any case, you would not be happy serving as a mandarin under the current conditions. The King and his court are completely under French supervision, and mandarins are nothing but French lackeys."

She would have gone on haranguing him, but he thought it was better to change the subject.

"What about you, where are you going?"

"I'm going to see one of my relatives who followed her husband to this province."

The ferrymen exchanged glances with each other, after which Tâm saw them taking renewed interest in the newcomers. The older one asked abruptly.

"What is your name?"

The young woman showed no surprise at the unusual question and cheerfully replied.

"My name is Ve, like the cicada, the insect."

"So it's you!" the man exclaimed. "We were told to expect you and your group."

"Who told you?"

"Commander Chính. He said last week that you'd be coming up from the capital."

The ferryman now had the full attention of all of his prospective passengers. Tâm remained silent, but the young woman who called herself Ve continued her lively exchange with the ferrymen.

"I've never met him. Can you tell me more about him and his rebels?"

And so, while they waited for the rain to stop, both ferrymen told the group about the rebels and their commander. Ve listened and asked questions that Tâm had not thought of. It was obvious she and her men were eager to join the rebels and had made the trip up from the capital with that sole purpose in mind.

After a while, the conversation gradually dropped off. The ferrymen had said as much as they wanted and the young woman knew she couldn't press them for more. Everyone sipped their tea and ate the boiled peanuts the old innkeeper brought out. Ve and her companions seemed lost in thought as they patiently waited for the rain to stop. Out of boredom, Tâm brought out his dictionary and started leafing through its pages. He alternatively closed and opened his eyes as he tried to commit new French words to memory.

Ve observed him for a while nodding her head appreciatively.

"You are an unusual scholar."

He half closed his book, surprised by her remark.

"Why do you say that?"

"I see you are trying to learn French. Most of the scholars I've known usually stay faithful to their Chinese characters and books and won't try to learn any other foreign language."

"What about you, do you know French also?"

"Yes, I attended a school taught by French priests," she replied. "I am not Catholic in case you are wondering. My parents just wanted me to learn the language."

"You are very fortunate then. There are not many parents who will allow their daughters to get an education, especially from foreigners."

At the mention of her parents, she kept quiet for some time. Her companions looked uneasy and kept glancing discretely at her. Finally, she shook her head and added cryptically.

"My parents are very progressive and open-minded. They would have been gratified to meet somebody like you, Teacher Tâm. I am a little surprised that you are learning French from that book by yourself. Isn't it quite difficult doing it that way? "

He thought of a way not to answer the question directly, but in the end gave up. Still his eyes betrayed his fleeting predicament.

"Actually, somebody helped me in the beginning and gave me this book so that I could continue learning on my own."

She lightened up as she saw through his temporary panic. With eyes full of glee and mischief, she chided him.

"And she let you get away, or was it you who left her? Do you now miss her?"

Her flurry of questions left him smiling awkwardly, but he remained silent while she kept her playful eyes fixed on him for several minutes before relenting.

"All right, you don't have to tell me," she said. "I'm sure she's a nice young woman and you probably think more about her than you are willing to admit, but I am not going to pry into your personal life. Ah, if only someone would think as much about me, even half as much."

She turned away with an exaggerated sigh, stood up and went to the door to look out.

By then Tâm was thoroughly embarrassed. After two months of trying not to think about Giang, a stranger had in a few minutes seen through his mind and his heart. He admired the intelligent and impetuous young woman who called herself Cicada. Was she was from some family of high court mandarins who fell out of favor and were now opposing the current regime? The two men who accompanied her seemed to look to her as their leader, while she acted like someone who had no fear, was quite outspoken, and could easily handle herself with total strangers under any circumstance. She was not much older than Giang, and she was willing to throw herself into a cause that many considered hopeless or already lost.

She came back from the door and went to her companions. She picked up the bundle that she was carrying before coming into the inn and turned to face the ferrymen.

"The rain is ending," she said. "We should leave now and go over to meet this commander Chính."

Vinh Qui

His students were busy using their writing brushes to reproduce the characters he had written on a large piece of paper hanging on the wall. The older ones were calm and relaxed as they wielded their brushes with well-practiced skill, while the younger ones showed determination and frowned as they tried to focus on their assignments.

Even though Tâm kept an outwardly impassive appearance, he was pleased with his class. After coming back to the village, he had immediately reopened the school and devoted himself to his teaching. The children felt the change in him and responded by turning into the finest students he had so far.

"Teacher, please have your tea," a soft voice said behind him.

A steaming cup was placed next to his right hand. He turned and nodded at Thi who never failed to bring up from the back of the house his favorite beverage in midafternoon. She smiled, already spinning around to return to her seat in the back of the classroom where the older students were. He brought the cup to his face and blew on it several times before sipping from it. The tea was still very hot and the cup went back to its tray.

Outside, in the street in front of the school, there seemed to be some commotion followed by excited voices and sounds of running feet. The rest of the class heard them too, and heads turned toward the open front door of the school. There were people of all ages hurrying to the other end of the village, almost diametrically opposite from where the school was on the narrow ellipse that defined the boundaries of the rural community. Soon the students were turning to face him, unasked questions hanging in the air.

"It must be the arrival of the *vinh qui* (glorious return) procession," he answered them. "Finish writing your characters, then we will all go out and watch."

The scholar who had passed the royal examinations was, by tradition and by right, accorded a triumphal homecoming or *vinh qui* to his native village. Located in an area famous for its scholars, the village witnessed such processions almost each time the examinations were held, which usually meant every three to five years. In times of political trouble and wars, as it was, there had been no procession for much longer.

He had already reconciled himself to the fact that one of those who passed the palace examinations was none other than Chí, a former classmate. From the time that they started in school to the time when they participated in the final round of examinations, Chí had always been a competent if not dazzling scholar. He worked hard, knew the Four Books and the Five Classics, composed decent prose and acceptable poems, and in general did all that he was asked to do, but he never managed to come close to the creativity and brilliance of the village teacher's son. After his father passed away, Tâm took over and became the village teacher. That was when Chí decided to go study in the big city of Hà Nội. He could not stand being taught by someone of his own age, even if the expensive teacher he later found turned out to be a disappointment.

Now his rival was the one making his triumphal return to the village, and Tâm was going to be standing as one just more person in the crowd welcoming him home.

As he led his entire school toward the center of the village, he silently told himself to stop dwelling on the past. This was an occasion for the village to be proud of itself and to honor its tradition of offering its best and brightest to serve the nation. His father would have been disappointed that he was not the one honored in the *vinh qui*, but he would have been proud that he was the one who had taught Chí and his own son since they were mere toddlers.

The returning scholar, recently appointed Prefect of a nearby province, halted his horse at the highest point of the small hill overlooking the village. He was still new to riding and his body, unused to the rigors of travel, was sore in many places. He was on the plump side, with a chubby face which normally would have been pale but was now rather tanned from days of exposure to the sun. From the daily fight against riding pains, he wore a constant scowl and the corners of his mouth were permanently downturned.

Captain Duẩn, the officer in charge of the detachment of soldiers escorting him, shouted an order and the whole column came to a stop. At the front, men were carrying a drum and a gong suspended from poles. They were followed by a group of village men who had walked the day before to the provincial city to escort Prefect Chí back to their village. The men were wearing ceremonial dresses and carrying poles adorned with multi-colored flags and signs announcing proudly the village's pride in their new *Tiến Sĩ*.

Soldiers carrying rifles were divided into a section that preceded Chí and another one that followed him. The captain was also riding a horse, but everyone else was walking as they had been since that morning. All welcomed the rest and took the opportunity to check on their dresses, flags or uniforms and equipment. They wanted to look their finest for the march to their final destination.

The sides of the road leading from the hill to the village gate had been weeded, and the road itself had been swept clean for the past several days by the villagers themselves, as ordered by the Village Chief, the father of the returning scholar. Some were still sprinkling water on the roadway to reduce the amount of dust that will be generated by the long procession. Chí saw that people were starting to line up both sides of the road, with even more in the distance leaving their fields or homes to come join the lines. He smiled with pleasure and decided to extend his rest at the top of the hill to give time for the stragglers to join the crowd. He wanted everyone in the village to see him make his entrance.

"Tell the men we'll rest here for a while," he ordered the captain. "In the meantime, have them continue beating on the drum and the gong to let people in the distance know we are coming."

The soldiers had been striking the drum and the gong at regular intervals all morning, but on their captain's order the sounds became rhythmic and increased in intensity. It was as if they were summoning a garrison to assembly, or calling on soldiers to man gates and ramparts to repulse an enemy attack.

Chí was sure his whole clan was already lined up in front of his house, with a multitude of relatives coming from nearby villages and towns. The only one he wondered about was his archrival, the village teacher who should have been the one returning in the *vinh qui*. Would he show up, or would he hide in shame in his schoolhouse?

In many cases, a returning scholar who was married would have his wife riding in a palanquin behind her husband in the procession. However, Chí was still single and there was no need for a palanquin. Despite his parents' efforts at finding him a good match over the last several years, he had remained a bachelor.

In the capital, many mandarins and even royals had given him subtle hints about marriageable daughters, but he had been too busy preparing for his new post to give them much thought. He had to take crash courses on provincial administration. He had to pay homage to so many dignitaries that he lost track of who they were and what each had said to him. He was not blind to the matrimonial alliances made possible by his achievement at the examinations, but for several years now an idea had been growing and solidifying in his mind and he was going to wait until he came home to carry it out.

Looking down toward his village, he saw no more stragglers. Both sides of the road were filled with people, and children were darting from one side of the road to the other, or climbed on trees to get a better vantage point. Their parents and the village's constables could do nothing but shout and threaten punishment. A group of people wearing black tunics and headdress, no doubt an official delegation, were milling around the village gate, looking toward the hill, probably wondering why there was a delay.

The new Prefect looked at his captain and indicated with a movement of his chin that he was ready to move forward. At a firm command from the officer the column started its descent toward the village.

As usual Thi was the last to leave the classroom and soon found herself walking beside their teacher while the other students preceded them, talking and laughing, happy at this sudden and welcome change from their daily routine. She glanced at him and saw the same calm expression he wore every day. He caught her eyes and, though she thought she saw a brief smile on his face, he did not say anything.

"Will he come to our school, Teacher?" she asked.

They both knew whom she was referring to.

"Thi, I don't know," Tâm answered.

"Shouldn't he come to pay respect to your mother, Teacher?"

"He may, but one can't tell. He is the Prefect now and he is a very important person with many duties."

Like the rest of the village, Thi knew what had happened in the capital. The news travelled fast and reached the village even before Tâm finally did after his long walk. She was among the many who felt that fate had treated her teacher unfairly, but from the day he came home he had not broached the topic with anybody. If someone asked him about it, he skillfully steered the conversation onto other topics, and after a while the questioners came to realize that he had built a wall that few, if any, could cross.

Recently when he asked for volunteers to learn the new Vietnamese script invented by foreign missionaries, he had looked at her directly and she had nodded right away. Several of the older students joined her and the small group stayed behind each day after class to learn to read and write the new script.

He told them that as soon as they mastered it, they would become his assistant teachers and spread around to teach the rest of the village. It was an idea that appealed to the entire group and energized them more than anything else in their studies up to that point. She could not help from smiling as she thought about becoming a teacher in her own right.

"What makes you so happy today, young miss? It's the arrival of the new Prefect, isn't it? Doesn't he look striking and handsome? Ha, ha, it's the truth, isn't it?"

The woman who shook Thi out of her daydreaming was Bà Canh, a neighbor, who was now laughing out loud, baring her black lacquered teeth, as she savored the discomfiture that her teasing had caused to the young girl.

"No, not at all," Thi quickly corrected the woman. "I was actually thinking of something else".

At that moment, she vowed to never blacken her teeth as some of the older women in her family had been hinting. When they were ready to be married, girls would go through several days of lacquering their teeth black. Most accepted this tradition, but not her, no matter what people would say.

"At least half of the young girls of your age in this village are wishing they could have followed him in a palanquin. But it's never too late, and, if you were to ask me, I know that you will have a very good chance of being called the Prefect's wife."

"I never said that I wanted to be … that," Thi protested vigorously, but the woman had walked away, slapping her hips while chuckling to herself. In frustration, Thi stamped her feet as she went to rejoin her group. She saw that her teacher was observing her from the corner of his eyes, but he turned away as she came nearer, and she was glad that he didn't ask her anything.

The drum and gong sounds were becoming louder as the procession moved toward where they were. The village teacher and his entire school stood in the shade of a poinciana tree, the younger ones in front and the older ones with their teacher in the back, all looking eagerly to the procession moving toward them.

The poinciana was past its flowering season and there were no vibrant clusters of red flowers completely covering the tree as they did a few months earlier when the examinations took place. Instead a multitude of green or black seed pods hung like mini scimitars from virtually every branch.

Preceded by the delegation of village officials who had greeted them at the gate, the pageant, swollen to almost twice its original size, proceeded slowly down the main road. The villagers were in a festive mood, some trying to shout over the sounds of the drum and its companion gong.

Prefect Chí and the captain were on their horses towering over everybody. While adults gesticulated and pointed out the newly appointed scholar to each other, children stood with open mouths, mesmerized by the sight of the soldiers with their shiny weapons.

The new Prefect was wearing a dragonfly hat and wore a deep blue ceremonial robe with round and silvery designs shining brilliantly under the bright sun. He rested his left hand on the pommel of a sword attached to his belt, while his right hand firmly held the reins of his horse. He was trying to convey an air of authority and confidence.

The captain escorting him, when he was not looking at the crowd, could not help casting nervous glances at his superior. The new Prefect had only recently learned how to ride a few days prior to embarking on his return trip and had requested that the captain followed him closely to prevent any mishap.

Passing by the group under the poinciana tree, Chí recognized Tâm standing in the crowd. Rather than acknowledging him, he scanned the people around his rival quickly. He found her in the back rows. She looked somewhat flustered and her eyes showed none of the curiosity or enthusiasm he had been expecting and at times seen in the rest of the village crowd. The captain, who had followed his gaze, also noticed the young woman who appeared hardly impressed by the pomp and circumstance of the *vinh qui* and its principal character. He made a mental note of it, conceding that this Prefect did have an eye for beauty.

The procession moved on, leaving behind billowing clouds of dust. Toward the center of town, it slowed down then stopped in front of a large house, a mansion surrounded by a high wall festooned with lanterns and braided long strings of red firecrackers.

The open front gate was topped by a newly painted sign filled with golden Chinese characters on a red background. The occupants of the house were standing under the sign in their finest clothes, clustered around a patriarch, an old man with wispy white hair but a healthy complexion and a body used to good food.

The Nguyễn Hữu clan was assembled and ready to greet their grandson, son, brother, nephew, uncle, and cousin who had brought honor and fame to the three generations of the clan. Someone lit the firecrackers and soon explosions and smoke filled the whole area as children jumped and shrieked with joy while several soldiers gathered

around the Prefect's nervous horse to calm it down and help him
dismount.

.

The Banquet

She walked home from school after her small group finished their daily Vietnamese script session with their teacher. It's only been three weeks, but Thi and the others were feeling very confident of themselves. In that relatively short time, they had gone from learning to write one by one the characters of the Roman alphabet, some with special accent marks, to penning in whole sentences that their teacher dictated while he paced back and forth in front of them.

What she liked best was when he picked out a poem in *Nôm* characters, and then read it slowly line by line as they wrote down each word. After years of learning, she was able to read and write *Nôm* characters herself, but to be able to write words with the same sound and meaning in the new script in a matter of weeks was simply amazing. *Nôm* involved learning thousands of Chinese characters, them combining them, one character for sound and another one for meaning, into a complex character representing a Vietnamese word. The new script consisted of only 23 characters, and she and her fellow students mastered it in a matter of days.

The *vinh qui* procession was over and everybody had gone back to the fields or to their homes. Only small children were visible, playing in front of their houses. Thi walked with her usual light steps, smiling at the children and acknowledging the few adults that she encountered with small bows. Her mind was on one of the most important persons in her life.

She remembered that day when someone had come to her shouting that the village teacher was back, and she with several other students had gone out to the main road to look for him. The whole village had heard of his failure at the exam, but nobody knew that he would be taking so long coming home. Some even hinted that he was hiding in the capital out of shame.

She knew in her heart that he was coming back, but did not share that feeling with anybody. Still when she finally saw him, thinner and well-tanned after his long march, it was as if a big burden of worry had lifted and dissipated. The students greeted him with unconcealed joy, and his face lit up when he saw them. They followed him all the way from the village gate to the school. Knowing that he was tired, she asked everyone to go home to give him room and time to rest. Thus their small procession ended, without any fanfare, but still she felt euphoric.

School soon resumed, and to be there for a few hours each day was the high point of her days before she went home to her domestic chores and duties. She would not have minded if life had gone on that way for as long as possible. Her teacher was home and that was all she cared about.

Toward the center of the village, she saw the imposing compound that was the ancestral home of the Village Chief. The house itself was a large two-story mansion, tall and imposing, unlike any other in the village. There was now a soldier guarding the front gate, and she made sure to walk on the other side of the street as she went by it.

"Where are you going, little girl?"

She turned and saw in the middle of the gate a young woman fashionably dressed in a dark blue silk tunic with a high collar, much more fashionable than the ordinary four-flapped brown tunic that most women usually wore. The dress followed the well-proportioned and ample contours of a well-fed body. Her hair was wrapped inside a tube of deep purple velvet fabric coiled neatly around her head, with a small tail sticking out stylishly on the right side of her head.

"Oh, Kim Liên, it's you!" exclaimed Thi as she recognized the new Prefect's younger sister who used to also attend the village school but quit after only a few years. Kim Liên was known for her sharp tongue and a penchant for taking on haughty airs when talking to people that she considered below her social status. She certainly looked more striking than me with my brown tunic and my flowing hair not held together by anything but a cloth tie, thought Thi.

"Where are the hens that your father said he would give us?"

The high pitched and harsh tone of the question surprised even the guard who turned to watch the two young women, one aggressive looking with both hands resting on her hips, while the other was obviously taken aback and unsure of what to say or to do.

"I have no idea of what you are talking about," Thi responded.

It dawned on her that perhaps the entire village was contributing to the banquet in honor of the new Prefect, and that her family had been asked to contribute a few chickens. Many officials and relatives of the Nguyễn family had been coming to the village over the past several days. They and the company of escort soldiers had to be fed, straining the resources of even such a rich family. As if to confirm her guess, Kim Liên kept up her verbal assault.

"He said he will have four of his fattest hens brought here this afternoon. I thought you were to bring them, but now I can see that you are just strolling about. So, once again, where are those hens?"

"I am just returning from school. Once I get home, I will ask my father about it. Then, probably one of us, either one of my brothers or I will bring them over."

Pointing an accusing finger at her interlocutor, Kim Liên continued on with her tirade.

"School? That was over hours ago. What have you been doing since then? Do you realize we have to feed hundreds of people? Every family in the village has been bringing gifts for the new Prefect, and many are now helping with the preparations and cooking. Your family better not try to get out of this!"

Suddenly, a strong and familiar voice came from behind Thi.

"Thi obviously knows nothing about what her father promised you, so let her go home first to find out. There is no reason to berate her now, is there?"

Thi turned around to look, and almost in unison the two young women shouted.

"Teacher!"

Kim Liên, who had been so shrill and self-important, at once took on a bashful air, smiling nervously while glancing at the village teacher. He had the stern expression that he sometimes used in class when dissatisfied with somebody's performance. His stare would go right through the student wilting in shame. It did not happen very often, but when it did, the whole class, not just the guilty party, would be subdued for a long time afterwards.

"Your brother sent for me, please tell him that I have arrived."

"Yes, yes, please come in Teacher," Kim Liên stammered as she began to walk backwards, her eyes downcast and her arms hanging limply at her side.

Relieved to be rescued from an unpleasant situation, Thi cast thankful eyes toward her teacher then said softly.

"Teacher, I am going home now."

She saw him nod his head as he stepped through the gate and followed the young woman of the house into the Village Chief's compound.

The sunset was resplendent with a sky filled with clouds in shades of orange, red, and purples. It was still early in the monsoon season and the banquet participants were able to sit outside. Aside from Tâm, however, nobody paid attention to the magnificent sky. People were busy eating, drinking, talking and laughing noisily. They were sitting around an assortment of tables and bamboo or wooden beds laid out in the open around the ancestral home but still within the compound walls.

The man of honor was at a long table closest to the house, surrounded on one side by the clan patriarch, his parents, and his uncles and aunts. On the other side were officials from the province down to the village level. Women were seated cross legged at separate beds arranged in a group nearer to the back of the house.

The village teacher chose for himself a spot far from the center of attention but close to the compound walls from where he could observe most of the banquet scene. People from the village recognized him and respectfully made room for him. He noted that Captain Duẩn was also nearby, while some of his men were gathered at tables by the door.

Tâm thought back to the meeting he had with his former classmate where Chí offered him a post in his administration at the provincial headquarters. The position would pay a good salary, plus undefined "fringe benefits". He would become Chí's right-hand man in all matters, civilian as well as military. Tâm wasted no time in saying no to his former classmate's offer, claiming in all honesty that he was very happy at what he was doing which was teaching at the village school.

Sitting a good distance away from the center of attention, Tâm knew that he would have been invited to the head table had he accepted the job offer. He had no regret, his decision having been made months ago to spend the rest of his life as a village teacher. That had been his passion from the very first day he took over from his father, and perhaps even before that. He loved the children and his goal in life was to be able to open up their minds to concepts and worlds beyond their village.

Maids and man-servants, as well as volunteer helpers were carrying trays after trays of food and drink from the back of the house to the tables as Kim Liên directed them with short orders and hand gestures. She was definitely in charge of the ancestral household, exerting authority even over older women like her mother and aunts.

At least in Tâm's memory, it was surely the largest banquet held in the village, even when previous scholars were similarly honored. The Nguyễn Hữu clan was among the most successful and influential in the province, holding considerable land over several cantons. Many of the people present at the banquet were their business partners and allies, and many in the rest of the crowd were in their debt for renting land or obtaining various services and credit from them.

There had been some speeches and toasts at the beginning of the banquet, most hurried on by applause from hungry dinner guests. When the first dishes were brought out, speeches were cut short or held off for a while as people dug into the large trays of roast pork, duck, chicken, and fish.

Sweet rice cooked yellow with mung beans was in abundance at every table, as well as rice wine of the purest kind. Faces were becoming red and redder as the night progressed, and the noise level of the conversation and laughter rose accordingly, even from the ladies' tables.

Tâm who had become used to eating sparingly during his long walk home was amazed at how much others were tucking away. The captain for one did not say a word while he kept bringing food to his mouth where it promptly disappeared as if thrown into a bottomless pit. He was in all likelihood following the time-honored tradition of soldiers to always be ready to eat as much as possible, whenever and wherever they could.

His face flushed a deep dark red, a man at one of the tables closer to the house was trying to stand up but he overestimated his sense of balance and had to steady himself on the shoulders of his neighbors. When he finally stood straight, he launched into a toast, his loud voice surprisingly firm in spite of his inebriation.

"I am an uncle of my nephew, the scholar who has won the palace examinations and has brought fame and honor not only to himself, his family, and our clan, but also to this village and to our whole North. Like many of you today, I went to witness his triumphal procession arrive home after a long voyage from the capital. It was a magnificent occasion, was it not?"

Heads were nodding and some were shouting their agreement with slurred voices. Most had stopped talking to listen to what he had to say, knowing there was more to come.

"However, honored guests, do you know what was missing?" the man continued, and then answered his own question. "What was missing was no fault of our own! It was not because our Village Chief did not organize his men in time, or because the rest of us were not prepared. No, honored guests, what was missing was a palanquin being carried behind my nephew's horse, a palanquin in which a beautiful young lady was following her husband home. There was no *Cô Tiến Sĩ* (wife of the presented scholar). Yes, most honored guests, this *vinh qui* we had today was missing one *Cô Tiến Sĩ*."

The audience exploded in laughter, eyes turning to Chí whose face now turned a deeper shade of red. He waved for his uncle to sit down, but the man would not be stopped so easily.

"Honored guests, my nephew has been so busy studying all these years that he never took time to look for a wife. His parents kept reminding him, his grandfather urged him to do something about it, his uncles and his aunts made numerous hints and suggestions. However, he was too intent on winning that royal honor, with the result that he came home to us without a spouse. I heard rumors that the court mandarins did not forget to mention the names of their daughters of marrying age. But, no, he had no time for that because the King gave him an important post in our province, and he did not want to waste any time to come back here to assume his functions. If he keeps doing what he has done so far, honored guests, my nephew will be the most eligible bachelor for the rest of his life. Ha, ha, ha!"

Many people burst out laughing, others shouted.

"Don't say that, it's his karma!"

"Give him time, let our scholar *learn* a few more things that he doesn't know yet!"

These last outbursts produced guffaws from some of the men who slapped one another while wives tried vainly to shush their unruly husbands. The uncle, pleased with himself for having stirred up his audience, turned on his feet, making a full circle before launching into a peroration to conclude his toast.

"Most honored guests, we certainly cannot let matters stay as they are, can we? This new Prefect needs help. The least we can all do is for you to join me in raising our cups, first to congratulate him for a glorious achievement, and secondly to wish him that the Red Silk Matchmaker will soon lead him to the lucky maiden who will be his bride."

The guests lifted their cups and many tried to empty theirs in one throw before slamming them back on their tables with exaggerated force. Almost immediately, conversation and merriment resumed everywhere.

Bored of standing up and directing the servants, Kim Liên stopped by the head table and leaned toward her father to whisper in his ear.

"My brother is no dummy and he is certainly not shy. He has his eyes on someone else already."

"Who is it? She's the daughter of what family?" Nguyễn Hữu Long, the Village Chief and the richest man in the village asked excitedly. "How come he hasn't told your mother and I? Don't you dare make up stories now, my daughter!"

"If you don't believe me, you can ask him yourself," she answered while pointing to her brother with her chin. "He's just sitting there being made fun of by these drunkards. Go ahead, and ask him."

She stood up, pouting in mock anger, and ambled away to resume her household managerial duties.

Family Matters

In a society where prefacing someone's name with a title was a
tradition, he did not find one that he really liked until his
fortune became well established. They used to call him simply Cả
Long, because he was the oldest child in his family. Then once he
became part of the Village Council (*Hội Đồng Xã*), the name switched
to Hội Đồng Long. The one that he liked best and settled on finally,
after becoming Village Chief, was Xã Long.

Village Chiefs were often the most powerful authority in the
countryside, and he used that position skillfully to his benefit,
becoming the wealthiest farmer in the province and a powerful local
official, feared and respected by all, including those mandarins
ensconced in power at higher administrative levels.

He was a tall and imposing man, with a square face where a large
nose and bulging eyes figured prominently, and with a general
constitution well suited to the rice fields or perhaps a military career.
When he was young, he was able to till twice as much land in one day
as men of his age. That was partly how he built up his fortune, working
his own family's acreage, renting out his labor to others, then, through
shrewd negotiations, began to expand his land holdings.

He soon stopped touching the plow or guiding a buffalo. He
started to hire others to farm his land as he began trading in rice and
joined the ranks of the merchant class. He was a cunning and ruthless
businessman, and used those character traits to great advantage in his
dealings.

Throughout the years, no matter what new venture he started, he somehow managed to always win the better part of a deal and add to his fortune and power each time. Those who opposed him were crushed sooner or later, while the rest came under his dominance, owing him favors and returning them by carrying out his orders with complete faith in his business acumen as well as his political wisdom.

He had hired the best craftsmen and builders to come to the village and rebuild the ancestral home, transforming it into the compound that it is now. Costly ironwood timber was purchased and hauled in from distant provinces to make the main columns and frame.

Feng shui masters were hired to design the garden surrounding the house, making sure that natural energy flowed through the compound, the house and the main rooms where the family lived. He believed that his business and his authority have both increased as a result. He was a man blessed by the gods and worshipped by his friends and minions. He was a real dragon, the literal meaning of his name, Long.

He was also practically illiterate, relying on others to read and write for him those Chinese characters that he never had the time or the patience to learn. However, once he became wealthy he married the self-effacing but well-schooled daughter of a poor teacher from a neighboring village, and their son had inherited from his wife a natural aptitude for books and learning. While he had wished for a boy physically more in his image, Xã Long immediately saw a future mandarin when the boy was just a toddler being informally educated by his mother.

As soon as they could, they sent their son to the village school where another young boy, the village teacher's own, had already started at an even earlier age. The two became rivals, with his son always struggling to keep up with the other boy. Xã Long did not like that, but he couldn't do anything to change the situation. His wife, who knew her Chinese characters, was able to help a little bit, but it didn't make much difference. Xã Long suspected the village teacher of favoring his own son, but he had no proof of any bias, and even if he did, what could he do about it?

When the old village teacher passed away, he sent Chí at once to a school in Hà Nội to study under one of the best scholars of in the old capital city. He did not want his son to be studying under his young rival who had succeeded his father and became the new village teacher. That move to Hà Nội obviously paid off. His son was now a *Tiến Sĩ* (presented scholar) and the new Prefect, while his rival had failed shamefully. Chí came home as a mandarin with a royal appointment, whereas his disgraced rival had to resume the life of a humble village teacher.

Xã Long already noticed the increase in deference and politeness accorded him in his dealings with workers, merchants, and government officials. People were whispering behind his back that he was the father of the newly appointed Prefect. There had been an increase in traffic of eager matrons from far and near coming to visit his wife, bearing small gifts and making open suggestions as to the matrimonial possibilities with this and that young lady. There used to be many visitors who came to his compound, but lately the traffic had doubled. He was sure that his wife would do the initial screening of the possible future daughter-in-laws, and that he would review the final slate and decide on the one lucky enough to be picked.

That is why his daughter's whispering toward the end of the banquet had kept him up until now. He was sitting in the family's hall, surrounded by his wife and his daughter, waiting for Chí to make his appearance. All, except may be Kim Liên, were tired but they were willing to endure it to find out the truth.

His daughter took her constitution and her character after him, Xã Long thought. She was taller than most women, with a full figure, and it was rumored that she could lift a heavy sack of rice as well as any strong man. Like him, she disdained bookish learning and stopped going to school as soon as she could get away with it.

Since then, she had, by sheer obstinacy, taken over the running of the household, demoting the older women to supporting roles. They and the servants were as terrified of her as they were impressed by her determination to get things done, from preparing daily meals to organizing that evening's banquet, an elaborate affair without equal in the village's history.

Lately he had started to let her accompany him in business dealings, and she proved to be as astute and fierce as he was, to the point where some people would rather deal with him hoping to get some concession or some advantage that they could never get from her.

He often wondered if anybody could be the man to tame this female tiger that he had brought up. If only his son could be as decisive as she was, he would have had nothing to worry about.

He decided to ask his daughter the question that had been on his mind.

"The girl you are talking about, isn't she the daughter of that farmer at the other end of the village, Cả Nguyên, the one that rents a few acres from us?"

"That's the one, Father. I know her from when I was still attending the village school. She started there when I was in my last year."

"Wouldn't that make her about ten years, younger than your brother? Not that it would matter anyway," he sighed, suddenly remembering a certain woman who was also quite young when he first and last set his eyes on her.

Kim Liên was quick to note the sudden change in her father's expression, but she had no inkling as to what caused it.

"Yes, and she has a cute face which makes her look even younger. She must have caught my brother's eyes from a very young age. People tell me she's the teacher's favorite."

"Which one? The old one or the young one?"

"Both in fact. She was like a daughter to the old one, and like a favorite sister to the younger one," Kim Liên answered, feeling some uneasiness about the second part of her answer. She remembered the village teacher admonishing her earlier that afternoon when he came to the defense of Thi. She had felt jealous then, wondering why the village teacher had come so readily to the defense of the object of her bullying.

"So, let your brother come and tell me and your mother that he wants the girl," her father continued. "Then we'll talk to her parents."

"Don't worry, husband. I will take care of it," his wife said, finally joining the conversation.

She was a thin woman, with a face that rarely showed emotions, but her eyes did not shy away from challenging her husband when needed. She was content to let him run his business, but she thought it was her privilege to worry about her children's future, especially that of her son, her favorite.

"You stay out of it and don't say anything at all," she said. "He does not have to marry that little girl, and in fact he can pick any wife from the list that I have drawn up these past few weeks. You know, if you had not sent him to the big city, we would have gotten him married several years ago, and you would be playing with your grandchildren now. If only you had listened to me."

"Listen to you? He would still be nothing in this village, if he had stayed here," Xã Long shouted, not liking his decisions criticized. "It's only because I made him go away that we now have a Prefect in this house. If he had married earlier, this may not have happened and he would still be holding on to his wife's pants!"

"In any case, that little girl would have been too young a few years ago," Kim Liên tried to steer them back to the subject at hand. "As it is, she's barely seventeen."

Xã Long was still furious and unrelenting toward his wife.

"What about your daughter here? Why aren't you worried about finding her a suitable party? She is now older than you were when we got married."

At this, before her mother had a chance to answer, Kim Liên quickly shouted.

"Don't you two worry about me!"

"I know, you and your father will decide whom and when you should marry," her mother said sadly. She had long ago given up on her headstrong daughter. "Village Chief, what should I do when your daughter won't listen to me?"

While his parents and sister were discussing his matrimonial future, Chí had a long talk with the captain in charge of the contingent of soldiers assigned to his protection. Not having the slightest military training himself, he wanted to be sure the officer understood that security matters were in his hands.

He was aghast at what he found. All the soldiers were in various states of inebriation. The more sober ones smiled at him stupidly, the rest were snoring loudly and the storeroom where they slept reeked of alcoholic fumes. No guards were posted anywhere as a result. The captain himself was red faced, fighting in vain to show that he was still in control of his faculties and his men.

He promised that he would have his soldiers stand on guard duty, but anybody could tell that there was no one in any condition to deliver on that promise. Fortunately, thought the Prefect, they were safe within the compound walls right in the center of a peaceful village that had not seen war in his entire life.

In a few more days, they would be moving to the provincial capital, and soon after that, as ordered by the King, he was to initiate a new campaign against the remnants of the Black Flag bandits.

Would he, a bookish scholar, be able to conduct a successful campaign against them? He had been told that a separate contingent was also converging on the capital and would be placed under his authority, thus giving him a sizable combined force. That was the only comforting aspect of the new and challenging situation that came with his appointment papers. Still, there were too many unknowns, and the initial euphoria of passing the examinations had given way to mounting feelings of anxiety and self-doubt.

Earlier that afternoon, he had experienced another disappointing encounter. He needed a Zhuge Liang to advise him, and his old classmate Tâm had many of the qualities, including intelligence and erudition, that the legendary adviser to Liu Bei in the Three Kingdoms was reputed to possess.

After noticing the village teacher in the crowd welcoming his procession, he had summoned him to his house. Liu Bei had gone to find Zhuge Liang three different times before being allowed to meet the Sleeping Dragon, but this was different. Even though he conceded that Tâm was very well learned and well respected, he had already known him for many years, and there was no reason for a Prefect with a royal appointment to have to call on a village teacher already disgraced by his failure at the examinations.

His former rival arrived with little ceremony in a well-worn tunic and without a headdress. Sitting in front of him, Chí had put on a show of modesty, conceding that but for a slight touch of the brush, the village teacher would have been in his place in that day's procession. The village teacher showed no reaction and just sat there waiting for him to come to the real purpose of the visit.

He offered the position of assistant to the Prefect and described in vain how his former classmate would benefit from it. Other people would have jumped at the opportunity to serve and to receive not only a steady official income but also the chance to amass a personal fortune with the fringe benefits resulting from such an influential position in the province. The village teacher, sitting with his back straight, listened to him without emotion, and in the end flatly rejected his offer.

"At least tell me why you don't want the post?" an exasperated Chí demanded.

"I don't want to leave this place without a teacher. This is where my father taught many generations of village children. I want to continue his legacy."

"There will be plenty of others willing to take over the village school," Chí retorted, raising his voice and waving his hands in frustration. "Our village is not that poor and we can attract the best teacher here. Now tell me what the real reason is."

"Another reason is that I have no desire to become an official and work in government."

"Why did you go take the examinations then?"

"I saw them as a personal challenge. I wanted to find out whether I would measure up to the best scholars in our nation. But I really felt better after I failed, and I am now very happy teaching again, helping children learn and grow to be better adults with a good education. I thank you for your offer and sincerely wish you success as a Prefect. The people need someone that will help and not be a burden on them."

Chí was puzzled by that last comment. "Of course, that's what a good mandarin is for, and I intend to fulfill my duties in exactly that spirit."

"Well, perhaps you could start by not forcing people to make contributions to your own banquet."

With those words Tâm stood up.

"What are you implying?" Chí remained seated but leaned back and pointed a shaky finger at the village teacher. "Who has been forced to do anything? What contributions? Don't you even think of leaving without telling me!"

"Your Excellency, please ask your sister, if you really want to know."

That's how their conversation had ended. As the village teacher walked out, the new Prefect sat in his chair, furious at his inability to come back with anything against this first accusation in his new career.

As it happened, throughout the rest of the day he did not get a chance to talk to his sister alone. During the banquet, he watched every dish being passed around and only reluctantly picked at one small piece from a plate of boiled chicken covered with green scallions that his mother placed in front of him and repeatedly asked him to eat. Afterwards, he was glad that his father summoned him to come to the main house. Knowing that his sister would be there, he went in, eager to get at the bottom of the matter.

The three of them were seated on lacquered chairs inlaid with oyster shell and made of the same ironwood used to build the house. As usual, his father and sister were doing all the talking, while his mother said little. His father immediately took the initiative.

"Your mother and I have been thinking about finding a suitable wife for you so that you'll have somebody by your side when you go to your new post. In fact, that's all that your mother has been concerned with ever since the good news about you came to us. But..."

"Father, Mother, you shouldn't worry," Chí interrupted his father, but Xã Long was not a man used to yielding to anyone in a conversation.

"Listen to me. You now are a grown-up man with an important appointment and a bright future ahead of you. Your mother has been talking with various families, inquiring about their daughters who may be worthy of you. But today your sister has told me that you already have your eyes on the daughter of the Nguyên at the other end of our village. You have known her for a long time, way back when you used to attend the village school. Is that true?"

Chí turned to his sister with a frown.

"Kim Liên, who asked you to get involved in this?"

"Never mind that," the father quickly came to his daughter's defense. "She is your sister after all and has only your best interest at heart. The important thing is for you to let us know whether what she said is true."

"I don't know," the young Prefect answered gruffly.

"What do you mean? Do you like her or do you not like her? It's that simple. Or, is your sister just relating to us some baseless gossip? Should your mother and I take appropriate steps and start the arrangements?"

As his sister looked intently at him before rolling her eyes and turning away, Chí took his time in answering the barrage of questions thrown at him.

"I don't know because I have never said anything to her."

"And that's the way it should be. You don't just go out, meet a girl, and propose to her on your own. Marriages have to follow our customs and traditions. We'll need to retain a matchmaker who will approach her parents to obtain her birth date and time. Then we'll consult an astrologer to see that your ages are compatible. If the stars are propitious, we'll have a ceremony to inform her parents officially of our marriage proposal and commitment. After that, we'll have another ceremony to decide on an auspicious date for the wedding, then another one to inform the girl's parents of the date. Finally comes the actual wedding day when you will go receive the bride from her parents and bring her back to our home. That's how it was done for your mother and I, and that's how it should be done for you too. Let us, the parents and the elders, handle these matters so that they are properly carried out according to tradition. If that's the one you want to marry, all you have to do it to tell us."

"Here I am, a Prefect appointed by the King, with power of life and death over thousands of people," Chí thought to himself. "But Father does not think that I am an adult capable of making my own life decisions."

His mother, who had maintained her usual silence, finally chimed in.

"Husband, it's not that our son does not want to follow tradition. Maybe he's not yet sure about his feelings for the girl. Are you, Chí? I am told she's fairly pretty, and she comes from a good family, but do we know about her character and her moral qualities?"

Seeing her brother remaining silent, Kim Liên answered for him with a malicious grin.

"What he really means when he said he didn't know is this: he is not sure whether the girl likes him or not. In all these years in Hà Nội, away from our village, he has been pining for her, but perhaps his love has been of the unrequited kind."

The expression on her brother's face told her the situation was exactly what she had described.

"Daughter, why do you tease your brother like that?" their mother said. Ever since she knew how to speak, Kim Liên had a knack for embarrassing and skewering her older brother without mercy at the slightest provocation and even without any provocation.

Xã Long also came to the help of his son.

"Nonsense! Who wouldn't want to marry your brother, the most eligible scholar, the one who won a royal appointment? Love has nothing to do with marriage. In this case, we are even going a little bit against tradition because we are asking your brother's opinion of the girl first. In my time, children just agree to the spouse their parents pick for them. Their ages, their destiny as revealed by the stars, the family positions, the morals of the groom and bride, all these factors contribute to a successful marriage. Love does not lead to but follows from marriage."

After satisfying himself that nobody was challenging his views, he added.

"Chí, you are much too reserved. You do not yet appreciate the importance of your position, and the full extent of your power and influence. Around the province, there are hundreds of families with daughters of marrying age and they all have their eyes on you. This Nguyên girl may not yet be aware of your interest in her, but let your mother and I send a matchmaker to her parents. In no time, you, my son, will have the wife of your dream, while you, my daughter, will have a sister-in-law that you can put under your tutelage, isn't that right? Or will it be the other way around, since as the wife of your older brother she will outrank you? Ha, ha, ha!"

"That, I'll have to see," Kim Liên joined her father in laughter, but she remembered that afternoon's scene when Thi did not look like someone to be easily intimidated.

Confronted by the whirlwind of questions and declamations surrounding his matrimonial prospect, the new Prefect forgot what he was going to ask his sister. He left the room to go and collapse onto his bed. He slept badly, turning and thrashing throughout the rest of the night. The bed, also made of ironwood, did not make a sound.

After everybody had left, Xã Long pulled and puffed on his water pipe then sat back in his chair reminiscing. The nicotine in the tobacco stimulated his sleepy brain and brought back things he had never shared with anyone. Unlike his son, he had always been bold and aggressive with his women, taking them by guile or, when necessary, by force.

He had not thought about it for many years, but he remembered exactly how it happened. After a late night banquet, he went to the outhouse to relieve himself in the early hours of the morning. When he reached it, he saw a woman walking by, with a swinging gait and light footsteps. She gasped in surprise and had to stop sharply when he confronted her.

Even in the faint mist of dawn, he could tell that she was comely and well-built, with shapely lines in the right places. He moved toward her and quickly had her in his embrace. She fought back to get out of his grip with a strength unusual even for a country woman. However, he was in the prime of his youth and, like a wild boar, pinned her on the ground and forced himself on her. Her cries for help followed by woeful sobs were wasted in the emptiness of the early morning. When he was finished, she got up, ran away, and disappeared into the fog, never to be seen again.

Gold Farmers

In 1865, after the Taiping rebellion, the Black Flags Army (*Quân Cờ Đen*) commanded by Liu Yongfu spilled over from China into Việt Nam, invited there by Emperor Tự Đức, the reigning monarch at that time. Although they initially helped the Vietnamese government pacify local uprisings and defeat French forces in at least two famous battles, they soon became the de facto oppressors in the areas that they controlled, levying taxes and pillaging at will. As the better-equipped French continued their attacks, the Black Flags began to suffer serious setbacks, incurring heavy casualties. Meanwhile the longer they stayed in Việt Nam, the more unreliable resupply from China became. Food could be obtained by force from the population that they terrorized, but weapons and ammunitions had to come from China, which itself was falling apart under foreign pressure and internal uprisings against the Qing regime.

Some of the Black Flags started to withdraw across the border to go back to their bases, or to go home because they were weary after years of fighting. Finally, when China and France signed the peace treaty of 1885, which ended Chinese influence and firmly established French colonization in Việt Nam, the Black Flags were given the order to withdraw to China. Most did, but a small number remained in the country where they merged with local anti-French groups or bandits in order to survive.

The same night of the banquet for the new Prefect, a man came to a small house separated from the rest of the village by many fields in all directions. The isolation was intentional and mutually agreed upon by the owners of the house and the rest of the villagers.

There were many terms for what the occupants of the house did for a living, from mispronounced to lofty words, depending on how polite one wanted to be. The man and woman who lived in the house practiced a trade that was essential to most human societies, namely getting the night soil produced by humans and carting it away to a safe distance where its sight and smell would not offend the visual and olfactory senses. What they worked on was referred to as "gold", or simply as "fertilizer" with a different intonation. What they carted away was laid out on their own fields, and left there until most of the smell went away via evaporation. Sunlight and especially its ultraviolet rays did the rest of the work in killing bacteria and converting the human waste into a useful product.

Later on, the so called "gold" farmers resold the naturally treated waste as fertilizer to the village farmers. Collection was something they did every day of the year, except when they were sick or during the Lunar New Year or Tết festivities. Generations of the same clan had been doing it for hundreds of years in this village and in the surrounding ones. While farmers willingly paid for their services and the products of those same services, most people looked down on these practitioners, much as the Dalit in India or the Eta in Japan were for centuries. They were the tainted and unclean outcasts to be avoided and denied normal human contact regardless of their value or usefulness to society.

The woman in the house, Phạm Thị Cơ, came from a long line of gold farmers, while her husband, Vũ Văn Khang, was an outsider who married into the clan. Unless they were willing to marry distant relatives from other parts of the country, the young men and women of gold farmers often had difficulty attracting mates who would not mind being drawn into a career that most people considered disgusting or demeaning.

For what would they say when someone asked them what they or their parents did for a living? People always gave them a wide berth when they encountered them on the road with their bamboo poles and their two buckets of "gold", so what chances did they have to strike a conversation and become acquainted with a person from outside of the clan? Therefore, from time to time, clan members, mainly from the younger generations, would leave and go to distant provinces to work in other occupations, and never come back to their roots.

In Cơ's case, her parents decided to marry her off at the age of 16 to a boy who was only half her age. He came from a poor family with too many mouths to feed, and his parents gave him away so that the rest of them would not starve. After the simplest of marriage ceremony, Cơ lived a chaste life with her boy husband, sleeping at his side like a big sister with a younger sibling. This lasted for many years.

The couple was sleeping when a hand knocked lightly on their door. She heard it first, listened for a second knock then rose from the bed to grope her way to the front door of their house.

"Mother, it's me."

She hurriedly opened the door, and as soon as it was wide enough the black shape of a man slid into the house.

"Don't make any noise and let your father sleep," she whispered.

She managed to light an oil lamp and brought it closer to her son before taking his hand and leading him to the kitchen in the back of the one-room house. She seized his shoulders, looking into a handsome face with bright eyes and a sensuous mouth. She saw a little bit of herself in it, briefly regretting the beauty that had faded from her own face under the cumulative effect of time and the punishing work she had to perform day after day.

"Why are you coming here at this hour of the night? Are you well? Are you hungry?"

"Mother, I came to see you," Vũ Văn Chính replied and tried not to wrinkle his nose at the faint smell that he used to be so familiar with when he was growing up in the house. "I am fine, everything is fine, and I already ate. How are you and Father?"

She looked back to the dark corner where her husband slept, then said.

"We are still the same, but we are not getting younger. Your father and I can still handle our work, but who knows a few years from now. What about you, are you still trading with those merchants?"

Both of them knew what she meant. He was their only child, and when he left both husband and wife realized that there would be nobody to continue their work after them. For her, it meant that five generations of gold farmers would come to an end and she was powerless to do anything about it. It was out of the question for them to have another child. She was too old for that and besides they had tried for many years before but she could never conceive again after giving birth to her only son.

Every time he stopped by to visit them, she would gently remind him of the problem of succession that his going away had left her. At first, he kept making it clear that he had left the clan for good. Lately, he had not even tried to reject her. He simply talked about other topics, as he proceeded to do then.

"Business is good, and my partners and I are on the verge of making a good deal soon. A few more like this one, and we'll have our future assured! By the way, I heard the village has a new mandarin and he had a big homecoming today. The Nguyễn Hữu clan will be even more unbearable from now on."

She kept silent, contenting herself to peer into her son's face, one where thin lines due to a combination of age and perhaps hardships had begun to appear. He continued.

"They say he does not measure up to Teacher Tâm, and he'll be a bad mandarin and a burden to society."

"Son, we don't pay much attention to what people say, and it's not going to affect us one way or another anyway."

Chính continued, ignoring her comment.

"When I was attending the village school, I knew that Teacher Tâm's father tried his best to encourage other students, like the Village Chief's son, to compete with his own son, but nobody could ever surpass him in any subject. Not only that, but brother Tâm was always willing to help the rest of us study, while Chí never came to anybody's aid. He always kept to himself, as if he was too good for the rest of us."

"Too bad you did not continue with your studies, son. You were doing well until you quit and left home," his mother sighed.

"I did not want to attend the school for free without making any contribution, like all the others did. It was embarrassing, even though neither Teacher Tâm, nor his father before him, ever raised the subject. What good would education do for me anyway, if I were to continue our clan's occupation? As it is, at least I am using some of what I learned in my business dealings."

The sleeping father turned on the creaking bamboo bed and mumbled in his sleep. Mother and son kept quiet until the sound of regular breathing reassured them that he had gone on sleeping.

"They say that you are associating yourself with some seedy characters," she had lowered her voice even more. "Is that true? Are you sure you are all right?"

"Mother, don't listen to what people say. I am fine, don't worry about me."

She wanted to ask him why he never came to visit her in daytime, instead of sneaking in at night. She needed to tell him of her doubts and her fears, but she knew from previous visits that it was pointless. She was afraid that too many questions would only drive him away even more. Finally, deep inside her, she was afraid of finding out the truth about her son's career.

He interrupted her thoughts.

"Mother, I have to go now."

"Wait until it becomes lighter, I'll prepare something for you to eat."

"My friends are waiting for me, I have to go now."

"You are not going to drink or party with them, are you?"

He almost laughed out loud before whispering into her ear.

"Actually, we are going to go join the new Prefect's party."

"Don't joke about that!" she exclaimed. "They never invite people like us. Besides, I heard he even brought soldiers with him, and they will chase you away for sure if you come near them."

"Mother, go back to sleep, and stop worrying about me."

Just as quickly as he had come in, Chính slid out of the house and disappeared into the darkness. His mother stood at the half open door, forlorn and uneasy at her son's bantering.

In the darkness that her eyes had gotten used to, she went to kneel before the small altar where she kept a bowl filled with rice and ash for burning incense in front of a small clay statue of the Buddha. She took out her prayer beads, and began reciting the Tâm Kinh (Heart Sutra) that the village teacher's uncle had taught her. The 260 words came to her easily, and though she would never have claimed to fully grasp their meaning, their sounds and rhythm eventually soothed her. She went over the final mantra several times, each time weaker than the previous one, until her mouth only exhaled breath and no sound.

Yết đế Yết đế Ba la Yết đế Ba la tăng Yết đế
Bồ-đề Tát bà ha

(Gone, gone, gone over, gone fully over.
Awakened! So be it!)

When she finally went to lie down beside her husband, she saw that his eyes were open and looking at the ceiling. His question was not unexpected.

"Did he tell you what he was really doing for a living?"

"No, he didn't," she sighed.

Later that night, Kim Liên was returning from the small bath house next to the kitchen where she had taken a bath and changed into loose fitting clothes in preparation for going to bed. Her unbanded hair was hanging loosely, reaching all the way to the small of her back. The rest of the house was asleep, with sounds of loud snoring coming from the direction of the storeroom where the soldiers stayed. She gritted her teeth, hoping that she wouldn't hear the disgusting noises once she reached her bed. Suddenly, just before she got to the main house, she saw dark shapes appear at her right. Before she could scream or say anything, a hand was firmly clamped over her mouth while both of her arms were forcefully pinned down. The men, who worked in total silence, soon had her tied to one of the pillars supporting the roof extending from the main house to the kitchen. A piece of cloth was strapped across her mouth before being bound tightly in the back of her head. Terrified and trembling she watched in fascination as the men moved toward the storeroom where the soldiers slept.

She thought there was going to be a fight or at least some kind of commotion once the bandits went into the storeroom. To her consternation, nothing happened for what seemed like a long time. Eventually, the men returned, each carrying rifles or other bundles unfamiliar to her. As soon as they cleared the door, they ran toward the rear where she knew there was a gate to the gardens and fields at the back of the house.

Finally, a man who acted like their leader, came out. He walked directly to where she was. In the darkness, she saw that his face was covered with a black cloth like the rest of his men. He untied her from the pillar quickly but left her gag on and did not touch the remaining ties around her arms and chest. He dragged her up firmly, then started walking away, pulling her by a strand of her ties. She groaned but no sound came out, and she had no choice but to follow him, feeling like a clumsy buffalo following its owner. She tried to drag her feet to slow down the bandit, but he just tugged harder. As she tripped and pitched forward, the man turned around and steadied her with one arm. He shook his head without saying a word, a dagger suddenly appearing in his hand. With one motion, he made her understand that he was ready to cut her throat if she did not come with him quietly. He then turned forward and yanked at the chord with renewed vigor, leading her into the night.

It was mid-morning before the weary household finally woke up and made two shocking discoveries: most of the soldiers' rifles had disappeared, and the young mistress of the house was nowhere to be found. Her clothes, those she had changed from before going to bed, were scattered near a pillar. Four of the hens contributed by the village and kept for the day's meals had also vanished.

The young Prefect was furious. He rebuked the captain while soldiers went into all directions looking for the missing young woman and weaponry. There were many footsteps on the small dikes separating the fields in the back of the house, but they could have easily been made by the farmhands who had been up at sunrise and gone to their work all around the village.

Xã Long, accustomed to handling crises, managed to keep his anger under control and began assuming his role of village leader. He ignored his wife, her tears and wails, and, seeing that his son was not accustomed to decisive action, took things in hand. He sent servants to go to the village notables, including the village teacher, as well as the traders, landowners, and those who farm his landholdings. He asked them to seek out their own contacts to find out who the kidnappers were and, if possible, where they went. He told them to enlist all available village hands to search for his daughter in the four directions, with the village at the center and reaching as far out as possible.

The searchers went from house to house asking if anybody had heard or seen anything the previous night. Unfortunately, the only sounds and sights that most remembered were from the noisy banquet and the drunken guests as they left for home. The volunteers ranged far and wide, going into the surrounding villages to ask anyone that they saw. Rumors spread swiftly as people assembled in small groups and exchange information, real or imagined. Some were sure that Xã Long's daughter had fled to join the Cần Vương movement, taking away half of the soldiers and their arms with her. Others knew that she had a lover in the Black Flags and went to join him in the mountains bordering the province to the Northwest. By the time the rumors got back to Xã Long, they were even more elaborate and as far from truth or reality as possible.

As soon as he was contacted, Tâm gave a day off to the whole school and, after sending the younger children home, asked his older students to join him in the search. Before starting, he walked around the school and looked in all directions to try to see where the soldiers and people from the village had gone. They were everywhere, some in the village going from door to door, others out on the main roads, and even more in the distance in animated conversations with field hands.

Out to the West of the village, the hardest working couple was straining under their loads of night soil, walking firmly with their rhythmic gait toward their own fields. As usual, nobody was following them, and they were probably unaware of the village's unfolding crisis. He wondered if anybody had thought of asking them. Since they were among the first people in the village to wake up to do their work, was it possible that they saw something, anything, connected to the kidnapping of the Village Chief's daughter? As an uneasy feeling began to take hold inside him, Tâm told his students to team up and form small groups before fanning out throughout the village. They did so quickly and he watched them walk away for some time before he finally headed in the direction where he last saw the couple of gold farmers who were then mere dots on the horizon.

Although he was fit and walked swiftly, he still found it hard to catch up with his targets. He followed the rice levees, zigzagging through the green sea of undulating rice plants, trying not to lose sight of the couple. Hearing the sound of footsteps behind him, he turned and saw Thi hurrying after him. He stopped and waited for her.

"Teacher, let me go with you," she said as she caught up with him.

"Are you sure? I am going to talk to Chính's parents other there."

She nodded, remembering the brawny and cheerful lad who preceded her by a few years in the village school. Since he left the school and the village a few years ago, she had not thought much about him until just then.

"Fine, let's walk at full speed and try to catch them," Teacher Tâm said.

By the time Tâm and Thi reached their house, the husband and wife had dumped their loads onto a field, and then washed their hands and feet quickly to prepare to receive the visitors they had seen walking toward them. People rarely came near them, and they were wholly unprepared for the village teacher whom they had not seen in several years. The pretty young girl accompanying him looked vaguely familiar, and was probably from the village, but they could not tell from what family. Neither appeared to mind the strong smell permeating the area, or at least they did not show it. Standing in front of their house, the couple bowed respectfully to Teacher Tâm. The husband looked younger than his wife, who was almost as tall as him. Though she was clearly older, her face was pleasant to look at and she smiled brightly as she spoke first.

"Teacher, we are honored that you came to visit us. Is there something that we may help you with?"

"Well, something happened in the village," answered Tâm. "You probably have not heard about it yet, but the Chief's daughter is missing, and everybody is out looking for her. The soldiers accompanying the new Prefect also reported that they lost some of their weapons."

Before he could go on, the woman paled and suddenly grasped her husband's arm. The latter looked uneasily away, unwilling to meet the village teacher's eyes. The couple stood rooted in place, mute and nervous, their expression betraying the fear that came over them. Tâm turned slightly to one side and looked back at the rest of the houses in the village spreading from North to South in the distance. Thi glanced at the couple, then at her teacher, already guessing most of the truth.

For a long time, Tâm had been hearing rumors that his former student had joined the mixed band of bandits and Black Flag remnants based in the nearby mountains and forests. Initially, he had not given them much credence. An educated man would never turn to banditry, he thought, and Vũ Văn Chính, although he quit school early, had a good mind and a good-natured temperament. Chính came from one of the poorer families in the village, but his parents were honest, worked hard, and were willing to send their son to the village school to get an education, rather than relying on him to shoulder part of their work. Both Tâm and his father had declined to accept any tuition or contribution in kind from the family and allowed their son to attend the school free. The boy showed promise, and there was hope of a better future for Chính. However, one day he stopped showing up for class, and soon afterwards the rumors began. In a small village, there was usually some truth in most rumors.

Now, the reaction of both parents after he had barely told them what happened the previous night could only confirm his worst fears. He turned toward the mother.

"You have to tell me how your son is involved in all this. Tell me everything, for I need to know the truth to see if there is some way I can help you. "

Worries

Being the only daughter and the youngest child in the family of farmer Cả Nguyên had many advantages, not the least of which was being spoiled, thought Thi. Her father called her his princess, her brothers teasingly addressed her as Your Highness, and all spared no effort to please her. Everybody always tried their best to spare her the slightest physical exertion, even though she was no longer a child, and had all the strength needed to do most things.

She was visiting her taro field, a small plot of land next to their home that her oldest brother had tilled for her. She had planted the corms, in neat and evenly spaced rows, and then declared that she alone would tend the field. She weeded it every chance she got, fertilized it from time to time with chicken manure, kept it watered when there was no rain, and harvested the mature bulbs for family consumption and for others. For her, the taro plot had another benefit. The plants grew quite fast and reached their full height within a few months. She could sit among the tall plants and nobody could see her under their lush canopy.

Red dragonflies fluttered and darted around her. She gazed dreamily at them, knowing that they were doing their job of eating smaller insects harmful to her plants. In flight, their movements mirrored her worried thoughts. They went up and down, or sometimes flew sideways to the left or right. That's what she had been doing since the village teacher left. She had been alternating between worry and hope. She had thought much about why he had decided to go on his mission, coming up with various reasons, none of which satisfied her.

Like the dragonflies, she kept veering from one reason to another, not settling on any.

Right after they took leave of Chính's parents, she had gone home in haste. The house was deserted. She entered the kitchen and took out a taro bulb that she had boiled in the morning. She quartered it, wrapped the quarters in banana leaves and tied the bundle with a thin strip of bamboo, then ran back to the school as fast as she could. The village teacher was preparing to leave and was packing a small travel bundle to carry with him.

As soon as she saw her, his mother lamented.

"Thi, your teacher is leaving again! Can you believe it? And it seems like he just came home yesterday. If only he had told me in advance, I could have made some rice balls for him. As it is, I have nothing for him to take."

"Mother, it's all right," Teacher Tâm said. "It won't take me so long this time, and I can buy what I need along the way."

"Teacher, please take this," Thi said haltingly as she tried to catch her breath, offering her package with both hands. "It's some taro that I cooked this morning."

"Thi, you shouldn't have. And this is really too big for one person..."

"That's because you have never seen a whole taro bulb from her plot," his mother explained. "When she brings us the sweet taro soup or the fried patties that you like so much, you can never tell how big the corms were. She is such a good gardener, in addition to being a talented cook. She will make somebody a good wife some day. "

If there was a hint somewhere in those last words, her son did not catch it or, if he did, he chose not to respond.

After that, he had left the school, leaving the two women standing at the gate, watching him until he went out of sight.

Squatting in her taro field, well hidden from casual eyes, Thi was pulling weeds reflexively. Her thoughts kept returning to the village teacher and the improbable task that he was undertaking. He had asked her not to tell anyone about the conversation they had with Chính's parents, and she understood why. But she worried about the danger he would be facing. Stories about the cruelty and violence of the Black

Flags were well known throughout the country. She had never paid much attention to them, but now, as she recalled hearing about them, she was uneasy.

From the day that she entered the school village, brought there by her father, she had looked up to Tâm. He was the same age as her oldest brother, who had also attended the same school but quit after only a year, claiming himself fit only for farming and physical labor. Her two other brothers were given a similar chance, and both quit after the same half-hearted attempts. While they were still studying, she discovered that she could learn the Chinese characters by just peeking at their homework. They gave her the nickname of Miss Character (*Cô Chữ*) and nobody was surprised when she asked to be allowed to go to school, one of the very few girls to do so.

She became the favorite of both the old village teacher and his son, Tâm. The former treated her as if she were a daughter that he had always wished for but never had. The latter treated her like a baby sister from the time she entered the village school, playing with her as well as helping her with school work. She in turn made sure he never needed to show or explain to her anything more than once, while freely enjoying herself with a surrogate brother who didn't mind giving her piggy back rides or participating in the children games that she pulled him into.

Things changed when the older teacher passed away and Tâm suddenly had to assume his father's duties. While nobody inside or outside of the school challenged his qualifications, he was no longer playful with his students. He began acting toward her more like a teacher and less like an older brother. He became reserved after school, although his mother continued to call her Little Thi and treated her like the member of the family that she had been all those years.

After initially feeling rejected and upset, Thi came around to understand why he had changed. Still, deep inside her she longed for the simple joys of childhood and the special bonds that existed between them. When he left to participate in the national exams, she had looked forward to his triumphal return. She kept glancing involuntarily toward the point where the road emerged from the hill to descend toward the village, hoping to catch the first sight of him. When news came that he had not succeeded, she waited patiently for his return to go to the village school and console him.

She was surprised to see him apparently quite happy to be back in the small village school, ready to teach again. He was well tanned and thinner, but otherwise suffered no ill effect from his travel. His clothes were almost threadbare, his hair had grown longer and was tied in the back of his head, unrestrained by any headdress. He looked less like the ascetic village teacher that he was before he left, and had become more open and kinder to all. He still maintained a discreet distance with her, but she was accustomed to that. Deep inside, she knew that turning back to the times of their childhood was no longer possible.

Prefect Chí went to see his father and found him seated at a small table in a corner of the main room, drawing a long puff from his water pipe. As the older man exhaled the smoke, his half-closed eyes were fixed on his son, who couldn't see through the billowing smoke and guess what his father's mood was.

"Father, we still have no news about my sister. We have been searching everywhere for the past two days. We questioned everybody in the village, as well as those from surrounding villages, and haven't come up with anything significant. I myself have participated in some of these searches, and I can tell you that my men have been very thorough."

"I knew all that. What else do you want to tell me?"

Xã Long had come to realize that his son still had to learn a lot from the school of life. The detachment of soldiers had unearthed nothing but unverified rumors, while their captain was only very imaginative with newer and more exaggerated excuses for losing their weapons and for the kidnapping of Kim Liên.

His son had also given a lot of orders and ran around here and there to no effect. Xã Long too had been very active, sending out couriers and contacting his business associates in all four directions to ferret out any possible information about his daughter. His network, which worked so well all these years, provided little help this time. He also had come up with nothing that was credible, becoming irritated with himself, his son, and anybody else that came near him.

"I am going to have to leave today for the provincial capital," his son continued. "I've delayed my departure too long already, and I need to go there as soon as possible. I will not forget my sister's situation, and in fact, I will have more resources available to me once I arrive at my new post. Another contingent of soldiers will be arriving from down South and will meet me there."

"Will they be the same kind soldiers that came with you here? People who do nothing but eat and get drunk at our expenses? People who talk in their strange Central accent and scare everybody that they question? Nobody understands half of what they say anyway!"

"Those who will be arriving will have better officers," his son countered, conceding the poor quality of the men and the captain who escorted him home. "There will even be some French officers and soldiers with them."

The Village Chief remained skeptical and he raised his voice in exasperation.

"Are a few more Frenchmen going to make that much of a difference? What do they know about our country and fighting these rebels? Remember that the Black Flags defeated them a few years ago."

"Father, don't shout," Chí raised his hands in panic. "Even walls have ears! I need to prove myself as a Prefect, and I will carry out my duties as well as I can. Meanwhile you run this village and stay out of politics. Let's just try and get my sister back and not worry about anything else."

Xã Long reluctantly agreed with his son.

"Yes, let's try and get her back here before she's caught in the middle with the rebels on one side and you and the French on the other. I don't know what I would do if anything were to happen to her."

His daughter was a female image of himself, he thought. With her gone, he could not concentrate on his daily Village Chief duties and business dealings. His wife was also distressed but could do nothing but sigh and tear up. If only his son had half of the spirit and the toughness of his sister! Except for passing an examination, what good was all this bookish learning without any practical and down-to-earth experience?

Seeing his father deep in thought, Prefect Chí attempted to change the subject.

"Father, I will be leaving soon, perhaps before midday. Afterwards, will you and Mother have time to talk to the Nguyên family?"

The Village Chief looked surprised. He had not thought at all about the subject for the past few days.

"So we are back to this issue of your own future then. I haven't forgotten about you. Your mother and I have not started anything yet, but I have known Cả Nguyên for many years. He is a good farmer and a reasonable man, and he should be more than happy to have you as a son-in-law. Who wouldn't be?"

Chí smiled for the first time since the day after the banquet.

"If you need me back here, send word up to the province, and I will come down at once."

"Of course, but these matrimonial matters usually take time. We'll need to consult an astrologer, select auspicious dates, make the arrangements, inform relatives, and there are tens of thousands of other little details. But, don't you worry! I will take care of everything for you. Now you just have to go and prove yourself to be a worthy Prefect for the King."

The Rebel Base

He managed to find his way toward the hills where Chính and his band were assumed to be based. It was not too difficult, since all he had to do was to retrace the steps that took him from the ferry back home just a few weeks earlier. He still remembered well his conversation with the ferrymen, and the young woman who came up from the capital to join the rebels. While they had not mentioned the exact location of the rebel base, he knew roughly where it was.

At the end of the second day, he came to a small town on the banks of the Red River. Men and women were working in the fields and life appeared to be normal in this corner of the land. He was tired and as soon as he saw the first inn, he wanted to stop and rest for the night.

To call it an inn was very generous. It was little more than a rustic house with apparently two rooms, the front one with low bamboo tables and chairs for travelers. He had heard that in this part of the province the Black Flags used these so-called inns for their own purposes, staffing them with sympathizers or their own men. He wondered whether he would be able to obtain from the inn owner some information about the daughter of the Village Chief and where she was taken. He also needed to rest and buy some food because the small supply he brought from home had dwindled to almost nothing.

The inn was deserted. He went to sit in one corner, wondering whether he should call out for the innkeeper. As if reading his thought, a woman came out of the back room and went directly to his table. She looked different from the people he had seen so far. Although she was dressed in the same type of brown of clothes as other women, she stood out with a complexion that was fairer than most. Her eyes shone brightly even though her face was partially hidden by the square cloth that she wrapped tightly over her head. The first words she said showed that she was not an ordinary innkeeper.

"Teacher, welcome to our humble inn."

He was surprised that she had recognized him as a teacher, because he had tried not to look like one by wearing well-worn and faded clothes. She ignored his expression and continued.

"You must be weary from your journey. Would you like something to drink, and maybe something to eat also? Today we don't have any meat, but we offer very tasty vegetarian dishes."

Something in her looked or sounded familiar. She spoke in the accent prevalent in the region, yet the words were pronounced with a precision that was unusual. He could tell that she was not a local, but he failed to guess where she came from. Her bearing was also too refined and cultivated for a mere inn maid.

"I would like some tea and whatever food you happen to have, anything simple and not expensive."

She left to go fill his order, and he heard her mumbling to herself, loud enough so that he could hear her.

"A poor village teacher, no money, sure …."

He ate the surprisingly tasty dishes, and drank tea served in a black bowl, which at first appearance looked crude. He held the bowl and examined it, admiring its uniform and smooth glaze contrasting with its irregular shape. This is no ordinary place to be serving tea in this kind of bowl, he thought to himself. The tea was green and milder than the amber or dark brown tea that he was used to drinking at home.

The inn started filling with men arriving in the company of a woman who went at once to the back room. The men sat at the remaining tables, and talked among themselves in low voices, paying him scant attention. The inn maid was entirely at ease among them, going around taking their orders. Other women brought out the drinks and food. Soon rice wine had loosened tongues, raised the volume of conversation, and the sound level in the small room rose.

The inn maid came to his table as he was finishing his meal. She looked definitely familiar and he wished she did not have half of her face hidden so he could take a better look.

"Teacher, I hope you don't mind the noise," she said with a light laugh. "These men have no respect for anybody once they start drinking."

Before he had a chance to respond, she had turned to the men and admonished them.

"We have a scholar as our guest today. You should try not to disturb him!"

The room felt silent, and Tâm felt embarrassed by the change and the attention it drew upon him.

"Please don't say that," he said. "I am just a traveler who is passing by."

They all turned to look at him.

"Are you on your way to your school, Teacher?" asked an older man.

He became wary and did not want to provide them with more details than necessary.

"Actually, I left my village school two days ago."

His questioner stared at him, contemplating for a brief interval his next question.

"Where are you heading to then?"

All eyes were now concentrated on him. The inn maid was standing toward the back of the room, a look of concern on her face. For the past few hours, as he was approaching the town, the village teacher's sixth sense had warned him that he was being watched. He saw no guard post or sentries, but he knew that his movements could not have been ignored. So this was it, this inn would be a first test of whether his instinct was right and whether he was on the right track.

"I am trying to find one of my former students. His name is Vũ Văn Chính. If you happen to know where I can find him, please let me know."

A long silence ensued, during which the inn maid and the men's leader exchanged glances. The rest of the men remained still, waiting for some unspoken signal.

"Then you are his village teacher, the one that he told us about," the older man said.

Without even waiting for Tâm to admit his identity, he continued.

"Why are you here? Did they send you? Did the new Prefect send you?"

"Nobody sent me. I came on my own, after speaking to Chính's parents. I need to speak to him and ask him to release the Village Chief's daughter."

"Why is that your concern? Are you related to her?"

"We are not related, but I am afraid that if she is not released, sooner or later the Village Chief will find out who's behind her kidnapping, and the first to suffer will be his parents."

"I believe that he did not intend to kidnap her," he continued. "He and his men raided the Village Chief's house to steal weapons and ammunitions from the Prefect's soldiers. This kidnapping was not in their plan."

Seeing no objection or denial, he went on.

"If so, why would you want to keep her? You've already obtained what you needed. She will just be a burden, and if anything happens to her, it will reflect badly on your group. As it is, people are already frightened of the Black Flags."

The older man immediately cut him short.

"We are not the Black Flags, although they sometimes claim to be our allies. We have our own just cause, and we certainly don't behave like they do. "

"Then, are you the Cần Vương members who are fighting the French?"

There was no answer, but Tâm could tell from the look on their faces that he had guessed right. He noted that they had slowly surrounded him, blocking off any avenue of escape. They no longer touched their food or drink. Earlier they were probably only making noise and pretended to be drunk. He looked at the inn maid, and saw with surprise that the woman who came with the group was now standing at her side. The inn maid had removed the square cloth from her head, and suddenly he recognized her as Cicada, the spirited young woman he met only a few weeks earlier. She was smiling at him and her eyes were as mischievous as he remembered them. Before he could speak to her, the woman at her side calmly gave an order to the men's leader in the famous court accent of Huế.

"Please send someone to bring commander Chính and escort the Village Chief's daughter down here."

"Yes, Your Highness," the man respectfully answered before giving signals to two of his men to leave and carry out the order.

Tâm was stunned at this sudden turn of events. Was the woman a member of the royal family, a princess perhaps, or a high court lady? Was it possible that his former student was now a leader in this movement, with men under his command? He got ready to stand up, but the two women had moved toward him and, with a gesture of her hand, Cicada indicated that he should remain seated.

"Remain where you are, Teacher Tâm," she said in that accent that he had not heard since he left Huế. "I knew you would recognize me sooner or later."

Pointing to the woman next to her, who was a little older and had an obvious air of authority, Cicada half-jokingly said.

"This is the inn owner."

The woman ignored her and smiled warmly at Tâm.

"Commander Chính told me about you. He speaks very highly of you, and I must say that I agree with his sentiment. As for what happened in this inn, I hope you don't mind the precautions we have taken. We always have to be on guard against the men the government sends to spy on us. Cicada recognized you from the moment you stepped into this place, but she wanted to put you to the test anyway, mainly to tease you. You know how she is."

"I am most grateful to you, Your Highness," he said.

She took off the square cloth draped over her head, revealing carefully combed and shiny black hair tied into a bun at the back. She looked like an older version of Cicada, and he wondered whether they were sisters or somehow related.

"Please don't call me that. The men can't help using those stilted forms of address when talking to me, but I prefer that you simply call me Cô Nhân instead."

As the rest of the men finished their meals, several women came out and started clearing the tables. All showed genuine respect for Cô Nhân and Cicada, and quickly carried out their work.

An evening fog had descended, engulfing the countryside around the inn with an eerie cloak of darkness. Only several candles provided small auras of light in the inn. Cô Nhân came to sit in front of him, then Cicada came with a fresh pot of tea and two more tea bowls. She set them on the table and sat down.

"I saw how you appreciated the tea bowl," she stated as she poured fresh tea into their bowls.

"It is unusual and I couldn't help admiring it. I didn't expect to find such beauty here, so far from the capital" he said contemplating the steam rising from the bowls. Then he added pensively. "Our nation must be going through trying times for a commoner like me to be sitting here having tea with you."

Looking up, he saw a poignant expression on Cô Nhân's face. She tried to smile at his veiled compliment.

"Had my uncle been crowned King, you would not have failed your examination. He would have done away with those silly rules about using taboo names," she said, reverting back to the northern local accent.

"Who knows, you may have been a high court official at this moment, having matcha in Japanese tea bowls and conversing with like-minded people. My uncle would have used you as a loyal and capable official entrusted with national duties worthy of you."

"I don't deserve such praise," he protested. "I am only a village teacher. With my limited talent, there is not much I could do to help our nation."

"You are too modest, Teacher," Cô Nhân said. "We have heard about how you, and your father before you, have devoted yourselves to educating the village children. Your work is just as important as that of the generals and officials who are fighting the military and political battles."

"How can you compare me to those gallant people?" he protested.

"You know well from the ancient teachings that there are many forms of courage. In your own case, aren't you the brave one who came here without hesitation, knowing that you would be entering a bandits' lair? How many would have done what you did?"

"By the way, the Village Chief's daughter is not that easy to handle and commander Chính will be happy to have her taken off his hands," Cicada said with a cheerful laugh. "She is strong willed, very vocal, and does not seem to be afraid of anything. In fact, she's somewhat like the commander himself at times."

"She takes after her own father," Tâm explained. "If she were a man, she may very well become a Village Chief in her own right."

"We hear that her father is a cunning and powerful man who's not afraid of exercising his authority and bullying the common folks for his own benefit. Our nation certainly does not need more of his kind," Cô Nhân said forcefully.

After a pause, she added. "It will be tomorrow morning before your former student and his unintended captive arrive back at this inn. Please stay here until then. The maids will bring you beddings and blankets, for the nights are chilly in these parts."

She and Cicada rose at the same time, and they both quickly left by the front door of the inn. A number of men emerged from the darkness and followed them out into the dense fog.

He slept fitfully during the night, curled up in a corner of the room and fighting the cold air drifting down from the surrounding hills. The quilt they lent him barely kept him warm.

He got up early and went through his normal routine of exercises. Once done, he sat at the corner table and waited while watching the sunrise and admiring the hues of red and orange through an overcast sky. When there was enough light, he took out a small book to read but found that he could not concentrate on it as he normally could at home.

He was hoping to see Cô Nhân or Cicada again to ask them how the rebels were preparing their defenses against an attack. He remembered Chí mentioning he had to hurry back to the province to meet with other troops coming up from the South via another route. Would the new Prefect be leading the assault on this rebel stronghold? Could a man chosen through examinations and lacking any military training or experience give orders on strategy and tactics without sounding ridiculously naïve?

A familiar voice interrupted his daydreaming.

"There you are, Teacher Tâm! Was it too cold last night? Were you able to sleep?"

"Thank you, Cô Nhân. I was able to sleep fine."

She sat down opposite him, with her guards standing nearby. On her order, the servants served tea and steaming sticky rice mixed with mung beans neatly bundled in banana leaves. She waved her hand over the food.

"I usually don't have anything but tea in the morning, but you'll need sustenance for your trip home. While you are eating, may I borrow the book you were reading?"

He handed her the book and, before she could open it, he explained.

"It's a book given to me when I was in the capital. It is printed with common everyday phrases or sentences in both Vietnamese and French. I am using it to learn both the new script and French at the same time."

Cô Nhân leafed through the book for a few minutes, stopping at some pages to read.

"When I was a child, French priests at court were holding classes where they taught us French and this new way of transcribing Vietnamese," she said. "Many members of the royal family did not want to learn from them because they feared that the priests would try to convert us to Christianity. My father, on the other hand, made all of his children attend the classes. He thought we should try to learn as much as possible from the French. He believed that we should open up our society to Western ideas, and especially to their science and modern technology."

"Yet, today the same people who turned down the missionaries are now cooperating with the French colonial administration," she continued. "Meanwhile, we have become rebels in these parts, and the new King is sending royal forces, accompanied by French soldiers, to eliminate us."

"The French must be putting pressure on the court mandarins to solve the problem that your movement has created," he said. "However, rest assured the people, as well as many scholars, are supporting you."

"That may be true, but the question is: how much longer will they support us? If we can't win the next few battles, will they continue to have faith in us? Teacher Tâm, what do the ancients say about winning the people's allegiance? If I remember correctly, purity of ideals is necessary but not sufficient for the ruler to maintain his reign."

Seeing that he had finished eating, she stood up and led him outside. Followed by her guards, they walked for a short distance until they came to a bridge spanning a river with flowing water almost black in color. He saw that where he had stayed the previous night was but a small part of a larger town on the other side of the bridge. There were fortifications consisting of thick mud walls topped by bamboo spikes encircling the town as far as he could see. Beyond them townspeople were bustling with their everyday activities.

"Why are the main fortifications located only on that side of the river?" he asked.

"Most of the townsfolk live over on that side," Cô Nhân explained. "Where you stayed last night is only a small part on the outskirt of the town. When the enemy comes, we will stop them there before they reach the bridge. If worse comes to worst, we will retreat and defend ourselves from behind those fortifications. We'll be prepared for them."

"What if they use their cannons on you?"

"We'll be able to withstand them, but we don't expect them to be able to carry very many heavy guns with them," she replied.

Before he could react, she pointedly asked.

"Do I have your promise that you will not tell anyone about what you see here? The enemy surely knows where we are, but we prefer that they remain in the dark as to how well, or how poorly, we are preparing our defenses."

"You have my word," he replied without hesitation. "I am not involved with the current government, nor do I want to be. Can you tell me who is the general commanding your forces?"

"He's my husband, and he is one of the names at the top of the list of persons that the court has declared as rebels. So far he has won every battle against the generals that the court has sent against him."

"He is not here, right now," she continued guessing his next question. "He is traveling to muster more troops and especially to obtain additional weapons and supplies. He has under him able commanders, one of whom is your former student. But the men need to be fed and equipped suitably, so he is always making sure that we have the required provisions and the proper logistics to support our forces."

That means he probably went to China, Tâm thought, but didn't say anything as they crossed the bridge and reached the other side of the river. More armed men were waiting for them and led them down a narrow and steep path to the riverbank beneath the bridge. As he came closer, he saw Cicada walking beside a strongly built young man that he recognized as Chính. Other than being a little bit taller and more mature than a few years ago, he was his smiling self, with the same slightly crooked grin that used to be his trademark when he was still attending the village school. He wore no weapon or even a uniform, but from his appearance and the deference the other men showed him, he was their obvious leader.

"My Lady, Teacher," Chính greeted them, bowing deeply to both Cô Nhân and the village teacher.

Cicada looked radiant at his side, and Tâm suspected there was something deeper between his former student and the young woman. He was happy and impressed by the young man's confidence and bearing.

"Have you been well, Chính? It's been several years."

"I have never been better, thank you, Teacher," he answered with a laugh. "I must say, however, that my life will be easier once you get this nag over there off my hands. She has been complaining and shouting insults at us day and night."

"Who are you calling nag, you miserable bandit?"

The voice came from a small hut some twenty paces from where they were, but Tâm recognized at once Kim Liên's voice. Both Chính and Cicada laughed and shook their heads. They all walked toward the hut. As they reached it, Tâm peered inside and saw the Village Chief's daughter sitting on the ground with a black blindfold over her eyes, her arms bound to her side. She was disheveled and her clothes were rumpled, but she appeared otherwise unharmed.

"Someone is here for you," Cô Nhân declared. "We are letting you go today."

"I can't see anybody or anything," said the rebellious young woman. "I have been blindfolded ever since I was kidnapped by your gang."

"I am here, Kim Liên. It's me, Teacher Tâm."

She started to sob, as if a dam of frustration, fear, and resentment had burst open.

"Teacher! Please take me home!"

He looked at Chính and was going to ask about removing the blindfold and her ties, but Cô Nhân spoke instead.

"Teacher Tâm, we ask you not to remove any of her ties for at least a couple hours after you leave this place. We are providing a boat that will take you downstream and save you quite a bit of walking. You won't go back the same way you came, but this trip will be less physically demanding for you. It will also be easier travel, especially with someone tied up as she is. You both can get on the boat that is coming to shore right now."

A sampan approached, guided by a woman maneuvering a single oar and a small girl sitting at the bow holding a rope. Chính helped the still shaky Kim Liên stand up. They moved toward the boat, with Chính leading his captive by the fabric cord that tied her hands. By the time they reached the edge of the water, the little girl had thrown the end of her rope to one of the armed men who held it firmly to prevent the boat from drifting away. Another man was holding on to the back side of the sampan. Kim Liên let out an audible gasp as Chính suddenly lifted her up with both arms, waded in the water and deposited her unceremoniously aboard.

There was no time and not much else to say, so Tâm thanked Cô Nhân and Cicada, patted Chính on the shoulder, and then climbed into the boat. Without delay, the sampan driver maneuvered it into the river current and the boat began to move downstream. Tâm turned his head back, looking at the group standing onshore, wondering if and when he would see them again.

"Teacher Tâm, can you remove this thing over my eyes, please?"

The captive's voice reminded him that she was sitting at his side in the middle of the boat.

"Kim Liên, let's wait a little bit longer."

The rower, who had until then ignored them, her eyes staring ahead as she poled and guided the boat, spoke.

"You should not remove the blindfold and her ties until I tell you," she said.

He understood that she had been given her orders and were carrying them out firmly. They were all quiet from then on. The little girl remained at the bow, glancing back at them every once in a while.

At mid-morning, they had reached the confluence with a larger river, which he guessed was the Red River. The little boat did not hesitate to navigate onto the wider watercourse. The current was even stronger, and he sensed that the woman was letting the boat float along with it, only using her oar to point it straight ahead. Once they lost sight of the tributary they came from, he was allowed to untie and remove Kim Liên's blindfold.

"Your arms will feel numb for a little while," he told her.

"Where are we?" she asked as her eyes blinked rapidly to adjust to the sudden daylight.

"We'll be near Hà Nội later this afternoon," said the boat owner. "From there, you can walk home in less than a day."

Once released of her bonds, Kim Liên had become less belligerent, saying little, perhaps overwhelmed by the events of the past few days. She stole a few quick glances at Tâm, several times on the verge of asking him questions, but she did not speak again for the rest of the trip.

During the afternoon, the little girl had moved back to where they were and offered them tea and glutinous rice cakes cooked in tight wrappings of arrowroot leaves. As they ate, she took over from her mother so that the latter could also eat and rest a little bit. The mother stayed at the bow, watching and occasionally making small corrections to help her daughter's steering.

Tâm had turned around to look at the girl and her mother work together to control the boat's direction. The woman's face was not particularly striking except for an expression of confidence and inner strength. He noticed that before eating the woman made the sign of the cross. Observing her more closely he saw that she wore a small wooden crucifix on a metal chain around her neck, under her four-flapped tunic and the traditional undergarment bodice underneath it.

"You belong to the Christian faith, don't you?"

"Yes, Teacher," she responded, her eyes still concentrated on her daughter. "My entire family is, for as far back as I can remember."

"Even during the reign of King Minh Mạng?"

"Even before that, although I am told that my grandfather was martyred and our clan lost all of our land and possessions. We now make our living on the river, carrying passengers and goods."

"Then your husband is also a river man?"

Her reply took some time, and there was a subtle hint of emotion when it finally came.

"He got himself killed in a battle several years earlier."

He was lost in thought for some time after that, not knowing what to say. His companion had dozed off again, no doubt catching up on sleep that she had been missing for the past few days. He took out his book and started reading from it. The woman had resumed her post and the little girl came back to the middle of the boat, looking curiously at what he was reading. To his surprise, she began reading out loud a Vietnamese sentence from the book. After finishing it, she giggled and looked at him with eyes full of intelligence and a candid smile. He shouted back at her mother.

"What is the name of this pretty daughter of yours, and how old is she?"

"Her name is Hồng, and she's seven years old."

He was surprised at how young she was, and also wondered who taught her to read so well. "Who taught her the new Vietnamese script?"

"Father Phan from our church taught her, and I also help her at home."

"Hồng, can you write also?" he asked the little girl. She giggled nervously and her mother had to answer for her.

"She is barely starting to, and I am not too good at writing myself so that I could teach her properly. I would like to send her to school, but of course we can't afford it. If only her father were still alive…"

The village teacher was silent for some time, thinking how strange it was that one could find such gifted children in the most unlikely places and not just in scholars' families or in the comfortable homes of the affluent. Dozing next to him was the daughter of a wealthy and powerful Village Chief who had all the means and opportunities to attend school but chose not to. Meanwhile the child of a hard working but poor woman yearned to be in school but would probably not have the slightest chance of doing that.

Later that afternoon, the boat made a turn to another tributary of the Red River. After navigating for just a short time, it came to shore, docking near the trunk of a tree that had fallen partially into the water. The woman tied the sampan to the trunk then helped her two passengers get off. Before doing so, Tâm reached into his pocket for money and offered it to her.

"Thank you for taking us in your boat. Please accept this for our fare," he said.

The woman promptly declined, pushing his hand away. "You don't have to pay me, Teacher. Cô Nhân has already taken care of everything."

She pointed in the direction of the sloping riverbank.

"If you don't know where you are, walk up to the top of that dike that you see from here. Once there, turn North and keep walking on the dike until you come to a road. Keep following that road and you should reach your village before night fall."

He was surprised that she knew the waterways and even the roads leading to them so thoroughly, as if she carried maps in her head.

"What about you, won't it be hard work for you to go upstream from here?"

"It will be harder, but the tide is going to reverse its direction in a little while and then it won't be too hard."

"Will the tide help you all the way home?"

"Yes, it will even though its effect is not that strong by the time we reach home. All the boat owners on this river know this and take advantage of it whenever they can."

Before leaving, he offered her what he had been considering all throughout the last part of their journey.

"You can send your daughter to my village school if you want. You won't have to pay any tuition, and my mother will be happy to take her in."

The Matchmaker

The whole compound erupted in shouts of joy at the sight of Kim Liên who seemed to suffer little from her ordeal. Xã Long wasted no time thanking Tâm profusely and invited him in for refreshment followed by dinner. He declined dinner but did sit down for some fresh coconut juice. While he was still drinking that, servants brought out fruit and all sorts of sweets, piling them in front of the two weary travelers. In between peppering his daughter and her rescuer with questions, the Village Chief kept shouting orders for the servants to bring out even more refreshments.

Once the initial cacophony of sounds and activity had decreased to a more normal level, Tâm stood up.

"Village Chief, thank you for your hospitality, but I need to go home and let my own mother see me." He also knew he had to go see Chính's parents and let them know that they no longer needed to worry about their son.

"Of course, Teacher Tâm! Forgive me for not thinking and trying to keep you here too long. But you will have to come back when my son the Prefect...Heavens, we forgot to send somebody to tell him the good news."

He pointed to one of the servants and shouted.

"You, get ready to leave for the province right this instant!"

The man darted a quick glance outside at the waning daylight, but knew he could not refuse the Village Chief who had already begun giving his instructions.

"Tell the Prefect that his sister has been freed by the bandits and has come home accompanied by Teacher Tâm. Tell him that she is unharmed. Tell him," Xã Long did not finish as he turned to Tâm. "Where did they hold her, Teacher?"

"I truly don't know," Tâm answered, noting the change in Xã Long demeanor and tone from a grateful father to that of an authority figure. "They had me wait overnight and brought her from somewhere else."

The Village Chief frowned at Tâm briefly before saying.

"I expect you to eventually give me and the Prefect a full account of what you did and what you saw."

He then faced his wife, changing his frown to a grin.

"There is another thing that we must not forget, wife. Did you contact the matchmaker?"

"Yes I got in touch with her right after as we discussed it with Chí, but we've been waiting for Kim Liên to come home first before starting anything."

"Well, she's home now. So send word to that woman to come to our village and go see the Nguyên about their daughter."

Tâm stood up to leave, brushing off entreaties from Xã Long's wife to stay a little bit longer. He went to see Chính's parents and told them that they no longer needed to worry about their son's action. Then he went home to the village school.

The two women were waiting for him. They were busy cooking an early meal to welcome home the village teacher. Thi had been going in and out of the kitchen at every chance she got to peer out in the direction of the school gate hoping to see him appear through it. News traveled fast in the small village, and within minutes of Tâm entering the Village Chief's compound she had known about it. She went at once to the village school to inform Bà Lân, the village teacher's mother.

Finally, he came through the gate, the expression on his face revealing nothing of the joy of coming home after a successful mission. It was somber as if something was worrying him. However, he brightened when he saw her.

"Thi, what are you doing here?"

He went to the back door where she was standing and stopped just before reaching her. Her eyes were bright as she smiled and stepped aside to let him through.

"Teacher, you are home finally! Your mother and I have been so worried about you."

She wanted to tell him how many times she had gone to the foot of the hills and looked up at the path, hoping to catch sight of him before anybody else did. However, as his eyes fell on her, she blushed and kept silent. He noticed the change in her expression and stopped as if he wanted to say something. Somehow no word came to him, the teacher who was normally so eloquent in front of his students. His mother's voice broke the spell.

"Teacher Tâm, what are you doing standing by the door? Come inside so I can see you. Take a look at what Thi and I have prepared for you."

Heartened by his mother's call, he exchanged a glance with Thi, and then laughed out loud.

"Let's go in so I can tell both of you what an adventure it has been this time for the Village Chief's daughter."

A few days later, Thi had returned from school and finished feeding the chickens and collecting their eggs for the day. She put some eggs into a basket that she was going to take to the village teacher's mother. Her mother was preparing the evening meal and did not look up when she entered.

From the corner of her eyes, Thi first saw them coming out of her neighbor's house. Bà Canh accompanied by an older woman dressed in a dark purple silk tunic walked slowly toward the front gate of her house. The older woman was somebody she had never seen in the village.

"Mother, we have visitors."

Her mother hurried to finish dicing the fat purple kohlrabi that they grew in their vegetable garden.

"Who are they, Thi?"

"Our neighbor, Bà Canh, and an old woman, a stranger."

Her mother at once stopped her work, dropped her knife and stood up. She washed her hands quickly, dried them, and ran to their bedroom where she rummaged for a tunic to put over her clothes and prepare to receive the visitors.

"Bà Cả Nguyên, are you home? Anybody home?"

"I will be right there," her mother shouted. Lowering her voice, she craned her neck back to the kitchen and instructed Thi.

"Daughter, make some tea and bring it out when it's ready. Oh, how I wish they had warned us so we could be better prepared. I look like a mess and you... You are fine."

Thi had not often seen her mother so excited.

"Who is that lady? Do you know her?"

"It's Bà Bí, the matchmaker!" the mother whispered before turning to go.

A day earlier, through their neighbor, she had heard that a matchmaker sent by the Village Chief was going to come by for an introductory visit. Her neighbor told her the news with a broad smile and in a friendly tone that she found a little surprising. Though they were good neighbors, Bà Canh had always acted as if she were an older sister that her younger neighbor should defer to in all matters.

There had been gossips about the marriage prospects of the Village Chief's glorious son when he came home from the examinations. Although mildly interested, she had not paid much attention, never thinking that her still young daughter could be a candidate for daughter-in-law of the most powerful family in the village. However, when her neighbor mentioned the matchmaker's visit, she had been filled with tumultuous emotions.

The marriage would make sense and would benefit the family fortune, if the Village Chief would reduce their land rents just a little bit for his prospective in-laws. She had already been thinking of how nice it would be for her hard-working husband and sons to live better and start enjoying their lives more. She could even see herself being dressed in a nice silk dress and visiting with the likes of the Village Chief's wife and other well-to-do ladies. Just a little taste of some top-reaching fruit that she could only dream about up to that point.

On the other hand, she knew her husband did not hold Xã Long in high regard after losing many battles to him on land and rent issues. He and his sons toiled year after year and the most they could hope for was to keep the land they already had, while Xã Long kept expanding both his land holdings and the power he held in the village. She hoped that her husband would contain his pride at least once and agree to their daughter marrying Xã Long's son, the new Prefect.

What would Thi think? The mother had no idea, or rather did not want to face the truth. On one hand, she was hoping that Thi would not object to the marriage proposal. On the other hand, she admitted that her daughter would make up her own mind, and that her husband would support his daughter no matter what.

Thi understood why her mother became so frantic on hearing the visitors' call. She ritually went through the motions of boiling water and preparing tea. After pouring the water into a teapot containing dried tea leaves, she put it on a tray with three cups and brought the tray out to the front room.

"This is my daughter Thi," her mother announced proudly as if nobody knew who she was. "Daughter, pour out the tea and offer it to our guests."

"So this is Lê Thi," the matchmaker said in a gravelly voice, watching closely the subject of her mission. "She is a fine beauty indeed."

If only she had done her hair right instead of having it hang freely like that, and those teeth should have been blackened, the old lady thought. She still looked like a child! Surveying the rustic house with its crude country furniture and the plain mother sitting across from her, the matchmaker kept thinking of the earthy expression that she did not often have the opportunity and the circumstances to use: this young maiden was a pearl sitting atop a pile of buffalo turd.

Thi did not keep her gaze lowered but peered straight into the eyes of the older woman as she handed her a tea cup. They were squeezed in narrow slits like some feline animal judging when to pounce on its prey. Seated next to her, Bà Canh, the neighbor, was her usual self, beaming like a simpleton, so pleased to be part of a scene that could lead to such interesting gossip topics.

Her duty done, Thi retreated to the kitchen. She picked up her egg basket, went out quietly through the back of the house toward the open fields and began walking in the direction of the village school. The rice fields were undulating in the wind, looking like green waves crashing against their dikes. Big purple and black clouds hung low in the sky, their fringes turned gold by the setting sun. As she approached the village school, the wind picked up and she knew that the rain would soon follow it.

She did not find him in the school room, but saw him instead amid their garden plot. He was diligently using his hoe and did not notice her coming. He did not look the part of the traditional scholar, but was instead the very image of a hard working field hand, his shoulders and arms moving in unison with the hoe as it tore up the earth, his shirt soaked through with sweat.

She quietly went to the rear of the school house, where a big room served its diverse functions: bedroom, sitting room, dining room, storage room for school supplies, and a semi-enclosed kitchen at the very back. She knew it well from the many times she had been there carrying out small chores from preparing tea to storing and arranging school supplies. His mother treated her like her own daughter, letting her have a free rein of everything in the house.

"I brought you some fresh eggs," she said by way of announcing herself.

The old woman peered out from the kitchen door, smiling as she said.

"Thi, you are so kind to us, always bringing us gifts like this. Thank you, but are you sure your parents don't mind?"

As she stepped into the kitchen, Thi shook her head.

"Of course not! They want you to have them."

Her tone and expression did not escape notice of the village teacher's mother. She had watched and dealt with generations of youngsters as they passed through the school gate. She was well attuned to their moods and passions.

"Did something happen, Thi?"

The young woman that she first saw as a toddler many years ago was putting the eggs inside a bowl. She opened the kitchen cupboard, put the bowl inside, and finally turned to face the village teacher's mother.

"The matchmaker came," she said.

After he finished smoothing out the last row of the garden, he stopped to rest, surveying the garden but not really seeing it. The sky had darkened as the late season rain was beginning to fall, whipped obliquely by the wind. He hurried to the well to clean up then went inside.

His mother and Thi were seated on his mother's bed tucked in a corner of the room. The young student was crying as his mother held and patted her hands, murmuring words to her. He stopped at the door, not sure whether he should go into the room or not. His mother looked at him and nodded, silently telling him to come in.

He went to sit in his chair by the desk that his father had built out of bamboo with his own hands. As he dried himself, he took in the sight of the two women, one with wizened and kind features, and the other with a face that was on the verge of leaving childhood but still retained much of the same sweetness that was there when she first came to the school.

She had her eyes downcast, not looking at anyone. He could not remember whether he had ever seen her cry, and the distress that he felt on seeing her tears quickly grew in his heart. She was one of the rare humans who managed to bring joy into her surroundings, especially in this village school where two generations of his family had nurtured her mind and were the beneficiaries of her devotion to them.

"The Village Chief sent a matchmaker to her house today," his mother said. "She is there now, on behalf of the Village Chief and his son, the new Prefect."

From the moment that he left the Village Chief's compound, he had known that day was coming. He had kept it within himself, trying and failing to push it back into some subconscious level. He had rationalized that he should have been happy for her. Marrying a high-level mandarin such as a Prefect was the dream of many young women.

"She says that she does not want to get married."

Would he remind her of the time honored Confucian teaching that a woman should obey her father, her husband, and her son in that order? That marriages should be arranged by parents and that duty overrules any personal inclination or preference? That this system had worked well for centuries for innumerable couples, leading to stable families and societies? As one of the pillars of moral authority in the village, it would have been the proper advice for him to give.

Thi spoke up for the first time since he went inside.

"Auntie, I am so sad. What am I going to do? What am I going to say to my parents? Why can't my life go on as before? I just want to continue my education, and be here in this school with you and Teacher."

She lifted her moist eyes to look at him, and he knew then that he couldn't say what duty demanded of him.

His mother tried her best with words that she always fell back on when nothing else could bring comfort to someone in distress.

"My child, people grow up and move on the path that their karma has laid out for them. I have seen many like you come here to the village school, and then leave after a few years to fulfill their fate in life. Most left willingly, a few did so reluctantly, afraid of what they had to face in the world. But they all went on to live very happy lives. I have known you all these years and I know that you are very gifted and have a kind heart. Life can only have good things in store for you."

Thi stared at the floor, slowly shaking her head. Before he could stop himself if he had thought more about it, Tâm said in a low voice but clear enough to be heard over the din of the rain pounding on the roof and the ground outside.

"Thi, you should go home and tell your parents what you just told us. Let them know how you feel and what you think about the direction your life should be taking."

The two women turned their faces to look at him. His mother appeared a little shocked, while Thi, eyes still glistening with tears, also showed surprise. Yet, as she gazed at him, she stopped crying and her face slowly brightened up.

"She can't go home now," his mother interrupted the moment. "It's raining hard outside. You stay for dinner, Thi, then when it stops raining Teacher Tâm will see you home."

Thi stood up and tried gamely to smile.

"Thank you for inviting me to stay, but may I ask you for one favor?"

"And what is that, Little Thi?"

"Let me cook dinner. You have done enough for today, so just stay here and don't even lift a finger until dinner is ready."

Once it stopped raining, Bà Bí left to go make a report to the Village Chief. She had stayed in the Nguyên's home longer than normal because of the weather. The father had come home from the fields as soon as it started pouring. While his beaming wife brought him up to date, Bà Canh and the matchmaker exchanged understanding smiles. The husband did not receive the news as enthusiastically as his wife, saying instead something unusual.

"We must first tell Thi and find out how she feels about this."

"Let me tell her to come up now."

She went to the door to the back of the house and called for her daughter.

A few minutes later, it was clear that the girl was nowhere to be found. The mother gamely explained that she was probably caught in the rain somewhere else and was waiting for it to stop before coming home.

The matchmaker was not surprised. It was normal for prospective brides to be shy or even fearful of her, as if she were an ogre. Some went into hiding until she left, which was clearly what this Nguyên daughter was doing.

"That's all right, I don't need to see her again," she assured the parents. "All I need now is for you to give me the date and time or her birth. I will give that, together with the Prefect's date and time of birth, to the astrologer. That man will soon let us know whether the two are compatible. We'll just have to wait until then."

She was already thinking of how she may use the astrologer to negotiate a better fee with the Village Chief. The stars and their confluence could at first be hard to read, leaving some uncertainty about whether the two prospective spouses were well suited to each other. Then, if the groom was steadfast on getting the bride that he had his eyes on, for an additional fee the matchmaker could be convinced to get a second astrologer's interpretation, one more auspicious and conforming to the will of heaven. She had been doing her trade throughout several provinces for years, and that ruse had yet to fail her.

The few astrologers that she used did not mind her practice at all since they also benefited from it.

As it turned out, she had to remain at the Nguyên's house longer than she wanted. Bà Canh, even though she lived next door, also stayed, unwilling to miss anything that the matchmaker said or the stories that she told. In the course of travelling far and wide to visit and negotiate with many families, Bà Bí knew more than most people what was happening in society, especially among the powerful and well-to-do. Mention almost any name to her, and she was ready with their life stories and anecdotes about them.

In this village, another interesting prospect was the Village Chief's daughter who had just returned from her kidnapping ordeal. Turning to Bà Canh, the matchmaker attempted to find out more about Kim Liên.

"The Village Chief's daughter, does she have any marriage proposal yet?"

"Ah, that one, she scares away all of the men who come near her," Bà Canh answered with a laugh. "She has her father's temperament, and she is as strong willed and aggressive as he is. That's why she's still single, even though most girls of her age would have been married by now."

"She's not bad looking, dresses properly, and her family is well known and powerful," Bà Bí declared. If only this family's daughter would try to model herself on Kim Liên, instead of keeping her white teeth and that ridiculous hairdo.

"To tell you the truth, the only one who could possibly be a good match for her is the village teacher," Bà Canh added in the conspiratorial tone that she used when passing along gossips, meanwhile ignoring the surprised looks from Thi's parents. "People say that the only man she respects, outside of her father, is Teacher Tâm."

The matchmaker was now even more curious.

"Then what is he waiting for? He must be the same age as the new Prefect, no?" Glancing quickly at the parents, she added for their benefit. "But the Prefect is by no means old. We all know he had to spend many years studying in order to be where he is now and to make his family and this village proud."

Bà Canh was impervious to any reaction she may have caused, and went on blissfully.

"Well, after he got the bandits to release her and brought her back, people say that the Village Chief may start something. You know that the Chief himself married the daughter of a school teacher, don't you? For now though, his first priority is going to be his son. Once that's over, it will be his daughter's turn next. There's your next client, matchmaker lady!"

They had not gone through the back as Thi did earlier but along the main road. Tâm carried a small lighted paper lantern attached to a bamboo stick. The night air was cooler and clear. The rain had ended and left behind many puddles. It was impossible to walk in a straight line and they had to circle around too many pools of water.

She followed him closely and at one point grasped his free hand for support. He turned toward her, but she had already released her grip as she sidestepped another puddle. They looked at each other for a moment, each surprised at the unexpected contact. He smiled as he remembered the childhood games he played with her and the times that he carried her on his back or in his arms. She seemed to warm to his smile and extended her hand. He willingly took it and led her forward once again.

When they reached her house, they stopped and slowly let go. Both remained still, not knowing what to say, yet each with their own thoughts swirling in their minds. There were lights in her house, so perhaps the matchmaker was still there.

"Thi, go inside."

"Yes, Teacher."

He watched and waited for her to walk through the gate and go inside her house. Only then did he turn around and go back to the village school.

In the darkness, neither of them noticed the matchmaker who was observing them from the other side of the road.

When he came home that night, Tâm found his mother waiting for him, seated upright on her wooden bed in a corner. Not waiting for him to sit down, she cleared her throat and began.

"Thi was very upset today when she came here."

He went to his desk and sat down to wait, looking at the open book that he had left there earlier. He saw and recognized the printed words on paper, but their meaning eluded his distracted mind.

"I know that you have always behaved correctly like a teacher, especially these last several years as she grew up and became a young woman. You may not have known it, but I have been watching you, and I know that you have maintained the proper distance and restraint required of your position. If not, I would have reminded you of your duties right away."

He looked into the darkness outside, wondering whether escorting Thi home earlier was improper. Was it wise for him to hold her hand even when the excuse was a slippery road filled with rain puddles? Several months ago, he had let circumstances steer him into a relationship with another young woman. After his failure at the examinations, he had been strongly advised to cease all contact with her and go back to his village. He had tried and had not yet forgotten that bitter experience.

"We both have known her for many years now, and she has become part of our family. Your father used to dote on her, until the very end of his life. I myself have grown accustomed to her presence, and she has been like a daughter to me."

She paused and looked around their room, as if she could see Thi in it.

He remembered the little girl who loved to play house and often enough managed to get him involved in her childhood games. His mother also indulged her, letting her have free rein to the kitchen and eventually to the whole house. She was indeed the daughter and the sister they had shared their life with.

"She had never been as distraught as she was today when she told me about the Village Chief sending the matchmaker to talk to her parents. In fact you have seen her yourself when you came in afterwards. She only quieted down after you said that she should let her parents know about her own feelings."

She let a moment pass then looked directly at him.

"What about you, Teacher Tâm? Let me know what your feelings are."

He was ready with an answer.

"Mother, I only wish the best in life for her. But Thi herself, and her parents, will have to decide what that is. I cannot encourage her to disobey her parents."

After a long moment she sighed, disappointed but not surprised at her son's response. He had at times been moody since he came back from the capital. She had first attributed it to his disappointment in the examinations, but seeing him dedicate himself to the adoption of the new script and working actively with his students to propagate it, she sensed there was probably another reason. She wanted to ask him about it, but she held back as she saw how busy he was with teaching and preparing for his classes.

"You are right. That's what I am thinking also, and, if he were alive, your father would have agreed with us."

She wondered how much time she had before she had to go and join her husband in the afterlife. She did not want to leave Tâm until he had someone to care for him, someone like Thi. She would have liked that very much, but did her son leave a door open for that wish of hers? She was afraid not, but she had no idea why he would be that way. Maybe something had to happen, and she had no idea what it would be. A moment later, she let out a long sigh.

"Son, I don't know why, but I keep thinking that your life and hers will have many challenges from now on. What did you two do in your previous reincarnations to would cause it?"

It sounded similar to something that he himself once said to Giang. It was as if a dike broke, and the memories came rushing back to him, and he could do nothing to hold them back.

The Village Temple

It stood by itself on the river bank, a fair walking distance from the village. Though every year the river overflowed and submerged the land around it, nobody had ever seen water reach the temple gardens, let alone its steps. Perhaps that is why people were not surprised when they had to descend toward the river along a narrow path before climbing again to pass by the gardens and eventually reach the crude stone steps leading to the temple which was perched oddly on a rocky outcrop overlooking the river and its banks.

The gardens held a surprising variety of vegetation from flowers to vegetables. To the back of the pagoda several varieties of bamboos grew with stem colors ranging from black to green and yellow. For a quarter century the abbot had tried planting different varieties of flowers and bamboos until the only surviving ones were those that could withstand both flood waters lapping at the temple grounds and the waterless months of the dry season.

The temple was unassuming and consisted of a small, almost bare room with a floor that was nothing more than hardened clay. At the back of the room, a small and well-worn wooden statue of the seated Gautama Buddha was placed on a low altar. A large, seemingly crude, ceramic bowl was placed in front of the statue and filled with sand so that incense sticks could be stuck in it by worshippers. The only other decorations consisted of fresh flowers brought in from the garden outside and delicately and artistically arranged. People usually glanced quickly at the flower arrangements without giving them a second thought. However, a few found out that the more they looked at the arrangements, the more beautiful and captivating the flowers became, until those who were thus mesmerized had to be practically dragged away from them.

There was no statue of deities, monsters, or folk heroes commonly seen in other temples. There was no scroll painting or lacquered panels depicting visions of Nirvana or historic events in Buddhism history. The temple contained the bare minimum needed for meditation and praying. Worshippers were not sought after or encouraged, yet they still came because of the reputation of the abbot.

He was Lê Duy Khánh, older brother of the village teacher's father. He was an ordained priest who had decided to leave the shelter of the large temple where he had shed his hair and taken his vows to go spend the rest of his life as an ascetic in a more humble place. As a novice studying Buddhist scriptures and striving to understand the teachings of the Buddha and his disciples, he had seen the widening gulf between those teachings and what was actually being practiced.

The priests around him cared more about building up the temple's coffers than about enlightening anyone, including the novices, or about helping the faithful who came to the temple. They relied on a mixture of superstition and drawn-out ceremonial practices to numb the senses and scare or mystify those who came to pray and present their offerings. Those few who made large contributions, especially monetary ones, were given lavish attention by the most senior monks. Elaborate prayer sessions followed by vegetarian feasts were held for them and all sorts of blessings were bestowed on them, their families, their careers or their business enterprises. Those who could or would not contribute much were largely ignored and left to fend for themselves with the deities or demons scattered here and there as statues or paintings in the large temple.

As soon as he could, monk Khánh went looking for a place where he could practice his religion in a way that was as close to Buddha's teachings as possible, and devoid of any of the material trappings and ceremonial baggage of places like the one where he was ordained. Because of his eccentric character, and also because his family made hardly any monetary contribution during his training, his superiors gladly set him free. The temple thus had one less mouth to feed, and everyone was spared his constant remonstrations and his reproachful eyes.

He went to the place where his brother had settled in as the village teacher. His brother led him to an abandoned and run-down temple, almost hidden behind thick vegetation.

The temple, a decrepit relic of the largesse of a King of the Lê dynasty in the 18th century, completely neglected and virtually unknown to outsiders, was exactly what he was looking for. Because of its location, the temple looked mysterious and attractive, but it did not have room to grow. Abbots with even a hint of ambition could not live there for any length of time without feeling stifled by its physical location and size. After the original monks had passed away or left for worthier places of worship, the temple was abandoned. Anything of value was stripped and carted away, and the temple was condemned to a slow natural death, to be smothered by weeds and worn down by the elements.

He was a relatively young man then and set himself the task of restoring the temple and its grounds. It took him many years of virtually unaided labor, although his brother did come occasionally for help with tasks that one person alone could not cope with.

When the temple was restored to a livable state, he started working on the grounds around it, planting flowers and vegetables for beauty and sustenance, while using bamboo to shore up the South side and to prevent erosion from dragging the temple down into the river. He was a middle aged man by the time those tasks were completed. During the years of physical labor, he maintained a Zen like regimen of meditation, physical and martial arts training. Once he was old enough, his nephew, Tâm, came to train with him.

As the years passed, abbot Khánh's reputation as an ascetic practitioner of Buddhism grew. He, however, considered himself an ordinary man who happened to choose the path of self-denial and sacrifice while others struggled to raise a family or went in pursuit of fame and fortune. He did not consider himself better than others because of that. He had no family of his own, and his mere existence required very few material things.

The only disciple that lived with him was an old man who drifted in one day and would not leave. The old man was never heard to say anything. He was a deaf-mute who contented himself with tending the gardens and making the simple vegetarian dishes that they ate together. He was the one who created the simple, delicate, and yet captivating flower arrangements. How he acquired that talent was a mystery to all.

A soft aura of holiness enveloped the abbot because of his ascetism, but what attracted the ordinary people to him was his willingness to listen to them and dispense advice to help them solve the mundane as well as the more complex problems of their lives.

Those who came to consult him did not realize or did not seem to mind that while he always listened, and occasionally asked questions, rarely did he say or tell them what to do. They would kneel in front of him while he sat immobile in the full lotus position, sometimes with his hands held in the cosmic mudra, his eyes closed. They poured out their hearts and souls to him, and answered his questions when he asked. Then there was a prolonged period of silence until the visitors suddenly realized that he had, without saying so, led them to the right conclusion or choice. Most then smiled or laughed and left after thanking the abbot. A few frowned and went home unhappy, until circumstances and later events showed them that the abbot had in fact given them helpful advice through his questions, or had in fact predicted some of the events in their lives.

As the years went by, the abbot gradually gained the reputation of being a holy man who could foretell the future. He always denied that he had any such power, but his fame grew despite himself.

In the cool morning of a late autumn day, Cơ, the gold farmer, came to the temple. She had bathed and changed into fresh and clean clothes. From the back, a casual observer would have thought she was a young woman, slender and graceful with the swinging gait that came from carrying her daily harvests on a bamboo pole. However, her face, sad and lined with fine worry wrinkles, betrayed the ravages of decades of the daily remorse and anguish that she had endured.

Cơ walked in and saw the abbot praying before the Buddha. She knelt down behind him and remained there, listening to the sound of the *mộc ngư* (wooden fish) that the abbot was tapping rhythmically with a striker. He eventually finished his sutra, and slowly turned around to face her. She lifted her head, and he saw that her face was covered with tears.

Even though people referred to him as abbot, he had no official Buddhist title, and she had always addressed him as Teacher, a common enough title that he did not object to.

"Teacher, I have done all that you have told me to do. I pray every day, but … I am suffering even more than before."

He waited for her to continue.

"My husband does not say anything, but I think he knows."

Through his half-closed eyes he observed her and, beyond her, the world that she brought with her when she came to the temple.

"My son has joined the rebels. He kidnapped the Village Chief's daughter and only released her after Teacher Tâm went to look for her. The new Prefect is now leading royal soldiers to fight against him and his band."

In spite of his seclusion, news from the outside still managed to reach him. He already knew what she was telling him, but he kept silent and let her relate everything to him at her own pace. Her suffering was one more proof that the world indeed was a sea of sorrow, that all was suffering as the first noble truth of Buddhism stated. But what about the second noble truth according to which desire, attachment, anger, and ignorance were the causes of suffering? What did this woman ever do that led to her present fate and the emotional and physical hardships that she had been enduring for all those years?

Finally, she stopped her monologue and became once more the reserved and self-effacing woman that she was every day, the one that people would rather not approach despite the essential chore that society depended on her to carry out. She waited for him to speak to her.

Under certain circumstances, when all was lost and there was nothing left but to accept the consequences, silence was the best that he could offer. He knew that she came to the temple hoping for not much more than understanding. She too knew that was what he usually offered. That, and perhaps help with learning and understanding certain passages from the sutras. This time, he wanted to give her more. He closed his eyes and waited a long time for his thoughts and visions to become ordered and coherent.

"Your son will meet with adversity and danger, but he will be able to overcome both with your help."

He opened his eyes and fixed them on her. She reflexively bowed and stared at the ground. He stared into the emptiness beyond her black hair streaked with a little bit of gray and partially hidden by a shawl she had draped over her head.

"You are the only one who will be able to help him."

She lifted her eyes in surprise, trying to fathom what he had just said. His face was somber but she also saw a kindness in it, as if he wanted to tell her she should reveal the truth that she had been hiding, and that if and when she did so, no calamity would befall her. After a brief moment of silence, she realized that was all he was going to say.

She closed her eyes and tried to empty her mind of most thoughts just as he had taught her, but once again, the guilt of what she had done kept resurfacing from the innermost depths of her conscience. It began many years ago when she realized that she was carrying in her womb an unwanted child.

Her husband was still a shy boy who had barely entered into manhood, and who had up to then lived a chaste life with a wife much older than him. On her own, she had to lead him into consummating their marriage, leaving him bewildered for days after. Later, when the baby was born, she made it a point to make him carry the infant in his arms, hoping to seal with that act his fatherhood status.

Despite her efforts, she was never able to conceive again, and Chính grew up to be their only child. Over the years, her husband slowly distanced himself from Chính. Occasionally, she would catch him looking without expression in the direction of her son, but he would turn away his eyes as soon as she approached. The uneasy and unspoken tension in the house eventually led Chính to leave home as soon as he thought he could live on his own. She was frantic when he did so, but her husband remained reserved and untroubled, as he had been through most of their existence together. That was when she began to come to the temple. The abbot listened to her story without commenting, and began to teach her how to pray and meditate.

When she reopened her eyes, he was no longer there. She knelt again before the statue of the Buddha and murmured her prayer. After that, she left her offerings on the ground: a long log of soap and some sweet rice cakes. Since he never took any money from her, she always left things that she thought would be useful for the two old men living by themselves in the temple. She made the soap out of coconut oil and lye from wood ash, and the cakes from young sweet rice. Most villagers prized her soap and but few knew about the green rice cakes. She rarely made them after her son, who was their most voracious consumer, left home.

On her way back, she saw the abbot and his disciple working in the gardens, two old men engrossed in their manual work and oblivious to her presence.

Confrontation

Xã Long gripped the arms of his chair as if he could pulverize them into sawdust. His face was flushed red and distorted. His wife, seated next to him, was more reserved, but she too was shocked by the news that their son's marriage proposal was encountering obstacles. In one quick and violent motion, he stamped his right foot heavily on the floor.

"Who said 'no', that little brat or her parents?"

Bà Bí was used to dealing with such emotions, and in fact welcomed his outburst as it played right into her plans. The harder she made it appear, the better off she would be when the marriage eventually took place, and she was wholly confident that she would be able to make that little peasant girl bend. She also derived perverse pleasure in tormenting the Village Chief with her skillful scheming. It was not often that she had the opportunity to toy with local despots like Xã Long.

"It's mainly her, Village Chief. She is saying that she does not want to get married."

"What is wrong with her? What do her parents say?"

"They were receptive at first, and were happy at the idea of their daughter marrying the Prefect, but now I am not sure."

"That spoiled girl! How does she dare to say no to my son? He is the Prefect of this province! The King himself bestowed on him that title!"

"Husband, there is no need to shout," his wife finally spoke up. "The matchmaker can hear you quite well, and you don't have to convince her of anything."

He turned his anger on his wife.

"And you, what are you doing sitting there? Do something about this . . . refusal. Your son is coming home any day now. Do you want to be the one telling him that he can't get married to the one that he wanted?"

She ignored his ranting and stared at the matchmaker instead.

"Did they give a reason? Is there someone else?"

As she finished her sentence, their daughter slipped into the room. Alerted by the shouting, she wanted to find out what it was all about. The matchmaker ignored her and calmly replied to her father.

"I think there maybe someone else, but I can't be sure."

"Do you know who?"

"He's a village teacher, Teacher Tâm."

The Village Chief at once growled.

"What, him again? How could he? What . . . ?"

He did not finish, wondering why the village teacher was suddenly playing such a prominent role in their family life, first with the rescue of their daughter, and now becoming an obstacle in his son's matrimonial plans.

Kim Liên, who had been listening attentively, decided it was time for her to speak up. Since the kidnapping, she had lost interest in the village teacher, but she could not resist the opportunity to find out what was happening between him and that Nguyên girl.

"Bà Bí, how can you be so sure? Did she or her parents tell you?"

"No they didn't, but people like us naturally know about these things."

The younger woman kept pressing her.

"He's known for being interested only in his teaching and the village people have long thought that he would remain celibate all his life or at least for a very long time."

"Well, if you want, I can go back and find out more from the girl's parents. Before that, I will consult the astrologer to make sure we won't be wasting our time if she and your brother's ages turn out to be incompatible."

"Can you do both of those things as soon as possible?" Xã Long said irritably. "I want this resolved by the time my son returns."

"Yes, of course, Village Chief."

Before she left, she made sure that they paid her in advance for the astrologer fee, inflated by a good premium for her services.

In the morning, Teacher Tâm sat in front of the class and started reading a passage from Mencius.

"Kao Tzu said, 'Human nature is like whirling water. Give it an outlet in the east and it will flow east; give it an outlet in the west and it will flow west. Human nature does not show any preference for either good or bad just as water does not show any preference for either east or west.'"

"What was Mencius' response?" he asked the class.

Most heads bent down, and glances were exchanged as students checked to see whether someone knew. After a long minute, he looked in the direction of Thi who sat at her usual place in the back. She did not hesitate to recite the quote from the book.

"'It certainly is the case,' said Mencius, 'that water does not show any preference for either east or west, but does it show the same indifference to high and low? Human nature is good just as water seeks low ground. There is no man who is not good; there is no water that does not flow downwards. Now in the case of water, by splashing it one can make it shoot up higher than one's forehead, and by forcing it one can make it stay on a hill. How can that be the nature of water? It is the circumstances being what they are. That man can be made bad shows that his nature is no different from that of water in this respect.'"

As usual, she was the one who could easily quote from the classic books. He could not imagine what the school would be like without her. If women were allowed to compete in the examinations, she could have easily outranked many scholars, including Prefect Chí, and she might very well have won the top honors.

He had seen her when she came in that morning. She bowed to him and attempted a brave smile on a face with slightly puffy eyes. There were many questions that he wanted to ask her, but he was also determined not to intensify her personal crisis, so he kept silent.

To give himself time to think, he instructed everyone in the class to copy down the quote from Mencius as best as they could, allowing Thi to help them along as needed. Later on, he was going to elaborate on the more complex excerpts, hoping that someone in the class would question him on them. On many occasions, Thi was one of those who would do so, but he wasn't sure whether she was going to speak up that day.

Toward mid-morning, he saw a woman leading a child approach the school with the hesitant steps of someone not familiar with the village. As they came closer, he recognized them and walked out to the gate, his students' eyes following him. He was the first to call out.

"Little Hồng, has your mother finally decided to let you come attend my school?"

The little girl fixed her big eyes on him, nodded, and her cautious smile was the sweetest one he had seen in a long time. He bent down and swept her up in his arms, laughing at her surprise and delight, breathing in the fresh scent of the river child. Her mother stood, smiling shyly as she gazed at the schoolhouse and the curious students watching them. Any fear or apprehension she had until that moment disappeared when she saw her daughter's expression, and the obvious kindness of the village teacher.

Since the time they transported him on their sampan, her daughter had asked about him and his school almost every day. She had finally given in to her daughter's wishes, even though it meant she would be alone on the sampan. Privately she also thought that her daughter will be safer in a village far away from their home, beyond the reach of the fighting between government forces and the rebels. Should anything happen to her, at least her daughter would be kept out of harm's way.

"Let's go inside," the village teacher said. "It's about time for our recess anyway, and I will introduce you to my mother and all the students."

As he put the little girl back on the ground, Thi moved forward and smiled affectionately as she took her hand. Hồng looked back first at her mother, then the village teacher. Both nodded, silently telling her that it was all right, and there was nothing to fear. She wavered for a brief second before finally going hand in hand with her newfound friend through the classroom door.

"This is Hồng who is joining us as of today," Tâm said. "We'll recess now, and during that time those in the front row will make room for her. If necessary, one of you can move down one row."

Thi remembered her first day in school, when she sat next to Tâm who, at that time, was still a student.

"Teacher, could she sit beside me instead? That way nobody has to move and I will be able help her directly."

"That's an excellent idea!" he agreed.

He noted that his student was then her usual self again, as active and helpful of others as she used to be.

The sampan driver left as soon as she was confident that her daughter could stay at the school with the village teacher and his mother. She promised that she would be back often to visit.

That evening, after dinner was finished, Tâm sat at his table and opened the book that Giang had given him. Hồng was still getting familiar with the surroundings, following his mother around as the older woman pointed out things for her to know and remember. However, it had been an exhausting day for her.

His mother, who was now called grandma, suggested, "Hồng, you must be very tired, so it's better for you to go to bed now. You are sharing that bed with me, so get on it first and go to sleep. I will lie down at your side a little bit later."

Before climbing on the bed, Hồng went up to Tâm.

"Teacher, may I say my prayer first? I always pray before going to bed and my mother said I may do it as long as I keep my voice down and don't disturb you."

"Of course, little girl, you can pray any time you want."

He led her toward the bed.

His mother glanced at him, her eyes communicating surprise. They had heard of the Christian tradition, but this was the first time a child was going to pray so innocently in their presence.

Religion to the village teacher and his mother consisted of an amalgam of ancestor worship and Buddhism, each practiced ritually on special occasions or holidays. His mother maintained an altar in the house where she burned incense to the memory of her husband and their ancestors at the beginning and in the middle of each lunar month. On some of those occasions, Thi used to bring fruit or cakes as offerings. She usually left them at the altar, muttered a short prayer, and then all waited for the incense to burn completely before consuming the food. Tâm only lighted incense sticks and prayed to his father's memory on his death anniversary, relying the rest of the time on his mother to do all the traditional rituals. He himself took almost no strong interest in religion, despite the fact that his father's brother, Uncle Khánh, was the abbot at the local temple.

Hồng knelt by the side of the bed, inclined her head forward, and then said a prayer in such a low voice that neither of them could hear the words, except for the beginning of the prayer:

Lạy Cha chúng con ở trên trời,
(Our Father who art in Heaven,)

When she finished, she crossed herself, climbed on the bed and lay down on one side. She did not close her eyes right away, looking dreamily at his mother then at him.

He remembered that he had seen and read the words of the prayer before. He went back to his book and soon found the Lord's Prayer in both the new Vietnamese script and in French. He studied the Vietnamese words that she had just recited. Next he tried the other version in his hesitant French:

Notre Père, qui êtes aux cieux ;
Que votre nom soit sanctifié ;

(Our Father who art in Heaven,
hallowed be Thy name;)

From behind him, the little girl continued in perfect French, her voice pure, the words enunciated precisely:

Que votre règne arrive ;
Que votre volonté soit faite sur la terre comme au ciel.

(Thy kingdom come;
Thy will be done on earth as it is in heaven.)

He rushed to the bed and sat down beside her. She covered her face with her hands then slowly released them to look at him earnestly.

"Hồng! You know that prayer in French? How?"

"Father Phan taught me."

"Who is Father Phan?"

"He is a French priest."

Tâm turned to his mother.

"Mother, did you hear that? She learned French from a priest, and she for sure speaks it better than I can"

His mother was speechless, shaking her head in disbelief. She walked over to sit down on the bed also. She extended her hand to caress the little girl's face, drawing back a loose strand of hair. Hồng's eyes filled up with tears and two drops slowly made their way down her cheeks.

"Why are you crying, little Hồng?"

"I miss my mother so much."

Before the two adults could say anything, she added.

"But she wants me to be here, and I am happy to live with you and Teacher Tâm."

The old woman tenderly wiped away the little girl's tears. They remained at her side, the village teacher lost in thought, his mother lovingly rubbing the little girl's back until she finally fell asleep.

After school the following day, the matchmaker came to visit. Bà Bí was all smiles and bowed to Tâm repeatedly, until he finally understood that she wanted to be alone with his mother. He went out to the garden, taking Hồng with him so that the two women could be left alone.

The matchmaker took her time coming around to the subject that drove her to the village school. She talked about herself and how she came to be a matchmaker covering the entire province. She recounted the marriages she had arranged for such and such families in the province.

Tâm's mother listened politely to the long introduction. When she could no longer bear the excess of information that Bà Bí was pouring out, she interrupted.

"You honor us with your visit, but what did you have in mind?"

The question triggered another lengthy account of the matchmaker's most recent mission, one with the goal of getting the Village Chief's son, the new Prefect, wedded to the most beautiful girl of the village. And who might that be? Well, none other than the most capable student in the village school, the one renowned not only for her beauty, but also for her intelligence and scholarship. She was of course the daughter of the Cả Nguyên family at the other end of the village. That family, as well as their neighbors, were of course delighted when the matchmaker had approached them and told them about the Prefect's intentions. Who could possibly say no to him?

Finally, Bà Bí got down to what she had come for.

"I hear that Teacher Tâm, who is another eligible and fine bachelor in the village, may have some matrimonial plans of his own. If so, why have you ignored me? I am always ready and willing to work on his behalf."

"You must have heard wrong! My son has no such plans."

"However, there is no smoke without fire, is there? You know, nothing escapes my eyes and ears. But, don't worry. He is after all the same age as the Prefect, and it's time for both of them to get married. I am just somebody who could help him find the right person."

"But, it is not true. This year has been quite challenging for my son, as you well know, and all he wants now is to concentrate on doing his job as a village teacher as best as he can."

Soon after those words, the matchmaker left without much ceremony. She had the information that she wanted.

The Village Chief

A lone in his main hall, he greeted the matchmaker with an expressionless face, hiding his emotions well beneath a calculated coldness. His son had sent word that he could not come home right away because he was busy planning for an offensive against a rebel base, probably the same one visited by Teacher Tâm recently.

Xã Long was trying to figure out how he could make the village teacher reveal what he had seen or heard, so that he could relay back the information to his son. His own sources of information from business associates and traders who passed by his village had so far been vague and unreliable. Many people supported the rebels and protected them by withholding any information about them from strangers.

Bà Bí interrupted his ruminations.

"Village Chief, I have good news for you, several pieces of good news in fact."

He just stared at her and said nothing, waiting for her to continue. Familiar to dealings with figures of authority, the old woman was unperturbed by his demeanor. He behaved like a despot in the small village, but she had dealt with many like him before.

"First, I have the reading results back from the astrologer. He said that your son, the Prefect, and the Nguyên girl are very compatible. The stars could not be aligned any better for them."

Actually the astrologer had first told her that marriage was out of the question for the two. The positions of the planets and stars on their astrology charts were all wrong no matter how he chose to interpret the charts. Bà Bí had anticipated the bad reading and knew how to play the game. She used part of the money she had pocketed on the previous visit to give an additional amount to the astrologer and asked him to take a second and more careful reading. The man happily complied and revised his conclusion to the one that the matchmaker reported to Xã Long.

The Village Chief nodded his head to one side, indicating that he had never doubted that the stars could be anything but favorable to his son's future. The year was already turning out to be extremely auspicious for Chí, with him passing the examinations and winning the royal appointment. Before he could urge her to continue, his wife and daughter entered the room, drawn there by news of the arrival of the matchmaker. They had overheard what the old woman had said and his wife was already beaming with pleasure.

"Bà Bí, tell us the rest of your good news," said Xã Long.

"Well, the village teacher's own mother told me that he has no intention of marrying the Nguyên's daughter."

"That is good news?" inquired a skeptical Kim Liên.

"Of course, young Miss. It means that your brother has no competitor, and that the Nguyên's daughter has no choice but to obey her parents."

Kim Liên saw through the obfuscation and persisted.

"But are you saying she may still be smitten with the village teacher?"

"No, I did not say that, young Miss. Not at all. However, in my profession, we know that many times young people have these romantic concepts of their future partners in life. It is my duty as matchmaker to dissuade them of their fantasies and make them realize that they should rely on the wisdom of their elders and let their parents make the right choice for them."

Kim Liên rolled her eyes upward.

"I don't think you'll find it easy with that girl, but you are the expert. What do I know about getting people married to each other? Father, Mother, it's up to you now."

Xã Long was a shrewd businessman who knew that he had to obtain as much information as possible before trying to close a deal.

His instincts were telling him that his daughter was right and that the matchmaker needed to do some more work.

"Bà Bí, go to the Nguyên and talk to the girl, then report back to me. This marriage, if it comes about, is not between two parties with equivalent social standings. My son is a Prefect after all, and we have the right to insist that he will only marry a woman who is absolutely committed to him. There should not even be a hint of scandal. After all, what does she has to offer but her virtue? Her family is nothing compared to ours."

The matchmaker had already anticipated his response. She kept her smile and replied.

"I was on my way to see them already, but I thought I should tell you first how things went with the astrologer, and where things stood with the village teacher. I understand your concerns, but don't worry about anything. I will make sure they, and especially the daughter, fully understand how fortunate they are for even being considered by your family."

The matchmaker timed her arrival so that all the members of the Nguyên would be at home. To make sure, she stayed over at their neighbor's house and watched until the father came back from the fields and the family had time to consume their evening meal. While waiting she queried Bà Canh for additional information on the Nguyên.

She learned that they were a hard working family of farmers who owned some land and rented additional acreage that the father and their two sons tilled. In good years, the small clan prospered, and in bad years they held their own through skillful management of their crops. The daughter, Thi, came late in the parents' life and was the one that everyone, parents and older brothers, cherished. From an early age she had proven herself to have a scholarly inclination.

Unlike her brothers she insisted on attending the village school where she proved herself to be a star in her own right. In addition, her sweet temperament and attractive appearance endeared her to many in and outside of the village school. Thus in a family where brawn and brute force were essential to the clan welfare and prosperity, Thi alone shined because of her intelligence and grace. A pearl indeed, sighed Bà Bí, and one that was making her job more taxing than all the other unions that she had helped bring about. She crossed the road and went into the open door of the Nguyên house without much ceremony.

The father was not idle even after dinner. He was sitting in his chair weaving a fish trap out of strips of bamboo piled near him. Now that the new winter rice was planted and growing, catching fish had become his primary concern and he was busy making one more trap to be placed in the canals and streams crisscrossing the countryside. He stood up reluctantly as the matchmaker was admitted into the front room. His wife was already fussing around with a chair that she offered to the old woman, who declined and climbed up on the wooden bed where the family usually sat for their meals.

"Please remain seated and continue your work," Bà Bí urged Thi's father. "Don't mind me, I just need to talk with your wife for a little bit, then I'll be on my way."

Thi was sitting in a corner at a small table with a book and some paper on which she was writing diligently. She reluctantly laid down her quill and was about to stand up and leave the room, but the matchmaker hailed her back.

"Thi, don't disappear like you did the last time. We also need to talk."

"Go and bring some tea, and then stay up here with us," her mother told her gently.

A few minutes later the women had two cups of steaming tea placed in front of them. Thi went back to her place, picked up her quill and resumed transcribing a poem from the old to the new script. The matchmaker did not miss what she was doing, intrigued by the strange characters that appeared in quick succession under the tip of the quill that Thi was wielding so expertly.

"What characters are those that you are writing?"

"It's the new Vietnamese script that Teacher Tâm has taught us to write."

Bà Bí clucked her tongue derisively. "They don't look at all like Chinese characters to me. Why is he teaching you that?"

Thi stopped writing and looked up at the matchmaker.

"Eventually, he wants us to teach it to others, and bring education to as many as possible. This new script is very easy for people to learn in a short time. His goal is that the whole village will soon know how to read and write."

Bà Bí made it a point to draw out a long sigh.

"The whole village indeed! Well, scholars like him are well known for their lofty goals that have no basis in reality."

She next turned to the mother who was lost in her own thoughts.

"Let's get back to the reason for my visit here tonight. First, some good news: the astrologer told me that the positions of the planets and stars under which your daughter and the Prefect were born make the two of them perfectly compatible."

Thi cast her eyes down, the uneasiness that had started with the arrival of Bà Bí now rising gradually. She did not see that her father was frowning while her mother was speechless with joy at the good news. The matchmaker, her lie unchallenged, as she knew it would be, did not wait to exploit her advantage.

"The Village Chief's family and the Prefect of course, are very interested in moving ahead with this matter, so I hope that you will agree with me that we can all proceed with the next steps. They are prepared to welcome your lovely daughter into their clan, and you must admit that this is truly an honor for her and for your family."

"Father, mother, I do not wish to get married," Thi said firmly, staring unflinching at her parents, then at the matchmaker.

Her mother gasped audibly and her father contemplated his unfinished fish trap as he nodded his head slightly. Bà Bí again clucked her tongue and shook her head.

"I don't know why, but that's usually the first reaction out of most young maidens like you. In your case though, I am curious: is there someone else that you wish to marry instead?"

As no answer was forthcoming from Thi, the matchmaker stared at her icily.

"I just came from a visit to the village school. Teacher Tâm's mother told me that he has no plan for marriage, and does not intend to marry anybody in the foreseeable future."

For a fraction of a second, Thi was taken aback by the matchmaker's undisguised ill will. She recovered quickly and decided to ignore the bait by remaining silent. In the past few days, Thi had gone through a range of emotions and her resolve had been strengthened in the process. She knew she was going to follow her teacher's advice and tell her parents what her true feelings were to this marriage proposal, but she also did not want to do that in the presence of an unfriendly person who intruded upon their life. Her parents on the other hand exchanged worried glances with each other, and then looked at their daughter to gauge her mood and see what her reaction was.

An uneasy standoff ensued between the wizened matchmaker and the unwilling object of her scheming. After a long interval, Bà Bí changed tactics.

"I take it from your silence that there is no one standing in the way, and that you will do what all children do. Children must do what they are told, and go sit where their parents tell them to."

At that instant, when it was least expected of him, Thi's father spoke up.

"Bà Bí, you heard our daughter telling us that she does not want to get married yet. She knows what she wants, and we are not going to force her to change her mind."

The matchmaker and Thi's mother looked at him in surprise, but he had said as much as he wanted. As far as he was concerned, there was no need for further discussion. Thi had made her decision, and he agreed with her.

For several years now, he had watched his daughter grow up, gaining in self-confidence and exhibiting a natural poise to match her intelligence. While his wife was the excellent housekeeper that she had always been, she simply did not begin to compare to her daughter in knowledge and even in wisdom. In the last few years, he had come to rely more and more on Thi, letting her help him make the right decisions in matters big and small, from what crops to plant to how to do business deals with the likes of the Village Chief. If she now wanted to turn down this marriage proposal, he was willing to trust her instinct and judgment in the matter.

The matchmaker fought to control her irritation. She wanted to give an admonition and tell those stubborn peasants how dim-witted and foolish they were. However, in the end she just got up without any ceremony and pointedly spoke to Thi.

"I am not taking no for an answer. I am going to give you a few days to think it over while I take care of some other details. When you are ready to change your mind, tell Bà Canh to let me know, and I will come see you again."

She was almost out of the door before Thi's mother recovered enough from her panic to run up and accompany her to the outside gate.

"Please, don't be offended," she said, her voice so low it came out like a whisper. "I want to apologize for my daughter, but you probably already know that once her mind is made up, nobody can sway her."

The frustrated matchmaker pretended that she didn't hear her and continued walking out to the main road. She had planned to report to the Village Chief that same evening, but instead went home enraged beyond description.

Father Phan

Tâm sat in front of the class looking at his students using their abacuses to solve the problem he had given them:

"A bamboo tree was broken by the wind and the upper section fell to the ground, remaining attached to the main trunk. The part of the trunk still standing measured 12 *thước*. The distance from the trunk to the tip of the fallen section was 5 *thước*. How tall was the bamboo before it fell?" A *thước* was equivalent to about half a meter or yard.

The clicking noise of the abacus beads hitting their frames was all that could be heard as the students did their calculations. Thi who already knew the answer was watching Hồng.

He saw that Thi had looked up and was trying to get his attention. He stood up and walked to where they were. Hồng was writing on a piece of paper characters that he could not recognize. She took her time and stopped occasionally as she appeared to do some mental calculations. Finally she wrote down two characters, and looked triumphantly at Thi and the village teacher.

"The answer is 25 *thước*," she whispered while the other students could still be heard moving beads up and down their abacus rods.

He saw that Thi was as surprised as he was. He knelt down, took the piece of paper and examined it carefully.

"What did you write down, Hồng?"

A shadow fell on them before they heard an unfamiliar and deep voice.

"Teacher Tâm, she is doing arithmetic with Arabic numerals."

He looked back to the door and saw a foreigner standing next to Hồng's mother. Both smiled and bowed to him deeply. Their backs were loaded with packages wrapped in cloth and tied firmly together.

"Mother, Cha Phan!" the little girl shouted. She stood up and ran into her mother's open arms.

The foreigner was wearing Vietnamese clothes, and even wore a conical hat. Under it was a face weathered by age and exposure to the sun but with bright green, friendly eyes. His hair and the thick beard on the lower part of his were reddish brown. He did not appear at all like other foreigners Tâm had met in the capital, who were well-fed and well-dressed men quite at ease among the aristocrats of the courts. The foreigner standing before him was the common man's priest and he dressed like a common man, except for the black color of his clothes.

Father Phan was smiling affectionately as he looked at the little girl clinging to her mother. By this time, the whole class had lost its concentration with everybody turned around and looking at the scene taking place at the school door. The village teacher announced an unscheduled recess to receive the visitors and give the class time to settle down from the unexpected diversion.

He invited the foreign priest to sit, and they faced each other at the front of the empty classroom. Thi, Hồng and her mother had gone to the back to visit with Bà Lân. Hồng's mother had brought several packages containing clothing, foodstuffs and sweets for her daughter. As they were being opened, gasps, laughter and cries of pleasure could be heard from the back of the house.

"Hồng is an amazing child, Father Phan. She reminds me very much of one of my students, Thi, the one who just served us tea, and has been helping Hồng getting familiar with this school and catching up in her studies."

"Indeed, I noticed that the two of them seems to be a very close pair, as if they were sisters."

Tâm looked at the priest who, if not for his physical appearance, would be like any other Vietnamese man.

"She has mentioned your name a few times, and told me you are the one who has been teaching her not only our new script, but also French and what I just saw today, arithmetic using a different number notation. In fact, there is a lot that I can learn from what you have taught her yourself. While I was in the capital a few months ago, I met a young person who was educated by Jesuit priests. Would you be from the same order, and can you tell me how you came to be acquainted with Hồng's family?"

The foreign priest sighed, like Vietnamese often do in their conversation.

"I am a Jesuit too, as most of us are in this country. As to how I came to know Hồng and her mother, it's a tragic story. Her father was killed in a battle with a French naval group when she was barely one. I was a chaplain at the time and was present on one of the French ships. At the end of the battle, I saw her mother bury her father, with Hồng crying nearby… I've tried to help them as best as I could since then. I even asked my order to let me stay as a priest at a small church in a village near where they lived. That village, as a result of missionary activities going back to the 16th century, is one of the few in your country where most of the population is Christian."

He paused for a short time, as if gathering his thoughts.

"Unfortunately, there is only so much that someone like me can do. The reality is that since her husband's death, Hồng's mother has had a very hard life, trying out different ways to earn a living, until she ended up being a sampan driver just like her husband used to be. She wanted for a long time to give her child a good education, and I tried to help by teaching her child a few things. What she really needs though is to attend a school like yours, where she can be with other children. When her mother mentioned your offer of taking Hồng in, I encouraged her to accept it and bring her little girl to you right away."

Tâm nodded his head slightly.

"She may be helping me more than you can imagine. Her arrival, for example, is very timely. I have embarked on a program to spread literacy among our people by teaching them the new script. She has been very helpful in that regard, since she already knows the alphabet. I am using her as an example to convince the rest of the village, including the adults, to learn to read and write with the new script."

The priest had been observing Tâm during the conversation. What he saw was a serious and intense young man, not unlike what he had been when he first joined the Jesuits. He thought of the ways he could help him further his ideals and bring changes around him, in a country where the status quo was the official policy and where changes often met with punishment instead of rewards. It was too bad that the village teacher had failed the royal examinations, for he would have made an excellent mandarin. On the other hand, would an honest man like him have been able to make his way unscathed through the maze of court politics and corruption?

"I have heard much about you and your school from Hồng's mother. You certainly go beyond what most village teachers are willing to do, and you seem to care even more for your students, even those who cannot afford to pay you. If you will let me, I would like to help you in any way I can."

The village teacher reflected for a moment, contemplating what he wanted to tell the older man who had crossed continents and oceans to come to his country. He was a kind and benevolent priest, but he nevertheless came from a country which was using its military might to colonize and exploit his weaker homeland.

"Your country has colonized mine by force and as a consequence it has become quite unpopular with many of us. Some are even now taking arms and are rising up against the monarchy in Huế and the colonial powers that wield the real power behind the throne. I am not sure whether armed resistance is the only answer, or will even be successful in the long run. I have been thinking quite a lot about what role I should play in all this."

"And what role would that be?"

He now had the French priest total attention. In the deserted classroom, the two men watched each other with curiosity and mutual respect. The priest was intrigued by the young man, so unlike any that he normally dealt with, especially among the scholars and mandarins. The village teacher pondered whether he should share with the older man thoughts that he had so far kept mostly to himself, finally deciding he could.

"We cannot just continue to teach the Four Books and the Five Classics to our young people and think that would be enough to make our country strong and able to cope against Western military power and your civilization's scientific and technological superiority."

He stopped and looked wistfully at the small world that could be seen through the school door. Under a blue sky with just a few clouds, the greenery of rice fields and trees contrasted sharply with the hazy backdrop of the distant hills. The countryside looked peaceful, and yet he had to wonder how long it would remain so given the undercurrents of Western might that had taken hold and were chipping away at the foundation of the old society.

"My father taught the children of this village for almost three decades. Some of his students have gone on to win glory by passing examinations at the national level. Even before that, our entire province has always been famous for the quality of the scholars and mandarins it produced. Yet, since the beginning of this century, people like them have not been able to help our monarchs resist foreign domination. Our ruling class of scholars has made no difference whatsoever while your country is conquering mine."

"Many of us hate the word backwardness when it is used to describe the state of our society. To any and all we proclaim our pride in our 4,000 years of civilization, in the glorious achievements of our past heroes in defeating the Mongols and in pushing back the Chinese invaders more than once. We blame our current woes and weakness on outside influence, but isn't that like a general blaming the enemy for his defeat? Whom can we blame except ourselves when we cannot maintain our freedom and independence? Why should we keep proclaiming that we have a superior civilization when we let invaders take over our government and run our lives?"

His gaze returned to the priest, resting on the black wooden crucifix hanging on his neck.

"Your religion gained a foothold in our country when King Louis XVI helped the founder of the Nguyễn dynasty come to power. Since then, your faith has won quite a few adherents among our population, while our monarchs made the mistake of wasting their time and efforts to stop the spread of Christianity. While doing that, they failed to modernize our nation and we have lost 30 or 50 years compared to a country like Japan, which under the Meiji Restoration has been modernizing its economy and its political and class structure since 1866. I've heard that Japan has now caught up with the industrial

West, that it can now field both land and naval forces as sophisticated and powerful as the best ones in the world."

The priest could only nod his agreement as the village teacher came to the end of his monologue.

"I don't know how much one person like me, a failed scholar, can do when our whole system of government must be transformed. I need your help here, where I at least have some influence and can make an impact. I am a scholar and a teacher, but I no longer have faith in our traditional educational system. Help me educate our children and widen their horizons. Tell me what I should learn and do, so that I can teach them what they need to know to cope with life in the 20th century."

Much later, the French priest left, impressed by the young man who was not a Christian but didn't hesitate to share his thoughts with him and ask for his help. He still had several more places to visit in the North, places where Christianity had gained a foothold and was spreading, slowly but surely. After that, he was to return to the capital and make a full report to his superiors.

The Prefect

Commander Chính found it hard to keep Cicada out of his mind. The remarkable young woman who came up from the capital to join the rebel cause had gladly volunteered to serve in a most perilous mission. At his request, she had agreed to go play the role of housekeeper for the new Prefect. Her mission: to ingratiate herself to the newly appointed mandarin and find out as much as she could about his plans for attacking the rebel base. The two men who accompanied her served as couriers to convey to the base whatever information she obtained, as often as necessary.

Before she left, while a nervous Cô Nhân went over cautionary advice and warnings, Cicada appeared to be at ease, even lighthearted. She commented in the pure Northern accent that she had learned to speak with since arriving at the base.

"Commander Chính, you don't seem to be sorry to see me go."

He was caught by surprise and found himself at a loss for words.

"It's all right," she added in a mocking tone. "I will somehow get back at you when I return."

"Cicada, I do worry ... about you ... going on this mission," he stammered. "I have thought a great deal of what might happen if you were caught or somehow found out."

Her suspicious look bored right into him.

"What if something did happen to me, what would you do?"

"I will of course come rescue you."

She was not going to let him off so easily.

"And if I were killed before you could rescue me?"

He peered into her eyes, trying to convey to her the new emotions that he had begun to feel toward this striking young woman, so unlike anyone that he had ever met. After an uneasy silence, she lowered her eyes, and he hastened to say.

"Then I will never forgive myself for letting you go."

She snickered and gave him another disdainful look.

"Ha, fancy words indeed. I doubt you will even miss me for a few minutes."

Cô Nhân had been listening to this latest exchange and knew that her friend had felt attracted to the young commander from the moment she met him. She also suspected that he was not immune to her attention either, and she tried to ease their discomfort with words of encouragement.

"Let's not be so gloomy, you two. Cicada, I expect to see you back here after a successful mission. Commander Chính, let her go while you prepare our men for the fight ahead. She will provide you with the best intelligence you can possibly have, and that's like winning half of each battle already."

After that scolding and a long last look at him, Cicada left. Chính, who had steeled himself against any emotional attachment, felt a sudden distress. He stood motionless, long after Cô Nhân had turned around to go back to her quarters.

He wished he had not been so cold to her when she first arrived. He regretted he had not sought her out more when she was staying with Cô Nhân and the other women. He wanted to reach out, grasp her, and bring her back, but it was too late. She and the two men who accompanied her were already mere dots in the countryside beyond the last guard post.

Prefect Chí had been told by his father that a distant relative would come to see him when he got to the provincial capital and that he should use the man as his personal aide. What he wasn't prepared for was the large delegation of dignitaries gathered in front of the Prefect's mansion. Standing at the front of the delegation was a short and rotund man about his father's age with bright eyes and an obsequious smile.

"Welcome Prefect, welcome nephew!" shouted the man as the rest of the delegation joined him in bowing to Prefect Chí as he dismounted and handed over his horse to a soldier.

The man went to him and whispered that he was Uncle Hoan related by marriage to the Village Chief. He then introduced Chí to the dignitaries, proving himself to be a wily and suave man quite at ease in such circumstances. Whenever he did not know someone's name, he would tilt his head up, closed his eyes, and frowned until the man volunteered his name and title. Upon hearing that, Uncle Hoan instantly opened his eyes in recognition and continued as if he had known the man being introduced all along. Introductions done, he dismissed the dignitaries in no uncertain terms.

"Honored officials, as you all know, His Excellency the Prefect has just completed a long and exhausting trip to come assume his royal appointment. He should now be allowed to rest, so I suggest that we all go back to our offices and wait for His Excellency to make our acquaintances within the next few days. As he wishes, he will of course be in touch with any of you if and when you are needed, but for now let us allow him time to settle down in his new quarters."

Uncle Hoan had arrived to the mansion the day before. In the short time he had been there, he had persuaded everyone to look upon him as the most important man after the new Prefect. He secured an office and began issuing orders to all the functionaries, soldiers, and servants assigned to the mansion. The previous Prefect had left more than a month before, and the leaderless staff was very eager to please his replacement. In the space of a day, Uncle Hoan had imposed order out of chaos, identified the main players on the staff, and already had the outlines of what he was going to do to make his nephew's life worthwhile for both of them.

He was known elsewhere in the province as a wily merchant often doing a delicate balancing act between dishonest manipulations and shrewd dealings. He was ensnared by the law a few times, but always managed to disentangle himself from any mishap by throwing away a small fortune in bribes to government officials. After his latest escapade, one involving a failed attempt at smuggling Chinese goods across the border, he had been idling away his time until a messenger from Xã Long brought him the news of his nephew's appointment as

Prefect and a request to help the young man settle in. Uncle Hoan had interpreted that request to include helping his scholar nephew govern in the most mutually profitable manner, for him, for his nephew, and of course for the whole clan.

Prefect Chí walked into a mansion that had been left bare by the previous occupant. However, the staff had been cajoled and threatened into getting at least the minimum essentials for him to settle in while Uncle Hoan was arranging for the rest.

He found that a hot bath was already prepared for him in a room at the back of the mansion. He was overjoyed at the sight of the tub filled with steaming water, and welcomed the chance to get rid of the horse smell that had been with him ever since he left his home village. He disrobed and settled himself in a wooden tub filled with steaming water. A servant took his dusty clothes away to be washed, and he closed his eyes and tilted his head back. He was not too sure of which side of the family Uncle Hoan came from, but he felt comforted that he had someone looking for his welfare and interest. Just as he was about to doze, he heard the uncle's eager voice.

"Go on in, there is nothing to be afraid of."

He opened his eyes to see Uncle Hoan pushing a young woman into the bathroom. She was quite attractive despite her coarse brown peasant clothes. She was also trying to suppress her laughter at seeing his mounds of flesh floating in the tub.

"Go on, greet the Prefect. Your Excellency, this is Cicada who is going to be your personal servant."

Cicada bowed and, still giggling, slipped out of the room.

The next few days went by so quickly that Chí did not realize that more than a week had already passed when he finally sat down to tally his first action items as the Prefect of a province. Uncle Hoan had brought back one by one the officials and dignitaries who had welcomed him on his first day in office. There had been daily banquets, uncounted speeches to give and many more to endure as everyone tried his best to sound eloquent and capable in front of him. In the evening, all he could do was to crawl into the bed that Cicada had turned up for him and fall asleep as soon as his head hit the pillow.

When he woke up in the morning, she had his clothes and breakfast ready and waiting. She carried out any order he gave her diligently, always with a smile and never complaining. One day he caught himself wondering whether Thi would be like Cicada once married to him. He could not come up with an answer, and the image of the young maiden back at the village disappeared just as suddenly as it had come.

Since his mission was to punish the rebels, he left most of the administrative duties to Uncle Hoan, concentrating on preparing for the military campaign due to start as soon as the additional troops from the capital made their way to the province. He reminded Captain Duẩn to find whatever was necessary to replace the guns that his men lost and to prepare the provisions and their transport carts.

In this provisioning effort, Uncle Hoan was most helpful as he appeared to know every businessman and where everything was in the province. All Chí had to do was to approve and to stamp with his seal the orders requisitioning or purchasing what was needed. This business of governing was much easier and more enjoyable than what he had thought it would be. He enjoyed using his Prefect's seal and the sound that it made as he brought it down forcefully on the various pieces of paper presented to him. However, what he did find truly pleasurable was the food served to him every day.

Although he enjoyed the banquets with scores of guests in attendance and an abundance of dishes, what he liked best were the private meals prepared for him by a cook under Cicada's supervision. She had discovered that he did not particularly like the boiled chicken or pork dishes often served in this part of the North. From his student days in Hà Nội, he had developed a liking for rice noodles with charcoal grilled pork, which became an addiction and eventually included all sorts of grilled food ranging from fish to fowl.

Therefore, whenever he dined alone with Uncle Hoan, Cicada invariably had the cook take out a clay oven and light up some charcoal over which she grilled most of what he ate: poultry, fish, pork, beef, and the onions, squash, eggplants, and other vegetables that went with them. The new Prefect would start salivating when the smoke and smell reached his nostrils and could not keep still until the food was served.

Such a fare, accompanied by liberal amounts of wine made from black sweet rice, never failed to transport Chí to the gates of heaven where he often lost all of the day-time inhibitions that he felt when playing his new role of Prefect. He laughed out loud, openly discussed his plans and politics with Uncle Hoan, and, at the end of the meals, his face flushed, his eyes bloodshot, he even stared overtly at Cicada clearing the table before serving tea.

One night, Uncle Hoan could not help but notice his nephew's obvious ogling of the servant.

"My nephew, you like this Cicada, don't you?"

"Yes, indeed. Beside you, she is the most talented person on my staff, and she is more pleasant to look at than you, I am sorry to say."

They both chuckled and exchanged knowing glances. After waiting for the servant to be out of earshot, Uncle Hoan whispered.

"It's going to be difficult, since she tells me she's already married."

"Is that so? That is unfortunate," mumbled the young Prefect.

"However, my dear nephew, if you want a woman, you just let me know and I'll find someone for you. Several dignitaries have already asked me about your matrimonial plans, and there seems to be no shortage of families with daughters ready to become your wife."

"Uncle Hoan, I only need one young woman from my village. However, you don't have to help me. My parents are already taking care of it, and I hope to be married to her as soon as this campaign is over."

At the end of this last sentence the new Prefect let out a long and quite audible sigh, sounding lovelorn and sad.

Cicada who had by then returned with tea decided to ask the question she had been keeping to herself.

"Your Excellency, when will you then begin your campaign?"

"I will start out as soon as the rest of my soldiers arrive here from the capital," replied Chí without even thinking. "Cicada, I didn't realize you were even interested in these kinds of matters!"

She stared at him with bright eyes full of reproach, a serious expression on her face.

"It's because I worry for your comfort. You know that I am here to serve you, but, once you go on your mission, who is going to take care of you?"

Prefect Chí was dumbfounded at this sudden outburst from the usually reserved servant. As their eyes met, he thought that hers projected an unusual inner strength. That was even more surprising, but he could not fathom where it came from.

"My soldiers will take care of me, of course."

"But, my dear nephew, it'll be a far cry from the care that she has given you here," Uncle Hoan roared with laughter, fueled in part by a good quantity of rice wine he had consumed. "Those peasant soldiers eat the coarsest of food, and what they prepare is even worse. Enjoy what you can here, Your Excellency, and come back to Cicada as soon as you have punished those rebels."

Cicada bowed to Uncle Hoan to thank him, and retreated to the kitchen.

The five hundred additional troops arrived, led by a royal captain accompanied by two foreign officers dressed in French uniforms. Prefect Chí did not know about the two French officers, but held his surprise in check. Fortunately, the older and more senior of the two could speak Vietnamese fairly well, and the new Vietnamese captain seemed to be able to speak enough words of French to act as a sort of interpreter. Uncle Hoan and an assembly of mansion staff, including Cicada, left their posts to come watch the foreigners arrive. However, the new officers, after presenting themselves to the Prefect, quickly left to supervise the disposition and quartering of their troops and weapons, which included several horse drawn cannons.

Prefect Chí, who had never seen so many soldiers in one place, turned to Uncle Hoan.

"These soldiers need to be housed and rested first, don't you think? You should go and help the officers find their ways around, and provide them with anything they need. We are not going to be leaving for at least two days."

"Yes, Your Excellency," said Uncle Hoan. He turned to the staff gathered around him. "Men, you come with me, and you, Cicada, stay here to serve the Prefect."

She seemed a little disappointed at not being asked to help, but said nothing. Instead, she turned to the Prefect.

"Your Excellency, will you have those officers as you guests for dinner tonight?"

"That's an excellent idea. Why don't you get everything ready for that and I will send somebody to tell the two French officers to come join me tonight. After their long trip from the capital, they deserve some of that nice grilled meat that you prepare so deliciously."

He clapped his hands in satisfaction, already anticipating the feast to come.

She threw him an amused glance and scurried away toward the back of the mansion. There, before doing anything else, she took out a brush and a piece of paper and wrote down a long message with a steady hand and precise brushstrokes. That done, she went to find the man that the rebels had placed inside the Prefect's mansion to assist her. She entrusted the message to him and asked him to go deliver to his commander as soon as possible. Then she resumed her role as Cicada the servant.

Retaliation

His daughter's health had been a subject of concern since she came home after the rebels released her. Her illness came and went from day to day. She could be her lively and aggressive self one day, then become lethargic and morose the next. On those days, she simply curled up in bed and turned away everyone trying to talk to her. After some time, it could last from a few hours to several days, she would come out of the slump and go make her presence felt again around the house or outside.

The village herbalist had been summoned to come to the Village Chief's compound, only to be sent back by Kim Liên who refused to see him. Nevertheless, he wrote a prescription because he felt compelled to do so. He was paid for it and for the package of dried herbs, mushrooms, and medicinal roots that he left behind. Servants dutifully prepared an infusion with the ingredients, but the young lady of the house refused to taste any of it.

"Is my daughter better today?" Xã Long asked his wife.

"She's still the same," the Village Chief's wife dutifully replied.

After a brief hesitation, she decided to share with her husband a thought that she had been keeping to herself.

"You should not talk in front of her about your son and his campaign against the Cần Vương or the Black Flags rebels."

"Why shouldn't I talk about that? The King himself put him in charge of the campaign."

The royal appointment meant the highest honor to Xã Long, and he never missed a chance to mention it to anybody since his son came home covered in glory and splendor. The campaign against the rebels was nationwide, and he made sure that everybody knew that his son was playing a very important if not vital role in it.

"She physically cringes every time you do, and she becomes sick afterwards. It is obvious that she does not like all this talk of wiping out or killing the rebels."

"My dear wife, you are wrong. I know my daughter. She is tougher than many men and I doubt she would be affected by my kind of talk. She would enjoy it even."

"Well, I am just telling you what I observe."

Xã Long was used to his wife yielding to his opinions, so, without wasting a moment, he went on to a more pressing subject.

"Has the matchmaker talked to you again? Have you seen her at all? It's been a long time already, and I've been busy with many other things, but we should not forget about Chí's marriage."

"That matchmaker is another one who has been acting strangely. No, I haven't seen her since the last time she was here. I don't know why, but I hear people say that the Nguyên girl is being obstinate, and the family will not accept our proposal."

The Village Chief stared at his wife with incredulous eyes ready to pop out of their sockets. He was speechless for a while, his wife seeming to wilt before him. Then he shouted at the top of his voice to unseen servants.

"Go find Cả Nguyên and tell him to come here this instant!"

Not much later, his daughter appeared in the doorway, apparently recovered from her last bout of melancholy. She looked at neither parent as she went and took her seat. Kim Liên knew when a crisis was taking place and she was determined not to miss it for any reason.

Cả Nguyên wore his ordinary work clothes that he did not have time to change in his hurry to respond to the Village Chief's summon. The rice was growing and there was not much for him to do, other than doing some maintenance work on his tools and fixing things in and around the house. He had an idea of why Xã Long wanted to talk to him, and he had thought about how he was going to respond. His wife implored him with her eyes before he left, but he pretended not to notice her.

Xã Long, his wife, and their daughter were seated as he came in. Nobody said anything at first, and he was left standing in front of them crossing and uncrossing his arms nervously. After a long minute Xã Long's wife, realizing the apparent lack of simple courtesy, stood up and asked him to sit down on one of the vacant chairs. She also asked a servant to bring up tea. As soon as she finished her order, Xã Long went directly to the crux of the matter.

"I sent a matchmaker to talk to you and your wife, and I haven't heard anything from you yet. That old lady has been hiding from me ever since she said that she was going to talk to you. So now that you are here, let me ask you this directly: is there a problem?"

Cả Nguyên tried to choose his words as carefully as possible.

"Village Chief, we are honored by the fact that you have thought about us."

"Go on," Xã Long pressed him.

"It is not that we don't want to accept the honor, but in reality our daughter is too young and should wait for a few more years before she is ready for ... what the matchmaker proposed."

"Meaning she does not like him," interrupted Kim Liên. "Meaning she has lost her heart to somebody else already."

"Oh, no, please don't say that. She's too young, and nobody would even ...."

Xã Long had brought his anger under control while waiting for the arrival of his land tenant. He knew that the Nguyên were farming their ancestral land and had expanded by renting some acreage that belonged to him. Because it was marginal land, he had so far given them low rates and was going to wait until it was brought up to better farming quality before charging them higher rates.

"Uncle Nguyên, tell me then how many more years before your daughter will be ready of marriage?"

"I don't know, Village Chief. That's too hard for me to say."

"You can look at growing rice and tell exactly how many days before it's ready for harvest, can't you? But you can't tell me when you can give away your daughter's hand in marriage? Come on, try harder and tell me: will it be one year, or three, or five?"

Receiving no answer, Xã Long went on as he relished the discomfiture of the man squirming in his chair. He brought the teacup to his lips, but before sipping from it, casually delivered his sentence.

"Fine, I agree that you won't be able to give me an honest answer. Therefore, here's what you will do: starting this year, for the land that you are farming for me, I will have to increase your rent from 20 to 40 percent of the harvest. Next year, it will be 50 percent for two years, and then 60 percent after that."

Land rent was based not on the actual harvest, but on what the landlord thought the land should yield. Three years before, Xã Long had specified the yield, but given a low rent rate to compensate for the poor quality of the land. He knew that doubling it alone would make it extremely difficult for his tenant, and raising it to 50, let alone 60 percent, would be impossible for any farmer to bear.

"But Village Chief, that land is very poor. As it is, we can barely remit what we owe you each year!" Cả Nguyên almost shouted in protest.

Kim Liên took advantage of the fact that Xã Long was savoring his tea. She knew her business facts and had no qualm about finishing what her father had done to the agitated farmer. She smiled mischievously as she spoke.

"Uncle Nguyên, you will have no problem. After all, you and your sons are reputed to be the best farmers in these areas. Over the past three years, you have brought those fields to yield almost as much as the other ones with the good advice that your daughter has given you. My father is only now catching up with your progress. We just don't want any of our other tenants to complain about those very low rates that you have been enjoying up to now."

"Please, no ..., you are mistaken. That land is still marginally productive, even though we spend more of our own labor on it than on any of our other fields. It has been back breaking work for my sons and me to clear the brushes and pull out the stones that keep coming to the surface every year. Then we had to build irrigation ditches, and small dams to contain the water. We had to perform hundreds of other tasks that you probably are not even aware of."

The Village Chief saw no point in negotiating anything when the opposing party had already said no from the beginning.

"I do know more than you think. Don't forget that in my youth I used to farm and did the same things that you claim you are now doing. You don't have to teach me anything. You must excuse me now, but I have some other business to take care of."

Xã Long and the dejected Cả Nguyên stood up at the same time. The visitor went out the front door, his head hanging low, while the host went to look for his water pipe after throwing a triumphant look to his wife and daughter.

"I will gather the Village Council in a few days, and then I will deal with the village teacher," he told them.

Kim Liên left her parents to go out to the kitchen area. She felt recharged by the brief exchange she had with the father of her rival, or perhaps her former rival since she now only had lukewarm feelings for the village teacher. Her mood did not last long. As soon as she walked through the open area where she was attacked and made a captive of the rebels, her elation dissolved instantly. She stopped on the spot where she was grabbed from behind and a powerful hand clamped itself against her mouth, while a low but confident voice told her not to resist.

The blindfold wrapped around her eyes prevented her from seeing him, and her vision was not restored until it was lifted by the village teacher. Still, she had little doubt that he was handsome, and she would recognize that voice and that laugh anywhere. At times, she could even feel the strong arms that wrapped themselves around her, the same arms that lifted her from the ground and deposited her in the sampan. How she loathed that man! What would she give to be able to see him and make him cringe like so many of the people she dealt with in the village?

She lowered her eyes and let out a sigh. Of the two men she admired the most, outside of her father, the village teacher was one. She already knew that he was lost to her. Actually he had never belonged to her, since that girl from the Nguyên family had preempted his affection from the very first time she entered the village school. That was why during all that time travelling down the river with him in the sampan, he barely paid any attention or talked to her, preferring instead to engage in conversation with the boat owner and her little daughter.

The rebel was the second man, an impossible dream. She would never be able to look at him except as an enemy or an outlaw whose head sooner or later would adorn the top of a bamboo pole. Did he care? Did he even have an inkling of how she felt about him? She shook her head and let out another sigh.

Her mother came up from behind, surprised to see her normally active and strong daughter out in the open and acting like a love-struck schoolgirl.

"Daughter, what are you doing here? What's troubling you?"

Kim Liên recovered quickly from her moment of despair.

"I was going to get something to eat, but I just now lost my appetite. I am going back."

She turned around, avoided her mother's eyes and went to her room.

The news of the disastrous defeat inflicted by the rebels travelled fast. Barely a day after the crestfallen Prefect returned to his provincial headquarters, the whole village was fully aware of what had happened. People were stopping one another on the road or in the fields to share the latest rumors that were going around, each time gaining in scale and distortion.

By the end of the day, rumors had it that a small force of rebels had ambushed the Prefect column as they were nearing their base. The government troops expected only a few poorly organized bandits led by ruffians of questionable military skills. They advanced as if they were on parade, unaware that their movement, strength and disposition had all been made known to the rebels. First, the government column was shelled and cut in two disoriented halves. Then the survivors were pinned down by accurate fire from rebel sharpshooters behind dug-in positions. The rebels were using not old muskets but rifles with longer range and better accuracy.

The Prefect, his officers and soldiers ran for their lives, leaving behind most of their weapons. The French officers and soldiers had no option but to flee as well, abandoning cannons that they didn't have time to set up or position. All the provision carts were lost, providing a welcome bonanza to the rebels.

Xã Long was devastated. He locked himself in his house and turned away all visitors. His wife, when she heard the news, ran to find him to see if he knew anything more that could reassure her that their son was safe and unharmed. Instead of answering her questions, he growled menacingly, causing her to beat a hasty retreat out of the room. The only person he did not chase away was his daughter.

However, Kim Liên knew his moods well and, after taking a quick look at her father, wisely decided not to ask him any question. The news and rumors strangely cheered her up. She knew who had humiliated her brother, and she was quite happy that it had not been the other way around. She would die if her brother had captured the rebel commander and brought him back in a cage, or worse, as a head at the end of a pole.

Giang

Her father casually informed the family that a visitor was coming for dinner that evening. He revealed little about the stranger aside from the fact that he was a priest who had come back from a long pastoral visit to the Northern provinces. Giang was at once intrigued and wanted to find out more about the visitor, but she wanted to wait until she could actually talk to him. Anything that her father could relate would be second-hand information in any case.

She had fully recovered from her mysterious illness. She had resumed her weekly visits to the orphanage and had resumed her duties at the stall in the Đông Ba market with Mai. Their father now had an armed soldier following them close by when they went to or returned from the market and there had been no incident of any kind.

At the orphanage, talk and gossips about Found and her new status in Minister Toản's household were becoming less common, the surprise and novelty having slowly worn off. At times Giang couldn't help herself picturing Found following Tâm around like his shadow whenever he came to the orphanage, but she knew that such images were of a time that had gone by and would never come back. The little girl was being pampered by her mother and, hopefully, by her grandfather, the Minister of Rites. Tâm, her idol had returned to his village, perhaps never to set foot in the capital again.

Since she came out of her lethargic state, Giang at least she went through the motions of resuming her daily activities. There was a large emptiness in her life, a feeling she kept hidden inside her. Her sister Mai had some inkling that something was not the same with her sister as before and, several times already, had tried to talk to her about it. Each time Giang had steered the conversation away to other topics. Mai did not persist, reasoning that her sister's attitude was the result or side effect from her long illness.

Giang did not want anybody, especially her mother, to know that she was biding her time and waiting patiently. She thought of Tâm daily, and her heart ached each time she thought about him. Almost everywhere she turned, there was some reminder of the times they spent together during a summer that was too short and yet filled with so many memories.

The orphanage had not changed in any way, and some of the children still mentioned him and the historical legends he told them. The tower of the Thiên Mụ pagoda was visible in the distance, and twice a day the 108 sounds of its bell carried itself over to her house. Her grand uncle, the abbot at Thiên Mụ, once told her that the number of bell ringing derived from the six senses. Each of the senses had positive, negative, or indifferent reactions, making 18 feelings. Each of the feelings could be pleasurable or not, resulting in 36 passions. Each passion in turn could be experienced in the past, present, and future, totaling108 afflictions. The sounds usually woke her up in the early morning, and she often wondered how many of the afflictions could best describe the loneliness that she felt then. Rather than calming and comforting her, the bell sounds intensified her longing and sadness.

One day she rode the filly to the beach at Thuận An, retracing the steps she and Tâm had taken together from the capital to the seashore only a few months earlier. She walked on the beach aimlessly then sat in the same place where they had spent an afternoon, when everything was so idyllic and life was smiling on both of them. A storm was gathering and a cool wind blew in steady gusts from the ocean to the shore. The waves which were starting to change into white caps did not help her mood, leaving her as disconsolate as before. On her way back, the sky darkened dramatically, and it started raining heavily to the accompaniment of violent thunder and intense lightning. She saw a small roadside temple and stopped there to find shelter. She tied her horse to a column, patted its head and asked it not to break loose and run away in fear. Fortunately, the filly was placid and obedient, and after a moment Giang entered the small temple to escape from the drenching rain.

There was nobody inside, and the temple's single room was bare. There was no altar, no statue, but the back wall was covered with a faded painting of a benign looking goddess standing on a giant lotus flower in the middle of a pond. On an impulse, Giang crossed herself and knelt down in front of the painting. She looked at the goddess for a long time, letting tear drops slowly roll down her cheeks. Alone in the abandoned temple, she cried for the first time, not as child, but as a young woman making her first steps into adulthood. She prayed and unburdened herself of her worries and yearnings, disregarding her church's admonitions against idolatry and worshipping other religion's deities.

The countryside and the temple in it were plunged into darkness but frequent flashes of lighting kept the back wall illuminated with a brilliant, unearthly light. The goddess seemed to be looking at her with understanding and compassion, and at times she thought she saw the hint of an encouraging smile on the benign face. When the storm was over, Giang felt revived and much better than she had been in a long time. She went home determined to take charge of her life.

She heard her father's carriage and went down to greet him and the visitor. Her mother and Mai were already in their living room. Soon Special Envoy Bonneau walked in, escorting a gaunt and deeply tanned man in a black soutane, with thinning hair on his head and a thick, almost unruly, reddish beard. Father Stéphane kept a friendly smile as introductions were made. His eyes slowly passed over Mai before lingering curiously on Giang. Together with their mother, both sisters were wearing evening Western dresses, but they looked as different as two perfect strangers could be. One was taller with a Western build and facial characteristics, and a slightly mischievous although honest look. The other was almost all Vietnamese, except for her eyes and an open and warm expression that he did not often see, except in small children who had not yet been told to distrust foreigners and keep away from them.

"Françoise, your eyes give you away as your father's daughter. Otherwise, you could almost pass for a Vietnamese," he said, and then turned back to Bà Trang. "And thank you, Madame, for giving the world two such charming girls, each one so beautiful in her own way."

Bà Trang laughed lightly and shook her head.

"Father Stéphane, they do *appear* charming, and I need to say no more. But let's proceed to the dining room where we can talk over the simple meal we have prepared in your honor."

The meal was anything but simple, and the French dishes were a reminder of home for the priest who had become accustomed to the spicy food of Central Việt Nam. Toward the end of the meal, while cheese, fruit and coffee were being served, the small talk around the table had dwindled in intensity. Bonneau raised his voice slightly to get everyone's attention and explained the priest's presence at the table for the benefit of his family.

"Father Stéphane, or Cha Phan as he is known in Vietnamese, has been in this country for over a decade. He speaks Vietnamese just like a native, and he has lived or travelled to all corners of the North, the Center, and the South."

As he talked, he glanced at his older daughter with a glint in his eyes. Something in them told Giang she needed to devote all of her attention to what was going to be said.

"Father Stéphane recently came to his order's headquarters here in Huế with a special request to his Jesuit superiors. They are the ones who relayed his request to me, and that's why I wanted to invite him here today so that we can hear what he has to say in his own words. Father Stéphane, tell us what you need and why."

"The list of what I need is not long," the priest began. "It includes school materials, such as notebooks, pens, pencils, slate boards, chalk, ink, and books. Books printed in the new Vietnamese script are welcome, but French textbooks on any subject would also be welcome. The teacher of the school that will receive all these materials is a bright young scholar who wants to wean his students from classical Sino-Vietnamese studies, and turn them toward the West. He wants to modernize the educational system, starting with his own village school."

He saw that Françoise, or Giang, was watching him keenly and hanging on to his words.

"I suspect that you are already familiar with this village teacher," he added. He was starting to understand why Special Envoy Bonneau had invited him to come for dinner and meet his family.

"Is his name Lê Duy Tâm?" asked Giang weakly.

"Yes, the same one who was unfairly failed in the palace examinations, jailed briefly and beaten, before being pardoned by the King."

"Did you see and speak to him? How is he?"

Giang ignored the silent signs that her mother was making to tell her to restrain herself. Her father watched his daughter, surprised at the sudden intensity of her emotions. He had wanted her to hear the news directly from the priest, hoping to cheer her up, but her reaction revealed something else that he had not seen in his daughter before. The priest, a keen observer of human emotions, became aware that he was perhaps witnessing a family drama happening right before his eyes.

"I saw him indeed. He is fine and safe in his village, and has resumed his life as the village teacher. He has started to teach his students the new script and they are doing well. He is a good man, very dedicated to his chosen profession. If it was Christianity that he was pursuing, he would have been an exemplary Jesuit."

His comment made everybody smile and brought some color to the face of the young woman so keen on finding out about the village teacher. To indulge her, he described in details what he saw in the few hours that he was with Teacher Tâm.

The village school contained only the essentials for a frugal existence and none of the luxurious paraphernalia and modern conveniences of a French colonial mansion in Hué at the end of the 19th century. The French priest was impressed by Tâm when he met him, and he lauded his idealism mixed with the practicality imposed by the demands of his career as a village teacher. He was surprised that he was still single at his age, but he did not have the time or the inclination to ask why. Now, he knew or at least he thought he knew.

He wondered how a poor scholar from a village so far from the capital managed to win the heart of the privileged daughter of the French Special Envoy. He had to admit that he himself saw in the village teacher many traits and characteristics which made him somewhat of an exceptional man, but were they enough to capture someone's heart? He remembered Blaise Pascal saying "the heart has its reasons which reason knows nothing of." Being a man of the cloth, he thought that was as close to an explanation as he would ever get.

"He is well liked, or shall I say worshipped, by his students. They would do anything for him. When I was there, they were going to help him teach the older adults how to read and write in the new script. They were very excited about the idea, even if all of them, including their teacher, had only recently learned it."

He paused to sip his coffee, noting the smile and dreamy look on Giang's face. He did not know that she was the one who had taught Tâm, so he continued.

"He is also using a little girl that he sort of adopted as an example for his class and for the entire village. She is the youngest of his students, but she can already read and write in the new script without any trouble."

"You said that he adopted her?" asked Giang.

"Yes and no. She's staying in his house, the school house, but she does have a mother who comes visit her every month. That little girl, whose name is Hồng, is someone that I have been trying to help for a few years, after her father was killed in a battle with French troops. She's a gifted child who deserves to receive an education in a school setting, rather than following her mother around on her sampan. Teacher Tâm had no trouble taking her in as a student, and in fact he was the one who suggested the idea. I convinced her mother, who was initially hesitant, to take him up on his offer."

At that point Bà Trang could not resist asking a question that had been in the back of her mind. "So, Teacher Tâm does not have a wife?"

"None that I could see. He just lives with his mother behind the school, just the two of them. Now they have Hồng with them, and perhaps she adds something to their life."

Giang looked away wistfully, lost in her own thoughts.

"I wish some of the court mandarins were as tolerant as Teacher Tâm," said her father. "So many Vietnamese have lost their lives, and this country has wasted so much time, because those in powers were obsessed with killing Christians. Not that it has stopped or even slowed down the spread of Christianity, as you well know, Father

Stéphane. Your order keeps expanding and setting up roots everywhere in this country."

"And sometimes we have done so at a dear cost," sighed the priest. "In any case, that's what keeps me so busy travelling from one province to another, and I will keep doing my work for as long as I can, God willing."

"Cha Phan, when are you returning to the North?" Giang asked, addressing him by his Vietnamese name.

"Well, I need a few more days to gather all that I am supposed to bring with me, especially for Teacher Tâm. Perhaps you could help, Special Envoy, and allow me to get some of the supplies and materials originally intended for your own schools here."

"Of course," Bonneau replied. "Consider it done."

"Then, I should be on my way within two weeks at the latest, and probably sooner," the priest addressed Giang. "Is there something that you think I should take with me on this next trip to give to the village teacher?"

Giang answered without any hesitation.

"With my parents' permission, and if it will not inconvenience you too much, I would like to go with you."

The room suddenly became very quiet. The priest looked at each of his hosts. Bonneau had extracted his pipe from somewhere and was trying very carefully to clean it. His wife had turned her face away so that he couldn't see what her expression was. Was she upset, angry, or sad? The younger sister was smiling at her older sibling, her head nodding in support and admiration. Giang, he had decided not to use her French name anymore, was staring at him with eyes the color of the deep blue sea, and eagerly waiting for his answer. He saw in them something innocent, sincere, but at the same time resolute, almost defiant.

After the Jesuit priest had left and everyone had retired to their rooms, Special Envoy Bonneau finally took pity of his wife. She was on the verge of tears as a silent crisis had been building within her without any outlet as long as their guest was still among them. When they were at last alone in their bedroom, she collapsed into a chair and began sobbing. He went to her, but she extended an arm to push him back. The woman who had always maintained an iron hand on the household as well as on her business had been defeated by her own daughter. She managed to ask him in halting words.

"Why … didn't you … tell … her … not to …?"

He took his time answering her, for he himself didn't know what the real reason was. There were several and he didn't know which one really mattered in the end.

"Would it have made any difference?" he finally said. "Short of locking her up in her room, what can we do?"

"She's your daughter!" Bà Trang argued with a surprising vigor. "How can you let her go off and … see that monster that has bewitched her?"

Bonneau reacted more forcefully than he had intended.

"My dear wife, you must calm down. This is unusual for you. The one that you should call a monster is the Minister of Rites' son, the one who raped his father's wife. The same one that you tried to get our daughter to marry! You must rid yourself of that insidious fortune-teller story that your uncle, the abbot, concocted, without any basis in fact. He only wanted to tell you what you wanted to hear and in the process slandered a good and innocent man! Don't you understand that?"

The outburst calmed him down somewhat, and he took one of her hands and patted it, seeking her eyes with his.

"I know you had the best intentions, and that's why at the beginning I did not interfere with any of your plans. I should have, because somewhere along the lines you forgot what your real goal should have been. Instead of making sure that Giang will be happy, all you cared about was to get her married to some scion of a powerful mandarin family. Most of all, you just wanted a son-in-law who was not that village teacher."

As she obstinately shook her head from side to side, he continued.

"I have been thinking for the past few months about the two of them. Call it karma, or call it something that God in His infinite wisdom has decreed, but her fate somehow is tied to his. We should not interfere. Short of taking some drastic and cruel action, we cannot and will not change it. Look at what happened when you took her to Tourane to meet the Minister and his son: she showed that she was as headstrong as you are and capable of decisive action by coming back here as soon as she heard that her loved one had been arrested. And we almost lost her when she felt into that state halfway between dreaming and being in a coma. When she woke up from it, I could tell that she had been transformed and was no longer the child that we used to think she was."

The couple went on talking quietly. He applied his skills at persuasion, honed by years of serving as Special Envoy to the Vietnamese court. He knew when to press his advantage, when to retreat and come back from another angle, never giving up his objective. He asked her to look at their own past, at how many obstacles they had to overcome on both sides, Vietnamese as well as French, before they were finally allowed to become husband and wife.

After hours of tossing and turning in bed, Bà Trang finally fell asleep as the first rays of the sun began to illuminate the horizon. After what seemed like only a few minutes, she reopened her eyes and shook her husband awake.

"You must go talk to Cha Phan."

Bonneau kept his eyes shut and asked in a tired voice.

"This early in the morning? What is it about?"

"About Giang travelling to the Tonkin to find the village teacher."

He opened his eyes wide.

"Are you finally agreeing to let her go?"

"Yes, but you must tell him he must act on our behalf and make sure nothing bad happens to her."

He sighed but was inwardly elated at the change in his wife. The constant undercurrent of tension for the past few months was finally giving way to reason and pragmatism. He looked at her puffed eyes and the new wrinkle lines that have started to appear on her still beautiful face.

"Go back to sleep, I know just what to do and what to tell him."

The Village Council

It had been almost a month since his son's embarrassing defeat in his first battle command, and now Xã Long was ready to take action. In the late afternoon, after the monsoon rain had brought the temperature down a little, the Village Council members came promptly at the village communal house as he had requested.

The *đình* or communal house was the most important structure in the village, with an imposing roof supported by 60 thick ironwood pillars and solid walls that some said could withstand even direct gunfire. With his own money and the free labor contributed by the villagers, over several years Xã Long had funded and led the restoration of the communal house, transforming it from a modest and rather ordinary looking building into an imposing one that was the pride of the village and something of envy among all the other villages in the region. It had seven rooms, the largest of which was the communal hall where ceremonies or theatrical performances were performed, and where the Village Council usually met. It also served as a sort of court of justice where disputes were settled and sentences were occasionally doled out to those who violated village rules and regulations. One room had no windows and an entire wall consisting of ironwood pillars, closely spaced together. It served as a temporary detention facility for criminals arrested in the village and held there until they could be tried and sentenced, or until they were transferred to a higher provincial authority.

While waiting for the notables to settle down around him, Xã Long contemplated the scene and its main players.

The Village Chief was normally the lowest ranking member of the Council, an executor of the decisions taken by the other notables. The most influential member was traditionally some elderly and retired mandarin who, because of his knowledge and experience, was entrusted with managing village affairs wisely and efficiently. The largest landowners, the wealthiest craftsmen, and at times a respected village teacher formed the rest of the Council.

A younger man, Tuấn, chosen for his physical abilities and allegiance to Xã Long, served as the village's constable. Under the direction of the Village Chief, Tuấn enforced the Council's orders, and, together with some burly young men, his part-time constables, acted as the local police to punish or take into custody those who dared go against the established rules and regulations.

Over the years, Xã Long had built up his power base through persuasion, bribery, force, and varying combinations of all three as each situation warranted. He dealt with many villagers out of business necessity or as part of his official functions. He had a good network of allies and used them as his eyes and ears.

Furthermore, because he was the wealthiest businessman with the largest landholdings and a successful rice milling business, every family in the small community sooner or later had to deal with him. Many had to pay him part of their crops as land rents or fees for using his mill. Some owed him money he lent to help them after a meager harvest, a severe drought, a massive flood, or to pay off their gambling debts.

Others benefited from favors that he judiciously doled out from time to time to win friends and neutralize foes. The Village Council members were among those who owed him the most favors.

The elderly former mandarin, Phạm Văn Khê, who should have presided over the Village Council was now a mere rubber stamp for the Village Chief. That is because Xã Long discreetly supplied him at nominal cost the opium that he smoked. This man, whose scholarship was exemplary in his youth, now had a memory that often failed him conveniently at the most crucial moments. Whenever a critical issue was to come before the Council, Xã Long told one of his servants to make sure that the old man smoked his pipe beforehand so that he would come peacefully and meekly to the meetings, ready to speak out in favor of the side that his benefactor had chosen to take. He could cite with ease historical precedents and royal or local rules to support that side. Since he was the recognized authority in such matters, his pronouncements were usually final and ended further discussion.

The council members who were also wealthy landowners got preferential treatment and discounted rates at the rice mill controlled by Xã Long. They never suspected that the mill cheated them of some rice to make up for the lower rates. Perhaps some did harbor such suspicions, but they wisely kept their own counsel. Live and let live, as some were known to say. Therefore, when the Village Council debated and made decisions, they scrupulously observed Xã Long, swinging over to his side or strengthening it with their own opinions when needed.

The one man that Xã Long could not control was the old village teacher, Lê Duy Lân, Tâm's father. For many years, he was the most respected person in the village and, by popular demand, became a member of the Village Council long before Xã Long's time. Although not a wealthy man, the policies and measures that he urged the Council to take always benefited the whole village. He did not have to bribe or pressure anyone, yet the Council members listened to him as their wisest and incorruptible member. The only force he held was moral, and the only persuasion he needed was his frugal life as the teacher of everyone's children or grandchildren. Nobody could accuse him of hidden motives or a conflict of interest since he never benefited from anything that he advocated.

Fortunately, shortly after Xã Long had maneuvered himself into the Village Council, the old teacher passed away. His son Tâm was too young and had more than enough to deal with in trying to continue in his father's footsteps as a teacher. He had no time for the Council, and neither Xã Long nor the rest of the notables thought of asking him to fill in for his father. Some, the Village Chief included, were in fact relieved that they did not have to deal with another honest man in their group.

When his son Chí passed the palace examinations and rode home in triumph, Xã Long knew that his power was absolute. No one could challenge him on anything, not that anybody wanted to try. People bowed to him much deeper than before and an endless procession of well-wishers and sycophants began gathering at his home.

Yet he was unhappy. Here he was, sitting in the communal house and preparing to make the Council decide and take action against the one who so ably succeeded his father at the village school, the same one who failed in the examinations that his son took in the capital. Did that failure diminish him in the eyes of the villagers? No, by all measures, he had become even more popular, especially once he and his students started teaching the older people in the village how to read and write in the new Vietnamese script. Meanwhile, his son was soundly defeated in his first battle against the rebels, becoming the object of disparaging comments and even humiliating jokes in the village and perhaps in the entire country. Things were not supposed to be happening that way, but Xã Long was determined to use his influence and wield his power to turn them around.

Councilman Khê always started the meetings before artfully handing them over to Xã Long. On that day, he was at the top of his form after smoking his opium and taking a long nap. He woke up refreshed and ready for the Village Council assembly. Sitting next to Xã Long, he took his time looking at each of the other notables, nodding appreciatively as if he was reviewing and approving each person. He spoke slowly in the deep and strong voice of the mandarin that he used to be, projecting it clearly and effortlessly toward everyone.

"We are assembled here today because of an issue that has been brought to my attention by the Village Chief. Rather than telling you what it is, I will ask the Chief to do that a little bit later. However, before he begins let me first ask you to give him your full attention to what he is going to relate and describe to you. The issue has never arisen in our village before, but now that it is, we cannot overlook it. Maybe some of you would not even recognize it as real problem. Let me assure you: it is real and it is without doubt a threat to our community and our way of life. People have come to the Chief and made him aware of it. He has conducted his own investigation and has confirmed the existence of such a threat. He has never been wrong before, and I can assure you that he is not wrong this time. I now yield to him, and let him make clear to you what this is all about."

He turned to Xã Long and dipped his head slightly, satisfied with the interest his short speech has elicited among the Council notables. A few were straightening their backs and craning their necks forward, their eyes fixed on the Village Chief, eagerly waiting for him to speak. He did not disappoint them. Referring to Khê by his old title, he began.

"What Prefect Khê is referring to is the beginning of a not so subtle campaign to convert the people in this village to Christianity and to transform our village into a Catholic community."

The audience gasps were almost as loud as various exclamations by the Council notables.

"What? How could it be? Impossible! This cannot be tolerated!"

Xã Long continued evenly.

"I can tell you exactly who the instigator of this campaign is. He is none other than our village teacher, Lê Duy Tâm. Yes, the same one who recently went to the capital and failed so shamefully in the examinations. The same one to whom we send our children or grandchildren every day to get an education."

He stopped to let the meaning of his words sink in. He noted with satisfaction that a rising uneasiness was gradually replacing the initial surprise on many faces.

"Under the pretext of teaching everyone in the village how to read and write, he has used our older children to help him carry out his evil plans. The adults are being taught not Chinese characters but the new script that the foreign missionaries created to help them in their conversion work. Some of you may think that it is not such a bad idea, and under normal circumstances one could agree with that."

He raised his finger and wagged it in the air.

"However, do you know what materials our village teacher is using to teach, first the children, and now the adults? Constable Tuấn will show you what he has found in the village school."

The constable, uncomfortable at being put at the center of attention, reached down to his side and brought up a well-worn book that he held up high for all to see.

"This is a book in two languages, French and Vietnamese, both written in the foreigners' script. Constable Tuấn will now pass the book around for each of you to look at."

Tuấn cautiously handed the book over to an elderly landowner who goes by the name of Bác Thông. The man started examining it and opened the book at its first page. Xã Long waited just a few seconds before continuing.

"Now, I know that none of you, even with your traditional training in Chinese and Nôm characters, will be able to read this book. I can't either. I just know it is in two languages because there are two types of printing on it. One is straight, the other is slanted. The former is in all likelihood a French word or words, and the latter is its corresponding Vietnamese word or words. Or it could be the other way around. As the book is passed around, I invite you to carefully look at its cover. Since Bác Thông is holding the book, let's start with him."

The notable who was leafing through the book promptly closed it.

"Can you tell us if you can read anything on the cover, Bác Thông?"

After a careful examination of the cover, Bác Thông slowly replied.

"I can't read anything, but I think I recognize the number ten. It's the largest character in the middle of the cover."

Xã Long could not suppress his laugh, though he had not intended to ridicule the notable.

"You are right, but only if the book were written in Chinese. It is, however, a French-Vietnamese book, and what you are recognizing as the number ten is actually the symbol of the cross, the foreigners' symbol for their religion. Please pass the book around so that all can see what I am talking about."

While the Council notables took turns examining the book, Xã Long signaled for the constable to be ready for his next call.

Each notable looked at the book's cover and nervously passed it on to his neighbor as if handling a burning cinder. No one wanted to hold on to a Christian book.

Once it came back full circle to him, Xã Long continued.

"That's the book that our village teacher is using to teach our children, and soon the older people in this village."

Several voices were heard at the same time.

"How could he dare?"

"Who authorized him to teach the … Christian religion to our children? When did this all start?"

One of the voices did manage to ask a simple question.

"How do we know that the village teacher actually used the book?"

Xã Long was prepared with the answer.

"It's good that you asked that question. Some children have reported that he had the book with him, and our constable has managed to *borrow* it right from under his nose, so to speak. It's not as if Teacher Tâm made a secret of it or kept it hidden. He usually has it right by his side, and it is usually left out in the open in the classroom, whether school is in session or not."

He pointed a finger at the constable. "There is something else that I will ask constable Tuấn to show you."

At his signal, the man produced a piece of what looked like scroll paper and handed it over to Xã Long. He held it in front of him so that everybody could see what was on it. There were rows of neat and regular script running on the paper.

"Our very smart constable also managed to *borrow* this from the village teacher. He has been transcribing the Vietnamese version of the Christian book on this and other similar pieces of paper. He has not told anyone about it yet, but we understand that once the children can read fluently in the new script, he will use these transcriptions as textbooks. He is determined to use this new script to expose our children to the foreigners' religion. Let me hand these out to you so that you can see for yourself what I am talking about."

Of course, none of the notables could make sense of the writing on the pieces of paper. Unwilling to look at them any longer than they had to, they hastily passed them on to their neighbor. Xã Long was pleased with their reaction. Traditionally, a teacher was as revered as one's own parents were, but he had managed to sow the seeds of suspicion and ill will toward Teacher Tâm in his audience. And he was not yet finished.

"Honored members of the Council, I now want to bring to your attention another related matter. Recently, most of us have become aware that the village teacher has taken in a little girl to live with him and his mother at the school. He has allowed the girl to attend the school, just like any other child in this village. Did he ask us whether we could allow it? No. Did he even inform us about it? No. It's as if this Village Council did not exist, as if village rules and traditions no longer count. It's as if Teacher Tâm is running his own school without any regard to the community he lives in. I am sure you all know the famous phrase *'the King's laws yield to the village's rules'*. Well our village teacher is telling us *'the village's rules stop at the school's door.'"*

"Who is this child? Is she his daughter?" asked another elderly notable.

Xã Long recognized him as another retired mandarin who, in his youth, was famous for fathering a child in each of his posts throughout the provinces of the Center and the North. He absolutely did not want the man to develop a sudden empathy for the village teacher.

"No, she's not his daughter. Her mother somehow got the village teacher to accept her as a student, but that's the least of our worry. What we should be concerned with is the fact that she is a Christian, the first one that our village has ever known."

The room erupted. The notables were clearly agitated and could no longer remain calm and composed as they used to be at all council meetings. Everyone spoke, tried to ask questions, or started discussions with their neighbors.

"How can this be? Who let this happen?"

"Has he gone crazy?"

"He failed the examinations, and now he has done this to our village? We have given him and his father their livelihood for over thirty years, and he dares treat us like this?"

"Close down the school now, unless we all want to follow that evil religion and kick our ancestors' altars down."

Unperturbed, Xã Long let them talk among themselves and vent their irritation while he took his time in sipping his tea before he resumed his accusations.

"Yes indeed, that girl is a Christian living right among us. Some have seen her making the sign of the cross and praying, not surreptitiously, but quite openly in the presence of Teacher Tâm. He has brought her among us, and the question you want to ask is not who she is, or where she came from. No, what you want to ask is why did he bring her to our village?"

He let his eyes scan the face of each one in the room, challenging each notable to answer his question. Because he was getting tired and did not want the meeting to drag on, Councilman Khê responded.

"It's quite obvious: he is using her to bring the foreigners' religion to our village."

"Why would he do that? Isn't he like the rest of us? He is not a Christian, is he?" another Councilman wondered aloud, not to anyone in particular, but Xã Long felt the questions were meant for him to answer.

"Who knows what goes on inside his mind or his heart? However, facts are facts, and no one can deny that this little Christian girl is living among us. What is even more troubling and revealing is that a few weeks ago, the girl's mother came to the village school accompanied by a French priest, a bearded man who called himself *Cha Phan.* He had a very long talk with the village teacher. What did they discuss? Nobody knows and Teacher Tâm is not saying."

Xã Long was cautious now. The French priest obviously had the backing of the colonial powers, and he did not want to say anything against him that could be reported unfavorably to the authorities. After all, his own son, the Prefect, was working hand in hand with the French to fight against the last remnants of the Cần Vương movement.

He had met Vietnamese Christians in his business dealings and had come to admire them a little bit, not only for their hard work, but also for their cohesion and their loyalty to their own people and faith. Another characteristic was that they were willing to learn and adopt Western ways and techniques, often well ahead of other Vietnamese with deep-rooted fears of modern innovations.

His target was the village teacher, not the little Christian girl, nor the foreign priest, not even the book and documents that the constable had obtained. They were only objects or images for him to use in manipulating the elders on the Council and drive public opinion against his real enemy. The actual threat was not Christianity, it was one man who stood in Xã Long's way, contemptuous of his authority and possibly having contributed to his son's setbacks both on the battlefield and in his personal life.

"Now, whom should we blame? The little Christian girl? The foreign priest who came to our village? Should we not instead blame our village teacher who invited them to come in the first place? Remember: he never informed us or asked for our opinion and consent in these matters. For him our Village Council might as well have never existed and you, the Notables who represent the whole village are irrelevant to him. For him, we on this Council are no better than water puppets."

Right on cue, Councilman Khê, still impatient for a conclusion to be reached, decided to provide his comments to move things along. He began launching into his tirade in a low voice.

"Let me say this, Village Chief: as much as we used to like his father, we must accept the undeniable fact that his son has not lived up to the trust that our village has put into him."

"First, according to our customs and traditions, some going back hundreds of years, no stranger can be admitted into our midst without obtaining the approval of the Village Council. That Teacher Tâm failed to do so is a serious offense all by itself."

His voice now rose higher.

"However, what is even more serious is his attempt to undermine the moral and religious foundations of our community by trying in an underhanded manner to sow the seeds of Christianity in our midst. For thousands of years, Confucianism and Buddhism have been the two spiritual pillars of our society. In this century, our emperors have pointed to the Christian religion as the enemy that seeks to undermine our nation and destroy our morals. That foreign religion teaches its converts to abandon the cult of ancestors and to give their hearts and souls completely and unconditionally to the service of the one they call Jesus."

At this point, he was practically shouting, his face dark and furious against the perceived enemy of the village.

"Are we just going to sit back and let the village teacher do as he pleases? Are you willing to accept that in the future, after you have left this world, your children or grandchildren will not burn incense sticks in your name, but will instead light candles to worship foreign statues in the foreigner's churches?"

He paused to take a deep breath and calm himself down, his own words having awakened in him the anger that he was famous for when he was the highest mandarin in the province. The other Council members were likewise agitated and irritated by the vision of the bleak future he had painted for them. He harangued them one last time.

"Village Chief, what do you propose for the Council to do about this problem? We need to contain it right now before it spreads out and becomes so extensive that we won't be able to stop it."

Xã Long had his answer prepared.

New Challenge

After waiting many days for the warship to be ready at Thuận An, just before boarding they were told that still more heavy weapons and their accompanying troops were to embark before them. Special Envoy Bonneau father explained to his daughter that the troops were reinforcements needed for some looming battle against rebels in a province neighboring the one where Tâm lived. Under the command of a newly appointed mandarin, the forces the royal government sent to crush the rebels had been routed and the Resident General wanted French troops to lead another assault on the rebel base. He assured Giang that where she was going would not be affected by the fighting, and there was no reason for alarm.

Once aboard, they encountered bad weather at sea and the warship was pelted by heavy rain and strong winds every day without respite. Giang suspected it had veered off course, although none of the naval officers would admit to it. Instead of the normal two to three days for the voyage, it took them a week before the monsoon gave them some respite and they finally saw land again.

Since she decided to accompany Father Phan on his trip North, as the days became weeks, and the weeks dragged into a month, Giang became more and more apprehensive. She and Father Phan had done everything that her father had recommended, but had encountered nothing but one delay after another. If she had taken the land route, the same one that Tâm had taken, she could have been with him by now.

Whenever she was by herself, she thought about Tâm, the one for whom she was leaving her home and her family. She kept going over the moments they had spent together during the summer. At times, she remembered the strange sensations she felt when he was with her. She could almost still feel his arms holding her tightly as they rode back from the beach at Thuận An. She needed to see him again, look into his eyes, and reassure herself that she had not been mistaken about how he felt toward her. She could not believe that the summer had only been just a dream or that he was a man like Lamartine who had promised to return to Graziella and never did until well after she had passed away.

Just before she left, her sister had teased her.

"You'll find out that he went home and got married to some peasant girl. What will you do then?"

"Oh, you are so wicked! He told me he had nobody waiting for him at home, except his mother."

Mai sister burst out laughing.

"Mother says that's what all young men say, and that you will believe what you want to hear anyway."

Seeing the expression that came on Giang's face, she hurried to add.

"I am on your side, really. I'm just repeating what I overheard her say to father."

"She does not know, nor does she understand Teacher Tâm like I do."

As soon as they arrived in the port of Hải Phòng, the main port in the Tonkin, they went ashore while the warship took on more troops. Military priority overruled everything, and the officers were in a hurry to load the men and their equipment. She saw one officer who looked somewhat familiar, and recognized him as the recently promoted Captain St Arnaud who worked as an aide to her father. Her sister used to complain that he had never tried to talk to them even though he came to their house often to see their father on official business. He was in charge of the contingent of French and indigenous troops from Cochinchina. He, of course, did not see her or, if he did, completely ignored her.

The port city was formerly known as Ninh Hải, until the French renamed it Hải Phòng shortly after it was ceded to them in 1874 via the

Treaty of Sài Gòn. Since then the city had become a veritable French naval base. Giang observed that it was thriving and showed abundant signs of Western influence, from the new buildings and houses built in Western style to the presence of a sizable French community in the city, all living in colonial affluence and splendor. Both she and the priest were glad when they were at last able to leave it and start the land leg of their voyage.

Giang was keen to get away from the sight of French men and women, and even children at times, parading down the streets as royalties, proud of being French and disdainful of the natives. There were even farcical sights of ample French women dressed in frilly Victorian clothes sitting smugly in chairs straddling two long bamboo poles carried by a dozen small Vietnamese women. The French women smiled and laughed while their carriers struggled gamely to maintain a synchronized pace and avoid a spill of their passengers.

In the brief time she spent in the city she had experienced first-hand how humiliating it was to have to yield the right of way to a Westerner, or be talked to in pidgin French and treated like a lowly servant when seen in the company of the French priest. She understood that was because she was dressed in local clothes and wore a conical hat that hid half of her face, looking for all practical purposes like the priest's servant. Still that did not lessen the annoyance she felt at being treated in that manner.

She had no idea of what would happen once she got to Tâm's village. At the start of her trip, she was busy with preparations and with the steady advice given several times a day by her parents and even by her sister Mai. During the voyage, the rough weather and tall waves had all her worried attention, even though she did not get seasick. Now, only a few days perhaps from her destination, a feeling of dread was slowly taking hold of her. She did not have the strange dreams she did when she felt sick on her return from Tourane, but her instinct told her that something could yet go wrong when she would finally be reunited with him.

Thi took a break from her copying. She and several of the older students were making textbooks in the new script by transcribing famous Vietnamese poems and folk verses. They were to use the textbooks to teach reading to the adults in the village. So far, the campaign for literacy had met with a degree of success that nobody had thought possible.

Teacher Tâm said he wanted to start on a small scale before expanding the campaign to the entire village. They were able to persuade the first ten adults to come to the village school in the evening. She and four older students were assigned two adults each, and under the supervision of their teacher they helped the older people learn the alphabet and practice reading and writing simple words. The next step was to introduce them to popular Vietnamese poetry and folk sayings written down in the crude textbooks they were making.

She looked up to the front of the class. Teacher Tâm was looking pensively, almost dreamily, out the window. What was he thinking about? Was he still sad about failing the examinations? In previous years, she would have gone sit by his side and start talking to him about school or about any topic that came to mind. Since he came back from the capital, she had stopped doing that, only bringing him his tea then coming back to her seat. She did not mind that the new little girl in the village school, Hồng, had taken her place and was now the main recipient of his attention and affection.

The talks at home about the marriage proposal from the Village Chief's son had unsettled her greatly. She had told her parents very firmly that she considered herself too young and was not yet interested in marriage to anybody. Her father had related to her what the Xã Long's reaction had been during their meeting. He also said that he was considering cutting back on the fields that they rented from the Village Chief, reducing the family income in the future. The more she thought about it, the more sickened she became at the thought of the Village Chief throwing his weight around to impose his will. She knew that young women were sometimes forced into a marriage not to their liking, but usually it was their own parents and families who pressured them into it. In her own case, her family was supportive of her decision, and the only pressure came from a man who thought he could make anyone bend to his will. It was as if the village was the fiefdom of Xã Long, and she, her family, and everyone else had to do as he dictated.

Tâm was unexpectedly tense that morning. He searched his memory to find out why, but could not come up with anything. The school was buzzing with activity, all students carrying out their assignments in their usual industrious manner. Little Hồng was learning rapidly, making up at incredible speed the years of schooling that she missed. Thi and the older students were very proud of their extra work teaching the adults the new script. The latter often came up to him to express their gratitude and to tell him about their progress under the tutelage of people who were the age of their children or even grandchildren. Even his own mother was involved, trying to learn the new script in the evening with help from Hồng, the youngest member of the school.

He was keeping a new roster of the adults who were learning to read and write to keep track of their progress. When they started, he didn't know how long it would be before they knew enough to be considered literate, but it looked like it would be sooner than he thought. Next he wanted to begin distributing the hand-copied books he and his students were making so that those villagers who became literate would have something worthwhile to read. It was a modest beginning, but it had set the school humming like a beehive. If there were enough villages like theirs, wouldn't the entire country benefit as a whole? That would be the perfect entrance into the 20th century.

On the threshold of such an accomplishment, one that he valued even more than passing the palace examinations, why was he then uneasy? It was the same feeling he had at times when he was walking back from the capital and unknown danger was looming ahead. It was as if somebody was trying to warn him and steer him away to a safer path, or even show him what to do and say to get out of a thorny situation. After he came home and related it to his uncle Khánh, the monk thought for a long time before answering.

"Some things cannot be explained. Just accept them as they are. If you want, you can think that someone is trying to protect you."

"Who would that be?"

The monk had ended their conversation with his typical enigmatic answer.

"You should already know."

Recess had just begun and it was Hồng who saw them first.

"Cha Phan!" she shouted and jumped up to run out the door.

Thi's eyes followed her and she saw two visitors, the bearded French priest and a young woman who was not Hồng's mother. Cha Phan lifted the little girl up and hugged her affectionately. The young woman smiled but she was peering inside the schoolhouse, searching for someone.

Thi was amazed at her eyes which were a deep blue, unlike any eyes she had ever seen before. The newcomer, wearing a conical hat, was dressed like a Vietnamese and appeared to be one, except for those eyes. She heard footsteps behind her and turned to see her teacher step out of the back room. He went to the front door before stopping sharply.

"Giang!" he exclaimed.

The young woman also came to a stop before reaching the front door. She stood still, gazing at him with a hesitant smile, as if she was trying to gauge his reaction.

"Teacher Tâm," she said softly.

He stepped out into the yard, went to her, reached for her hands and took them in his. She blushed but did not pull back while keeping her eyes fixed on his, those blue eyes that he had dreamed about so often.

"Is it really you, Giang? Did you come all the way from the capital?"

She nodded at each of his questions, and then quickly bit down on her lower lip as her emotions finally overwhelmed her and her eyes started filling up with tears.

Following the foreign priest's example, the students went outside and kept busy unloading the books and supplies from the horse cart the two visitors had arrived in. They carried packages inside, bypassing the front room to go directly to the back by the side door. Without anyone telling them, consciously or unconsciously, they were giving the teacher and his visitor whatever little privacy was possible in the schoolroom with its doors and windows wide open.

They stood facing each other in the deserted room, for a moment oblivious to the world around them. For them time had stopped, the world no longer existed, and they were finally together. There was a lot of movement outside, but they neither saw nor heard all the coming and going around them.

"I thought I would never see you again," he said. "I never thought you would come here, and yet here you are. Why? How?"

He kept his voice low, unconsciously wanting to protect their intimacy. He was no longer holding her hands but he could not keep his eyes off her as a hundred questions raced through his mind.

"You left without telling me," she reproached him softly through her tears, unable to repress a smile that revealed her happiness at seeing him again. She already knew then that he still felt the same about her. "So, of course, I had to come find you."

He wanted to put his arms around her to make sure she was not an apparition, to feel her warmth, to listen to her breathing, to hear her heart beat. Still, his customary reserve prevented him from giving a free rein to his emotions, and he merely stood mesmerized at her sight. He noticed how thin she was compared to a few months earlier.

"You seem to have lost some weight. Was the trip up hard on you? Have you not been well?"

She shook her head.

"We were on a ship and the journey was not strenuous at all like it was for you who walked home from the capital. But I did become ill right after you left, for about two months. I am fine now, nothing to worry about. You too look thinner, Teacher Tâm. I tried to keep you safe in my dreams when I was sick, but perhaps you still had to endure a lot."

His uncle's words came back to him, and suddenly he knew she was the one whose presence he felt during his trip home from the capital.

"So it was you who watched over me during all the time I walked home. I always felt a presence of someone beside me, someone who encouraged me when I was depressed, who helped me overcome danger and obstacles. It was you!"

She continued to smile, but suddenly frowned and asked.

"Why did you leave without saying or writing anything?"

It was as much a reproach as a question. He had mulled over the answer many times over the previous months when he was trying to justify to himself his abrupt departure from the capital.

"Giang, I left because I thought that was best for you. The worlds we live in are just too far apart, and after I failed at the examinations there was little I could do to bridge the gap between a simple village teacher and you, the daughter of a most prominent family in Huế. It was hopeless, and perhaps it still is. I told myself that it was best for me to go home, that it was best for you to listen to your parents and obey them. I thought that by now you would have been married to …."

"To that mandarin son who fathered a child with his stepmother?"

Her blue eyes were peering intently into his.

"Teacher Tâm, even if he were not who he is, even if my mother had managed to find the best possible match for me in the capital, I would still come here today to be with you."

Her voice and words were spoken with a passion that he had not expected. Once again he regretted his decision to literally flee from the capital. What he did was contrary to his upbringing, even if he had rationalized it by saying it was in her best interest. He had let the shame of failing in the examinations, of being jailed, and the insulting admonitions of secretary Kham affect his judgment and behavior. He had not only underestimated her, he had also hurt her. He remembered her tears when she first saw him a moment ago, and he felt remorseful for causing them.

"Giang, will you ever forgive me?"

"Teacher Tâm, I already did the moment I saw you."

He reached out for her hands again. He had barely touched her skin when he heard his mother's voice.

"Son, aren't you going to introduce your visitor to me?"

They had forgotten where they were and were jolted out of their short-lived intimacy. Both turned around. Giang at once bowed to Bà Lân, then lifted her head and her blue eyes gazed intently at the old woman, frail but steady on her feet. Her motherly eyes shone brightly, an aura of kindness emanating from them.

"Mother, forgive me for not introducing our guest to you right away," he said. "This was so unexpected, I had no idea she was coming. Anyway, this is Giang. She's the one who taught me the new script in the capital a few months ago."

Turning to Giang, he added. "Perhaps I should call you Cô Giang?"

His mother laughed good-naturedly, quickly surveying and assessing the younger and taller woman who was speaking with her son in the unfamiliar accent from the Center. She had overhead some of their conversation but had trouble understanding all of what the visitor was saying.

"So, you are the one who caused all this commotion in our village!"

Giang was startled but kept her composure.

"I just arrived here a few minutes ago. What could I have done in such a short time?"

She had switched to a pure Northern accent when talking to his mother, and Tâm noticed it immediately. His mother laughed genially before giving her answer.

"Well, indirectly anyway. Indirectly you have caused some of the older folks in the village to come trudging here every day to be taught how to read and write by their children or grandchildren. Don't worry though, they like it. They want to learn. They are proud of themselves to be still learning something useful at their age. Even I have my own private teacher, that little Hồng who is so smart, well beyond her age. Cô Giang, we should all be thanking you."

"Ah, it's all right then, though you almost gave me a scare. I thought I had done something bad without knowing it."

"No, of course not, you did nothing wrong and I'm glad that you have come to visit us today. My son, who was so moody before, certainly seems quite happy to see you," she said then switched to another subject.

"How did you manage to speak with a Northern accent so well?"

"Cha Phan told me I should try to speak with a Northern accent when I am here if I wanted people to understand me. I had always listened carefully to Teacher Tâm when he was in the capital this past summer, and I became familiar with the way he talked. These past few days I have tried to imitate the Northern accent in conversations with people I met on the way here. I hope I am not doing too badly."

"Oh, you are so amazingly good at it! And those blue eyes of yours …," she shook her head but did not finish her sentence. Instead she turned to her son.

"I will not interrupt your conversation any further. I am going back inside, and in a while, I'll have the little one serve you some tea. You go on talking with Cô Giang since you must have a lot of catching up to do after all these months."

The old woman turned around and went to the back of the house, and when out of earshot, mumbled to herself.

"Is she the one? Is she the one he's been waiting for?"

Later on, they all gathered in the classroom. The French priest sat between the village teacher and Giang, with Thi and Hồng next to her. Other students stayed in the background, observing the scene in silence. They welcomed a rest after unloading and storing away the books and supplies that Cha Phan had brought. Tâm's mother stayed at the back, busy as usual with her daily chores.

Giang tried to look at the students one by one, seeing in their faces a natural curiosity and an openness to the stranger in their midst. She noticed that the older girl, Thi, remained quiet and reserved. She was a beauty but, unlike girls of her age in the capital, her beauty was neither affected nor artificial. It was almost understated, like a wildflower that only close inspection would reveal nature's wonder. She was following her teacher's expression and movements closely, like an attentive student, or perhaps more than that. Giang looked from her to the village teacher, then back. Thi caught her eyes, smiled and perhaps even blushed before getting up to go to the back room. Tâm was busy chatting with Cha Phan and saw nothing of the visual exchange between Thi and Giang.

The little girl, Hồng, fascinated by Giang's appearance and presence, did not try to hide her curiosity. She observed Giang with dreamy eyes and a faint smile on her lips. After some time, she crept up to the village teacher and whispered something into his ear. After listening to her, he turned to Giang.

"Hồng wants to know how long you intend to stay with us."

She smiled at the little girl and answered truthfully.

"I will go back with Cha Phan whenever he does." That was the understanding she had with her parents and the priest, and she knew she would be going back to the parish's church and stay with the nuns as she did the day before and probably during her entire stay.

Hồng appeared disappointed, and without warning ran away to the back. She returned a few minutes later and whispered something else to her teacher. After listening to her, he announced.

"My mother would like to invite you and Cha Phan to share our noontime meal. Please accept, and then stay with us at least until the afternoon turns a little bit cooler."

The French priest answered for both of them. He had never seen Giang in such high spirits and wanted to give her as much time as possible with her village teacher.

"Thank you. We'd be delighted to have lunch with you, if it's not an imposition on your mother."

Giang stood up and extended her hand to Hồng.

"I will then go and give her a hand. Come on, little one. Lead the way and I'll follow you."

Hồng happily dragged her away.

The Village Chief led his group, consisting of constable Tuấn and his three part-time helpers, toward the school. Xã Long felt excited but in total control. He had tucked into his belt a fully loaded six-shot revolver acquired from a Chinese trader. He only carried it around when he wanted to make sure people recognized his power and authority.

He had chosen his men well. Tuấn was completely devoted and loyal to him. The other three were young men who normally worked for him as field hands. He had provided the constable with a shiny rifle, bought from a Black Flag deserter. Tuấn, who did not get to carry it often, let alone use it, had the weapon slung across his back. The three part-time constables did not merit any firearm, but carried instead short wooden poles that could be used as clubs if needed. One of them also held a shiny bamboo cangue used occasionally on criminals, especially those inclined to violence. The village teacher was well known for his martial arts prowess, and Xã Long was not taking any chance.

People seeing the group could have easily thought they were on their way to apprehend a dangerous thief or a hardened criminal, which would be a rare occurrence in the village. Xã Long did not care, for the anger he had built up within him had replaced common sense and obscured his normal judgment.

They walked fast, and anyone tempted to follow them had been dissuaded from doing so, with a sharp command or sometimes with just a withering look. They arrived at the village school shortly before noon and saw that the students were still in the classroom. There was an empty horse carriage in front of the school, an unusual sight. Stopping at the front gate, on the Village Chief's signal, constable Tuấn called out.

"Lê Duy Tâm, you are hereby ordered to present yourself before the Village Council."

He had seen them coming for the last few minutes. He rose to his feet and went to the door. The surprised students turned their heads around, and two of them, Thi and Hồng, stood up soon after their teacher did. Giang was still in the back, helping his mother prepare lunch, while the French priest was out strolling around the village.

Tâm stepped out, positioned himself in front of the door, and took into account the men, their weapons, and the cangue. His heart sank. He wondered bitterly whether the Minister of Rites had sent Xã Long to re-arrest him. He stared at the Village Chief, waiting. Xã Long grasped the grip of his pistol, then shouted.

"Lê Duy Tâm, you are to follow us to the communal house."

Constable Tuấn urged his men to move forward. However, impressed by the village teacher's calm and his air of authority, the men remained in place.

"Please tell me, what is the reason for this?" Tâm asked.

"The Village Council has given us the order to arrest you for violating village rules and for trying to propagate the foreign devils' religion," Xã Long answered in as brutal a manner as he could express, as if the village teacher was a common criminal.

By that time, Thi and Hồng as well as other students had spilled out into the courtyard and surrounded their teacher. The little girl grasped one of Tâm's hands and used it to try to pull him back inside the schoolroom. Giang, hearing the noise and commotion, ran out, and asked the students to move and let her stand beside their teacher. She looked at the Village Chief and saw an excited and fierce looking man glaring at her.

Her appearance startled Xã Long. He usually knew everyone in the village, but she was a total stranger and apparently a bold one who showed no fear at his sight. They stood still for a moment, until the Village Chief recovered from his surprise and shouted.

"I repeat for the last time: Lê Duy Tâm, you are to follow us and appear before the Village Council at the communal house. Constables, carry out your duties."

The constables shuffled forward but they still did not feel confident, awed by the presence of so many people arrayed in front of them, even if most were children. Tâm raised his hands.

"No need for that! I will follow you. I will gladly appear before the Village Council, if that's what you want."

"No, don't go!" Giang implored him before turning to question the Village Chief.

"On what authority are you doing this?" she asked. "What has Teacher Tâm done?"

Xã Long was not used to anyone questioning his motives and became visibly angry. Whenever he gave an order, people immediately carried them out and, if they dared, they would ask questions afterwards. The blue-eyed young woman glaring at him certainly had not learned to respect him. Xã Long always knew or controlled all the facts when he dealt with people in the village. In this case, her sudden appearance at the village school was a new element that he had not counted on. Nevertheless, he was not going to alter his plans because of her.

"You will find out soon enough before the Village Council. I am acting on the Council's behalf. You are not from this village, so you may not know it, but the Council is the sole authority here. Even the King's orders have to yield to the village's regulations."

Tâm saw Xã Long's hand firmly grasping his pistol's grip. His men might have been reluctant to make use of their weapons, but their leader appeared to have no such qualms. With so many children and women around, he wanted to defuse the situation at once.

"Village Chief, give me just one instant," he said, then turned to announce to his students.

"School is over for today. You may all go home."

A subdued chorus of voices answered him, and the obedient students began moving back inside to pick up their belongings. Remembering how the Village Chief had tried to put pressure on her own family, Thi was starting to wonder whether what was happening to her teacher might somehow be related. She felt tense and moved toward Bà Lân who had by then come out and had heard the brief exchanges between Giang, her son and Xã Long. The old woman was at a loss and saddened, but like her son, she remained calm.

Tâm looked at his mother, then at Giang who appeared dazed by the sudden turn of events.

"Giang, will you stay here with Mother until I come back?"

She nodded at once but her eyes showed the distress that she felt at this sudden and disturbing development. It did not escape the notice of both Bà Lân and Thi. The older woman drew Giang closer to her, while Thi grasped one of her arms as if to support her and share her anguish. As Tâm walked out, Giang lost her defiant composure and tears appeared on her face.

"Why must he go away so soon?" she cried. "I just barely saw him again."

The old mother no longer had any doubt that the young woman who appeared out of nowhere that morning was the one that her son was waiting for. She did not know what had brought them together. How did her son, a resolute bachelor, manage to travel South and come back entangled with a young woman who braved half of the country's length to seek him out in his own village? Could it have been some debt one owed the other in a previous reincarnation? If so, the wrath and persecution of one Village Chief would only delay what fate had already determined.

"Giang, he will be back. You'll see, he will be back."

He went out to the front gate where the Village Chief and his men were waiting. Awed by the village teacher's composure, the constables moved back to give him room to walk through their group. Xã Long saw that his men either forgot or could not bring themselves to put the cangue around the village teacher's neck, but he wisely ignored that oversight.

He was more restrained and had let go of his pistol. The constables had lost their swagger and could not look either at their boss or at each other. After all, the village

teacher was a respected figure in the community, not a burglar or a bandit like the one who kidnapped the Village Chief's daughter. Children worshipped him while their parents respected him totally. The reaction of the children, the dejected and even terrified look on their faces told the constables that they had taken part in an ill-conceived mission.

Having left school to go home, many students then retraced their steps to see what was going to happen next. Shocked and troubled by what they had witnessed, they stood silently on both sides of the main road. A moment later, they saw their teacher coming out of the school gate, surrounded by the five men who came to arrest him. The group walked in the direction of the communal house with many students following behind at some distance.

Three women and a small girl stood at the front gate of the school and watched in agonizing silence as the one they cherished was being taken away to face a new and unknown challenge. He should only be gone for a few hours and would come back at the end of the day after having cleared himself of whatever he was accused of. At least that's what they all hoped at that instant, having nothing else to grasp at.

The Battle

For the second time in his short career as Prefect, Chí found himself throwing a lavish party to the French officers who had arrived the day before, bringing reinforcements for another attempt at defeating the rebels and destroying their base. When they showed up for the party, the new arrivals were cold and aloof, no doubt looking down on a Prefect who had failed so miserably his first trial by fire. Chí was acutely aware of their attitude. He had already instructed Cicada to put out the best wines and food that she could requisition, with the help of Uncle Hoan of course. The new Prefect knew very well the importance of keeping the warriors happy, so he told her and Uncle Hoan to spare no expenses.

It had paid off, and after only half an hour, the French officers had lost their inhibitions. They ate with gusto, drank heavily, smiled at him, and laughed and sang drinking songs in their own language. Conversation flowed as smoothly as the wines making their rounds from one goblet to the next.

Prefect Chí only understood an occasional word of what the French officers were saying to one another, and had to rely on one of his captains who knew a little bit of French to translate for him. Still he missed practically all of what was being debated or joked about at the table. Nevertheless, he was happy. He hoped that by being a good host he would soon make the foreigners forgive him the serious gaps in his military knowledge and his atrocious behavior on the battlefield.

Cicada was busy circulating around the table, directing the servants and helping to serve the wines and refill the glasses, a full-time job that she relished. This duty gave her an excuse to linger around the French officers and listen in to what they were saying and, after a few rounds of drinks, they were saying a lot. They started by belittling the Prefect who understood nothing of their criticisms, and soon went on to brag about themselves and the superiority of their Foreign Legion. She kept them well supplied with wine, silently bidding them to say even more and reveal the details of their plans for the upcoming assault on the rebel base.

One of the new arrivals was a captain who wore a thin mask of disdain on his face whenever he looked at his host. He drank little and was aghast at his fellow officers' freewheeling, wine-induced talk. A graduate of the French military academy at St Cyr, Michel de St Arnaud had been in the country five years. He was an officer in the Foreign Legion and had taken part in some of the last battles against the Black Flags in the Tonkin. He had been wounded, not too seriously but enough to get him assigned to the staff of the Special Envoy in Huế.

He spent a year recuperating and trying to please the Special Envoy, but he considered his time spent in the capital generally wasted. Around him, French colonial troops, mainly the Foreign Legionnaires, were winning the last battles against pirates, bandits, and rebels in the Tonkin. In the meantime, all he did was to dress up smartly every day and accompany François Bonneau to countless ceremonial functions and events. He missed his Legionnaires, even though many were not French but Germans, Italians, Russians, or Hungarians and others from North Africa. He was therefore overjoyed when Bonneau decided to send him back to the Tonkin to participate in a punitive expedition against one of the last rebel strongholds.

He was appalled when he found out that Prefect Chí, who was the apparent head of the royal Vietnamese troops, was one of the mandarins that he had come to despise during his time in Huế. They had no military background or training, and yet were given military responsibilities that they were totally unqualified for. He had the same contempt for them that Genghis Khan had toward the Chinese generals chosen by examinations, the scholar warriors that the Mongols hordes easily crushed on the battlefield.

He was not at all surprised when he learned that the first operation that the new Prefect led was compromised before it even started. The rebels knew exactly what the royal troops were going to do and laid a carefully prepared ambush for them. When the majority of the troops advanced into their trap, the rebels started firing from concealed positions spread out almost along the entire length of the government column. Their enfilading fire sowed havoc and panic around the clueless Prefect and his officers. The government forces ran for their lives and escaped to their rear, leaving behind practically all of their guns and ammunitions as well as their provisions. The small company of French troops did not even have time to set up their cannons and had little choice but to join the fleeing soldiers in their retreat.

It was a classic ambush, one that could have been taught at any military school, and St Arnaud was determined that his side would not have to learn the lesson twice.

He had been carefully observing Cicada throughout the night. She was pretty, worked hard and had an uncanny ability to anticipate all of his wishes and serve him whatever he wanted, sometimes without waiting for him to ask. She treated the other officers likewise, getting wine and food to their plates as if she knew beforehand what they wished. He observed that she lingered in the dining area and did not miss any of the information that his fellow officers carelessly threw about as they bragged about their prowess.

St Arnaud shouted to a lieutenant sitting on the other side of the table.

"I see you are not drinking red wine like most of us here."

"Well, I found this Riesling, a white Alsatian wine which is very dry and more to my liking. Some of the Legionnaires introduced me to it."

"Ah, I do wish I could taste that wine myself, but I don't see it anywhere on the table."

"Captain St Arnaud, all you have to do is to hail that pretty girl over there, tell her what you want, and she'll bring it to you."

"Good idea. I'll try to get her the next time she comes by."

Both had to shout back and forth across the table to be able to hear each other, but St Arnaud was sure someone else also heard them. He made a show of digging into his food, and waited. Sure enough, within a few minutes, Cicada brought him a new glass and a bottle of the Alsatian Riesling wine.

He got up brusquely, seized her arm and forcefully dragged her out of the room. She winced in pain but was too stunned to protest. Nobody had ever treated her like that. His grip was powerful and she found herself unable to resist. Most of the officers present were smashed and thought St Arnaud had decided on his conquest for the night. They cheered him on with gusto. Prefect Chí saw it all, but he too was inebriated and all he could do was to stammer incoherent words as his favorite servant was taken out of the room.

Without Cicada, the dinner party soon lost its spirit and quickly came to a halt. The French officers got up to return to their quarters. The drunken Prefect went to his, fell into bed and passed out as soon as his head hit the pillow.

The following day he was sleeping well past his usual time, when Uncle Hoan entered his bedroom after knocking and getting no response. He shook his nephew until he opened his bloodshot eyes.

"Nephew, you must get up right away. The French are leaving."

Prefect Chí yawned and stretched before asking with irritation.

"What? Why are they changing our plans? We were not supposed to start our move until next week."

"I don't know, but something changed early this morning. Their soldiers are right now boarding three gunboats, and they have told your officers to have our own troops do the same in one more hour. If you want to to be with them, you should get up now and go down to the river right away."

Half of Prefect Chí wanted his revenge; the other half did not want to leave the comfort of his new home under the care of Cicada. Then he remembered his last sight of her at the party.

"Where is Cicada?"

Uncle Hoan lowered his voice.

"The French have her in custody. They say that she understands French perfectly and that she's a spy for the rebels."

The news instantly shocked the Prefect out of his morning lethargy. His mouth hung open, and he was unable to move or speak for some time. Finally, he managed to say.

"How could she be a spy? They must be mistaken. She's my most loyal servant."

"Don't say that too loud. The French captain who arrived from the capital has been interrogating her since last night."

Prefect Chỉ got out of bed and started to get dressed. He almost called out for Cicada to help him get ready, but his uncle's words finally sunk in. He wondered where she was and whether the French captain had her tortured.

"Are they going to suspect us too?" he asked anxiously.

Uncle Hoan did not like the question's unspoken meaning. He had hired Cicada, but she was referred to him by someone else, and he had no idea of her background and her past. With hindsight, he knew she was too good to be true: a servant with extraordinary abilities who worked hard, smiled all the time, and demanded next to nothing in wages. He had been inflating her salary for the last several months, each time pocketing the difference between what he gave her and what the government paid. Hopefully, his nephew would not find out and nobody else would dare question him about it. Only Cicada knew what he was doing but she had yet to make an issue of it.

"No, Prefect, we are not under any suspicion. How could you know that she speaks French fluently? You hardly know a few words yourself."

He promptly seized on those words to distance himself from the woman spy.

"You speak the truth, Uncle Hoan. I really know nothing about her."

Since that first glorious victory against the royal forces and their French allies, Chính had only heard from her once. The courier Cicada sent a few weeks later told him that there was going to be another attack. She reported that it would involve a more substantial French participation, and she promised to send him details about it as soon as she knew what they were.

He longed to see her and wished she would leave her post soon and return to the safety of the base. For the first time in his life, he found himself worrying about the safety of a woman other than his mother. When he had carried the Village Chief's daughter and deposited her into the sampan that was to take her home, the feel of that full body in his arms had failed to make any impression on him. On the other hand, with Cicada he wanted to take her into his arms but didn't dare for fear of offending her. Maybe when he saw her the next time, he would not be so timid. Yet, the brave rebel commander, the man who feared nothing, wasn't sure whether he would be bold enough to attempt what his heart wanted.

One late afternoon, to escape from those thoughts that were dragging his spirit down, he started on an inspection tour. He crossed the wooden bridge and went out to the first lines of defense on the other side of the river. Since an eventual attack would come via the main road leading into the city, he had sent more than half of his forces over to that side. There they had taken over all of the houses, opened holes in walls so that they could move easily from one house to the next, dug in their positions, set up guard posts, and reinforced their defenses. Every night ambush parties were sent to protect the base even further out.

The base itself was a small town on the opposite side of the river, surrounded by defensive walls built with clay and sharpened bamboo spikes protruding from them like quills on a porcupine. It took back-breaking work from his men over most of the summer to build those walls, and afterwards the town looked from the outside like the impregnable fortress that he wanted it to be.

Since their first victory against the government troops, Chính constantly reminded his men that the next attack was sure to come and they needed to be ready for it. After crossing the bridge, he went from one guard post to another and found most of his fighters at their assigned positions. They knew they were the first line of defense, tasked with keeping the enemy from ever reaching the bridge and crossing it to invade their base. Should there be a need for it, Chính was ready to order the rest of his forces over the bridge to join the fighting. Or he could also command everyone to fall back to the base and fight from its ramparts. There were plenty of guns, ammunitions, and provisions stored inside the base, enough to enable them to put up a strong defense and wear out their attackers over time.

He would be even better prepared if Cicada could send back some new intelligence. It had been quite long since the last courier, and he was getting worried. Without her, he was blind about the movement of the government troops.

As he walked over the bridge to go back to the base, the setting sun was putting up a colorful show in the sky, and a fantastic reddish glow filled the horizon. He looked toward it, then down to the river flowing placidly under the bridge. The water reflected the sunset and the redness of the sky made the river look like it was filled with blood. He hoped it would also be that red, when the French and their royal allies came to die before the rebel's ramparts, their blood flowing in rivulets down to the water.

Following the advice of Special Envoy Bonneau, St Arnaud did not use the land route to move his forces. The gunboats allowed him to get his forces to the battle site faster via a route the enemy rebels were not expecting him to take. If Cicada was still active as the enemy's spy, she could have forewarned them, but he knew that he would be invading the rebel base before they could get wind of her capture.

In a way, he admired the brave woman who for many hours had resisted his torturer, a dark North African skilled in inflicting maximum pain with a minimum of effort. She had finally bit her tongue in half and was bleeding to death when he last saw her. She still had not told them anything that they didn't already know: there was a base well defended with many rebels who counted on her for giving them intelligence on the government troop movements. While no other details could be extracted from Cicada, it was enough for St Arnaud. He was going to exploit the element of surprise to the fullest by moving his troops in the manner Bonneau had recommended.

He told his Legionnaires to get on two of the gunboats with only their weapons, ammunitions, and whatever else they could carry on their backs. Additional support troops, ammunitions and provisions were to come later in a third vessel as soon as it was finished being loaded. The royal Vietnamese troops and their Prefect could come along if they wanted to, but he was not going to delay anything to wait for them. He didn't really need them to win the battle, but he felt obligated to at least offer them the chance to join the fight.

It was late afternoon by the time they were finally able to leave. He calculated they would reach their destination in the middle of the night, under the light of a full moon. Travelling upriver and at night would give St Arnaud a double tactical advantage against the rebels who assumed the colonials only moved over land routes during daytime. The river was still flowing strong from the recent monsoon rains, but the steam-powered gunboats were able to navigate upstream without difficulty.

St Arnaud thought the noise the warships made would have been enough to wake up the entire rebel base. However, the wind which worked against the ships' movement also carried away their sounds. The assault forces arrived in the early hours of the morning to find the base silent, its inhabitants and defenders sound asleep. He landed his forces just outside of the mud walls surrounding the city and was amazed but relieved that no guards heard or saw them. That confirmed his suspicion that the rebels were only prepared for a direct attack along the main road on the other side of the river, and not for any threat coming from the river itself. Several of his men prepared charges to blow up a section of the walls while another group took their explosives further upstream and placed them at the foot of the wooden bridge. Meanwhile the Legionnaires and the royal troops took their positions and waited as the dawn sky began to take on hues of purple and red.

Finally, when the charges were ready, St Arnaud had one of his Legionnaires blow his bugle. A few seconds later, the dynamite charges erupted in a series of deafening explosions. When the smoke cleared, an end of the bridge had collapsed into the river while one part of the walls had crumbled leaving a still smoldering wide gap. A collective cheer went up among the Legionnaires and they rose to charge through the breach in the walls. The royal troops followed them, gingerly at first. Prefect Chí who had forgotten to cover his ears was temporarily deafened and disoriented by the dynamite explosions. St Arnaud came over and pointed him to where their men were charging. The Prefect understood and meekly followed the French captain as the latter, pistol in hand, began running after his Legionnaires.

The rebels who tried to rush toward the still standing sections of the bridge on either side of the river soon found that they could not go anywhere and most were strafed by machine guns placed at the bows of the ships. Others were brought down by French snipers who positioned themselves at the top of the mud walls and were beginning to pick their targets one by one.

The base was overrun shortly after sunrise by the combined French and royal Vietnamese forces. The rebels were totally unprepared for the sudden rain of cannon shells and machine gun fire coming from the boats on the river and from the French and Vietnamese soldiers who came ashore and poured through the walls. The attackers shot their way through the city and sent people fleeing in all directions. It was complete chaos and panic. After the initial surprise, a few rebels were able to fire back, but there were too few of them. More than half of the rebel force was on the other side of the river, marooned there by the collapsed bridge, pinned down and rendered ineffective by the gunboats crews who fired on anyone attempting to shoot back or swim across the river.

In the pre-dawn darkness, the rebels who could ran toward the mountains and jungles surrounding the base. Those who remained and showed any sign of resistance, even as much as a gesture of defiance, were methodically killed. The Legionnaires gave no quarters and shot anyone they encountered, sparing none, not even the women and children who could not flee in time. They also torched every house and thick smoke rose and darkened the sky blotting out the sun.

Commander Chính tried to organize his troops but could only rally a handful of his men. One of them told him that Cô Nhân and her women were killed in the first few minutes of fighting. Chính and his men fought as they retreated to a warehouse where they had stored ammunitions and gunpowder. Surrounded on all sides and without an escape route, the small group of rebels vowed to not surrender and to fight to the death.

They had plenty of weapons and ammunitions on their hands, which allowed them to put up a fierce fight and pour out a volume of fire far greater than their numbers warranted. The government forces were stymied and had to halt their advance. While the rest of the base was becoming quiet as most of the defenders had been killed or had fled, the warehouse's occupants successfully kept their attackers at bay. As casualties on his side mounted, St Arnaud arrived on the scene, looked at the situation, and made the kind of quick and smart decision that he was known for.

He ordered snipers to keep shooting continuously through the thick smoke at the warehouse while he had two cannons brought up from the rear. It took over an hour, and when they were finally in place, he ordered the barrels lowered and the big guns aimed point blank at the warehouse. The first volley created a cloud of dust and smoke, but as soon as that dissipated, firing from inside resumed almost with the same intensity as before. The second volley resulted in a deafening explosion followed by a multitude of minor ones. The weapons warehouse continued to explode for a good half hour, after which everything went quiet. The last pocket of rebel resistance had been silenced.

St Arnaud and an emboldened Prefect Chí went over to look at the crumbling walls which were all that was left of the warehouse. Soldiers in front of them occasionally poked with their bayonets to make sure that the scattered bodies lying about were definitively dead.

The Prefect felt squeamish at what he saw, but he kept quiet. He was walking at the side of the French captain who towered over him by a head. He had found in St Arnaud the model of a warrior that he only read about but never saw before, and he set himself the goal of following the French captain, observing his military mannerism to try and imitate later.

In front of them, all of a sudden they saw a Legionnaire brandish a weapon and call out.

"Captain, this one was carrying an American rifle, a Winchester!"

They came close to the Legionnaire and the corpse lying prone on the ground. He gave his captain the American Winchester to look at. The French infantryman was equipped with the Gras rifle, a competent but single-shot gun that had to be reloaded after each firing. On the other hand, the Winchester was a lever-action repeating rifle capable of firing up to 15 cartridges without having to be reloaded.

"We haven't seen too many of these American guns here in this country," said St Arnaud. "He must have obtained it from the Black Flags when they retreated to China. No wonder there was so much firing coming out of this storehouse. Turn him over so I can see his face."

The Legionnaire used his foot and hands to do what he was ordered. As soon as the corpse landed on its back, it moaned. St Arnaud instantly pointed his pistol at the man who remained unmoving but was indeed breathing. He noticed that the man was covered with dirt but had no apparent wound and no trace of blood anywhere but on his face, which was blackened and covered with scrapes.

"This one is still alive, soldier. Take him prisoner and I will interrogate him later. Tell our doctor not to let him die."

"Chí," the man on the ground called out. The rebel had opened his eyes and was staring at the Prefect who had bent down to take a closer look at his face.

Prefect Chí straightened up immediately. Since becoming Prefect, few people, not even his own parents, had dared to call him by his personal name. The man on the ground coughed, spit out some dirt then laughed quietly.

"Chí, we meet in such unusual circumstances! Do you remember me?"

"No," replied Prefect Chí in an exasperated tone. "I don't know you. Who are you?"

St Arnaud and the Legionnaire exchanged glances with each other. They understood nothing of what was being said in Vietnamese, but it was obvious that the rebel knew who the Prefect was.

"Go get me the interpreter," St Arnaud told his soldier.

Aside from those who fled, Chính was the sole survivor. Cô Nhân and the tightly knit group that ran the base and commanded its fighters were all dead. Their leader, Cô Nhân's husband, had not been heard from since he went to China to seek help several months ago. The force of the warehouse explosion threw Chính outside and miraculously saved his life while all of his men were killed. He would have rued the fact that fate had spared him, except for one thing. He did not want to die until he found out what happened to Cicada.

In front of the French and everyone else, Prefect Chí never admitted that the rebel prisoner was an old classmate. However, the French captain seemed to understand the situation and was in fact slightly amused by it. He let the Prefect conduct the interrogation, catching the meaning of what transpired through an interpreter.

St Arnaud knew that the prisoner was not going to reveal anything of military value. The rebel base was obliterated, but the French and royal troops were at the end of their supply lines. Their mission was essentially accomplished, and all he was planning to do was to go back the same way and on the same gunboats that had taken them to the rebel base. He watched with mounting amusement his counterpart, the chubby mandarin, becoming more and more agitated as the prisoner taunted him verbally. After a few minutes of shouting, the red-faced Prefect turned to the French captain, and through the interpreter, made a request.

"Captain, this rebel is originally from my village. He is the one who kidnapped my sister a few months ago. For that crime, and for the fact that he belongs to a group that openly disobeys the King's orders, I want to take him back to my village and have him appear before the Village Council so that he can be tried and executed."

"You do with him as you please, Prefect," St Arnaud agreed. "However, I would like you to ask him one question for me."

"Certainly, what would you like to ask him?"

"Ask him if he knows Cicada."

The French captain's request jolted the Prefect. He had forgotten about her during the battle, and suddenly he understood why St Arnaud had rushed to the battle shortly after interrogating Cicada. Had she been forced through torture to reveal something about the rebel base? Did St Arnaud decide to attack while he knew that the rebels were deprived of their most vital source of intelligence? The best way to find out was to ask exactly what St Arnaud requested. Prefect Chí turned to the prisoner.

"The French Captain wants to find out if you know a young woman who goes by the name of Cicada?"

Chính immediately opened his mouth to say something, but no sound came out. His eyes went from the Prefect to the French captain, trying to judge how much they knew. The thin smile on St Arnaud's face told him that he had already found out about Cicada.

"Where is she?" he snarled. "Did the French kill her?"

Through his interpreter, St Arnaud answered coolly, observing and enjoying his captive's reaction to his words.

"After she told us everything about you, she took her own life."

The primal howl that arose from the prisoner was not only piercing and overpowering. It also deeply affected everyone present, Vietnamese and French alike, making them experience and feel the depth of despair and the intensity of grief reached by a fellow human being, even if he was the enemy. Chí was the first to turn away, followed seconds later by St Arnaud who was surprised that his words could inflict so much pain.

The Trial

People set aside their daily routines and gathered in small groups or went to their neighbors' houses to gossip and exchange rumors. Fortunately, or unfortunately, the harvest season had not yet begun, and many could stay and work around their houses while chatting with their neighbors about what had happened, from the shocking arrest of the village teacher to the arrival in the village of the young woman known as Cô Giang.

The schoolchildren were on the whole distraught. There was of course no school, but a few at a time would drift to the village school or the communal house, perhaps in the vain hope of seeing their teacher back at his old place or being released from his prison in the communal house. They thus wandered around the village, aimlessly.

In the first few days, parents went in the evening to talk to the village teacher's mother. All she could tell them was that there was absolutely no reason for her son to be arrested. He was doing his best to educate the children in the village. Somehow Xã Long had misrepresented his actions to the Village Council. The parents nodded, sighed, and then left, convinced by her words and eager for the Village Council to meet and resolve the matter as soon as possible. Nobody failed to notice the young woman who remained in the background and kept quiet. In the light of the oil lamps, her eyes were a darker blue, but they were bright and penetrating.

When Tâm did not come back as they had expected, Giang went to the communal house to see him and bring him some food. She sat on the ground across from him, separated by the narrowly spaced ironwood columns that formed the wall of the cell where he was held. As he nibbled on the food, they could see and talk to each other, going over all that had happened in their lives from the time they were separated in the capital months ago. However, obviously upset and dejected by his imprisonment, he said little once they came to that subject. To try and lift his spirits she chatted about what was happening in the village.

Little Hồng was gone with the French priest back to his parish to keep herself out of the Village Chief's reach. Father Phan was very understanding and had no trouble allowing Giang to stay in the village with Tâm's mother. He was as perplexed as anybody about the Village Chief's intentions, and he said that he would be ready to come back to help clear things up, if his presence would help rather than hurt Tâm's case.

Giang was getting along fine with Tâm's mother, and had more or less settled in the schoolhouse. She slept in his bed and performed small chores around the house. Thi dropped by every day together with some of the older students. They sat in the schoolroom and continued transcribing poems using the new script. They asked about their teacher and, from time to time, asked her for help with their assignments. She freely gave it, happy to be useful that way.

On the third day, she asked him the question that had been on everyone's mind.

"Teacher Tâm, how long are they going to hold you here?"

He tried to sound positive and optimistic.

"They assured me the Village Council will meet in few days. As soon as I can go in front of the Council, I will clear up this misunderstanding."

She watched him eat the package of sweet rice and black beans that his mother had cooked, saying that was one of his favorite dishes. A few months ago, on the beach at Thuận An, he was savoring the simple lunch of grilled prawns and sweet rice that she had prepared. How things were different then! Both of them were so carefree, and thought nothing of facing the world around them. That world had now revealed to them its ugliest sides, and she wondered whether life would ever be the same for them again. A Vietnamese was defined by his village, and not just the physical location and boundaries of it, but also by the families and the people whom he grew up with. The village was everything in his life. What was going to happen to Tâm if his village sided with the Village Chief and against him?

With a heavy heart, she left him in his cell to go back to the village school. As she stepped out of the communal house she saw Xã Long who had just arrived. He blocked her way and his voice was imperious.

"What are you doing here?"

He had seen her at the village school but was still trying to find out who she was and why she was there. Her blue eyes and pale complexion suggested Western lineage, but if so what was she doing in a Vietnamese village so far away from the big cities where the French lived?

"I brought some food for Teacher Tâm," she answered, not stepping aside but waiting for him to move out of her way.

He was neither happy with her answer nor with her obvious disdain for his status.

"Who gave you permission to do that?"

"Nobody, but since you don't feed your prisoner, I had to bring him something."

Xã Long shouted toward the communal house.

"Constable Tuấn, come here!"

The constable had seen his boss arrive and block the way of the young woman. He was waiting at the door to see who was going to win the confrontation. Xã Long was well known for his rough and abrupt behavior, but the young woman from Huế showed no fear. Mustering an ingratiating smile on his face, he approached his boss.

"Village Chief …"

"I forbid you to allow anyone to go inside the communal house to visit or bring anything, including food, to the village teacher. Nobody can go in unless I approve, is that clear?"

"Yes, Village Chief."

Giang forcefully stepped forward and walked straight ahead. At the last moment, Xã Long had to move aside to avoid colliding with her. She went on her way, leaving the two men in front of the communal house, one enraged, and the other grinning inanely.

When she arrived back at the village school, his mother had just returned from a round of visits to the Village Council members. She knew the Notables from the time her husband was on the council. She had gone to the home of each one to plead her son's case and came back tired and empty handed.

"They are all without a spine," the old woman told Giang. "They barely listened to me. Some would not even open their doors, sending their servants out to tell me they were not home. The Village Chief has them in his pocket, and they won't do anything without his approval."

Giang told Bà Lân of her encounter with the Village Chief.

"That man is a little tyrant. He now forbids me to bring food to Teacher Tâm."

Bà Lân, exhausted from her visits to the Council members, shook her head in disbelief and said.

"Let me take it to him tomorrow. Let's see if they will stop me."

However, the following day Bà Lân got up feverish and feeling weak. She tried to stand up but could not gather enough strength to do so. Giang came over to help her get back on the bed. She went to her trunk, sent to her by Father Phan, opened it and looked for the medicines that her parents had insisted that she brought along on her trip. She gave a potion to the distraught woman and comforted her.

"You should rest today and I will take care of all things, including visiting Teacher Tâm later on."

"I wish I could go with you, but I don't think I can today," she said. "I just hope you won't get into any trouble."

"Don't worry. I know how to deal with that kind of people."

She went to the kitchen and started to prepare some gruel for the sick woman, while looking around to see what she could later bring to Tâm. Until then she had only been in a kitchen to observe how servants prepared and cooked the food. On rare occasions, her own mother would let her and Mai try their hands at making some pastry or dumpling. She realized that she was going to have to do everything herself since both mother and son were now entirely dependent on her.

The village school paled in size and stature to the mansion that her family occupied in the capital. However, she liked its compactness and in the short time since her arrival, had acquainted herself with its nooks and crannies. She was certainly happier in the small schoolhouse than she was in the mansion, even though the one person she came to see had been taken away almost as soon as she arrived in the village. Like everyone else, she had first thought that his going to the communal house was only a matter of hours, and that he would already have been back. However, the hours had turned into days without any indication as to when his ordeal would end. She knew she needed to do something, and an idea was starting to take shape in her mind. A woman's voice interrupted her thoughts.

"Young lady, is the mother of Teacher Tâm home?"

Giang looked up and saw a woman standing at the back door. She was taller than most Vietnamese women were, and she seemed shy and diffident. No longer in her prime youth, she was still a handsome woman, who could look striking despite her self-effacing manner and the simple but spotless clothes she was wearing.

"She is not feeling well today and she's resting inside. Is there something that I could do for you?"

"I heard about Teacher Tâm's arrest, and I just came to ..." the woman hesitated briefly. "I wondered ... if there is anything I can do to help. I also brought some green rice cakes. He has always liked them."

She was holding several packages neatly wrapped in banana leaves. She came inside the kitchen and gave them to Giang.

"You shouldn't have, but thank you!" Giang said. "I was going to bring him something to eat, and he'll surely enjoy these, but first tell me who you are so that I can let him know who gave him these cakes."

"You can tell him that I am Cơ, mother of Chính, a boy who used to be one of his students... You must be Cô Giang, the young lady from Huế. People in the village have been talking about you."

Giang nodded her head, her eyes twinkling.

"Won't you stay a little bit longer and have some tea with me. Then you can tell me what the villagers have been saying about me."

Cơ looked toward the door leading to the living quarters behind the schoolroom.

"I would like to ask you to let me come in and pay my respects to Teacher Tâm's mother."

Giang nodded and led the woman through the door. Bà Lân was awake and greeted the visitor without getting up.

"Chính's mother, it's nice for you to visit us."

Cơ approached her bed and knelt down.

"I am so worried for you and for Teacher Tâm, and I wanted to come see you. And here you are, sick and …"

"I am only a little bit tired. Many bad things have happened recently around here lately, and I am just feeling down because of them," the old woman replied. "Now tell me what they are saying in the village."

The visitor looked nervously at Bà Lân then at Giang before finally speaking.

"I don't hear everything, but I think mostly people keep wondering who Cô Giang is, what she's doing in our village, and things like that. They are not saying bad things about her, and some are even praising her for staying here to support Teacher Tâm."

Bà Lân sighed.

"That's right. She's not even from our village, yet she's willing to stand up for him, when others, for one reason or another, are abandoning him. You at least came to see us, and I am grateful for that."

Cơ hurried to say.

"Not at all, the least I could do is to come visit you after all that Teacher Tâm has done for me."

"Is that so?" Giang smiled to encourage the visitor to go on talking. "Now you have to tell me what he did for you."

It took some time, but the village's gold farmer, whose son was a rebel commander, told her. She hesitated in the beginning, but as she spoke, the words slowly began flowing with ease. Perhaps she needed to confide and share her pain with another human being, or maybe it was a natural empathy that she felt for the younger woman, but Cơ felt that she didn't have to hide anything from Giang.

Giang walked along the village main street, going toward the communal house. The Village Chief had forbidden her to bring food or go in, but she was determined to fulfill her mission, regardless of what might happen.

Along the way, a group of children left their houses to follow her from a respectful distance. They were students at the village school whose parents had been giving them small tasks to keep them busy while school was out, but most of the time the youngsters used their newly found freedom to roam around the village. Giang saw them from the corner of her eyes and smiled at them. She didn't mind them tagging along for they were not bothering her or creating any nuisance.

Upon arrival at the communal house, she went straight to the main door. When she was only a short distance from it, Constable Tuấn appeared and blocked her way.

"On orders from the Village Chief, no one is allowed in," he said in his sternest voice.

"I just want to bring Teacher Tâm some food," Giang said. She heard the children stop and whisper among themselves behind her.

"No food is allowed."

"You are not feeding him anything, are you?"

"That is none of your concern," the constable responded curtly.

The Village Chief had told him that one of his servants would bring food. None had yet to appear, but he wasn't about to tell that to the stranger facing him.

"Will you at least give him these food packages?" she asked, even though she already knew the answer.

"No, go away."

"Very well, I will wait here until you let me through."

She knelt down on the ground, spread out a flap of her dress and put the packages of food on top of the cloth, bent her head slightly, closed her eyes, and clasped her hands in front of her as if she was praying.

"You, you there! What are you doing?" Tuấn stammered.

The children ran home and spread the news throughout the village. By noontime, even those out in the fields had heard of the young woman's vigil. People went and stood in front of the communal house to watch Giang, to witness with their own eyes that she was actually there, kneeling and unmoving. Then they went and called on still more villagers to come.

Everyone knew what she was protesting. The children were unusually quiet and respectful, men were shaking their heads, and among the women, some were moved to tears. A woman brought a bowl of tea and tried to give it to Giang. She opened her eyes, thanked her, drank a little bit then closed her eyes again. As the sun rose in the sky and the heat intensified, people felt sorry for her, but they could do nothing but watch and discuss the matter among themselves.

"Why is the Village Chief not allowing her to visit Teacher Tâm?"

"He should come here and take a look at her."

"Yes, and I would give up anything to have somebody take my side like she does. Teacher Tâm is so fortunate!"

"How can you say that? Isn't he in jail? What is so fortunate about that?"

The constables took turns standing by the main door, barring anybody from coming in. They had thought at first that the young woman they had stopped at the door would soon go away. Instead, she remained where she was, kneeling under the sun, unmoving and unmovable. There was no rule against what she was doing, and Xã Long was not there to tell them what to do about her.

Abbot Khánh seldom ventured outside of his temple grounds, but it had been over a week since his nephew had come and the abbot was becoming concerned. Since returning from the capital, Tâm had been to the temple at least once a week, often bringing with him Hồng, the little girl. While he practiced his martial arts or worked on the temple grounds with the abbot and his helper, she roamed around, picking flowers, digging up sweet potatoes, chasing dragonflies, or making herself useful with small chores that the men asked her to do to keep her busy and entertained. Neither the village teacher nor his newest student had been at the temple lately, and the abbot found that unusual. His sixth sense had been nagging at him, and he finally gave in to it. He decided to go to the village school and find out for himself what was the matter.

As he was getting ready to leave, the woman Cơ arrived at the temple and walked in haste toward him. She clasped her hand, bowed to him quickly, and then tried to speak at the same time that she was trying to catch her breath.

"Teacher, your … nephew has been taken into custody by the … Village Chief."

So that was it, he thought. For some time now, he had sensed that something was going to affect Tâm's life. He had at first thought it was his failure at the examinations, but when Tâm came back and the uneasy premonition would not go away the abbot was puzzled and couldn't do anything but wait for the karmic forces to reveal their design.

"Why? What crime did he commit?" he asked.

"People say the Village Chief is accusing him of promoting the spread of the Christian religion."

The abbot frowned and waited for Cơ to finish.

"There is also a young woman who came up from the capital a few days ago to see Teacher Tâm. She is kneeling before the communal house to plead for his release."

At once he began walking and left the temple grounds. Cơ was usually strong and fast but she found herself having trouble keeping up with the old monk.

Shortly after noontime, the crowd saw abbot Khánh make his way toward Giang. He was composed and his footsteps were steady as he moved to the front of the communal house.

Although he didn't know much about Giang, he had guessed most of the truth about her. His nephew had been a changed man since he came back from the capital, and he had long suspected some emotional entanglement that his nephew would not speak about. Even before he met her, the abbot had to admire the boldness of her decision to come to the village. As soon as he saw her, kneeling but unbowed, he knew he could count on her resolve.

As he reached her and stood next to her, she tilted her head up. Tâm had told her about him so she knew who he was. He was a monk like her grand uncle, but he was much thinner and appeared both kinder and stronger. She saw in his eyes the same determination that she was looking to build up within herself. She knew that she had found an ally whom she could count on to help her end Tâm's predicament.

They were seen talking for a few minutes. After that exchange, the monk knelt down next to her and assumed the same stance she had taken. His head was bowed in prayer, and his hands were clasped in front of him, fingering a string of prayer beads.

"What now?" constable Tuấn cried out. "Why is the abbot kneeling down with her?"

He was thoroughly dispirited. When the day started, his official duty was simply to look from time to time on the village teacher in his cell. He and his men were neither prepared for the passive protests taking place right before their eyes or for the growing number of people who were watching them. He shouted at the constable standing near him.

"Go to the Village Chief's house. Tell him that at least half of the village is here to watch these two ... supplicants."

The crowd had increased in size with the arrival of the abbot, and more people were still arriving.

Tâm was in his cell meditating and had been in the lotus position from mid-morning. The constables had looked briefly on him before going outside. He heard faint sounds of their talking with somebody on the outside and he had guessed that person was Giang. After a while, when he didn't see her come in, he began meditating.

It had been several days since the incident at the school. When arrested, he had hoped to present himself before the Village Council and clear himself right away of the ridiculous charges Xã Long had thrown at him. Since then there had been no council meeting, he had not even seen the Village Chief, and neither constable Tuấn nor any of his men had any useful information that they were willing to share with him.

Giang came to visit him twice a day, and she tried to be cheerful each time he saw her. He was watching for signs of stress or worry, but outwardly she showed none. Instead, she was the one who kept telling him that he would soon be cleared of all charges and released.

His eyes closed, he tried to focus his mind on her image. A mental picture came to him, the same one that he sometimes experienced along the Mandarin road on his way home. He had a vision of her kneeling on the ground, her eyes also closed, and she was trying to tell him something. He knew then that it was going to be a challenging and fateful day, but that she was going to be there with and for him. He felt comforted at the same time that a new reserve of energy spread out throughout his whole body.

Xã Long arrived at the communal house shortly after noon. Usually at that hour, the villagers were in their homes or resting under some shade in the fields. However, on that day he had to elbow his way through several rows of spectators surrounding the two figures kneeling in front of the main door. The crowd was restless and an indistinct hum pervaded over it, with people talking to one another in low voices. He heard words of sympathy or pity toward the two supplicants and the village teacher inside the communal house jail. People were so fixated on what was happening in front of them that most did not notice him pushing his way through.

Feeling his anger rising, he strode vigorously forward to stand in front of abbot Khánh and Giang, facing them and the villagers. Constable Tuấn stood behind him, alternately watching his chief, the two kneeling figures, and the villagers.

"What do you think you are doing here?" Xã Long shouted, his eyes bulging and more ferocious than on any other occasion. He wanted his words to be heard also by the villagers present, a not so subtle warning for all to mind their own business, disperse, and go home.

Giang opened her eyes, but it was the abbot who spoke first. His voice, honed by countless hours of prayer and chanting, was not loud but resonant and clear, reaching even ears at the edge of the crowd.

"We are here to ask you why you are detaining Teacher Tâm without allowing him to meet with the Village Council. He has not had a single opportunity to defend himself against your accusations."

"Abbot, who gave you the authority to question the Village Council's decision?" Xã Long roared back.

"I am his uncle. His mother is at the moment ill and lying in bed. This young woman next to me has been sent by her to see to it that her son is well cared for in your jail. All we are asking is that you convene the Village Council and have Teacher Tâm appear before it."

Murmurs rose from the crowd, many of whom were the schoolchildren and their parents. Some were as bold as to suggest that the village teacher be freed immediately and unconditionally. Others demanded that the Village Council be summoned right away. It was unprecedented. Villagers usually only assembled for annual festivities in the communal house, events that took place in a joyous atmosphere. Xã Long understood why his men were apprehensive with this crowd. People were unhappy and agitated, and some were starting to get visibly angry.

As the good businessman that he was, Xã Long knew when it was necessary to take a step back. He had wanted to wait until his son came home after his victorious assault against the rebel base. Then he would have been able to also implicate the village teacher with treasonous support for the rebels. But he could still do that later, and spring it as yet another surprise against the unsuspecting village teacher. He addressed the two people kneeling before him as well as the larger crowd.

"I will have the constables go invite the council members to come to the communal house, and we will have our meeting. Be prepared to accept the consequences. Don't say that you have not been forewarned."

Constable Tuấn led Tâm out into the large yard in front of the communal house where the Village Council sat on chairs hastily arranged in a semi-circle. There was not enough space in the communal house to hold such a large crowd, and Xã Long had no choice but to conduct the meeting out in the open. Mercifully, the weather was relatively pleasant, with the sun and the temperature not overly harsh.

Councilman Khê was in the middle chair, with the Village Chief right next to him. Khê did not have time to smoke his opium pipe and was agitated and in a foul mood. The rest of the council members were not pleased either with the hurried up meeting and stared at the village teacher with suspicion and hostility.

Tâm saw both Giang and his uncle, the abbot, standing in the front row of the packed crowd, kept a safe distance from the council members by the constables. She looked at him with affection and smiled. His uncle nodded confidently, following him with his eyes as he was led to stand in the center facing the Village Council. His students were intermingled with their parents in the large crowd.

As the most senior member of the Council, Councilman Khê signaled to the constable that he wanted the meeting to begin. Every precious minute that he had to spend at the meeting kept him away from his favorite activity. The constable waved two wooden sticks and rhythmically struck a big drum wheeled out and placed next to the main door. After three long rolls and a final flourish, he stopped and yelled at the top of his voice for the audience to stop talking and maintain silence. The crowd quieted down, and he did not have to repeat himself. Councilman Khê began speaking immediately.

"Teacher Tâm, it has been brought to the attention of the Village Council that you have committed two serious violations of the village rules, both of them centered on your desire to spread a foreign religion in our community. Do you admit to those violations and are you prepared to accept whatever this Council will decide as punishment for you?"

Tâm replied without the slightest hesitation.

"Councilman, I do not. It has never been my intention to spread any foreign religion in our community. If the council had asked my students, they could have told the council that the charges against me are completely unfounded. I would like to know on what basis you have made these accusations against me."

Xã Long gave a signal to the constable Tuấn who left the scene and went inside the communal house. Meanwhile Khê continued in his unpleasant nasal voice.

"Teacher Tâm, instead of teaching Chinese characters to your students, have you not begun teaching them the script invented by the foreigners for transcribing their religious texts into the Vietnamese language?"

"Councilman, I have indeed been teaching them the script created by Portuguese and French priests two centuries ago to replace the Chinese characters that we have been using up to now. In addition, my students and I have also started teaching it to some of the elderly people in our village. However, teaching the new script cannot in anyway be construed as spreading the foreign religion. During my trip back home from the capital, I have been made aware that a growing number of scholars in our nation, including some around the King, have recognized that the new script is much easier to learn than Chinese characters and can be a very effective means for spreading literacy among our people."

Khê smirked and waved a hand with brown fingertips to dismiss the idea.

"In over 30 years of public service in almost every province of our nation, I have never met any scholar who has told me that. Don't expect me to believe you now. However, let me go on to another subject."

He glanced sideways at the Village Chief sitting next to him, making clear where the next accusation was coming from.

"Did you not learn this new script from a French priest that you met while you were in the capital?"

Tâm had to smile on hearing the question. He turned to look at Giang. She nodded, agreeing to his silent question. He swerved back towards the council members.

"I can definitely answer no to your question, Councilman. I did not meet any foreign priest while I was in the capital. The person who taught me the new script is right here in front of you."

He pointed to Giang standing in the crowd.

"That is Cô Giang over there and I met her in Huế. She was my teacher then."

Even though she was uninvited, Giang spoke up in the purest Northern accent.

"Yes, I am indeed the one who taught Teacher Tâm the new script."

Councilman Khê and most of the council members stared at the young woman whom they had hear about but had not yet seen until then. Xã Long was the only one who failed to show any surprise. He did not know that she was the one who taught the script village teacher, but that didn't matter much to him.

He felt a rising irritation, and looked around to see if constable Tuấn had come back from the errand on which he had sent him. At that moment, the man showed up carrying in his hands a pile of paper on top of which rested a book. Still holding his bundle, constable Tuấn shouted and demanded that the restless audience stop talking and kept quiet.

After his last question, Councilman Khê ran out of strength and motivation. His craving for opium had finally overcome his senses and he had lost his train of thought and could not continue. He sat back in his chair, his mouth contorted in a grotesque rictus, his breathing labored, and his eyes glazed over. Xã Long, after nudging him several times without getting any reaction, threw a disgusted look on the old mandarin, and knew he had to take matters in hands. He started with a blunt rebuke directed at the village teacher.

"Teacher Tâm, whether or not you were taught by some French priest or by this woman is not really significant. What is important is what you used the new script as your teaching vehicle for something else."

He paused briefly. His voice was booming and the crowd felt its effect as eyes focused on the all-powerful Village Chief. While looking at Tâm, he pointed to the bundle that constable Tuấn was holding.

"Do you recognize what the constable is holding?"

Tâm frowned slightly.

"Village Chief, he is holding things that belong to my school: a book and pieces of writing paper."

"He obtained those things on my order, village teacher. So you agree that they are yours?"

"They certainly are, and you have no right to take them from the school."

Xã Long ignored his protest.

"Isn't the book a religious book used by Christians?"

Tâm could not help letting out a laugh.

"No, Village Chief, that book is a dictionary. The words printed on its cover, if you can read them, say '*Dictionaire Annamite-Français*' which means Vietnamese-French dictionary. Cô Giang gave it to me to use these past several months as I was trying to learn French. I am very familiar with it, and I practically know it by heart. The first word of our language on the first page is *A* which is defined as an exclamation. The second word is *Ác* which is translated as bad, wicked. The third word is *Ai* ... I could go on, but you get the point."

Xã Long did not get the point but went on with his questioning anyway.

"Those pieces of paper or more precisely what is on them: aren't they Christian religious sayings or even prayers that you have copied. Isn't your goal to have your students study them under the pretext of learning the new script?"

Tâm began to smile, unnoticed by the Village Chief who was giving an order to the constable.

"Constable Tuấn, I want you to hold up high one of those pieces of paper so that everyone can see it… That's it. I will now ask the village teacher here to tell the Village Council what is on that piece of paper."

Tâm only paused briefly.

"Village Chief, would you agree to let Cô Giang read to you what is on that piece of paper?"

Xã Long hesitated, wondering if he was going to fall into a trap. He looked from Tâm to the young woman. He was about to deny the request, but confident that he could not lose, he nodded and grunted his consent.

"Constable Tuấn, please bring that piece of paper closer to Cô Giang so she can read it," Tâm said.

Once the constable stood in front of Giang with the paper, she gently prompted him.

"You are holding the paper upside down. I can't read it like that."

There were jeers and laughs coming from the crowd. The constable's face flushed instantly.

"Please turn the paper like this," Giang gestured with her hands. "There… Now I can read what's on it."

She silently read the writing, smiled sadly, and then began reciting.

"Thuở trời đất nổi cơn gió bụi,
Khách má hồng nhiều nỗi truân chuyên.
Xanh kia thăm thẳm từng trên,
Vì ai gây dựng cho nên nỗi này?"

(When all through earth and heaven dust storms rise,
   how hard and rough, the road a woman walks!
   O those who rule in yonder blue above,
   who is the cause and maker of this woe?)

They were the first four lines of "*Chinh Phụ Ngâm Diễn Ca*" (The Song of a Soldier's Wife) by Đoàn Thị Điểm the famous female poet of the early 18th century. Many in the nation, including those who could not read Chinese or Nôm, knew the entire poem or passages from it by heart.

She said the last line slowly and came to a stop reluctantly. Her voice was not as sonorous as that of the Village Chief, yet most people heard her. She lifted her eyes from the paper and turned them toward Tâm. For an instant, they only saw each other. The longings they had for each other blotted out the people, the communal house, and the village itself.

It was as if the cruel world around them had ceased to exist, and the heartaches and the physical hardships that it had inflicted on them had somehow vanished, or no longer made any difference. There they were, alone in the world, hoping to be near each other and to whisper to each other the loving words they had been holding back all those months.

Years later, women in the village would still describe how Teacher Tâm and Cô Giang tenderly looked at each other, and how proud they were to have been there to witness that unique and priceless moment.

The Village Council and most people in the audience were stunned into silence. When he judged that the crowd had fully appreciated what it was that Giang had read, Abbot Khánh began to speak.

"Honored members of the Village Council, have you now seen a religious text anywhere? The book is a dictionary, and what was on the paper? Verses from one of our country's most beautiful poems! Does that justify the Village Chief coming to arrest our village teacher? Who is the guilty one here? Has the Village Chief intentionally misled you because he knew full well that none of you could read the new script?"

The council members squirmed and began casting glances at the Village Chief as if they were seeking his help. Xã Long stood up, shaking with rage.

"Silence," he roared at the top of his voice. The power and volume of that command ended all side conversations almost instantly. His bulging eyes glowered at the abbot, at Giang, and at anyone in the crowd who dared to stare back at him. Children recoiled and turned away in fear at his demonic mien.

"I will have the constables throw out anyone who speaks unless invited to do so."

He stopped and looked around slowly, challenging anyone who would not agree with what he had just said. Then he went on another line of attack.

"My duty today is to also point out to the Notables on the Village Council that for the past few months, a little girl has been living at the village school, as well as attending classes there. She is not from any family in our village, and in fact, we don't know much about where she came from, or who her parents are. This is because the village teacher has chosen not to let the Council know about her coming to our village."

"Our traditions and rules dictate that all strangers coming to our village be reported to the Village Council and to me. He should have done that, but he didn't. Why? Arrogance, disregard for the Council perhaps? Actually, the real reason is much more serious. She has been seen making the sign of the cross inside the village school. She has been heard reciting her prayers, invoking not the Buddha but the God of the foreigners. This little girl is a Christian."

After this long tirade, he pointed a finger at the village teacher. "Do you admit that you brought her to our village?"

"I did," Tâm replied defiantly. Although it was her mother who actually brought her to the school, he wanted to take full responsibility for Hồng.

"Then tell us why you didn't inform the Village Council of that fact."

"Village Chief, she is only a child and her presence among us does not require an official approval from the Council. She is not a laborer or a tenant farmer that could come in and displace one of our villagers, or claim a plot of land. She came to get an education, and she will leave to go back to her own village once she has accomplished that."

Xã Long was openly scornful of the explanation.

"Your true intention is to bring her here to start our conversion to Christianity? Isn't it?"

Tâm scrutinized Xã Long's face carefully to see if the man was deranged. He knew him to be a shrewd businessman, a capable leader whose intelligence and astuteness could not be denied. He was wondering what made the Village Chief distort reality and concoct such bizarre accusations.

"No, that was not my intention, and I don't think someone like little Hồng can be perceived as a missionary for a foreign religion. She is no threat to any of us. On the contrary, she has proved to be an asset for our school and a model for many of our students to learn from and to emulate. She represents not a religion, but a type of education that our nation needs."

Forgetting the Village Chief's command to keep quiet, people in the crowd were whispering to one another. Many had seen the little girl walking around the village or playing with other children, and had never thought of her as anything but cute and lovable. Parents had heard their children report to them about her amazing intelligence and the new skills and knowledge she possessed.

No one believed that their village teacher was using her to convert people to Christianity. Wasn't he going to his uncle's Buddhist temple almost every day, taking Hồng along with him? And didn't the abbot himself come and kneel by Cô Giang to pray for the village teacher release?

Xã Long did not like the crowd's reaction. He swiveled his head to both sides and addressed the council members who had maintained an uneasy silence while he was speaking.

"Honored councilmen, I cannot deny that Teacher Tâm is quite skillful with words. He has tried to convince us that the foreign book is a dictionary, and that the words copied on paper are those of a poem. He even had his so-called teacher read a few lines from the poem to us. It is almost believable, but let me point out to you that none of us can read the new script, and therefore there is no way for any of us to verify the facts of the matter. How do we know whether that woman was not reciting something she had memorized, and was just pretending to read from that piece of paper?"

He turned his head right and left to make sure the notables agree with him, and some nodded. Tâm took the opportunity to interrupt.

"Village Chief and honored councilmen, I would like to make a suggestion. At the school, we have been teaching some adults in the village to read and write the new script. I would like to ask any among those adults to come up here and read what's been copied on those pieces of paper that constable Tuấn is holding."

Without waiting for an answer, he turned around and called out.

"Is there anybody willing to come forward and read for us? Just like you have been doing in class? I know that some of you can do it."

He scanned the crowd, recognizing several men who had been coming to class in the evening. He and his students, including Thi, had personally helped each of them progress from recognizing the Romanized letter in the alphabet, to writing them out with trembling hands, then to reading them aloud, one word at a time, and finally an entire sentence. He remembered the thankful and proud smiles that appeared on those faces as they suddenly realized they could at last read and write. If only one of them would volunteer!

"Teacher Tâm, I will do it."

The crowd parted and an older gentleman stepped forward. He was Ông Bài, a retired mandarin who happened to be constable Tuấn's father. Since he came to the communal house that morning, he had been infuriated both by Xã Long's blatant attempt to frame the village teacher, and by the sight of his son helping the Village Chief.

Constable Tuấn was the old mandarin's greatest disappointment in life. When he was growing up, he was provided every opportunity to go to school in the hope of someday passing the examinations and becoming a mandarin in his own right. Instead he showed no interest in his studies and, when he got older, came under the influence of the Village Chief. He became one of the youth with more brawn than brain that Xã Long surrounded himself with.

The only consolation for Ông Bài was his grandson who was everything that his son was not. The lad loved school. While his father had picked the Village Chief to emulate, the boy's idol was the village teacher. He was the one who had urged his grandfather to learn the new script, and with plenty of time on his hands, Ông Bài willingly came to the village school for that purpose. At home, both he and the boy read the materials handed out by the village teacher, or practiced writing the new script together. Both were amazed and overjoyed to find that they were making progress much faster than what either of them thought was possible.

"Tuấn, bring me one of those pieces of paper that you have stolen from the village school," he ordered his son.

Constable Tuấn was going to protest his father calling him a thief, but kept his mouth closed under the stern look the old mandarin gave him. He pulled out a sheet of paper, approached his father, and meekly handed it over. Ông Bài squinted and held the paper at arm's length so that he could see clearly the words on it. Again the crowd was hushed and almost all the councilmen leaned forward to watch what was going to happen. After a long minute, Ông Bài nodded his head appreciatively and smiled with pleasure.

"This quatrain from *Chinh Phụ Ngâm* is truly my favorite! Let me read them for all of you."

> *"Cùng trông lại mà cùng chẳng thấy,*
> *Thấy xanh xanh những mấy ngàn dâu.*
> *Ngàn dâu xanh ngắt một màu,*
> *Lòng chàng ý thiếp ai sầu hơn ai?"*

(We look to find each other but cannot --
we only see those green mulberry groves.
Mulberry groves all share one shade of green --
of your own grief and mine, which hurts the more?)

He stopped, looked up at the Village Council, and with a trembling hand pointed an accusing finger toward his son.

"Honored members of the Council! I am ashamed to say that it was my son, constable Tuấn, who stole the book and these papers from the village school. He did it without my knowledge. My grandson has been going to the village school since he was barely five. He's now ten and he's the one who convinced me to come to the school in the evening to study the new script under Teacher Tâm. That's what I've been doing and that's how I am able to read these marvelous lines."

He paused briefly and shook his finger at constable Tuấn.

"I am sorry to say that my dim-witted son, who neglected his studies when he was young, has sided with the Village Chief and helped him collect this so-called evidence to frame an honest man and arrest him on totally fabricated charges. This book and these pieces of paper are not religious texts of any kind, and Teacher Tâm has done nothing more than encourage our children, their parents, and sometimes their grandparents, to learn to read and write in a new way. I wish I had been taught by somebody like him years ago. However, it is not too late yet. My grandson is the one who has followed his teacher's advice and encouraged me to learn again after all these years."

He looked for his grandson in the crowd. The young boy stood with a group of fellow students, smiling awkwardly, but did not turn away under the sudden glare of public attention. He was as proud of his grandfather as the old man was of him. Ông Bài again faced the Village Council and raised his voice to a new level.

"This travesty of justice that the Village Chief has staged for you today has gone on too long. I urge you to let Teacher Tâm go! Set him free before this whole situation becomes known beyond our borders, before our village becomes the laughing stock of the whole country. Do not let yourself be manipulated by this ignorant Village Chief."

The crowd erupted in shouts of support. The Village Council members looked at one another, recoiling and shrinking under the noise. The Village Chief threw a scathing look at his fellow council members, willing into them a spine and toughness of character that they all seemed to lack. He made mental notes to make sure to withhold favors from them in the future.

Privately, Xã Long cursed himself for believing in what Tuấn had reported to him about what was going on at the village school. He wished he had found somebody who knew the new script and asked that person to look at the materials the constable had stolen from the school. The events of the last few months, from his son's examinations success, his daughter's kidnapping, and last but not least his fruitless attempt at arranging his son's marriage, all that had distracted him and made him commit a basic error. As the astute businessman that he was, he had simply forgotten to validate his assumptions.

He knew then that he had to bring up the charge that he wanted to delay until the arrival home of his son. There was no other choice. If he wanted to save face, he had to do it at that instant. He raised both of his hands high above him and waved them to quiet down the crowd. As soon as they did, he launched on his final bid to destroy the one that he no longer considered a mere thorn before his eyes, but a real enemy that he needed to crush to preserve his authority and power.

"We are far from being finished with all the charges against Teacher Tâm. There could be different ways of looking at what he has tried to do with his teaching. However, I guarantee you that what I am about to reveal to you will show him to be a truly dangerous element in our village."

He paused for effect and the crowd became quieter, as it waited for his next words.

"We all know that after my daughter was kidnapped by the Black Flags, Teacher Tâm went somewhere to find her and bring her back to us. At that time I was very relieved that she was rescued and I sincerely thanked him for his effort."

People in the crowd were nodding their heads and some even shouted, "Right! That's the truth! Release him now!" He pretended not to hear them and went on.

"Some time later, when everything quieted down and our village life went back to normal, I began asking myself how he, a simple village teacher, was able to go see the bandits and talk them into releasing my daughter. We all know that the Black Flags are ruthless people who will kill anybody for any reason or for no reason at all. For some time now, royal troops have been sent all over the country, including our own region, to destroy the bandits and restore peace. Even my son, the new Prefect, has been given as his first mission the capture and destruction of the bandits and their lairs. He has thousands of soldiers at his disposal, but even then it has not been easy."

He bowed his head and pretended to reflect deeply to emphasize that last point. During his lifetime, the village had never experienced warfare, but he knew that people were still concerned. News and rumors about bandits and the Cần Vương opponents of the regime in Huế were constant reminders that the country was still not at peace after nearly a century of rule by the Nguyễn dynasty. No one liked French colonization, but those who tilled the land cared even less about seeing war on their doorstep and interfering with their lives.

"So, how is it that he was able to convince those bandits to set my daughter free? How is it that he was able to brave danger and risk his own life in a mission that no ordinary person, certainly none of you in this village, would dare attempt? Remember that I did not even ask him to do it. He went away on his own, and within a few days brought Kim Liên back. How could he do it so easily?"

He now raised his voice while pointing an accusing finger at Tâm.

"That's because he knew who they were. He chose to ignore the King's edict and has secretly dealt with the bandits. He is a traitor who lives in our midst. For all we know, he may even be one of them."

He stopped, and a heavy silence weighed on the crowd. People were either completely shocked by his claims or too overwhelmed by their implications. The Village Council members, who did not know Xã Long would accuse the village teacher of treason, were bewildered.

In the crowd, three women knew his accusation was a total distortion of the truth. Cơ, the mother of Chính, was the first one. She was too shocked to react, and was unable to move or speak.

Standing among the students, Thi felt like shouting out against the vengeful behavior of the Village Chief. She had been witness to the conversation between her teacher and the parents of Chính, and knew why her teacher went so discreetly to bring back Xã Long's daughter. He was not a rebel. All he wanted to do was to shield the Cơ's family from the wrath of the Village Chief.

Giang in the meantime realized the seriousness of the Village Chief's accusation. Xã Long, for some reason, was obviously willing to subvert the truth so he could punish the good deed that Tâm had done for his daughter and his family. Cơ had already told her why he had gone to find and talk her son into freeing Xã Long's daughter. Tâm was someone who usually went out of his way to help other people, disregarding how others may interpret his activities. Now the ungrateful Village Chief was accusing him of treason and, if Tâm could not refute that charge, he would be in terrible danger. Captured Cần Vương leaders and their followers were regularly decapitated or exiled to some remote island.

She shivered at that thought and, while her mind worked furiously to find something, anything to use against the Village Chief, her eyes fell on Cơ who was standing only a short distance away. The poor woman was just as distressed as Giang, her face showing obvious strain as her eyes darted back and forth between Tâm and the Village Chief. Abbot Khánh was standing next to her, but he was oddly calm. His eyes were closed as if he was praying or meditating.

Suddenly, from the back of the crowd, a voice shouted.

"The Prefect has come home! The Prefect has come home!"

Everyone turned to where the sound was coming from. They saw a large cloud of dust made by indistinct shapes of men and animals. They heard the sound of horses snorting and of soldiers with their guns and equipment, marching toward the communal house. As the troops came closer, everyone saw the Prefect riding proudly at the head of the military column. He was surrounded by French and royal Vietnamese mounted officers. Behind them, on a cart pulled by two buffaloes was a cage made of bamboo that was freshly cut and still green. In the cage sat a man wearing filthy rags and covered with dust and dirt. No one among the villagers, except one person, recognized him or knew who he was. As the crowd parted to let the column through, Cơ cried out softly.

"My son! Oh, my son!"

However, the apparition of the Prefect and the troops had captured the crowd's attention, and not one soul, except for Giang and the abbot, heard her.

The Rebel

Kim Liên started the day in a better mood than what she had experienced in the past few months. She had seen her father leave home hastily to go to the communal house after saying that he was going to "take care" of the village teacher once for all. She knew that her father had jailed Teacher Tâm and effectively closed down the school. That was the reason her spirits had lifted somewhat. She was happy that the man who was so indifferent to her had been brought down from his high pedestal, and that Thi, the little Nguyên girl that he favored, could no longer attend school and act as if she were above everyone else.

Only two matters were still bothering the Village Chief's daughter. First, she didn't know how the one who kidnapped her had fared in the second assault that her brother had made against the rebel base. There were rumors that Prefect Chí had acquitted himself well during this second sortie, but there were no other details. Were all the rebels routed and killed? Was that one still alive?

Secondly, she heard that a beautiful woman with strange blue eyes had arrived in the village and was staying at the village school. People said that Teacher Tâm had met her when he was taking the examinations in the capital, and that the two were in love with each other. At first, Kim Liên dismissed the rumors as absurd, but as people kept talking about the stranger from Huế, she had to concede that it was not just a rumor. Then when her father had to go and convene the Village Council because the woman had held her own protest and pleaded for the village teacher's release by kneeling in front of the communal house, Kim Liên definitively wanted to go see for herself who she was. Most of the village was already at the communal house anyway, and she was not going to stay at home and miss the spectacle.

As soon as her father had left, Kim Liên got dressed in her finest clothes, combed her hair, coiled it around her head, and put on her shoes. Her mother stopped her before she went out and inquired.

"Daughter, where are you going?"

"I am going to see what Father is up to," she answered. "You should come along too."

Her normally quiet mother suddenly spoke with exasperation.

"It's not right what he is doing!"

"Why do you say that?"

"Don't forget that my father, your maternal grandfather, was a school teacher too. I don't think Teacher Tâm has done anything wrong, despite what your father is accusing him of. A lot of people are starting to know how to read and write. You should be learning that new script also since you don't want to take the effort to learn Chinese characters."

"Well, not right now, and not from him anyway."

"Did you already forget that he's the one who went and rescued you from the bandits?"

I wished he hadn't done that, thought Kim Liên, and maybe by now I would already be acquainted with the rebel commander.

"What did you say?" asked her mother.

"I didn't say anything!"

"I heard you mumble something."

"No, I didn't. I am going now. You still don't want to come?"

Against her own inclination, Xã Long's wife agreed to follow her daughter. They arrived at the communal house and watched the whole Village Council meeting from the back of the crowd. When the crowd parted for the Prefect and the soldiers, they found themselves drifting toward the front of the crowd.

Prefect Chí was now taking center stage after his father and the Village Council made room to let him and the French captain sit down before the assembled crowd. The interpreter sat behind the two men. Xã Long, beaming with pride, placed himself on the right side of his son. Councilman Khê, exhausted and in need of his opium pipe, had been taken home. The rest of the Council sat silent, overwhelmed by the newcomers and mesmerized by the bamboo cage placed in the middle of the court in front of the communal house. A dozen royal soldiers holding their rifles formed a ring around the cage, their deeply tanned faces turned toward the crowd. Officers had directed other soldiers to take positions in the village, and had given the rest orders to set up a bivouac in the back of the communal house.

Xã Long stood up and gestured for the crowd to quiet down again. He had already exchanged a few words with his son and, as a result, he knew who the prisoner was. He was beaming, proud and as happy as a man on his wedding day.

"Members of the Village Council, this is a good day of an auspicious month. The Prefect, following the King's orders, has returned victorious from his campaign against the rebels. He captured the rebel commander and has brought him to our village. This is the same bandit who a few months ago kidnapped my daughter."

There was a ripple of surprise in the crowd. Many now understood why Xã Long was no longer in a somber and angry mood. He continued.

"Heaven has looked down kindly on us, and now we have both the bandit and the village teacher in our hands, and both of them will face justice."

The interpreter was doing his best to translate the Village Chief's words to the French officer. At this point St Arnaud gestured toward Prefect Chí.

"Who is this teacher in your village who's on the rebel side? Where is he?"

Instead of answering him, Chí reached out to touch his father's back. Xã Long turned around.

"Why did you arrest Teacher Tâm?"

His father pointed at the village teacher who was still standing in front of them, although with the arrival of the rebel prisoner, he was no longer the center of attention.

"He's accused of two crimes. The first one is for teaching a foreign script to spread the Christian religion in our village. The second one is for disobeying the King's edict and participating in rebel activities."

Chí could not believe what he was hearing. He knew right away that Tâm was teaching the new script to his students, and he was surprised to hear his father saying he was doing it to spread Christianity. As for participating in rebel activities, could it be possible that Tâm had turned into a different man after failing the examinations?

Chí did not particularly like Tâm in the past, but he no longer felt that his old classmate was a rival. Since Tâm's shameful failure at the examinations the old jealousy was largely gone, except perhaps as far as Thi was concerned. In truth, so busy was he with his new duties that he had not thought much about her for the past few weeks.

As the interpreter finished translating his father's last words, he glanced over at the French captain and shook his head, trying to convey an expression of disbelief. The Frenchman raised one eyebrow and shrugged.

Chí bent toward his father and whispered.

"Do you know that the King is going to promulgate a new edict saying that this new script will have to be taught in all schools throughout the nation?"

Xã Long was temporarily taken aback, but he recovered fast.

"All right, but Teacher Tâm did go to contact the rebels during your sister's kidnapping, did he not?"

Prefect Chí was getting annoyed with his father.

"Father, we'll have to talk about this later," he said, still keeping his voice low. "Go on with the other matter, the rebel that I brought back for you."

The Village Chief turned to the audience.

"So, now that we have this bandit before us, the Prefect has given me permission to ask all the questions I need to ask to find out the truth about my daughter's kidnapping."

Pointing his finger to the man in the cage, he shouted.

"Are you the one who came to our village to kidnap my daughter and steal weapons from the royal soldiers?"

The Village Chief's loud voice hardly disturbed Chính. He had seen his mother in the crowd and suddenly his defiance against his captors had turned to despair. He knew they were going to execute him, but he did not want her to witness his last moment on earth.

Over the past few days, he had longed many times to have died in battle, or for a soldier to stab or shoot him to death in his cage. Then he would have joined his companions, Cicada and Cô Nhân, in the land of nine springs, without subjecting his mother to the agony of seeing him being beheaded. Although his father was nowhere in sight, he also knew that his death would mean a final and crushing disappointment to the man.

"You there! Answer me!" the Village Chief persisted.

Angry at his own fate more than he was at Xã Long, Chính snarled back.

"Yes, I was the one who took your daughter away. I did not want to, but she was in the way. So kill me now and get this circus over with."

An anguished woman's cry arose from the crowd.

"No! Heaven, no!"

Another cry followed it.

"Father, don't!"

The first came from Cơ, the second from Kim Liên who was standing with her mother at the front of the crowd. With all her strength, Kim Liên had pushed through the crowd and the villagers, recognizing who she was, had to give way to her.

She had been watching the man in the cage with curiosity, wondering whether he was the one whom she had been yearning for. She had never seen her kidnaper's face, but the way the prisoner looked, with strong and sturdy limbs, and his behavior, like that of a trapped but proud animal, had almost convinced her. Her heart was beating faster, and color came to her face. Once Chính spoke up, her doubts evaporated. She could recognize that voice anywhere.

The Village Chief, having easily extracted his first confession, was triumphant. He ignored the two shouts, and went on with his questioning.

"Did Teacher Tâm go to see you about releasing my daughter?"

"He did, and you got your daughter back, didn't you? Kill me now, and be done with it!"

Xã Long wanted to prove the complicity of the village teacher with his next question.

"How did he know where to find you?"

"I have no idea how, but he's not one of us. He is no rebel," Chính replied.

Since arriving to the communal house, he had seen the village teacher standing before the old men of the Village Council, and he guessed right away that his former teacher was in trouble. Hearing the Village Chief's questions, he suspected Xã Long was trying to tie the teacher to his rebel band's activities.

Meanwhile, Xã Long had turned toward his other target.

"Teacher Tâm, how did you know that it was this bandit who took away my daughter?"

Tâm was not surprised. He understood what the Village Chief was leading to, and had expected him to ask that question eventually. He threw a glance at Chính's mother and saw the utter misery and suffering on her face.

"I didn't know it was him. I just went to the rebel base, hoping to find your daughter there."

Xã Long exploded in a derisive laughter, startling everyone around him. However, he stopped laughing abruptly and wagged his finger at the village teacher.

"Teacher Tâm, do you take me for one of your naïve students? Do you expect me, or any of the council members here, or the Prefect, to believe you?"

He turned smiling toward the council members seated behind him.

"That lie has given us the proof that we need. Our village teacher has been maintaining contact with the rebels, and did not have to guess anything. He knew exactly where to go and find my daughter. He's probably behind the whole plot to kidnap her. He's just as guilty of treason as that one that the Prefect has brought back to us in that cage."

He stopped as if to regain his breath, and looked at each member of the Village Council. Some met his eyes but could not bring themselves to disagree with his conclusion. Others just looked away or downward, unable to confront him. The presence of the Prefect and the French captain also discouraged many from speaking out.

Xã Long gave them ample time before taking their silence as an unspoken agreement to the accusation he had made. He nodded his head, and then turned around and announced grimly.

"I am going to recommend to the Prefect that this village teacher deserves the same punishment that he has in mind for the rebel bandit."

As his words sank in and before people grasped their implications, an ominous silence fell on the crowd. Then, all at once, a chorus of protest and shouts of bewilderment arose from all around the village council. The noise built up gradually, alarming the soldiers guarding the cage and unnerving many of the Village Council members. However, before anyone could speak up or take any action, a young woman stepped out of the crowd.

Giang had been observing the French officer for some time. No sooner had Xã Long finished pronouncing his judgment, she knew instantly the danger of the situation. It was obvious that the arrival of the Prefect had emboldened the Village Chief and he had gone all out to accuse Tâm of being part of the rebel movement. She understood why Tâm could not or would not tell the truth. He would never point a finger at the woman Cơ in order to defend himself. She also suspected that even if he did, the Village Chief was not going to give him up just because there was somebody else to take the blame.

There was only one more thing she could do. She did not look forward to it, but there was no other option left. For a brief moment, when the French officer lifted his pith helmet to wipe the sweat off his forehead with a handkerchief, she had recognized him. She left her place and moved toward him.

Within seconds, a French soldier ran out and blocked her way, his rifle pointed directly at her, his face a mixture of anger and surprise at her boldness. Before he could say anything, she addressed him in French.

"I am Françoise Bonneau, and I am a French citizen. Let me speak to Captain St Arnaud."

The astonished soldier stopped in his track. St Arnaud had also heard her, and only hesitated momentarily before calling out.

"Soldier, let her come through."

Captain St Arnaud was both amused and irritated by the happenings around him. He understood quite well what the Village Chief's theatrics meant, even though he had to rely on his interpreter to understand the words being said. The interpreter was not as fluent in French as on most other days, but he managed to do his job fairly well.

The Village Chief was gesticulating and yelling at the top of his voice, but did not appear to convince anyone, least of all his son, who kept shaking his head but would not contradict his father openly. On the other hand, many in the crowd were openly hostile and angry at the Village Chief.

St Arnaud wanted the vociferous old man to stop. He had allowed Chí to bring the prisoner to the village so that he could be executed in the presence of the villagers, as a warning to all that the colonial regime would not tolerate any act of rebellion. However, the Village Chief was more concerned with accusing a village teacher and having that man executed as well. If some personal vendetta was the basis for all that was going on, the French captain wanted no part in it.

As Giang moved out from the crowd and strode toward him, St Arnaud recognized her. Special Envoy Bonneau had told him that his elder daughter was on the same ship that carried him and his troops to the Tonkin. However, absorbed with his military planning and operations, he had completely forgotten about her. In the back of his mind he thought he had at times seen a woman trailing after the French priest on the ship. He had assumed she was a Vietnamese servant and paid her no further attention, and now it dawned on him that she was Bonneau's daughter.

Whenever he came to see the Special Envoy in the capital, he had mostly seen her and her sister from a distance. Bonneau had introduced them to him, but he had not actually spoken with them, either officially or otherwise. He was not too sure how to deal with children of mixed blood, and had kept out of their way whenever he could. His fellow officers and men associated themselves quite freely with Vietnamese women, mostly prostitutes, and therefore mixed-race children were not uncommon around their camp and even when they were on the march during operations.

Personally, St Arnaud wanted to have nothing to do with the native women and kept himself aloof by design. As far as he was concerned, his boss's daughters were natives, and he made it a point to stay clear of them also. However, seeing one of them in an unlikely corner of the Tonkin, he got up and greeted her properly.

"Mademoiselle Bonneau, what are you doing here?"

"Captain St Arnaud, I need to tell you about what that Village Chief standing near you is trying to do. He is twisting and distorting the truth to fit his evil intentions."

Standing face to face with him and looking him straight in the eyes, she proceeded to relate at length what he could not know about the tragedy taking place before his eyes.

As she spoke with the French captain, Xã Long glowered at her before trying to get the interpreter to tell him what she was saying.

"Who is she? What is she telling him?"

"I have no idea who she is, but it looks like the captain knows her," answered the interpreter. "He is treating her very respectfully, which is something I have not seen him do with most people. But they are speaking too fast for me to follow."

The man in fact saw no need to translate anything for the arrogant Village Chief. After all, he only worked for the French captain. He turned away from Xã Long and took what he deemed was a well-deserved rest. As a result, everyone, from the members of the Village Council to the curious crowd had to content themselves with just watching and not understanding a word of what passed between Giang and the French captain.

Prefect Chí was in the same predicament, but his thoughts were wandering to the not too distant past. He remembered the rumor about one of the scholars being romantically involved with the daughter of a powerful family in Huế. He realized that the young woman with an aristocratic bearing who was talking to the French captain was the rumored young woman, and the mysterious scholar who had won her heart was in fact his former classmate.

A few months earlier, he and his band of friends had laughed at the idea of Tâm being involved in such a relationship, but the proof of it was standing right before his eyes. It was actually true then that his former rival, the self-effacing village teacher, did achieve a feat that others could only dream and talk about.

He observed the young woman closely, occasionally glancing away to appraise Tâm anew. She was very attractive and her blue eyes were fierce. The more he looked at her, the more Western traits he saw in her, from her above average height to her fair complexion. He assumed she was the daughter of some Frenchman at court and a Vietnamese woman, maybe even one of royal blood. There were tens of thousands of royal daughters and granddaughters, and some were known to have been given in marriage to Frenchmen. Chí suddenly became alarmed. Had his father gone too far and bitten into more than what a Village Chief, or even a Prefect, could handle?

St Arnaud mulled over various options as the Bonneau girl talked. He was surprised at her amazing command of the language, even for a mixed race person, at the intensity of her feelings and the genuine concern she held for the village teacher. In a sense, he envied the latter for having someone like her on his side. Ever since he left home, St Arnaud had been on his own in the world, with nobody caring for him except perhaps his Legionnaires. He quickly shook away the thought to come back to the pressing matter at hand.

The story she told him brought some sense to the tragi-comic theater he had been witnessing. The Village Chief reminded him of a frog puffing himself up to look like a bull. He wondered whether he would eventually explode, like the one in La Fontaine's fable. St Arnaud could easily overrule both him and the Prefect. The latter was a neophyte not only in military matters, but apparently also in administration and in the not so simple act of governance. Since arriving in the village, the new Prefect had meekly let his father take over, apparently satisfied with taking a back seat and watching as a spectator.

Giang waited patiently, ready with more information for St Arnaud if he wanted. She had detailed how she came to know the village teacher, and the series of misfortunes that had been plaguing his life, starting with his forced failure at the examinations. She had asked him to use his power to prevent another act of injustice against Tâm. She purposely mentioned that her father would have done exactly what she was asking the captain to do.

"Mademoiselle, please give me a little time," St Arnaud finally said. "Be patient and worry no more. I came here to make sure that the rebel prisoner be properly dealt with, and I want to give this new Prefect a chance to do that. Then I will make sure that nothing else will take place. Leave matters to me, and your man will be freed when this is over."

That was the best she could hope for, Giang thought. She thanked the captain politely, and went back to where the abbot, Thi, and Cơ were gathered. To the silent questions she saw in their eyes, she only nodded confidently.

"Prefect, how are you going to deal with the rebel prisoner?" the French officer asked through his interpreter. "After all, this is what we came to your village for, isn't it?"

Prefect Chí hastened to reply.

"Of course, and I will deal with him right now, Captain."

He stood up and stared at his father, silently willing him to sit down.

Xã Long could not know what was said between the French captain and that mysterious young woman who had appeared out of nowhere to take the village teacher's side. He had a feeling that maybe things were not going to go the way he wanted. He did not trust his son to make the right decisions, but there was not much he could do. He sat down, threw up his chin, smirked, frowned and resigned himself to watch his son perform as a Prefect.

The prisoner's guilt was never in doubt, and Chí only wanted to bring him to the village so that his father could witness the execution. He also wanted to prove that he was quite capable as a newly appointed mandarin, one who could operate well beyond his normal civilian duties. Chí pulled out a scroll of paper on which he had already written a summary of the crimes committed by the rebel, and the sentence that was going to be pronounced against him. He started to read aloud.

As soon as he began, from inside the cage came a demonic laugh came, one that could be heard by all. The prisoner was standing up, hands on his hips, his disheveled head thrown back, shaking with mirth.

"You have no right to judge me, Chí! You did not defeat me, the French did. I know I am going to die, but let the foreigner sitting next to you execute me himself. You are just his puppet and his lackey."

"Silence!" Xã Long jumped straight up and roared. "I forbid you to speak!"

"Why, is the truth too difficult for you to swallow, Your Excellency the Village Chief? Your son, His Excellency the Prefect, is a bumbling idiot whom I sent running home in his first battle against us. This time, he merely followed the French who did the actual fighting. What right does he have to strut about as if he were the victor?"

Not waiting for any reaction from Chí and his father, he continued.

"As for the village teacher, why do you insist on destroying him? Out of the goodness of his heart, Teacher Tâm came to me to ask for the return of your daughter. He had no knowledge whatsoever about what my fellow patriots and I did. Yet, you who have never liked him in the first place, you are trying your best to accuse him of rebellion. How absurd! How low can you get, Xã Long? Have you any moral decency left in you?"

Chính turned toward the crowd.

"And the rest of you, are you just going to stand there and let your Village Chief do whatever he wants? They are welcome to cut my head off any time, I am ready for that, but nobody should touch even a hair on Teacher Tâm. What has he done, other than trying to educate your children? He and his father before him have always fought against ignorance and illiteracy in this village. Are you just going to stand there and let him die? Are you?"

He turned to face the Village Chief again.

"Xã Long, you think you are astute, but you are only an ignorant peasant good at bullying people. You can't fool me or anyone else, including your ancestors."

Mentioning someone's ancestors was the ultimate insult, and Xã Long reacted at once. He took a step toward the cage, with his hand raised in a fist, ready to strike at the prisoner.

"Shut your mouth or I will kill you with my own bare hands!"

As he came closer to the cage, Xã Long stopped abruptly, realizing there was only one effective way he could vent his anger. He turned around and bellowed at his son.

"I demand that this rebel be put to death immediately. You have allowed him to live long enough already! If you want, I will gladly kill him myself."

As soon as he finished those words, two women stepped out of the crowd and began to speak at the same time.

"Father, don't," the Village Chief's daughter blurted out then stopped. Kim Liên could not bring herself to proclaim openly why she wanted to keep the rebel alive.

At the same time that Kim Liên spoke, a sorrowful voice arose.

"Village Chief, you must not kill your son!"

Cơ walked toward Xã Long, her hands clasped in front as if she was praying and begging for forgiveness. Her face was bathed in tears. As she came between the cage and him, Xã Long instinctively stepped back.

"Chính is your son, you must not kill him!" she repeated.

"Woman, what are you saying? My son is the Prefect, standing right there," said Xã Long, his voice breaking.

Almost immediately, he sensed that something was going to happen that was going to alter his life permanently. A woman did not step out of a crowd every day to challenge him without cause. What she also said about the prisoner being his son was even more shocking, although his mind had not yet measured the full implications of that revelation.

"Did you forget?" Cơ asked him. "One early morning more than twenty five years ago, you forced yourself on me when I was collecting waste from the back of your house."

Xã Long dropped the arm that was pointing at the woman. He wanted to command her to stop. In fact, she did so when she was halfway between the cage and him, but she had not finished speaking.

"I gave birth to your son nine months later. He's the one now in that cage."

He had not forgotten. He knew that a woman and her husband went around collecting night soil from each house every morning. They went about their business, unseen by most since people avoided them as if they were lepers.

Although he never saw her face clearly, he remembered the tall woman that he wrestled to the ground to assuage his lust, which only intensified as she struggled and resisted. In his frenzy, he ignored the nearby stench and her pleas, using his strength to pin her down and overcome her resistance by brute force. Afterwards, he just walked away, leaving her on the ground sobbing and devastated. He never saw her again, and in all the years had only thought about her maybe once or twice.

"That's a lie," he said. "He's your son, and your husband's son."

"My husband had smallpox when he was young, and he cannot have children. Chính is my only child. He's your child."

Kim Liên heard Cơ's words as if they were a series of thunderclaps. Even though her father called the woman a liar, she knew the accusation could only be true. She knew why the rebel had reminded her of someone, from the sound of his voice to his overbearing confidence. Chính was the son of her father, and therefore her half-brother. She turned in distress toward her mother, but did not find her at her side. The Village Chief's wife had already melted back into the crowd and disappeared. Kim Liên started pushing through the villagers asking them if they had seen her mother. Someone pointed her to where she had gone, and she fled in that direction.

Chí stood motionless, too overwhelmed by conflicting emotions to say or do anything. Only his eyes moved, falling on his father, on the prisoner, then on the woman who had come forward to accuse his father of rape. He tried to search for ways to refute the woman's claims, but the deflated appearance of his father told him it was pointless.

Xã Long had changed noticeably in the space of a few minutes. His shoulders were slumped, and he was hunched forward. He wanted to do something, but none of the possible courses of action was appealing. He could not continue to call for the execution of his newly discovered son, one in whom he recognized signs of himself, from his sturdy outward look to the boldness and bravery even when faced with certain death.

This one would have been worthy of him, maybe even more than the one appointed Prefect. If only he could have known about him sooner. Why didn't she ever come to him to say that their brief encounter had produced a son, his son, their son?

She pleaded for his life, but what could he do? His other son, the Prefect, had to carry out the King's orders, under the watchful eyes of the French officer. With the whole village having witnessed everything that happened in front of the communal house, Xã Long knew that he could not cover things up.

The villagers were stunned and watched in silence, not talking or making comments among themselves. Abbot Khánh had opened his eyes when Cơ stepped out of the crowd to confront the Village Chief. Long ago, he knew the day would come when she would call out Xã Long for the vile crime he had committed against her. Many times she had come to his temple to pray and to get over the guilt she felt toward her husband for raising a child that was not his. However, she could never bring herself to do the obvious, which was to confront the Village Chief. She did not want her husband to find out the truth, and, especially in the beginning, she feared that Xã Long would take away her child.

She continued to suffer in silence throughout the years, watching her baby become a young man who left home to join the rebel cause. After a quarter century, with the life of her son at stake, she was finally able to go up to Xã Long. He watched her standing unbroken and unflinching in her resolve. Somehow, the truth that she had to reveal in front of the whole village had lifted a burden over her and she stood like a statue, towering over a dejected and broken Xã Long.

Fate had created a situation where the Village Chief was not the only ruling authority. Anybody could see that the French captain, although he didn't say much, wielded more power than anyone else. His interpreter had become very animated in translating to him the exchanges between the Village Chief and the woman who stepped out of the crowd.

No one but St Arnaud himself knew whether the truth that she revealed mattered to him. It didn't, and he just wanted to see how the new Prefect was going to handle the execution of his newly discovered half-brother.

The prisoner himself was also subdued. It pained Chính to see his mother standing there pleading for him, the darkest secret of her life brought out in the open for all to hear and see. He couldn't begin to imagine how much his mother had to suffer throughout all the years.

All his life he had often wondered why she seemed to keep something from him and why the man he called father appeared aloof and uninterested in him. He understood then why she always reminded him to keep clear of Xã Long. He had never liked the man anyway, and he would never take back the insults he had shouted at him. For as long as he lived, he would never acknowledge him as his father.

Departures

After a brief exchange with the French officer, Prefect Chí announced that there was no longer any reason to hold the village teacher. He said it had all been a result of misunderstandings between the Village Chief and Teacher Tâm, but to many it sounded like he tried to apologize for his father's behavior. He asked everyone to go home, and that was all people wanted to hear.

The students were jubilant to see their teacher vindicated and freed. They cheered, they laughed, some cried, and some ran away to tell others at home or out in the fields. The rest mobbed the village teacher to offer their congratulations until the royal soldiers reminded them to disperse as the Prefect had ordered.

Side by side, Giang and Tâm went back to the village school, escorted by students and parents. Along their route, people came to the front of their houses to bow, wave at him, or to join the ranks of those who escorted him. Others came to look at the woman with the blue eyes, the one who started the day's events in motion that led to the release of their village teacher. The walk turned into a triumphal return, not as noisy as was Prefect Chí's *vinh qui*. On the other hand, it was more spirited and it made many feel better about their village and the times they lived in.

He had travelled that main road many times, as a toddler when he followed his father around, and later as a scholar defeated at the examinations. The weeds had grown back in many places along the road which no longer appeared clean and smooth as it was for Prefect Chí's homecoming.

The villagers were not dressed in their best, and there was no drum, gong, or firecrackers. However, he saw that the sky was of the purest blue, and he breathed in the fresh air faintly scented with a multitude of fragrances from the ripening rice fields and the plants and flowers all around the village. Although he had not eaten all day, he felt no pang of hunger and his steps were light and steady. Freedom had never tasted so good, not even when he was freed by the King's eunuchs a few months earlier. At that time Giang was not with him, but now she was, and that made all the difference.

As she walked by his side, Giang was chatting gaily with Thi who was thoroughly awed by the way she handled herself since she came to the village. They seemed to be best friends who had known each other all their lives. To Thi, Giang was like an older sister, one who deserved every right to her teacher's heart and who had already taken a significant part in his life. Together, they laughed, waved at the villagers and the children, and smiled at everyone. However, when they finally lost sight of the communal house, Giang became unexpectedly serious and turned toward Tâm.

"Your mother was not feeling well when I left this morning. We need to hurry home."

They almost ran back all the way to the village school. They found her sitting on her bed, all dressed up to go out but seemingly exhausted. However, her face lit up when she saw them.

"I tried to go to the communal house, but I could not get beyond the gate, without feeling dizzy," she said as she tried to get up from her bed.

Giang and Tâm rushed over to help her, but she waved them aside.

"I'm fine, especially now that both of you are home," she added, pointedly including Giang as a member of the family. In reality, she was quite weak and had to sit back down. She sighed but continued to refuse help from anyone and told them go about their business as if nothing was the matter.

While Thi went to boil water for tea, Giang and Tâm took turns telling the old woman what happened at the communal house, each adding their own comments about how they saw events unfold throughout the day. The students gathered around them, listening carefully to fill in any gap in their knowledge of what happened at the communal house. At the end, Bà Lân asked.

"So, are they going to execute Chính?"

"The French captain gave them until tomorrow morning to carry it out," Giang answered. "However, who knows whether the Village Chief or the Prefect now really wants to do that."

"Maybe we haven't seen the end of it yet," Bà Lân said. "Who knows what Chính's karma is? After what happened to Teacher Tâm today, I now believe more than ever than Heaven has eyes."

After things had quieted down and most had left, Tâm went out to the back to clean himself, something that he had not been to do scrupulously during his imprisonment. Out of habit, he picked up the hoe and started weeding the rows of their vegetable garden. It didn't take long and, once that was done, he went to the well to wash away the physical and mental grime left on him. After putting on clean clothes, he felt reinvigorated and renewed.

He overheard his mother, Giang, and some of the students talking up front. There seemed to be a lot of coming and going but he didn't worry about it, his thoughts mainly revolving around Giang. Since she had arrived at the village school, except for a few minutes at the beginning, he had not had one untroubled moment alone with her. He found himself at peace with the idea that she had decided to come to the village. Without her, he would still be at the mercy of Xã Long, whiling away his time in the communal house jail.

Even more important, despite being a stranger to the village, he saw that she seemed to be accepted by many, from his mother to the students and their parents. He was not surprised, knowing how well she interacted with the children and the adults at the orphanage in Huế. His main concern was about the future. What was going to happen to the two of them? He wanted her to stay, but how were they going to accomplish that? What would her parents think? What would his mother think?

Giang's voice rose from behind him.

"Teacher Tâm, I saw you working hard in the garden. You must be hungry after that. Would you like to come inside for dinner?"

Surprised, he turned around wondering how long she had been watching him.

"I haven't had too much time to prepare our meal, so don't be disappointed with what we have," she added with a playful smile.

His hair was still wet, combed and tied in the back, and he looked almost like he did on the first day they met. The only difference was that he was wearing his modest teacher clothes and not the scholar's tunic and hat bestowed to him the capital. She had to restrain herself to not run to him and hug him.

Perhaps sensing the invisible signal passed between them, he came closer, reached for her hands, and lifted them close to his heart.

"Giang, I've been meaning to ask you something, but all of the events of the past few days have not allowed me to do so, until now."

Despite his serious expression, she was still smiling as she waited for him to go on.

"Now that things have quieted down, what are you going to do?"

She lowered her eyes but did not reply.

"Giang, I want you to stay here with me. Will you? Or will you go home?"

Her nails dug hard into his hands, and she lifted her blue eyes to look directly into his.

"Teacher Tâm, I came here to find you, to be with you."

"Your parents, what will they say?"

"They approved of my coming here."

They both knew then that there was no turning back for her, and that she was going to be with him from then on, for the rest of their lives. Perhaps it had been so ordained from the very first day they met.

They went inside together and found his mother sitting at the table he normally used for desk. It was covered by a surprising number of bowls and small plates filled with all kinds of food, from green rice to stuffed tofu, pickled vegetables, and other appealing dishes usually reserved for festivities.

"This is a meal worthy of the King himself," he exclaimed. "Mother and Giang, how did you manage to cook this much in such a short time?"

His mother smiled while Giang explained.

"While you were in the back, Thi and the students have been bringing in these various dishes. They kept carrying them in and insisted that we accept everything. They would not take no for an answer. All I really had to do was to arrange them on your table."

During dinner, his mother barely ate, satisfying herself with looking at them and pushing away most of the food that either Giang or her son offered her.

"You too haven't eaten all day, so go ahead and pay no attention to me," she said.

Afterwards, they cleaned the table, put away everything, and by the time they were done, the moon was already high in the sky, bathing the outside with its soft white light. Only one oil lamp shed a warmer light on the three human beings inside the village school. This was the first time in many days that they were finally alone together.

Tâm was standing at the door leading to the classroom at the front, thinking he was going to move there later and make it his sleeping quarters while Giang spent the night in the back room with his mother, as she had been doing from the first day she arrived. That would be the right thing to do, he thought. Although she had chosen to come to him and share his life, they were not yet husband and wife.

"Teacher Tâm, I need to talk to you," his mother said in a tired voice. She was sitting on her bed and beckoning Giang, who was still in the kitchen, to come closer.

"You too, Giang. Both of you. Come near me."

Giang hurried over and sat on the bed near her, while Tâm pulled a chair close and lowered himself into it. His mother began as soon as she had their undivided attention.

"My children, listen to me carefully. I don't know how much longer I will be with you in this world."

"Mother, don't say that!" he exclaimed.

"What is ailing you?" asked Giang in alarm. "We'll get you to see an herbalist, or I can ask Father Phan to let us take you to a Western doctor."

"It is too late for any of that," the old woman said. "Tâm, lately, your father has often come to me in my dreams. It is a sign that he expects me to go join him soon."

Before he could make any protest, she continued.

"This is why I want to settle with both of you something that has been on my mind ever since Giang came here."

She turned to him and touched him on his forearm.

"Let me ask you first, Teacher Tâm. Is Giang the one you've been waiting for all this time?"

He was caught off-guard, but nevertheless answered without hesitation.

"Yes, Mother. She's the one and I have known that ever since I first met her."

He glanced at Giang. She met his eyes, smiled and lowered her head. In the light of the oil lamp, he thought he saw a slight blush come to her face.

His mother directed her next question to Giang.

"You came all the way from the capital to see my son. Are your feelings toward him the same as his toward you?"

"Yes, they are," she replied, using almost the same words. "From the very first day I met him, I knew he was the one."

"Did your parents approve of your coming here?"

"At first, they didn't. But in the end they allowed me to go on two conditions."

Her answer startled them both.

"Can you tell us what those two conditions are?" his mother asked.

"The first one is that I have to obey Father Phan. He can tell me what to do, or what not to do, and I must listen to him."

She paused for a few seconds, and then added.

"The second condition is that if Teacher Tâm, for any reason at all, does not want me here, I should go back home immediately, and … never see him again."

He started to shake his head, but his mother knew what she meant and explained.

"I think your parents were only worried that you'd find my son already involved or even married to someone else. As you can see, that is not the case. Now, let me ask each of you one question. You first, Teacher Tâm. Do you want to spend the rest of your life with Giang?"

"Yes, Mother, without any hesitation" he said confidently. He held his mother's gaze for a second before moving his eyes to Giang as a tightening sensation invaded the area around his heart and spread over his chest.

His mother paused to gather all of her strength to ask the remaining questions that had been on her mind since Giang arrived at the village school.

"And you, Giang. Would you want to spend the rest of your life with him, here in this village or anywhere else for that matter, far from the capital and from your family, without the benefit of the way of life in which you have been raised since you were born? And with all the hardships and danger that you already know about, as well as those that may yet come in the months and years ahead?"

Giang was prepared since the questions were almost identical to those that her mother had asked her before she left home.

"To spend my life together with him is what I have wanted for a long time now, even if he did not believe me in the beginning," she replied, with a glance at Tâm. He knew that she was still gently chiding him for his hasty departure from the capital a few months earlier. She did not give him the opportunity to respond and went on.

"As you said, I have indeed led a privileged life up to now, but I have also seen what others, who are less fortunate, have had to endure. It would be rash of me to say that I fear nothing that our future may bring, but I can tell you that I am prepared for whatever fate has in mind for us. I was able to convince my parents that what I feel for Teacher Tâm is not just a young girl's passing fancy. And I now hope that my coming here to this village has also persuaded you of the sincerity and strength of my feelings."

Her eyes, a darker blue than normal, expressed a mixture of candor, pride, and willpower not often seen in a person as young as she was. He could see that her fervor and eloquence had truly won over his mother, who did not wait long to say what she had in mind.

"Then I wish to see the two of you married, the sooner the better."

They were taken aback by the urgency with which she had said those words, but she had more to say to them.

"Tomorrow morning, as soon as there is light outside, you must do the following things. Giang, send someone to ask Father Phan to come to this school as soon as he can. Teacher Tâm, you must do the same with your uncle, the abbot. I would like both of them to officiate at your wedding. We won't have time to let all the relatives know, so it will be a very basic and simple ceremony. Your uncle will represent our family, and Father Phan will act on her parents' behalf."

"Father Phan will be here anyway," Giang hurried to say. "I've asked the French captain to let him know about today's outcome at the communal house, and he should be bringing back little Hồng tomorrow. But, shouldn't we look after your health first and get you treated and well again?"

The old woman smiled sadly and repeated what she had said earlier.

"Giang, it is too late for that now. The only thing that I wish for at this time is to see you and Teacher Tâm married. I don't want you two to have to wait for the mourning period of three years, if I should leave this world before you two can become husband and wife."

They both saw that she was exhausted after those last words. Giang helped her lie down on her bed. The old woman gave her a grateful look before slowly closing her eyes. Giang stood up and gently covered her frail body with a blanket while Tâm turned down the oil lamp so that it barely shone.

They sat quietly side by side and kept watch on the old woman. In the stillness of the evening, he bent down his head. He silently wept because his mother's life was slipping away and there was nothing he could do about it. He also realized that the challenges to his ideals over the past few days were only the precursors of many more to come. Sensing and sharing his sorrow and worries, Giang leaned over to rest her head on his shoulder, her face also wet with tears. Their hands joined and they thus comforted each other.

That same evening, in another part of the village, the rebel prisoner was in his cage, unfettered by any chain or tie, but having no more than a half a man's length to move in any direction. Chính was leaning his back against the stems of bamboo narrowly spaced apart that formed the cage's walls. He let his mind wander as his eyes scanned the place around him.

They had placed the cage right next to the outhouse in the back of the Village Chief's mansion. He found it ironical that a few hours before his death he found himself almost at the same place where the

Village Chief attacked his mother. He thought bitterly that it was quite possible that he was sitting on the same piece of ground on which he was conceived.

He could still picture his mother, standing alone and desolate in front of the communal house, looking at him through her tears, the words she was trying to stay stifled by her sobs. Abbot Khánh had come forward to try to console her, but no soothing words could diminish her anguish and pain.

Before that, Xã Long had left, walking away like a man with a heavy load on his back. His son, Prefect Chí, came over to tell him that he would be executed the following morning. The soldiers then moved the cage and put it in the back of the Village Chief's mansion with four guards posted continually around it. His mother, the abbot, and everyone else were prevented from following him.

Of all that he saw happening at the communal house, the only thing that he was happy about was to witness the young woman speaking to the French captain, and whatever she said was enough to set the village teacher free. The way she carried herself, her obvious courage and determination, reminded Chính of Cicada. He knew he was approaching the hour when he would go join her, and he was looking forward to that.

From the corner of his eyes, he saw the Village Chief's daughter walking out of the mansion, accompanied by two servants, each bearing a tray laden with food. Kim Liên herself carried a smaller tray. He remembered her from months back, and he shuddered at the thought that he had actually abducted his own half-sister.

Addressing the soldiers respectfully as elder uncles, Kim Liên smiled broadly and said.

"I thought you may be hungry so I brought you some food and beverages. Please eat and drink as much as you want!"

The soldiers glanced at one another, and then all nodded their approval of the unexpected bounty. They lost no time in relieving the servants of their burdens. One kept guard while the other three lustily dug in the delicious smelling meat dishes and sweet rice.

She next went to the guard on duty.

"Please allow me to give this small tray to the prisoner. He is going to die tomorrow in any case, but we should still give him his last meal. Isn't that the right thing to do?"

The guard wavered, looking at his companions for help, but they were too busy dividing the victuals among themselves.

"We don't want the prisoner's soul to come back and haunt us, do we?" she insisted.

"I can't open the cage," the guard said as his last excuse.

"You don't have to," she said. "This small tray can fit between these bamboo poles."

The guard grunted his consent, and then went back to watching his comrades, wanting to make certain that they were leaving something for him. Kim Liên came close to the cage and knelt down to pass the tray through to Chính. He was indeed hungry, having been fed very little since being taken prisoner. He took the tray from her. It was covered with a small mound of sweet rice and roasted pork arranged tightly together over banana leaves. She whispered hurriedly to him.

"Elder brother, look under the banana leaves. Use what you find there once the guards finish eating. I drugged their rice wine so that they will sleep for a long time."

She got up and, after one last glance at the guards, went back inside the mansion. He could not fail to note that she had addressed him as elder brother, and called herself younger sister.

The following day was unlike any other day at the village school. News spread rapidly that Teacher Tâm was marrying Cô Giang in the kind of hurried wedding that took place before an impending death in the family. The students, their parents and almost the whole village, joined in helping organize the event.

Thi took charge of a group of students who went around sweeping and cleaning every corner of the school, inside and out. The altar was moved from the back to the front schoolroom. Wild flowers were brought in as the only decorations as there was no time for anything else.

After the altar was set up, abbot Khánh arrived on foot, followed shortly after by the French priest in a horse cart with Hồng at his side. The two religious men greeted each other cordially, and while the abbot went to see Bà Lân, Giang had a long discussion with Father Phan. He listened attentively to her, asking only an occasional question.

The students, though busy with their tasks, glanced in their direction from time to time. They saw the French priest leaving Giang to go over to abbot Khánh. The two religious men conversed quietly in a corner of the schoolroom, concluding with each party nodding his acceptance to some common agreement. In the village's history, there had never been a wedding with two priests from two different religions officiating. Everyone was not only curious but also apprehensive as to what would happen. Fortunately, the students' spirit remained unflagging and the work assigned by Thi kept them busy with little time for idle speculation about what was going to take place.

In the end, two ceremonies were held in the school room jammed with students and parents, with many on the outside craning their necks to look in.

The first ceremony, if one could call it that, was conducted by Father Phan standing in the middle of the room facing Tâm and Giang. The village teacher wore his black school teacher tunic, simple and muted. She wore a dress made of domestic silk that she had brought from home. It was the color of turquoise and matched her eyes. Her outfit could not by any stretch of the imagination be considered wedding attire, but that did not deter the women present from marveling at the grace and beauty of the bride.

Hồng, holding a bunch of flowers that she had herself gathered, stepped forward and offered it to Giang who took it with genuine delight. The little girl moved behind her and the ceremony began. Abbot Khánh stood next to Bà Lân who was seated in a chair, looking pale and drained, but determined to see the day through.

Father Phan appeared in deep thought for some time before he began speaking slowly in Vietnamese for the benefit of every person present.

When he and Giang left the capital, he had thought that the purpose of their trip was mainly fact-finding. His mission was to escort Giang, bring her to the village, and afterwards take her back to her parents before any major decision had been made by anyone. However, Special Envoy Bonneau had also told him that he and his wife entrusted him with the authority to decide and act on their behalf on any urgent matter that needed to be resolved *in loco parentis*, Bonneau's exact Latin expression.

The dramatic events of the past few days compounded by the urgency of a dying mother's request had pushed him to make such a decision, even if he had to broaden the powers that Bonneau had given him, and even if what he was about to do ran counter to his church's rules.

When he was a young priest on his way to the Orient, he had visions of going to a part of the world barely touched by Christianity. There he would be converting heathens and propagate God's word as generations of his predecessors had been doing for centuries when they crossed the boundaries of the old Roman Empire to reach the savage hordes living beyond the edge of civilization. What he had found in Việt Nam was quite different than what he had expected.

The young village teacher that he had come to know was certainly no savage, and although he was no Christian either, his personal character, his learning, his conduct were worthy of the best that humanity had to offer.

From experience, he knew that converting educated Vietnamese to the Christian faith required much more of an effort on his part, and that success was by no means guaranteed. In this case, any missionary fervor that he might have entertained toward the village teacher had been shelved to the back of his mind after their initial contact. There simply was no desire, expressed or implied, to be converted. There was also no need to convert the young man, the keen mind of the Jesuit priest had to admit.

"Teacher Tâm and Giang, I have been entrusted by the Special Envoy and his wife to do what I determine to be best in a situation like this. Giang, your husband-to-be is not a Christian, and therefore the canon laws of our church do not allow me to perform the official ceremony of marriage between you two. I would have to seek a dispensation for that, and obviously, we know that will not be done today. It may not even be granted in any case."

He paused and gazed deliberately at the faces turned toward the center of everyone's attention. He saw and felt the admiration bordering on adoration that the students and even some parents felt toward the village teacher. He sensed their concern about the precipitous events of the last few days, and the worry some still harbored about the uncertain future facing the young couple.

The attitude of the villagers and his sympathy and admiration for the village teacher made the misgivings he had about going against his church's teachings and rules seem almost inconsequential. He turned his head slightly to address himself at the young woman whose French name was Françoise but was known to all by her Vietnamese name.

"Giang, I have known Teacher Tâm for some time now and I believe him to be a man of virtue and integrity, worthy of the trust of his students, of their parents, of the entire the village, and even beyond. I would be lying to you if I said that the thought of converting him to our faith has never crossed my mind. Even my actions in helping him and this village school were not entirely altruistic and were motivated partly by my duty to proselytize our religion as long as I am a priest. He would have been a prized convert, one that would have earned my superiors' praise."

His frank words brought a flicker of consternation in her blue eyes, and they took on a questioning look. He smiled to reassure her of his good intention and to let her know that he was not going in any way jeopardize her impending union with the man that she loved.

"Giang, I have never said this before about any other person: I don't see why he needs to be converted to our religion to become a better man for society or a better husband for you."

He nodded, looking at one then the other, then continued.

"What is important if that the two of you are marrying each other of your own free will, without any coercion from any party. That is the second condition for marriage, and those of us who are here know that it is indeed the case."

There was an audible sigh from a young woman somewhere in the room, but the priest went on.

"Even though I cannot perform the official Catholic rite of marriage for you, I do have the full permission of Giang's parents to say that they would have agreed to your union if they were present here today."

"Teacher Tâm, your mother has also consented to have this wedding take place. I am therefore ready to ask that our Lord bless this union and consecrate it, and I am sure that He who looks down on all of us will not mind that I am not following a certain church rule, one that was established not by Him but by mere mortals."

He proceeded to recite a prayer in Latin. Even though nobody, except perhaps Giang, understood the words, those assembled in the schoolroom were moved by the sight of Giang and Hồng saying amen and crossing themselves at the appropriate points.

Abbot Khánh took over next. He had told the French priest that he was going to act not as a Buddhist priest. He did not recite any sutra or perform a Buddhist wedding ceremony, which he insisted, did not exist. Instead, acting as a senior member of the groom's family, he directed the brief Confucian ritual during which Teacher Tâm and Cô Giang kowtowed to the spirit of the ancestors, to his mother, and finally to each other. When that was done and they stood up, Bà Lân nodded and smiled with genuine happiness at her son and her new daughter-in-law. Then as the two newlyweds went around the room to thank everyone present, she went back to her bed, leaning on Thi and Hồng.

As if by miracle, trays of food materialized from somewhere and were brought in by the students. Even a new well-wisher came in with a manservant carrying a big tray laden with fruit and plates covered with glutinous rice colored a bright orange, the color coming from the seeds of the spiny sweet gourd.

Tâm saw that the late arrival was the Village Chief's daughter. While her manservant continued to carry his tray to the back, Kim Liên apologized for being late and congratulated the village teacher and his bride with apparent sincerity. She was a different person, humble, demure, and pleasant, not dour or angry as she used to be.

Before her arrival, Giang had already recounted to the French priest the events of the previous day, culminating with the unexpected revelation by the unfortunate Cơ that the rebel prisoner was the bastard son of the Village Chief.

"Father Phan, I wish I could find a way to help her," she said. "But so far I haven't come up with anything. I can't just go to Captain St Arnaud and ask him to let her son go free."

Although his mind had also gone searching for some other solution, the priest could only nod his agreement.

"Even if you did, he wouldn't agree to do it. Do you know when the execution will take place?"

"People say it will be sometime in the afternoon, in the back of the communal house. You are not thinking of going over there, are you? None of us want to be a witness to it."

"No, of course not," the priest said. He was thoughtful for a moment before reflecting aloud.

"I was thinking that sometimes God works in mysterious ways. Who would have thought that little Hồng is the one that brought me to Teacher Tâm, and from him to you, and to this day? Who knows what may still happen for the rebel prisoner?"

Father Phan observed Kim Liên from a distance. Due to his long presence in the country and his closeness with his many flocks, Vietnamese were no longer as inscrutable for him as they were for most Westerners. He had learned to read their emotions beneath their public facade, and he sensed that the Village Chief's daughter was nervous and in a hurry. True enough, within a few minutes, while no one but the French priest was paying attention, she vanished from the schoolroom as quickly as she had come.

Following her departure, Tâm's mother insisted that the students, their parents, and the two religious figures sit down on the schoolroom floor or outside to share a wedding meal which, although unplanned, did not lack for gaiety and atmosphere. There was no time to slaughter pigs or buffaloes, and only a few chickens were sacrificed to provide some meat.

Thi could not prepare anything herself, as she was busy making sure that every student had assigned tasks and that everything flowed smoothly, and she was completely successful in that mission. This also kept her mind from the emptiness that she felt in her heart as the object of her devotion and adoration since childhood was permanently beyond her grasp.

People ate their fill, and there was even rice wine going around for those who wanted it. However, the two newlyweds went to the back room to see the ailing woman. She told them she needed to talk to Abbot Khánh and urged them to go back out to the front room and not neglect their guests.

The sound of galloping horses drowned out the joyful atmosphere at the village school. Soon clouds of dust followed and settled on those outside the schoolroom before finding their way inside.

Tâm and Giang had just come out from the back room when they saw the French captain bring his horse to a halt right in front of the school gate. He was followed by several other mounted Frenchmen, all with angry looks on their faces. The newlyweds immediately went to stand at the gate. St Arnaud spoke to the bride in French.

"The rebel prisoner has escaped. Have you seen him, Mademoiselle Bonneau?"

"No, we have not seen him," she replied. "And I am no longer Mademoiselle Bonneau, I am now married to Teacher Tâm."

The French captain walked his horse in a small circle while shaking his head as if he couldn't believe what he was hearing. Giang quickly translated for Tâm the brief exchange between her and the captain.

St Arnaud shouted an order to his men.

"Fan out, and go around this school."

As several riders obeyed his command, Giang asked.

"What's happening? What are your men doing?"

"We are searching for the rebel. He was seen coming here with the woman who helped him escape."

"What are you talking about? Who's she?"

"The Village Chief's daughter. She helped him break out of his cage either last night or early this morning."

Both of them remembered Kim Liên accompanied by her manservant as she came to the school to offer her congratulations. Tâm recalled that when he saw the servant, even with the large tray that he was carrying on top of his head, the man looked vaguely familiar, but someone or something else drew his attention and he had forgotten about him. Apparently, Giang had the same recollection. She exchanged an alarmed look with him and grasped his arm for support. Before they could think of what to say, they heard the deep voice of Father Phan from behind them.

"Captain St Arnaud, she came to congratulate these two newlyweds. However, she didn't stay long and left right away."

St Arnaud inclined his head to acknowledge the French priest who stepped forward to stand beside Giang.

"Father Francis, in what direction did she go?"

"I don't know where she went. We were all very busy as you can imagine, and nobody even noticed when she left."

That was at least part of the truth, and it sounded plausible enough to St Arnaud. He swore loudly, and abruptly rode off after his men. Giang turned toward the French priest with eyes full of concern.

"Father, will they be caught?"

"I hope not, I don't wish any harm to come to that brave young man."

Later, the news spread throughout the village and those at the school learned the shocking story. When he found out that the prisoner had escaped with the help of Xã Long's daughter, Captain St Arnaud had slapped Prefect Chí in front of all present, including his parents. Xã Long tried to defend his son and was promptly struck down by another French officer. The Village Chief fell down hard and broke his right arm. The French then left to chase after the prisoner, leaving the Village Chief howling in pain on the floor.

That same evening, Bà Lân's condition worsened. Everyone, including Father Phan, had left the village school and only those closest to her were left. Abbot Khánh, who had not left her bedside since talking to her earlier, beckoned for Tâm and Giang to come closer. Without being told, they knelt down beside her bed as he stood aside. He clasped his hands and began to recite a sutra.

The old woman opened her eyes and looked for a long moment at her new daughter-in-law and her son.

"Teacher Tâm, I am going to be with your father soon," she said weakly. "Listen carefully to what I am going to tell you and Giang."

Both could only nod their heads as their faces betrayed the grief that was ready to burst through at any moment.

"You cannot stay in this village. After you bury me next to your father, you have to leave and go South with Giang."

Almost immediately, he protested. During his triumphal walk home after being released from the communal house, surrounded by happy students and parents, he had looked forward to resuming his role as village teacher.

"Mother, how can I leave you here? How can I abandon the school that my father founded?"

"Listen to me. The Village Chief is not going to leave you alone. It will be unwise and even unsafe for you to stay here. Sooner or later he will find a way to make your life difficult if not impossible, just like he did this time. He will seize upon the few words that Cha Phan honestly expressed when he said you would have been a prized convert to Christianity, and he will use them to persecute you to no end. I can rest in peace only after you are gone somewhere else beyond his grasp."

She paused and took time to gather her strength before continuing.

"Go South and find or establish a school in another village or city. There is always a demand for good and dedicated teachers, and people like you are needed every day, in any part of our country."

She moved her head and looked around the room until she found Thi standing next to the abbot, with her arms wrapped around Hồng. Both looked distraught and terrified at the impending departure of the old woman. Without being told, they moved closer to the bed and knelt down next to Tâm.

"I have known Thi since she was even younger than Hồng," she told her son. "She is gifted and quite capable of taking over this school after you leave."

Thi reached out to her and the old woman still had enough strength to take and hold her hand.

"Thi, this school will be yours. After my son leaves, you will become the village teacher."

"How will I be able …?" Thi started to object.

"Thi, you can do it, just like Teacher Tâm had to when his father passed away. I know he has taught you well and he has told me that if you were allowed to take the examinations you would have passed them in your own right. With you in charge, the children of this village will be in good hands."

Tâm thought back of the times his mother had remarked to him about how capable Thi was in everything, in her studies as well as in how well she handled the other students. She had always carried out his instructions capably and efficiently, and had no problem in motivating the rest of the class, whether younger or older than her, to follow her example. Without anybody being aware of it, she had in fact been his able assistant, helping him in more ways than anybody realized. In fact, since he came back from the capital, she had been, with her enthusiasm and her constant prodding of the other students, the main force behind his campaign to teach the new script and eradicate illiteracy.

His mother was absolutely right: Thi would be a perfect village teacher, even if she herself was not convinced of it. For her benefit, and for those of everyone else present, he looked at her directly and recounted the story of a famed scholar.

"Thi, in the 16th century, during the Mạc dynasty, Nguyễn Thị Du, a female scholar, disguised herself as a man and took part in the palace examinations. She not only passed them, she was the Laureate for that year, surpassing all the men scholars."

"When they found out that she was not a man, rather than punish her, the Mạc King appointed her as the preceptor of his wives, his concubines, and all the royal children. Later on, when Lord Trịnh defeated the Mạc King, instead of being executed like many others, she was retained as the preceptor of Lord Trịnh's own children."

"So, Thi, you will not be the first woman teacher, and you will make an excellent one for our village school."

As her eyes still betrayed some distress, he added.

"You have been assisting me and you have helped me in matters great and small in the running of our school. Without realizing it, you already have the experience of being a village teacher."

His words had a calming effect on her, and there was an almost imperceptible nod, a hesitant acceptance on her part. His mother also noticed it and managed to smile wanly.

She next turned her head to Giang, peering into her eyes and admiring them one last time.

"Before I knew you, I did not know whether my son would ever find the woman of his dream. Fate has brought you two together, and I can now leave this world without worry, knowing that he will have you next to him from now on. He already owes so much to you."

After another pause, she continued, her voice getting weaker.

"After this, you need to go home, and take your husband with you so that he can properly pay respect to your parents. After that, follow him wherever he wants to go, support him in whatever he does, bear him children, and raise them to be men and women worthy of our best traditions."

The last words came out in a whisper, and after one last look at her son, she slowly closed her eyes.

"Mother, don't leave us!" Giang said.

"Mother!" Tâm shouted. He grasped her hands but she had already given her last breath.

A dam burst inside him, and he sobbed openly, uncontrollably. Giang also gave way to her emotions, her tears now streaming down her cheeks as she grieved for the woman who understood her better than her own mother.

On the other side of Tâm, Thi wept for the kind woman who had treated her as if she had been her own daughter. She also grieved for what she knew was the end of a major chapter in her life. Her teacher, the man whom she admired and loved, was going to leave the village with his new wife, leaving her behind with a task she was still not confident that she was qualified for.

She could not blame him, nor could she blame Giang, the one who actually put an end to the nightmare and injustice inflicted on him by the Village Chief. Still, deep inside her, she wished that fate had in some way allowed her to be the one leaving with him.

Epilogue

Xã Long never recovered the full use of his arm and his health declined. However, he remained a wealthy man and a power to be feared in the village. Only his wife was not afraid of him. Although she never forgave him for siring a bastard son, she continued to live with him, but ignored him for the most part and never spoke a word to him again. She turned toward Buddhism and prepared herself for monastic life as soon as family matters allowed her to do so.

The Village Chief's daughter and her half-brother managed to elude the French. After hiding in his mother's house, they left and fled toward the hilly lands of the Northwest. Chính tried to gather the remnants of his band, and with the gold that Kim Liên had brought from home, began to organize another base to continue their resistance movement. This second attempt ultimately proved as quixotic and unsuccessful as the last one.

Chí lost his position of Prefect. He barely managed, with his father's help, to become a minor official in another province. He eventually married the daughter of a merchant, resigned from his post, and opened a school in the provincial capital. Neither his marriage nor his teaching career turned out well, and he spent the rest of his life a bitter man. His wife gave him no children, and despite his father's urging he could not bring himself to marry another woman. His school slowly lost students as people turned increasingly to the new script and abandoned the traditional Chinese-influenced studies.

When she came to congratulate Giang and Tâm, Kim Liên had Chính carry a tray of orange colored sweet rice on top of banana leaves, beneath which was a small fortune in gold taels. At her mother's insistence, and without her father's knowledge, the Village Chief's daughter gave the gold to the village teacher to atone for the ordeal her father had imposed on him.

The following day, when he discovered the gold, Tâm left most of it to Thi. As the new village teacher, Thi eventually used it to finance the expansion of the school and to hire other teachers to help her cope with growing student enrollment as the new Vietnamese script became widely popular.

Giang and Tâm went back to the capital where her mother organized a second wedding for them so that all of her relatives had a chance to meet him. While her clan looked suspiciously at Tâm, her husband and daughter Mai went out of their way to make him feel welcomed. Bonneau offered his son-in-law a prominent position in the colonial administration, but Tâm declined. Instead, he and Giang moved further South to the bustling port city of Tourane. Once there, he founded a new school in a poorer area of the city while she took over and managed her family business.

Made in the USA
Coppell, TX
25 January 2021